BALEFUL BETRAYAL

OVERWORLD CHRONICLES
BOOK TWELVE

JOHN CORWIN

ISBN- 978-1-942453-03-1

Printed in the U.S.A.

RAVEN
HOUSE

To my wonderful support group:
Alana Rock
Karen Stansbury

My amazing editors:
Annetta Ribken
Jennifer Wingard

Thanks so much for all your help and input!

Books by John Corwin:

The Overworld Chronicles:
Sweet Blood of Mine
Dark Light of Mine
Fallen Angel of Mine
Dread Nemesis of Mine
Twisted Sister of Mine
Dearest Mother of Mine
Infernal Father of Mine
Sinister Seraphim of Mine
Wicked War of Mine
Dire Destiny of Ours
Aetherial Annihilation
Baleful Betrayal

Overworld Underground:
Possessed By You
Demonicus

Overworld Arcanum:
Conrad Edison and the Living Curse
Conrad Edison and the Anchored World

Stand Alone Novels:
No Darker Fate
The Next Thing I Knew
Outsourced
Seventh

For the latest on new releases, free ebooks, and more, join John Corwin's Newsletter at www.johncorwin.net!

PAYBACK IS HELL

After the crystoid incident nearly destroyed all magic in Eden and killed a dear friend, Justin Slade wants payback. That means invading the angel realm, Seraphina, and squashing the usurper, Cephus, like a bug.

Unfortunately, another crystoid in Seraphina is preventing the Alabaster Arch from opening a portal into the realm. Using a sky portal from the last remaining crystoid in Eden, Justin launches a desperate bid to open the portal from the other side.

Cephus, however, is more than ready for a counterattack. Not only has he fortified his fortress, but he's built a new arch and plans to open a portal to the Void, releasing the Beast and Armageddon.

Enlisting the help of the Seraphim sky fishers and their fleet of flying ships, Justin has to repair the Alabaster Arch leading back to Eden and bring through the mightiest supernatural army Seraphina has ever known.

Chapter 1

Falling from a magical hole in the sky and into another dimension wasn't exactly how I thought I'd spend the day before my best friend's wedding.

I had way too much going on with my calendar, but that was expected nothing new when planning an interdimensional war that could determine the fate of angels and man alike. Glowing eerily far below us lay the ultraviolet dome of Murk erected by Cephus, usurper of power and traitor to his own people, the Darklings.

Tarissa, the capitol city of the Darkling nation, Pjurna, lay in ruins for at least a mile radius around the dome, many of its exotic structures, organically twisting skyscrapers, and gravity-defying designs nothing but rubble. The city had a violet crystalline sheen to it, the result of being constructed from the primal force of creation, Murk, the power favored by Seraphim of the Darkling persuasion. Their opposing kin, the Brightlings, used white Brilliance, the force of destruction, as their primary tool.

Though the forces seemed opposites, they were merely two sides of the same coin. During my first visit here, I'd learned more about Murk than I'd ever thought possible. Even the furnishings in most buildings were created effortlessly through the use of magical gems that focused aether into desired forms.

Cold wind whistled through my ears, tore at my hair, and pressed my goggles against my skin. The Templar Nightingale armor insulated me a little, but as I angled out of the lone beam of magic powering its charms, its protection began to fade.

"I thought the ring Shelton bought Bella was a little gaudy," Elyssa's voice said through my earbud. "And it all feels a bit rushed."

I gave my girlfriend a disbelieving look. "Is this really the best time to talk about that?" I spread my arms to let the webbing between my armpits and my legs catch the wind and angle me to the west.

Elyssa paced my flight as easily as if it were something she did every day, and raised an eyebrow. "Why is it such a touchy subject for you, Justin? Every time I bring it up, you talk about something else."

"It's just weird thinking of him getting married and having kids."

"You're sad, aren't you?" Elyssa dodged around a golden bird and flitted through a cloud. "You think he's going to leave you and the bromance will be over."

As usual, she hit the nail on the head, but I was too proud to admit it. "Nah, of course not." I pretended not to care and focused my vision on the ground still far below. The squirrel suits, as Shelton called our modified Nightingale armor, gave us enough lift to stay airborne until we were in range of our objective, a crystoid meteor soaking up all the magical energy in the vicinity.

Cephus had hit Eden with hundreds of crystoids nearly two months ago in an attempt to keep our army out of Seraphina so he could remain in power. The crystal meteors nearly drained Eden of all magical energy for good. As a backup insurance plan, Cephus had used a couple of the crystoids in his own city, Tarissa. Not only had it crippled the local militia, but it had taken the skyways out of service as well.

Our only way of transporting our army was by using the skyway connecting the Alabaster Arch on the floating island of Kdosh to the mainland of Pjurna. I had to take out the crystoid so the skyway would work again.

Elyssa groaned. "Boys are so weird when it comes to expressing their feelings."

"Hey, I express my feelings all the time," I shot back. "Like this morning when I kissed your nose and said you were my sweet little booger."

A snort sounded in my earbud. "I'm talking about with guy friends."

Lights glowed from within the shield dome protecting the Ministry of Research, offering a blurry view through the translucent material. Towering in the middle of the plaza outside the ministry building stood an arch that definitely hadn't been there the last time I'd visited. Even from this bird's eye view it looked larger than the Obsidian Arches we used in Eden for instant transport from one part of the globe to the other. Through the haze of the ultraviolet barrier, it looked almost purple.

I pointed it out to Elyssa. "Do you see that?"

"Cephus built an arch?" she said. "That must be how the crystoids opened those sky portals."

A hole opened in the top of the shield dome. Four Darklings on blazing wings of ultraviolet fire streaked our way. They wore black uniforms and creepy masks like something out of a cosplay convention. Unfortunately, they weren't a group of harmless nerds.

"Uh, stupid question," Elyssa said, "but how are they flying without any aether?"

I switched to incubus vision, which allowed me to see things invisible to the naked eye. Daemos—demon spawn—used it to scout for soul essence like the brightly blazing halo around Elyssa. Since I was also part Seraphim, it allowed me to see aether, the magical energy imbuing the air, the earth, and everything around me.

Seraphina was a realm so abundant with magical energy that sometimes chunks of land broke free and floated in the air over a vortex of aether. The concentrations of aether grew so great in some places it was visible to the naked eye. The sky should have seethed with energy. Instead, it looked depressingly normal. A bright beacon of aether glowed to the west, the aether beam from the crystoid. The meteor sucked up the energy and beamed it through a hole in the sky and back to the Ministry of Research, supplying the dome and those within with an endless supply.

It quickly became apparent what powered the Darklings pursuing us. Thin beams of aether speared from the dome and into the Seraphim, keeping them supplied with all the power they needed. The

3

lead Darkling swooped upward and for a moment, the beam wasn't on him. Instead of faltering, he continued to steadily rise. The aether beam swiveled to intersect him once again and it was then I realized why the brief lack of connectivity hadn't affected him.

Each Darkling wore small fanny packs glowing with concentrated aether. "They're wearing batteries on their butts," I told Elyssa. "They're being recharged by directed aether beams."

"They're catching up fast," she said. "How far to the crystoid?"

I looked west toward the beam of energy cast skyward like a Hollywood spotlight. "Another mile." The entire city of Tarissa floated over an aether vortex and the meteor rested near the edge of the skylet—the local term for a sky island. While the crystoid sucked up all the aether above the skylet, it apparently wasn't enough of an energy sink to disrupt the vortex.

Elyssa grimaced. "They'll catch us long before that."

I glanced at one of the sai swords sheathed on her thighs and wondered how she'd use them in an aerial battle. If we folded our arms or legs for even a moment, we'd plummet to the ground. Already the skyscrapers in the undamaged western section of Tarissa loomed only a few hundred yards below. If we lost much more altitude, we'd never clear the city without dodging through the maze of high-rises.

Elyssa seemed to read my mind. "Plan B?"

Beams of ultraviolet Murk whined past us. One struck Elyssa's rocket stick. Sparks showered from the tip. Another salvo speared past us, narrowly missing the webbing of my squirrel suit. We leaned left and right, dodging shards of energy.

"I think your rocket stick is toast," I told her. "Plan B isn't going to work." One rocket stick wouldn't hold two people very well.

"I don't suppose you want to talk about this?" I shouted at our pursuers, but the wind snatched my words and tore them apart. I motioned my head down. "We gotta do this the hard way. Plan C."

She raised a dark eyebrow. "Isn't this already the hard way?"

"Harder way," I clarified. "I'm glad we practiced with these squirrel suits."

"Oh god." Elyssa glanced down. "I just figured out Plan C."

4

I flashed a grin. "Hey, me too." With that, I tucked my arms to my sides and closed my legs. Without the wings to catch the air, I dropped like a lump of frozen turds from an airplane. My stomach hugged my spleen and held on for dear life.

Blazing wings folded tight, the Darklings dove after us, firing blindly and missing. Elyssa and I streaked down the side of a tower that twisted in a corkscrew spiral.

"Get ready," I said. "Three, two, one, go!" I spread my arms and legs and arched my back. The wind slammed into the wings, steering me inches from the shimmering surface of the building. Elyssa and I leaned hard right and whipped around the corkscrew, dodged left and threaded the narrow slit in the center of a heart-shaped building. Another hard dive and we twisted back and forth through a maze of high-rises.

For a moment, I thought we'd lost our pursuers.

Four shadows on the deserted pedestriums below gave us only an instant's warning that we'd been outsmarted. Rather than attempt to follow us between the buildings, the attackers maintained altitude and watched us from above. I craned my neck and saw them swooping in for the kill. A bolt of Murk exploded against the building ahead and to my left. Shards of crystal exploded in a deadly cloud.

Elyssa cried out and swooped right. Another blast of Murk blocked me from following. At the last instant, I dodged left to avoid receiving a face full of glass. I crashed through a window and got it anyway. My ribs bounced off a wall, the wind exploded from my lungs, and I rolled across the floor of an empty apartment before skidding to a stop.

Gasping for air, I looked up in time to see a Darkling aiming his glowing fists of death at me. I reflexively threw up my left hand to channel a shield, except—oops!—I didn't have any aether to power it. Thankfully, my enhanced Daemos reflexes weren't affected by the lack of magic. I blurred left. A spear of Murk crashed into the wall like a sledgehammer, punching a hole clear into the next room.

Instead of fleeing like anyone with a lick of common sense, I dashed forward and punched the attacking asshat right in the stomach. With an explosive grunt, he doubled over and flew backward out of the window. My hopes of him falling to his doom were thwarted when one of his companions caught him and carried him to safety.

I ducked back inside as Murk hammered the area where my head had been. This time I used common sense and ran through the hole in the wall and into a huge, empty room overlooking a park. I spotted a levitator alcove in the left corner that housed what passed for an elevator in Seraphina. I drew up short when I realized there was no glow of light emanating from the shaft. I peered over the lip and was greeted by a dark hole promising a quick trip to oblivion.

Unless there were stairs hidden somewhere, I didn't know how I was supposed to get to ground level. The window to my right exploded and a Darkling barreled into me. His momentum carried us crashing through the glass and outside into empty air.

"This wasn't what I had in mind!" I shouted as we plummeted earthward.

He tried to let me go forty stories above the ground. What he hadn't counted on was my demon strength and desperation. He spread his wings but they weren't enough to hold us aloft. We lost altitude, cruising high over the small park and crashing through a window across the street. He caught a wing on the window frame while I tumbled across the room.

Like many buildings I'd visited in my previous trip to Tarissa, it lacked permanent furniture since magical gems on the wall allowed occupants to furnish the room on a whim. Without aether to power the buildings, the rooms were empty unless someone left the furniture in place from the night before.

I wished for a sturdy chair to break over the head of my assailant, or even a couch to duck behind as he tried to pound my head to hamburger meat with shards of energy. Instead, I was forced to juke back and forth across the room, slowly closing the distance.

I tried to reason with him in Cyrinthian, but it had been a while since I'd spoken the language aside from the crash course I'd taken from none other than Cephus himself the last time I'd been here. "Cephus is destroying this city!" I shouted.

My attacker didn't acknowledge what I'd said—in fact he seemed to be emotionally numb to everything, though it could have just been the creepy mask he wore. I ducked beneath another attack, came up from below, and delivered a crushing uppercut. My fist launched him off the ground so hard he hit the ceiling ten feet overhead and thudded back to the floor.

"Sweet dreams, flyboy." I knelt and inspected his uniform.

The symbol on the chest looked familiar. I flashed back to the day I'd gone to the Ministry of Research to save Nightliss. The guards all wore the same symbol—a white line spiraling into black—the Void. "There is no god," one of them had said. "Only life and the Void."

I knew a bit more about the Void than they did, namely that it had a denizen of its own, a creature called the Beast. Though I'd never seen the creature, I'd heard it growl after accidentally opening a portal into that dark realm. That had been more than enough incentive not to investigate further.

"If there's no promise of afterlife, only oblivion, why would anyone be so eager to die?" I wondered aloud.

Now was not the time for introspection, so I tugged the mask off the soldier to reveal a shaved head with a freshly puckered scar across the temple. That wasn't what nearly made me lose my breakfast. One of the seraph's eyes was gone, replaced by a white gem.

Seraphim come in two flavors—Brightling and Darkling—each with an affinity for opposing primal forces. Brightlings utilize Brilliance, the force of destruction, while their Darkling kin who they treated like second-class citizens, channel Murk, the magic of creation. In my experience, Darklings were usually the good guys. After all, my best friend, Nightliss, had helped me fight her evil twin sister, Daelissa, and her Brightling forces.

Not in the case of Cephus.

During the Second Seraphim War, I'd come to Tarissa seeking the help of the Darkling forces against Daelissa's army. My first day here, I'd met Cephus, one of the three members of the Trivectus, the governing body of Pjurna. At first, he seemed the most reasonable of the bunch, but that was before he tricked me into helping him murder Ministers Uoriss and Thala, thus propelling him to power.

7

He hadn't stopped there, kidnapping Nightliss and experimenting on her all while I was blithely unaware. When I'd rescued her, she'd been so beaten and bruised—a pang of regret tore at my insides.

Rest in peace, Nightliss.

On our way out of the Ministry of Research, I'd seen things that would make even the most hardened veteran's skin crawl. Seraphim in cages, bodies mutilated from horrible experiments, some of them turned into creatures that no longer resembled anything humanoid. If this mutilated soldier was any indication, it seemed Cephus had found a use for his cruel research.

The seraph's one good eye blinked open. The gem in the other socket glowed and a thin beam of Brilliance stabbed out. I didn't move quite fast enough. Pain seared into my right cheek. Shouting in pain, I rolled off the seraph and wrapped my arm around his neck from behind like a wrestler, squeezing his throat between my forearm and bicep.

He flailed, scratching my face, his legs thrashing. I pulled back my head to avoid his hands until he went limp from lack of oxygen. My fingers found a slow, steady pulse on his throat. I wasn't ready to kill him just yet, especially if he was a brainwashed victim.

The next thing I did was undo the leather straps holding the aether pack to the seraph's back. Two crystalline prongs pressed against the bare skin of his back through a slit in the uniform. The pack felt insubstantial when hefted in one hand. I opened the leather wrapping and nearly dropped it like I'd just peeled open a spider egg when I saw what was inside—a small glowing crystoid. Upon further inspection, I realized its surface was smooth instead of spiky, its insides sparking with electric aether.

"That explains things," I muttered. Even when it wasn't being fed by the aether beam from home base, it seemed to hold plenty of juice. I touched the crystal prongs and felt a rush of power in my blood. Cephus had been a busy bee. Not only had he found a way to destroy magic in Eden, but he'd come up with these aether crystals to power his own troops.

He'd severely underestimated our ability to fight off the crystoid menace despite an army of robots and armed airships thrown against us. Nightliss's burned, bleeding body flashed before my eyes and the hatred of a thousand suns burned in my chest. The day I laid hands on Cephus, he'd get a free Bible lesson because I planned to go Old Testament on his rotten ass.

I wiped my eyes and raced for a window facing north. I saw no sign of the other Darklings and, even worse, no sign of Elyssa. We hadn't even reached the target, and already this mission had gone to hell.

Chapter 2

Finding Elyssa was my first priority.

Knowing that I'd abandoned the mission to focus on her safety would probably piss off my girlfriend to no end. She'd kicked my butt plenty of times and I was more than willing to accept another whooping if it meant she was safe and sound.

I knelt next to the unconscious seraph and frisked him to make sure he didn't have anything else of value. He didn't even have a bladed weapon on his person, which meant Cephus was more interested in manufacturing glass cannon soldiers with tons of firepower but little experience or chance of survival.

What he'd accomplished was as impressive as it was repugnant. No matter how powerful, Seraphim couldn't naturally fly. If I really concentrated, I could manifest angel wings, but all I could do was glide. The last time I'd tried to flap my wings and fly, I'd nearly killed myself.

Thankfully, I didn't have to rely on wings to get out of this building. I reached over my shoulder and slid a shiny chrome rocket stick from the sheath on my back. It was a little dented from fighting, but a flick of the switch confirmed it still worked.

I preferred boomsticks—high-powered flying broomsticks—to the gadgets from Science Academy, but heading into an aether dead zone required desperate measures. Unlike broomsticks, rocket sticks had fins on the tail for steering and a rear exhaust port for flames. This model wasn't as fast or powerful as my boomstick, but it would do the trick.

Pressing the neckline of my Nightingale armor retracted it down to my waist so I could strap the aether pack on my back. The second the crystal prongs touched my skin, I felt the beckon of raw aether. I tugged up on the waistline and the armor grew back into a skintight layer of protection, spreading beneath the crystal prongs and breaking contact with my back.

"You've got to be kidding me," I groaned. I'd hoped the armor would grow over the aether pack. Instead, it was doing what it had been charmed to do, sliding across the skin no matter what clothes or gear the user was wearing. Even though I had a short sword at my hip, using it to cut through Nightingale armor would be like cutting through a titanium-plated tank with a can opener.

That left me with one option.

I flew the rocket stick out of the broken window, the aether pack snug against my back. I was also as bare-chested as a male model in a shopping mall. Though I felt naked without the armor and my nipples went hard as diamonds from the cold air, I now had access to magic.

"Or I could slice someone real good with my nipples," I muttered.

Gaining altitude, I rose above the tallest buildings and looked around. A fresh rush of power indicated the aether beam from Cephus's fortress had found me and even now recharged the power pack. Since I couldn't possibly be mistaken for one of his unfortunate minions, it seemed likely the aether beams homed in on the aether packs and not the users.

My heart dropped at the sight of a black-clad figure on the streets below. I dove straight down, pulling up at the last instant when I realized the body belonged to one of the Darkling soldiers. It was a breadcrumb that might lead me to Elyssa.

The hairs on my neck rose and I had the distinct impression someone was watching me. Though the streets were completely empty of people, there were plenty of buildings to hide in. Unlike Eden, there were no planes, trains, or automobiles in Seraphina. The cities relied on skyways and cloudlets for transportation. Without magic, none of those had power, and as I'd discovered in the last building, not even the levitators worked. That meant if someone was watching me, they were probably doing it from ground level.

11

I rotated the hovering rocket stick in a circle, but saw no one. Since my eyes hadn't found anything, I used another of my super senses and focused on ambient noises. The faint but unmistakable explosions from channeled energy echoed in the distance. I swept the rocket stick west and zipped forward.

A moment later I stopped to silence the rush of wind in my ears. The cry of battle sounded closer now. The echoes through the canyons of empty streets made it difficult to pinpoint the source, but it seemed to emanate from the north. I twisted the throttle to full and zipped down the road. Movement caught my eye. I pulled hard right and veered down a wide avenue flanked by crystalline towers.

Elyssa and another figure fought two soldiers on the ground. Divots in the street and surrounding buildings bore evidence of the firepower the Darklings had employed, but Elyssa was no easy target. Before I reached the fight, it was over and the attackers lay unmoving on the street.

I hopped off the rocket too quickly, stumbling forward and wind-milling my arms to stay upright. "Elyssa!"

She caught me in a hug and pressed her lips savagely against mine. "Justin, what happened? Why are you topless?" Her nose wrinkled. "Your nipples are rock hard."

I caught a troubled look from her new companion and my eyes widened with shock. "Flava!"

"It is good to see you again, *Justin*," the healer of the Tarissan Legion said in a tone that didn't jibe with her words. "We hoped you would be here with your army months ago."

My stomach sank with the leaden weight of guilt. "I'm sorry, Flava. We should have come right after the war. Maybe we could have prevented the terrible things Cephus has done here and on Eden." *Maybe Nightliss would still be alive.*

Flava's eyes hardened. "You promised us, Justin. You said you would lead us against the Brightlings and unify Seraphina." Her hands tightened. "Now the Tarissan Legion is all but destroyed and the Darkling nation is on its knees. Even weakened after the war in Eden, the Brightling empire could swallow us with little trouble."

12

Elyssa stepped between us. "We're here now, Flava. That's what matters."

"Where is your army?" Flava cried. "Where is our salvation?"

I took a deep breath to quell the tide of sorrow and regret rising in my throat. "The blame is mine, Flava. The moment I had a chance, I ran away from war. I thought your people could defeat Cephus on their own and I would come later and help you against the Brightlings." I ran a hand down my face. "I had no idea Cephus was capable of this. He nearly destroyed all magic in Eden."

"Thousands died here," Flava said, her voice trembling with rage. "Ketiss is dead, the legion scattered to the winds." Teeth bared, she poked me in the chest with a finger. "There is nothing but doom on our lands. You earned your name, Destroyer. The Primogenitor has punished us for our inaction against the Brightlings."

Many Darklings worshipped the Primogenitor, the supposed creator, and Cephus had tricked the population into thinking I was the Destroyer, a bringer of doom who would help the Darkling defeat their ancient enemy. I'd thought Flava had been cured of religion. Maybe she was throwing this back in my face. She had every right to be furious with me.

Before I could respond, Elyssa spoke in a calm voice. "We're here to destroy the crystoid—the crystal meteor—blocking the skyway from the Alabaster Arch." Elyssa put a hand on Flava's shoulder. "We're here to undo the damage."

"Destroy it?" Flava said incredulously. "One of those abominations turned the city center into rubble and killed most of the legion. Had I not been surveying the meteor near the skyway, I would have died as well."

"My god," I murmured. "Most of the legion is dead?"

"Yes," she said through clenched teeth. "These crystoids will be the death of us all."

"We can safely nullify them," I said, forcing my voice to remain steady. "Can you get us to the one near the skyway?"

Flava shuddered and stepped back. "Do not tempt me with hope, Justin."

"Get us there and we can do it." I added steel to my tone and stepped toward her. "Nightliss died along with hundreds of others because I waited too long." I tried to hold back the sorrow, but tears blurred my vision. "I failed everyone, Flava—everyone!" I took a deep breath. "This time, I won't rest, I won't stop until Cephus is dead and Seraphina is set to rights."

"Nightliss is dead?" The rough pain in Flava's voice nearly sent me over the precipice.

I nodded. "There was a bomb that would have killed our entire army. She sacrificed herself—took the bomb far into the sky."

Flava bit her lip and nodded. "We have all paid the price for your inaction, Justin."

"It's not his fault!" Elyssa shouted. "Do you know what he's been through? What the war against Daelissa cost him even before we asked for your help?" She angrily thrust her swords back into her thigh sheaths. "If Justin hadn't stopped Daelissa in Eden, she'd be ruling your whiny ass right now."

The Darkling reared back like she'd been slapped and her eyes went hard—a far cry from the gentle soul who'd saved my life in the final battle against Daelissa. "Perhaps that is so, but we lent you our help and received none in return. You can see the brutal results."

"Well, unless you know how to time travel, we can't do anything but move forward. Standing here casting blame in our faces is only wasting time." Elyssa sighed and turned her attention to me. "I see you took one of the enemy aether batteries."

I gladly accepted the change of subject. "Yeah, but the armor goes underneath it and I need the prongs to make contact with my skin."

"I can't believe you don't know how to adjust that by now," Elyssa said. "Tug up and out on the hem."

I pinched the hem at my waist and did as instructed. This time the armor spread over the pack instead of under it. I met her raised eyebrow with a shrug. "Hey, nobody ever told me it was that simple." I nearly groaned with pleasure as my frozen nipples thawed.

Flava knelt next to the unmoving soldiers and studied the aether pack. "Cephus has grown bolder by the day, sending his minions to kidnap any Seraphim still living in the city."

I pulled off the soldier's mask and exposed the shaved head, scar, and eye socketed with a gem.

Flava gasped and stumbled back. "What is this monstrosity?"

"One of Cephus's victims," I replied. "I don't even think he was a solider before."

"He's engineering Seraphim into soldiers." Elyssa's voice seethed with disgust. "What happened to the city population?"

"They fled to the outer edges," Flava said. "Without the skyway, there is no way off the skylet."

Tarissa floated on a massive miles-wide skylet above a tremendous aether vortex. "If memory serves, it's about half a mile to the ground from the edge of the city?"

Flava nodded. "It is less now due to the crystoids, but not enough for someone to survive the fall."

"How many crystoids are in the city?" Elyssa asked.

"Two—one on the eastern edge, and the other to the west near the skyway." Flava pulled the pack off the unconscious seraph. "They are enough to disrupt the skyways in all directions."

"Where is the rest of the Darkling army?" I asked.

"I hope they still maintain our national borders," Flava said. "Ketiss thought we could defeat Cephus without withdrawing other troops from their positions. We lost contact with the outside once the crystoids hit."

"I wish he'd been right." I tugged the aether pack off the other soldier and handed it to Elyssa. "You might as well wear this in case I run out of power in this one."

Flava turned away and slid her tattered uniform down to her waist to strap an aether pack between her shoulder blades, then slid her arms back into the sleeves and fastened it in the front. The low-profile pack made a discernable bulge against her upper back, giving her the appearance of a hunchback. I decided not to share that observation since her admiration for me had dwindled from hero to absolute zero in the past few months.

15

Besides, I didn't feel like joking about anything right now. The people of Pjurna were hurting something awful and I had to complete my mission if there was any hope of fixing it.

"What about them?" Elyssa looked at the slumbering soldiers. "Can we do anything to restore them?"

Flava knelt and pressed her hands to the head of a seraph who looked barely older than me. Then again, he might be fifty years old. Seraphim like my mother could live for thousands of years, provided nothing awful happened to them. The destruction of the Grand Nexus had ended the First Seraphim War over two thousand years ago by sundering the link between Eden and Seraphina. In Eden, all the Seraphim had been reduced to infantile husks with an insatiable appetite for life force. On this side of the Nexus, the results had been less spectacular, but no less devastating, reducing the life span of any Seraphim caught in the blast to centuries instead of millennia.

"I might be able to heal him, but I dare not use all the power in this aether pack for him," Flava said after a moment of silence.

I looked up and estimated how high we'd have to go to catch a recharge from the aether beams. "I don't suppose you learned how to fly since the last time I saw you?"

Her eyes regarded me gravely. "I was one of many who trained so we could fight the archangels on even terms, but I have nowhere near the skill of Cephus's"—she looked with distaste at the scars on the seraph's face—"mutants."

Brainwashed they might be, but I hated to leave these soldiers without helping them. For the time being, it couldn't be helped. I'd learned the hard way that making command decisions sometimes meant sacrificing the lives of others. In this case, I didn't feel all that horrible about not helping the seraphs that had tried to kill me earlier, but I didn't want to appear insensitive.

"Once we destroy the crystoid, we'll have all the power we need to help them," I said. "We have to go."

"Agreed," Elyssa said without hesitation.

Flava frowned, but nodded. "The trek through the city is dangerous and the crystoid is guarded by more soldiers."

"Soldiers like them?" I motioned to the mutants.

16

Flava shook her head. "Unless the guard has changed, the crystoid soldiers are loyalists of Cephus and the Void, not like these poor souls."

"I guarantee they reported to Cephus that we're here." Elyssa clenched her teeth. "There goes our quick mission."

So much for stealth and finesse. Cephus's people knew we were here and they would be ready for us.

Chapter 3

The plan had seemed so simple. The last remaining crystoid in Eden was in the ocean, far enough away to be no danger to the noms—normal humans. Each crystoid beamed aether through a sky portal bridging the dimensional barrier between Eden and Seraphina and straight into Cephus's fortress.

The quickest way to transport an army to Pjurna was through the Alabaster Arch at the Three Sisters way station in Australia, but it wasn't functioning due to the crystoids Elyssa and I had been sent to eliminate.

Using the last sky portal seemed the best way for a covert mission to succeed. How Cephus had detected our small bodies against the expanse of the sky before we'd fallen even a few hundred feet was still a mystery. Once the other sky portals began to close, he must have expected an attack.

Flava led us down winding pedestriums, using cover and stealth every step of the way. We spotted more aerial patrols overhead and were forced to hide until they were gone.

"I have a feeling the guard on the crystoid will be tripled by the time we get there," Elyssa said.

"That is why we are not going there first," Flava said.

I gripped her arm and turned her to me. "Where the hell are you taking us, then?"

She jerked her arm from my grasp. "To find all the help there is in this world."

"Legionnaires?" Elyssa asked.

Flava nodded. "There are a few left. Perhaps enough to clear the way to the crystoid." She cast a scathing glanced at me and opened her mouth as if to throw another insult my way, but turned and resumed walking.

The hike seemed to go on forever, taking us in a southwestern route that curved to the outskirts of the city. Short domiciles sprinkled the land, varying shades of crystalline structures like the insides of a geode—a far cry from the towers of the city center. Small roads wound back and forth between the seemingly random placements of the buildings.

"How beautiful," Elyssa said, kneeling beside a bed of blue roses.

"Not so lovely if a flying patrol spots us," Flava said. "Hurry."

The buildings were tall enough to provide some cover, but not like the high-rises back the other way. "Seems harder to hide around here," I said. "Why not stay in the city?"

"Because nothing works in the towers," she said. "There is small aether well that supplies some of the houses here."

I switched to incubus vision and spotted a nimbus swirling in a courtyard dead ahead. Logic dictated that was where we'd find the remnants of the Tarissan Legion. The updraft rose for several yards before swirling away, drawn to the north by the crystoid. It seemed Cephus's big purple fortress—a pulsating zit on the fair skin of Tarissa—held a monopoly on aether in these parts.

"We are here," Flava said, motioning to what looked like an igloo formed from blue crystals. "Our last hope waits inside."

I really wanted to call her out for being melodramatic, but the scowl on her face told me she'd probably punch me in the mouth. "Lead on."

She removed a gem from the inside of her uniform's collar and touched it to another on the side of the igloo. A section turned to mist and she stepped inside. Elyssa and I ducked through the opening and followed. An empty, round room with a domed ceiling lay on the other side. The mist solidified into a wall behind us.

"Well, that was anticlimactic," I muttered. "Where is everyone?"

Flava touched the gem to the floor and it misted away as the door had. We followed her down into a tunnel. A few yards later it opened into a wide cavern. The rocky walls, stalagmites, and stalactites, were a welcome relief from the overuse of crystal in the city above. It was as if the city designers went out of their way to make everything look completely different from the good old bricks and mortar we used in Eden. Then again, most of these people had probably never seen the mortal plane.

A sera with glossy white hair, porcelain skin, and elfin ears stepped from behind a rock formation and looked at me uncertainly.

"Lanaeia," I said in a hushed voice, uncertain how enthusiastically I should greet her.

"Oh, Justin!" She flung herself at me, embracing me so firmly I felt the breath explode from my lungs. "We are saved!"

Elyssa cleared her throat. "I'm here too."

Lanaeia kissed my cheeks and moved to Elyssa, sparing no enthusiasm. "The tyranny of Cephus will finally end!"

Flava bared her teeth. "Why are you so happy, *girl*? He abandoned us."

Lanaeia's silver eyes flashed. "You dare call me a human child, *zhuka*? I lived thousands of years before you were even a spark of life in your father's groin!"

I held up my hands. "Whoa, people. No reason for name calling."

Several more Seraphim stepped from concealment. I recognized two of them right away. A tall blond seraph with fair skin swiftly crossed the room and embraced me. "Justin, I have prayed so long to see you."

"Joss, it's great to see you." I released him to exchange grips with his best friend, Otaleon, a tall seraph with dark hair and eyes. Elyssa and I, with the help of Nightliss and Jeremiah Conroy, had rescued them from the evil wonder twins, Qualan and Qualas, both thankfully killed during the war.

Otaleon offered me a grim smile, but didn't seem nearly as giddy to see me as Joss. "I know we already owe you much, Justin, but we had hoped to see your faces much sooner. Now Tarissa is laid waste, our comrades in arms lie dead, and Cephus grows his forces every day."

His grim assessment punched me in the guts, but I tried to keep things positive for my own sanity. I'd been in seemingly hopeless situations before and overcome them. Hopefully this would work out somehow. "Remember Daelissa's army? Remember her Goliaths and the mighty archangels?"

"I could never forget," Otaleon said in a calm voice.

Lanaeia gripped Otaleon's arm. "What Justin is saying is that even in the face of insurmountable odds, there is hope."

"Where there is hope lies victory," Joss said.

"Then why do I feel the weight of defeat?" Flava said. "I feel the hole in my chest where once my proud legion gave me all the hope I needed. The Destroyer has returned, but his soldiers are few."

"You're really starting to piss me off," I growled.

"I am beyond anger!" Flava shouted. "You left us all to die when you should have led us to victory!"

"You are too late," spat another seraph I didn't know. "Go home and leave Tarissa to die."

My inner demon surged and pushed my anger over the edge. "Enough!" I roared. An orb of Brilliance crackled in my right palm and Murk ensconced my left. The cavern glowed with the sudden light. "I will not let their deaths be in vain. We will organize and we will strike the guards around the crystoid. No matter what Cephus puts in our way, we will overcome it as we did the horrors Daelissa unleashed."

My inner demon lusted after the power of destruction, throwing itself against the prison of my will. Its thirst for Brilliance was what caused me to lose control my first time in Tarissa. I'd learned to control it since then, but quenched the blazing orbs in my hands so as not to tempt fate, and continued in a calmer voice.

"I understand your doubts." I stared down Flava. "Perhaps if I'd come with the legion immediately, we would have quickly defeated Cephus, or perhaps his trick with the crystoids would have destroyed the greatest supernatural army ever assembled. I ran my gaze over the others. "The crystoids nearly destroyed all magic on Eden. Thankfully, we were able to neutralize them and send our army after one of Cephus's allies."

21

I jabbed a finger in the direction I hoped was north, and pretended I was addressing the mighty army of elves from my live-action role-playing days of Kings and Castles. "Out there lies the final obstacle to the army that will sweep through this land and destroy the usurper. Cephus thinks he has the upper hand, but we'll show him the depths of defeat."

Cheers broke out from the thirty or so people in the room. Even Flava's scowl faded, replaced by uncertain hope.

I gripped her shoulder. "You saved my life in the final battle with Daelissa. You brought Elyssa back from the brink of death. I am so sorry I wasn't here when you needed me most, but I'm here now, Flava. After we destroy the crystoid and restore the skyway, I will return with our army and destroy Cephus. Will you fight with me?"

Flava blinked and tears rolled down her cheeks. "I am furious with you Justin, but I still believe. Of course I will fight with you."

Lanaeia raised a fist overhead, Brilliance blazing around it and declared, "We will all fight with you!"

Another roar rose from the group.

Elyssa and I had flubbed our mission and flown straight into a crap storm, but we'd finally reached an oasis of air freshener. Time to flush Plan A down the toilet and come up with an alternative.

"Does anyone have a map of the city?" Elyssa asked.

"I believe so." Joss dug through a case of multi-colored gems and withdrew a small green one. Holding it in his palm, he channeled a trickle of aether into the gem and a three-dimensional holograph of the city sprang up, displaying the city center with the government buildings.

"It is out of date." Otaleon pointed to the buildings in the image which were now rubble.

Joss waved a hand across the image and scrolled it west to the skyway. He pointed to a section near the edge. "The crystoid is here. Most of the surrounding buildings are no longer standing."

Elyssa studied the image for a moment then zoomed out to an overhead view. "Where are we?"

Joss pointed to the southwestern sector of the city.

"Looks like a five-mile hike to the crystoid," I said. "Any idea how many patrols Cephus has between us and it?"

"You can be sure he has as many as he can muster," Flava replied. "Since you defeated his nefarious devices in Eden, he no doubt knows you possess the key to undoing him here."

"Where's the other crystoid?" I asked.

Otaleon brought out a table so Joss could place the gem on it instead of holding it, and the blond Darkling zoomed out further to display the entire city. He pinpointed a spot near the eastern edge of the city.

"Where are the skyways leading out of the city?" I asked.

Joss touched the legend on the map and lit it with flowing lines running in all directions heedless of any buildings in their path. The first time I'd ridden the city skyway, basically a road of clouds, I'd nearly crapped my britches. If you needed to get somewhere not in the direct line of the skyway, a cloudbank broke from the main path and carried you there. It was the best mass transit system I'd ever seen.

"Are any of the skyways working?" Elyssa asked.

"Only parts of the southern route," Joss said. He drew a line with his finger to highlight about four miles to the far south. "That is only because of the Creator's Well."

I raised an eyebrow. "What the heck is that?"

"An aether fountain dedicated to the Primogenitor," Flava said. "It taps into the Tarissan Vortex."

Elyssa paced around the map, drawing symbols on it with her finger, seemingly oblivious to the muted conversations springing up in the room.

I walked up beside her. "You see what we have to do, right?"

"I don't like using an outdated map, Justin." She rested her chin on a hand. "It'd be nice to have at least one all-seeing eye to give us live intel on numbers and patrol patterns."

"We didn't have any of that to help us during the crystoid incident in Eden."

Elyssa blew out a breath. "Yeah, but we also had Templars intelligence operations to rely on." She waved me off before I could speak. "Yes, I know what we have to do." Her finger jabbed the eastern crystoid. "Take that out and restore some aether to the city."

"Do you think it'll draw away any guards from the western crystoid?" I asked.

"At first, but then he'll just double-down on the western one." Elyssa zoomed in on the southern area and traced a route through the lower part of the city. "Even if the skyways work down there, we should avoid them."

"I think eliminating the eastern crystoid is a waste of time," Flava said. "Cephus will be able to concentrate all his forces to the west if there is nothing left to guard in the east."

Elyssa frowned. "If the eastern crystoid is gone that means the skyways in those parts should function again. Where do they go?"

Joss fiddled with the map and the hologram began to fill in the surrounding land masses. "It would open up the eastern route to Karjun, and possibly the northern route to the Vjartik Mountains."

"Are there any legions in Karjun that could help us?" Elyssa asked.

Flava gasped. "Of course! The Second and Third Legions are in the north. They could possibly send troops to help if the skyway is functional."

"Unless Cephus has more crystoids to throw at us, he wouldn't stand a chance against another legion," I said. "Right now he's focused on the west because that crystoid disables the western skyway to the Kdosh skylet and the Alabaster Arch. He must have another crystoid on the skylet itself to keep the arch from working."

"How long would it take for troops to reach us?" Elyssa asked.

Flava increased the scope of the map until all of Pjurna was visible. It resembled Australia but the southern coastline bulged into the ocean and a large river split the southern part of the land mass. The Vjartik Mountains ran the length of the north, and the Great Barrier Vortex, a cauldron of boiling ocean water, guarded the western ocean from attack.

Darkling legions protected the mountain passes to the east. I knew all this because Cephus and Flava had briefed me the last time I'd been in town.

"The troops are here." Flava drew a red line on the map. "It would take no more than two weeks for them to reach us."

"Two weeks?" I stared at the map. "I thought skyways were faster than that."

"Two weeks, a month, who cares?" Joss said. "They will overwhelm the dictator and return the city to us."

"I have an army waiting in Eden, ready to come through the Alabaster Arch on Kdosh and invade." I found Kdosh just off the western coast on the fringe of the Great Barrier Vortex and jabbed it with a finger. "The minute that crystoid is down, I can fly to the arch and neutralize the crystoid affecting it. Once the skyway and arch are working again, I can have an army here in hours instead of weeks."

"Patience," Otaleon said. "We have waited months for you. Another two weeks will not matter."

"It might." Elyssa's statement drew a few arched eyebrows and wrinkled foreheads. "Flava, you told me that there were hardly any patrols just a month ago and that the flying soldiers began appearing a week later."

"Yes," Flava said. "First only a few, but more all the time."

"A week ago I counted less than twenty flying out of the Ministry of Research," a seraph said in Cyrinthian. "As I scouted the enemy yesterday, I counted nearly a hundred and fifty."

I saw where Elyssa was heading. "You think Cephus is mass producing these soldiers—but how?"

"I suspect he's kidnapping citizens and turning them," Elyssa said. "In a week he went from twenty to nearly eight times that amount. Within two weeks he could have hundreds or even a thousand flying soldiers. It's imperative we stop him as soon as possible."

I did the math in my head and realized if we didn't act now, even bringing in the other legions wouldn't be enough.

Chapter 4

Murmurs filled the room. Some of the Seraphim less-versed in English asked Flava to translate Elyssa's words.

"There are fewer than thirty of us total," Otaleon said. "Without magic we cannot fight even a hundred or more of these fliers who will surely be guarding the western crystoid."

Lanaeia frowned. "If we disabled the eastern crystoid and wait on the other legions, the fliers will overwhelm us, but we are already too few to fight the fliers that exist."

"That's why we need to reduce enemy numbers any way possible," Elyssa said. "Right now, Cephus has only enough troops to post an overwhelming force in the east or west. If he thinks the eastern crystoid is under attack, he'll likely send his fliers to protect it, leaving only his ground units in the west."

"Yes, a feint to the east might work," Flava said. She turned to a seraph I didn't recognize and spoke in Cyrinthian. "Nailan, how many crucibles do we have left?"

"A dozen," he replied.

Flava nodded. "We'll need a noisy diversion to the east. Can you manage it?"

"Of course!" He slapped another seraph on the back. "Philas and I can charge the crucibles and plant them overnight."

"How large are the crucibles?" I asked, my tongue reacquainting itself with Cyrinthian.

Nailan made a wide circle with his arms. "Four feet in diameter."

"Can I have two of them?" I asked.

26

He looked at Flava who nodded and then turned a questioning gaze on me. "Surely you don't plan to use them directly on the crystoid, do you?"

"Yes, but not in the way you think." I channeled small orbs of Murk and Brilliance and directed tendrils from each to weave together into a fuzzy gray ball. "This is Stasis, as I'm sure those of you who fought Daelissa know."

"Yes, and many of us still have the prisms that help us channel both Murk and Brilliance," Flava said.

Darklings usually couldn't easily channel Brilliance, and Murk was a challenge for Brightlings. Some, like me, had an inherent ability to channel both forces while others needed the boost crystal prisms gave them to amplify their latent abilities.

"The crystoids soak up Murk and Brilliance, but are susceptible to Stasis." I channeled a thin beam of gray energy into the floor. "I'll fill crucibles with Stasis, and if we can hit the crystoid with one, it should neutralize it."

"You'd have to do that from the air," Elyssa said, brow furrowed with concern. "We only have one rocket stick which means no one could watch your back."

"I hope our diversions will draw away most of the fliers." I released the channeled energy and the elemental globes faded away. "I should be able to swoop in, drop the bomb, and get out quickly."

Flava bit her lower lip and stared at the crystalized rock where Stasis had hit it. "We'll need everyone." She turned to Nailan. "Issue a general recall. We'll plan tonight and strike tomorrow at dawn."

Elyssa shook her head. "We need to act sooner and hit them in the early morning hours." She paced a few feet forward. "Even the enemy needs to sleep, and in the dark, Justin stands a better chance of slipping through their lines."

"We don't have time enough to prepare," Flava insisted. "I agree with your idea, but we should postpone it by a day."

"Cephus is off-balance right now," Elyssa argued. "Though he anticipated our arrival, he hasn't had time to consider that we might attack the eastern crystoid. The more time we give him, the better prepared he'll be."

"I don't agree," Joss said. "Cephus has had months to prepare for every situation. Another day won't significantly alter his defenses."

"On matters of strategy, I have rarely found Elyssa to be wrong," Lanaeia said. "She is as brilliant as her father."

Elyssa's cheeks blushed.

I agreed with Elyssa, but also saw the need to prepare our own meager forces. They'd be the ones off balance if we called them back in and suddenly thrust them into action. "I think a delay would be best."

Elyssa pursed her lips and gave me a displeased look. A shrug broke the tension. "I hope you're right."

Flava turned to Nailan. "Send your scouts and recall everyone. Fill the crucibles and we'll decide which areas to target."

He nodded. "At once." Nailan gathered several seraphs and departed.

Elyssa studied the map. "Is there a chance we could get an updated view?"

"With the aether flow cut off to most of the city, the map can't gather updated information," Flava said. "It captured the destruction around the Ministry of Defense, but not the other crystoids."

I glanced at the rocket stick. "Maybe I could do some scouting from the air."

"Alone?" Elyssa shook her head. "Out of everyone here, we can't afford to lose you. I'll go."

I gripped her hand. "I don't think so."

"Using the rocket stick means we might lose it, and that's the only way you can deliver an airborne crucible," Elyssa said.

"Nailan and his scouts already know the new face of the city," Flava said. "I will use their intel to show you which sections of the city are leveled, but it will take some time."

Elyssa breathed a sigh. "Sounds good. We should get started."

My stomach rumbled. It was well past noon and we hadn't eaten. "Got any food around here? Maybe some angel food cake, or deviled eggs?"

Flava didn't seem to get the humor and shook her head. "No, but we have panari and glurk."

I wrinkled my nose at the unappetizing name of the latter. "Uh, is it good?"

"Of course." She turned to Joss. "Would you show him to the dining hall?"

"My pleasure," Joss said.

"Can you bring me back something?" Elyssa asked me. "I'm going to stay here with Flava."

"I'll bring you a heaping plate of glurk," I promised her.

She arched an eyebrow. "Sounds delish."

Joss took me to the dining hall—a long cavern with a wooden table and brought out platters of fruit. It turned out I'd sampled glurk and panari on my last visit. Glurk, dense as peanut butter, resembled a tomato and had a nutty flavor like almonds. Panari, a sweet crunchy bread, pleasantly enhanced the glurk. I munched cruna, a purple pear-shaped fruit with the texture and taste of a sweetened avocado, and drank a thick green liquid called Guanabana.

"I like glurk," I admitted to Joss as he nibbled on quintos, olive-shaped vegetables with a sour bite.

"Glurk sits heavy in my stomach," the seraph admitted. "I don't care for it."

Otaleon joined us and sat next to Joss. "I am sorry if I seemed angry with you earlier, Justin. The war lies heavy on our hearts, but you bore a greater burden than most. If I had been in your position, I would not have been eager to embark another war."

I felt my shoulders sag at all the war had cost everyone, and the high price my reticence had exacted from one of my dearest friends. A tear gathered in my eye. "I ran away because I wanted to escape another war. Because of me, Nightliss is dead."

Joss put his hand over mine. "We are all immensely saddened, brother. Please, tell us how it happened."

Lanaeia appeared at the door. "I would also like to hear."

I wound back time to the tidal wave sweeping over the island where Elyssa and I were vacationing and how it was the slap in the face that brought me back to reality. I told them how the crystoids exploded violently when improperly destroyed and how they turned anyone who touched them into an insane malaether zombie.

29

John Corwin

"One of our scouts witnessed prisoners forced to touch a crystoid," Joss said. "We believe it was one of Cephus's sick experiments."

"I touched one by accident," I admitted. "Thankfully, I was able to channel the energy out of me and avoid any lasting harm." I'd blown a huge hole through a hill in North Dakota as a result.

"I did not realize Nightliss was so reticent to return to the war as well," Otaleon said. "You said she was conflicted about the death of her sister, Daelissa."

"She vanished, leaving the Templars and everyone else behind," I said. "It helped me rationalize my own departure."

"Nightliss was the Templar Clarion," Joss said, eyes troubled. "How could she simply leave?"

"Everyone has their breaking point," I said. "Even someone who has been around for thousands of years. Moses—the man you knew as Jeremiah Conroy—broke when Daelissa killed his wife Thesha. Revenge consumed him for millennia, and in the end, Daelissa killed him."

"I do not blame Nightliss," Joss said. "Had I not been turned into a husk in the final battle of the First Seraphim War, I likely would have run away as well."

Otaleon chuckled. "Who knew we would spend our next thousand years in the dark? Or that the dragons would eventually restore us?"

"Technically, you weren't restored by dragons," I said. "You can thank Daelissa for reviving you."

Otaleon smiled. "True."

"Daelissa revived me," Lanaeia said in a quiet voice, "but I would rather have remained a husk than serve such a cruel mistress." She wiped away sudden tears. "I'm sorry, Justin. Please continue your tale."

I moved on to our discovery that Stasis nullified the crystal meteors, but soon after we began neutralizing them, Frankenberg, a former chancellor at Science Academy protected crystoids with airship fortresses armed with lasers and battle bots.

30

"Once we realized Frankenberg was sending a fleet of airships to guard the crystoid in the Three Sisters, we found his secret base hidden in Antarctica and fought his army of megabots, airships and battle bots." I swallowed the knot forming in my throat as the most painful part of the story arrived. "We defeated his army and destroyed the control room in his base before he could escape, but a nuclear device was armed and we had only minutes to react."

"Nuclear?" Joss asked.

"The explosion would have wiped out everything for miles, and our entire army was within range," I explained. "Nightliss took an escape pod with the bomb. It flew into the stratosphere. She ejected, but the shockwave severely injured her." No matter how deep my breaths, I couldn't ease the knot of agony in my chest.

"She sacrificed herself for those she loved," Joss said, eyes glistening. "She gave the greatest gift she could."

"Her life for thousands," Otaleon finished. He squeezed his hands together. "You should celebrate her sacrifice, not mourn it, Justin. Nightliss would not want you to carry around such pain."

I tried to respond, but sobs choked my voice. I tried to think of something innocuous, like baseball. Instead, images of the small black cat I'd rescued from a rabid dog played back in my mind. That cat had eventually revealed itself to be a Seraphim in disguise—Nightliss. We'd been through so much together.

Tears rolled down Lanaeia's cheeks. "She was the best of us."

I nodded. "The hardest part is believing that she's really gone." I broke the dam of sorrow in my throat. "Anyway, we cleaned up the mess and neutralized all but one crystoid. Since the aether beam creates a sky portal leading to Cephus's fortress, we knew it would be the best way to get here."

"Agreed," Joss replied. "The other Alabaster Arches lead to Brightling controlled territory."

"Pjurna is hard to reach from other continents even in the best of times," Otaleon said. "Tell me, Justin, how did Cephus manage to create portals from Eden to Seraphina without use of an Alabaster Arch?"

"Our people are still scratching their heads about that one," I said. "Frankenberg said Serena was involved, a split instant before a demon-possessed man tore him to shreds."

"Why would a demon kill him?" Joss asked. "There are so many parts of this that don't make sense."

"I agree." Out of everything, that demon's actions had confused me the most. "As for the portal, Elyssa and I noticed an arch inside Cephus's fortress when we first arrived. I'm almost certain it has something to do with the sky portals."

"Serena also knows a great deal about portals and arches," Lanaeia said. "I once heard her talking to Daelissa about creating an arch that could open to all realms and all locations in case the Grand Nexus could not be restored."

"How do you think the crystoids were formed?" Joss asked. "What is to prevent Cephus from creating more?"

I shivered at the thought of him launching more into Eden. "It must not have been easy or I think he would've launched another attack by now. It's vital we stop him from any more shenanigans."

The others stared at me blankly.

"Before he causes more trouble," I clarified.

"Ah," they said simultaneously.

Now that I'd told my story, I wanted hear theirs. "Can you fill in the blanks about what happened after the last time I saw you?"

Otaleon took poured himself a glass of Guanabana and sipped it. "As you remember, Ketiss urged Commander Borathen to attack Cephus immediately so Tarissa could be secured."

"The commander thought it was more important to get the Overworld Conclave back in order first," I said. "He didn't want to leave behind an unstable government."

"Ketiss agreed and determined the Tarissan Legion could defeat Cephus." Otaleon sighed. "I had faith in his assessment, as did anyone else you might have asked before deployment. Many other reborn Seraphim, including the three of us, joined his quest."

"Despite my reluctance to fight another war," I said, "I truly thought the legion would have no problems."

32

Lanaeia looked at the floor. "Fresh from victory over Daelissa's mighty army, we thought we would crush him quickly."

"We arrived on Kdosh and took the skyway to Tarissa," Otaleon continued. "The shield around the Ministry of Research was impenetrable to our attacks. Cephus sent representatives to meet with Ketiss and urged diplomacy. Eager to avoid more bloodshed, Ketiss agreed to talks. What we did not realize was that this was merely a delaying tactic."

Joss bared his teeth. "Cephus is a vile trickster, Justin. Kill him when you have the chance."

Otaleon turned to his companion. "Can I finish now?"

"You always tell the stories," Joss said. "I'd like to finish this one."

The other seraph chuckled and sipped his drink. "Of course."

Joss looked surprised, but wasted no time continuing the story. "Cephus agreed to sign a treaty handing all power over to the Tarissan Legion so long as he was given a fair trial with no possibility of a death sentence."

"He told Ketiss he'd hand himself over?" I shook my head. "Sounds way too easy."

"Cephus asked for a formal arrest by Ketiss with the legion present." Joss clenched a fist. "It was a ruse to gather everyone in one place. Those of us who were not formally part of the legion were not present, while others were assigned patrols in the north and south."

Dread rose in my stomach as I realized where this was going. "And then?"

"Cephus came outside the ministry with a contingent of guards and stood just on the other side of the shield. Survivors said streaks of light shot straight up from the Ministry of Research and vanished in the sky." Joss crushed a piece of fruit he held. "While Cephus watched, the first crystal meteor smashed into the center of the legion, killing nearly everyone present."

I felt sick to my stomach. "That sick son of a bitch."

"He is no one to be trifled with," Joss said. "Though I trust your fighting abilities, I think we should be very cautious and not underestimate Cephus's cleverness."

"I witnessed his cleverness firsthand the last time I was here," I said. "He brought the other members of the Trivectus to meet me and convinced me to manifest my demon side to prove who I was. They panicked and called their guards. I, of course, defended myself. By the time it was over, I thought I'd killed the other two members of the Trivectus."

"I remember the story," Otaleon said. "In truth, Cephus had them killed during the melee."

"Yeah." My throat felt dry so I gulped some Guanabana. "I'm done underestimating this bastard."

God, I hoped I was right.

Chapter 5

It was well past dark when most members of the resistance were present and accounted for. The scouts updated the map with current geographical information, revealing a city pockmarked with destruction. The crystoids had leveled several city blocks at the eastern and western impact zones. The crystoid used to destroy the Tarissan Legion was gone, probably neutralized by Cephus after it served its murderous purpose.

Elyssa updated her plan with the help of Nailan and his scouts, marking areas around the western front for the explosive crucibles. Her Cyrinthian was proficient enough that I didn't have to translate much.

"The southern approach to the target is heavily patrolled," one of the scouts said. "Even if the diversion draws away most of their troops, it would be best to circle north."

"Why is the southern perimeter guarded so well?" Elyssa asked.

Nailan answered, "They know we are based in the south, but not precisely enough to find us." He looked around. "Have we still no word on Tryphiss?"

Philas shook his head. "She is still missing, sir."

"Three days," another scout said sadly. "I think she was captured or worse."

Nailan turned to Elyssa. "Tryphiss was our northern scout and would have more details about skirting the southern patrols."

"If Cephus continues producing troops at his current rate, we'll have no place left to hide." Otaleon's lips curled back with distaste. "Soon the entire city will be patrolled from the air."

"I have seen the internment camp inside the shield," another scout said. "Cephus captures nearly a hundred refugees a day, and the holding pen is packed with our people."

"How many soldiers guard each crystoid?" Elyssa asked. "Break it down into ground and air forces."

The scouts took turns marking the maps with a mind-numbing array of patrol routes, soldier counts, and more. I dozed off, only to be shaken awake by Elyssa some time later. The holographic map hovered in the air behind her, covered with more symbols and lines of attack than a football playbook.

I cracked a yawn and stood. "Figure it out?"

"I hope so." She tried to answer, but a yawn interrupted her. "I hope you enjoyed your catnap."

"How long was I out?"

"A couple of hours." Elyssa slipped her arm through mine and started walking. "Nailan and his scouts left to place crucibles so they'll be ready for the attack tomorrow night." She led me around a curve in the cave tunnel and into a corridor lined with doors.

"How do the numbers look?" I was almost afraid to ask.

"A hundred and three of us against seventy-two ground forces and somewhere between thirty and forty fliers."

"Yikes!" I felt her arm stiffen against mine. "I hope they take the bait."

Elyssa stopped in front of a slab of ultraviolet crystal and motioned at the small blue gem on the rock face next to it. "Do they use gems for everything here?"

"Pretty much." I zapped the gem with a small charge of Murk. The door misted and we stepped through it and into a nicely furnished room. Another jolt of Murk in the gem on the other side solidified the door. "Under normal circumstances, everyone wears a gem and it records everything around them and acts like a smartphone."

Elyssa frowned. "You can browse the web with it?"

"It's how all citizens download their angel porn." I flashed a grin. "Remember when I told you about my demon rampage my last time here?"

She nodded. "Yeah, you said it broadcast all across the city."

"On individual gems." I shivered. "It was like being on the nightly news."

"In other words, you got internet famous a few hours after arriving." She tutted. "You just had to make a name for yourself."

"More like infamous," I muttered.

Elyssa covered her mouth as another yawn broke free. "Where's the bed?"

I pointed out a slab of crystalized Murk in the corner. "Right there."

Her face fell. "It doesn't even have a mattress?"

"They don't use those here." I found a blue gem at the base of the bed and hoped it did what I thought it did. When activated, the Murk diffused into a white cottony cloud.

Elyssa's tentatively poked it with a finger and her eyes went wide. "It's so fluffy!"

"Try laying on it," I suggested.

She gingerly sat on the edge, as if afraid she'd fall through what looked like insubstantial mist. When it supported her, she lay back and moaned with pleasure. "This is the most comfortable bed I've ever been in. It's like sleeping on air."

I stripped off my Nightingale armor and slid into a pair of silky shorts left for me by our hosts. Elyssa slipped into a shimmering nighty.

"I miss my boyshorts," she said with a sigh.

I grinned. "You know, there's something I'm dying to try on this cloud bed."

Elyssa lowered a strap on the nightgown. "Oh? Did you want to jump up and down on it?"

"In a manner of speaking, yes." It turned out the cloud bed worked out very well for what I had in mind.

"I'll bet Shelton is cussing up a storm," I told Elyssa over breakfast the next morning. "We're supposed to attend his rehearsal dinner tonight."

"He shouldn't have scheduled it the day before an interdimensional covert operation," she replied as she peeled open a glurk. "I'm sure he'll understand."

"Yeah," I replied half-heartedly. "I really hate to miss it." Of course nothing had gone to plan, and instead of destroying the crystoid and escaping back through the sky portal in under two hours, we were stranded with our backs to the wall.

Elyssa's forehead pinched into a sad look. She reached over and patted my hand. "I'm sorry, babe. I know how much it means to you."

"I'm even gonna miss out on the bachelor party."

Her sympathetic expression faded. "Oh, really? What, pray tell, did you have in mind for him?"

I shrugged. "Cinder was planning it."

"Cinder?" A full-blown snort erupted. "Please tell me you're kidding. How would an emotionally challenged golem know what to plan for a bachelor party?"

"Adam and Ryland were helping him, I think." My voice sounded a bit defensive, but she was right. Cinder might be a sentient golem that looked human, but he didn't have a handle on emotions just yet. "It's not like we planned to go to a strip club or anything."

"If Ryland is helping him plan, you'll probably end up at a shifter strip club."

I wrinkled my nose. "You mean, lycans and felycans stripping?"

"You haven't seen anything until you've seen a naked woman with a wolf head."

I shuddered. "Eww, are you serious? Have you actually seen that before?"

Elyssa finished peeling her glurk and regarded me with a serious arch of her eyebrow. "Babe, I'm a Templar. I've seen it all."

"I can only imagine." I popped a quinto in my mouth and savored the sour bite. "I've witnessed a lot of awful stuff, but I've rarely seen the seedy underbelly of the Overworld."

"Maybe when this is over I'll give you the grand tour." She winked and took a sip of juice.

"When this is all over," I muttered. "It's never all over. There's always another bad guy climbing out of a toilet to rain poop on our parade."

"Despite the crystoid-induced tsunami, I still enjoyed our time in Thailand," Elyssa said. "Cephus might think he's a badass, but we've been through worse."

"Except it's not just Cephus," I said. "Frankenberg said Serena is involved, and you know how shifty she can be."

"I can be shifty too." Elyssa spooned glurk paste in her mouth. "And you also have that aether pack so you can use your abilities."

"True." I didn't know how much power it held, but it was better than nothing.

Elyssa recalled everyone after lunch for status updates. Nailan reported that his people had finished placing the crucibles and the route to the western crystoid had been scouted.

Elyssa's comment during brunch about the aether pack had given me food for thought, so once everyone finished their status reports, I brought up an idea I expected to get shot down immediately. "We have three aether packs," I said. "That means three of us with magic versus any of their fliers and ground troops who remain behind to guard the crystoid during the diversion. I think we should track down another of their patrols and steal their aether packs. Not only is that fewer soldiers we have to worry about, but more magic for us."

"How large are their patrols?" Elyssa asked.

Nailan responded. "They usually fly in packs of four."

"Justin has aether," Flava said. "He could surely bring a squad of fliers to their knees."

Elyssa tapped a finger to her chin. "Four more with aether on our side would be a big help."

It took a moment for me to realize they were seriously considering my proposal. "My idea is pretty straightforward," I said. "So long as their patrols aren't larger than four or five, we can easily handle them."

Elyssa checked the time. "We have ten hours before mission go. That means seven hours before we need to report back here and move into position."

"Plenty of time for what we need to do." Flava looked at me. "What is your plan?"

"Just walk around until a flier squad finds us," I said.

"We'll need an ambush," Elyssa said. "Nailan, can you show me some good places to do that?"

The seraph nodded. "Of course."

With our simple plan fleshed out, our small group set off to the northeast. Lanaeia wore one of the three aether packs. Flava and I wore the other two.

The scout leader vanished ahead into the empty streets for minutes at a time, reappearing to let us know what lay ahead, and scaring the crap out of me each time he unexpectedly popped from behind a corner. Elyssa seemed to be the only one who knew when he was about to make an appearance, but she enjoyed seeing me flinch too much to let me know in advance.

Deeper into the city, Nailan leapt from the branches of a tree and landed right in front of me. I leapt five feet straight up and nearly hit the branch he'd dropped from. As usual, he remained straight-faced, though I suspected he got a kick out of my reaction.

"Now I know you're doing it on purpose!" I hissed.

"There is a four-man patrol flying south one street over," Nailan said. "I believe this is our best chance."

Elyssa nodded at me. "Get in position."

I slid the rocket stick from its sheath and twisted the handle. The seat unfolded and the fins popped out of the rear section. "I'm going to drop a flier on you," I told Nailan.

He raised an eyebrow as if he had no idea why I would do such a thing. "Just don't damage the aether pack."

Elyssa pecked my cheek. "Be careful."

"Hey, I'm always careful," I said, hopping on the rocket stick. I hit the accelerator too hard and nearly rammed the tree, screeching to a halt just in time. I gave Elyssa a sheepish grin and jetted upward before she could sigh and roll her eyes. Rocket stick nearly vertical, I climbed steadily, the polished surface of a crimson skyscraper flashing past beneath me.

I rolled left and straightened out before I reached the top of the building and flew into plain sight of the mutant squad. Gliding serenely over the street, blazing wings spread wide, they noticed me, but seemed to take a moment to register I was an enemy. They wore spiffier outfits than their comrades I'd encountered yesterday—shiny black armor with the white and black of the Void emblazoned on their chests. The leader of their V formation veered my way without a gesture or a shout and the rest of his brainwashed minions followed.

I let them close within firing range then spun and plunged back down a perpendicular street. They dove after me, beams of Murk blasting from their fists. I pulled out of my dive just a few feet off the crystalline street and dodged back and forth like a drunken three-legged dog in a mosh pit as the pursuers did their best to hammer me into mush. Fist-sized balls exploded against the street, leaving divots and spraying shards into the air.

The plan was working brilliantly except for one major thing. The mutants weren't flying low enough, instead maintaining altitude about twenty feet above me, probably because firing from greater height gave them an advantage. Just a couple blocks away, two statues rose on either side of the street where my comrades lay in wait. I had to do something fast. The next building rose to my left. Sparing a bit of juice from the aether pack, I channeled a ramrod and blew a hole through the window.

Devoid of furnishings, the spare interior gave me plenty of room to maneuver. I paused inside a large room stretching from one side of the building to the other and glanced back. The mutants zipped inside, flowing from a V to a straight line without pause, and firing away the second they spotted me.

It worked!

Now I just had to make it outside without dying. The rocket stick proved nimble enough, and the enemy attacks plowed an opening through the opposite windows so I didn't have to use precious aether. I zipped outside and veered hard right to line up with the narrow strait between the statues.

My pursuers maintained low altitude and continued the chase. The statues whooshed past. I continued another thirty yards and spun just as the fliers streaked through. Elyssa and the others waiting on the other side struck.

Silvery darts sprayed from the wrist-mounted lancer Elyssa wore. One struck an enemy in the neck, finding the space between the helmet and the shoulder armor, and the Seraphim went limp. His body bounced along the street and came to a halt. Laneia creamed the last flier with a well-timed blast of Murk. Joss and Otaleon threw shimmering nets and caught one more, but the lead flier climbed upward toward escape.

"He'll warn the others!" Elyssa shouted. "Get him, Justin!"

"Already on it," I called, urging the rocket stick to full speed.

The soldier flung crystal shards of Murk at me, too many to dodge, so I used more aether and threw up a shield. His wings began to shimmer and his momentum faltered. Either he was running out of aether, or tiring from the chase. I flung a dense sphere of Murk and nailed him in the back of the head. The armor clunked with impact and the flier slammed into the building in front of him.

He hung suspended for a moment and then his wings flickered away. I caught him around the waist before he fell. The rocket stick's engine whirred loudly as it struggled to keep both of us aloft. I eased back the throttle and descended as gently as I could. Elyssa and the others held up their arms and I dropped the unconscious mutant the remaining ten feet so they could catch him.

We did it. I prayed these aether packs gave us the edge we desperately needed.

Chapter 6

Breathing a sigh of relief, I landed and folded the rocket fins and seat of the rocket stick back into compact form and shoved it in its sheath. The odor of overheated electronics stung my nostrils and I hoped I hadn't burned it out. Shelton had assured me it could carry two hundred pounds, albeit slowly. I wished Elyssa's hadn't been destroyed, because it would've come in handy.

Flava and the others began stripping the armor from the fliers. Flava shuddered when she revealed the mutilated face of the first soldier.

"What this stuff made of?" Elyssa asked, knocking her knuckles against one of the helmets.

Flava pressed her fingers to it and closed her eyes. "Highly concentrated Murk threaded with Brilliance."

"It's so concentrated that it's black?" I asked.

She opened her eyes and nodded. "Something so dense could not be channeled without the assistance of powerful gems."

"Cephus and his ministry are fully capable of such feats," Nailan said.

"They made a mistake by not padding the helmet." Elyssa showed everyone the inside of it. "When Justin conked that last soldier, his head ricocheted."

"Like a marble in a, uh, bucket," I finished lamely, unable to conjure a suitable analogy.

"Yeah," Elyssa said with a roll of her eyes. "A bucket."

Flava removed the helmet from the flier I'd knocked out and gasped. "It's Tryphiss!"

43

I grimaced as I looked upon the face of a youthful looking sera, head shaved and marred by the scar across her temple, a white gem gleaming dully from the right eye socket.

"Now we know what happened to her," Nailan said grimly. "She's been turned into one of these creatures."

"Creatures or not, they are our people," Flava said. "They were citizens we swore to protect."

"We've failed them," Philas said in a miserable voice.

"You're a gifted healer, Flava." I put a hand on her shoulder. "Maybe we can take Tryphiss with us and see if she can be fixed."

"Bring them all," Nailan said. "Otherwise they may return to their new master."

Elyssa looked at the unconscious Seraphim doubtfully. "Do you have a holding facility?"

Nailan nodded. "We can contrive something. I don't want to leave them at the tender mercy of Cephus." He spat the name. "There must be something we can do."

"Quickly, then," Elyssa said. She shot lancer darts into the still forms that didn't already have one. "Those will keep them asleep."

Joss and the others fitted the stolen aether packs to their backs, eyes widening as they felt the power coursing through them. Hefting the stricken Seraphim, we headed south.

When we reached the cave base, Nailan secured all the prisoners but Tryphiss. Flava laid her on a table and placed her hands on the sera's temples. After a long moment of concentration, she grimaced and pulled away.

"These white gems are similar to the prisms you gave us for channeling Brilliance," she said.

"They must not work as well," I told her. "Otherwise I think the mutants would have used destruction to fight me."

"I agree." She ran a finger across the pink scar on the sera's head. "Cephus implanted something here. I believe it's what grants him control."

Just thinking about it gave me the heebie-jeebies. "I thought Seraphim were all about magic and not wetware."

The last word didn't translate well into Cyrinthian, leaving a puzzled look on Flava's face. "I cannot fathom what he might have used. The Ministry of Research was often the focus of controversial projects."

"I've seen them firsthand." Nightliss's bruised and battered body sprang to mind before I could stop myself from flashing back to her rescue from the ministry. "Is it possible to reopen the wound?"

"That is not something I dare start now, only hours before the attack," Flava replied. "I need to do a deeper scan and that will take hours."

"We don't want your attention split now," Elyssa said. "Whatever Cephus did can hopefully be reversed."

"You were right about not waiting for another legion to arrive," Flava said to Elyssa. "Even if we win, there will be hundreds of citizens affected by Cephus's monstrous violations."

The gut full of guilt I'd carried around since the crystoid incident grew even heavier. "I should have stopped him right after I rescued Nightliss. I had the entire legion with me."

"You needed me to heal Elyssa," Flava said. "It was imperative we reach her immediately."

"I could have sent you ahead and remained behind with Ketiss." I pounded the flat of a fist against the wall. "If only I'd done it right then. We could have saved thousands of lives."

Elyssa crossed her arms. "To quote the great Harry Shelton, if ifs and buts were candy and nuts, we'd all be farting fairies."

"Isn't it 'fat as pigs'?" I said.

"Not according to Shelton." She looked at the stricken sera on the table. "You did what you thought was right at the time, Justin. As much as you wish you were a military genius or all-powerful, you're not. I understand that and Nightliss did too."

Flava looked down. "I am sorry for blaming you for everything, Justin." Her gaze wandered up to meet mine. "The only fault lies with Cephus. I am weighing you with guilt that is not yours."

Her words and Elyssa's lightened the load a little. Nightliss was gone and Tarissa all but destroyed, but nothing I did now could change the past—only the future. I would do everything in my power to ensure a beautiful future for Seraphina, or die trying.

Night arrived and it was time to leave. Since the only reliable way to measure time in the no-magic zone was with mine and Elyssa's arcphones, I hesitantly gave Nookli over to Philas so he'd know the precise time to start his attacks.

"Why couldn't you give him your phone?" I asked Elyssa after he left with his group.

"I have the battle plans on mine." She smiled reassuringly as she double-checked her Nightingale armor for any damage. "I'm sure you'll get Nookli back."

We joined the others. Flava wore Tryphiss's armor but without the helmet since she said it hindered her vision. A group of Nailan's people had already left for the east to stage diversions. Nailan came with us, his people carrying the two crucibles I'd filled with Stasis in black webbing.

I took all the aether packs with me on a rocket stick ride and flicked on my incubus vision. Sure enough, once I achieved line of sight with the ultraviolet pimple in the city center, thin aether beams speared into them, and hopefully charging them to full. Since Cephus's evil minions hadn't thought to put a battery gauge on the side, I tested each by touching the crystal prongs and sensing the energy bursting across my senses.

Man, this aether beam works fast.

Back on the ground again, I rejoined the others and handed out the packs. Flava's eyes glowed purple when she affixed one to her back. "Now we have a chance," she murmured.

"We always had a chance," I countered. "This just gives us more opportunity to hand out some ass-whoopings."

"I thought we agreed to harm the fliers as little as possible," Nailan said.

I shrugged. "Just a figure of speech. Hopefully, Cephus will call most of them to guard the other crystoid."

We reached the staging area, a building shaped like a nightmare-sized tornado. I didn't see how it remained standing with such a narrow base and wide top. We were less than a block from the western buildings flattened by the crystoid, and about ten blocks from the crystoid itself, though measuring in blocks seemed pointless since only rubble remained ahead.

Nailan conferred with his scouts, concern etched in his forehead. Not the word "concern", but the facial expression.

"What's wrong?" I asked.

"We expected more patrols," he said. "We avoided only four ground and three air patrols."

I hadn't seen any ground patrols since the scouts expertly led us safely past them, but I had seen the fliers. "We zigzagged a lot. Maybe we just got lucky."

He didn't look convinced. "It's likely they've concentrated most of their troops at the crystoid." Nailan whispered commands to two seraphs and they melted away into the night.

Elyssa checked the time. "Fifteen minutes," she whispered.

Those fifteen minutes stretched into eternity. Seconds after the clock hit three A.M., my super hearing picked up the low rumble of explosions echoing across the city. The others exchanged tense glances. I switched to incubus vision and found the crystoid's aether beam. It seemed massive this close to it—far larger, in fact, than the ones I'd neutralized in Eden.

"There they go," Elyssa whispered excitedly and pointed to ultraviolet wings streaking across the sky and to the east.

"I count at least forty," Nailan said.

I tried to count, but even with my enhanced vision, they were too far away and moving too fast for me to clearly pick out each flier.

Nailan noticed me squinting. "Approximating the number of enemies is a talent every scout must cultivate."

"I'm glad we have you," I admitted.

Nailan's scouts flowed from the darkness several minutes later. "Thirty Void soldiers and ten Void fliers remain," one reported.

"Now the odds are in our favor," Flava said.

Elyssa gazed at the twinkling lights vanishing into the horizon. "The fliers need another few minutes to get far enough away."

I turned to Nailan. "Is stealth an option for taking down any of the remaining guards?"

One of the scouts answered. "They are too tightly spaced around the impact crater and there are no lone patrols."

"Why is it always like that?" I muttered. In the movies, there were tons of stupid bad guys who patrolled all by themselves, only to be taken down one by one. "Just one time, I'd like to take out the guy at the back of a patrol and jerk him out of sight so fast, the others don't even realize he's gone."

Elyssa patted my shoulder. "Justin, you're an incubus, not a ninja."

"One day, Ninjette," I replied, using the nickname her brother Michael preferred for her. "One day."

She checked the sky, and the time on her phone. "It's time. Justin, get ready."

I unsheathed the rocket stick and flicked out the seat and fins. Nailan tied the webbing holding the crucibles to the bottom.

"Remember to hurl the crucibles as hard as you can," he said. "They look fragile, but they require sufficient velocity to break on impact."

"I'm familiar with them," I assured him. "Good luck."

"May the Creator see you through, Destroyer," Nailan replied.

"That's something I never expected to hear," I murmured to myself.

Elyssa pulled me in for a long kiss. "I love you. Be careful."

I pecked her nose. "Love you too, honey-boo bear."

She sighed. "I'm so happy no one else here understands that."

Chuckling, I hopped on the rocket stick. "I'll be sure to include affectionate lingo in their next English lesson." With a twist of the handle, I guided the rocket stick up along the side of the vortex building until I crested the top. There was no roof, only a dark hole through the center. Like my previous visit to Tarissa, I didn't understand how people actually utilized these buildings. Did Seraphim have nine-to-five jobs like humans, or did they spend all their time being magnificent?

In a city where furniture and other items could be created magically, and where the bathrooms magically disposed of waste, it didn't seem there was much opportunity for making money.

Hovering over the dark pit, I eased my way to the other side of the building so I could peek over the edge. When I saw the target, the breath caught in my throat. "That thing is huge!" Glowing malevolently, the crystoid resembled a spiky sphere, crystal shards protruding from all angles. Those on top angled straight up toward the sky portal. As Nailan had reported during our planning sessions, rubble surrounded the meteor on all sides, blocking the view from those on the ground.

It was why he hadn't known how big this thing was. The crystal meteors that hit Eden had started small and grown as they soaked up aether. The largest I'd seen had been the size of an elephant.

This one was the size of a herd.

Measuring at least twenty yards in diameter, it dwarfed anything I could have imagined. Neutralizing even the regular crystoids was no mean feat. The smallest of those had nearly jerked me off my feet and sucked me dry.

Though I'd filled the crucibles full to bursting with Stasis, they'd do almost nothing to this monstrosity. Hell, it might take several of us channeling Stasis to stand a chance of neutralizing it.

This required a complete change in tactics. Simply flying overhead and bombing the crystoid would do almost nothing. I had to warn the others so we could reevaluate the plan. I dove for the ground, hoping to intercept Elyssa before they reached the enemy lines. I'd barely started my dive when flashes of energy lanced through the night. Our people had engaged the enemy.

I was too late.

Glowing white spheres shot high into the air from the enemy positions, lighting the battlefield. More glow balls launched from the tops of surrounding buildings until it was bright as day. That was when I saw what waited at the tops of the other tall buildings around the impact zone. Shiny black armor gleamed. Ultraviolet wings blazed. Dozens of Void fliers launched from the rooftops toward my unsuspecting companions.

Cephus had anticipated this attack from the start and staged everything. He knew Nailan and his scouts had no way to climb the buildings without being spotted by patrols. Even I hadn't seen the enemy lurking in the darkness.

"War is fought in three-dimensions," Elyssa's father, Thomas Borathen, once told me. "When anticipating attack, never forget to look up and down."

We hadn't looked up.

Thomas hadn't raised a fool. I saw Elyssa leading a retreat inside the vortex building. She already knew this mission had gone sideways, probably from the moment the lights went on. I ducked back behind the lip of the vortex building, using the hollow center to hide in. The Void fliers glided to the ground, apparently unaware of me.

Cephus's ground troops marched from their positions and joined the other units that now surrounded the building. A platform supported by the shoulders of four fliers descended from another building, bearing a seraph that made me see red.

My hands clenched so tightly around the rocket stick, I felt the metal start to warp.

A tall seraph with a flowing black cape embroidered with the Void symbol smiled confidently as his chariot drifted just above the heads of his soldiers. Cephus ran a hand through his pitch black hair, combed down in the Roman style and spoke. "My dear rebels, this fight has gone on too long. You may have the help of the Destroyer, but as you see, it was not enough." His voice boomed, apparently amplified by the gem on the collar of his cape.

I heard Flava shouting back at him. "The Destroyer will make you eat those words, usurper!"

"Justin, my friend, stop cowering and come outside." Cephus waved his hand in a sweeping gesture. "Join me in my quest to rid this world and all worlds of their petty religions. Let us reveal the truth and lead all the realms into an age of enlightenment."

He sounded so damned reasonable, I almost wanted to join him.

Flava returned verbal fire. "You spout nothing but lies, Cephus! You mean to kill us all."

"Most of you, yes," Cephus said. "I will, however, spare Justin and any he vouches for. I want him by my side when the truth is unleashed upon all the realms."

"You would not know truth if it penetrated your backside," Flava said.

I nearly lost it, hearing her talk like that, and had to hold in a laugh despite the deadly situation.

"In a matter of days the Void will open," Cephus said in a dream voice. "Our master, the Beast, will finally be free."

A cold, hard lump formed in my stomach, freezing fingers caressing my heart. *This crazy mother effer wants to open a portal to the Void?*

"How would you do such a thing?" Flava shouted.

"Surrender and perhaps I will show you," Cephus said. He waited about a minute, but Flava didn't shout back at him. He sighed. "You disappoint me, Justin. I suppose if you will not give up, I will be forced to kill you all."

Cephus looked back and nodded toward another seraph. "They have five minutes, Tain Prahven." He shook his head sadly and then the fliers supporting his chariot flapped their wings and swept him away.

Tain Prahven touched the gem at his throat and spoke in Cyrinthian, "By order of Lord Cephus, surrender or die!" His voice boomed, echoing through the dead city.

I followed Cephus with my eyes, calculating if I could reach him before his fliers killed me. I could end this right now. On the other hand, if I chased him, Elyssa and the others would die.

Without aether power in the building, they had no way to reach higher levels, trapping them in the narrow confines of the first floor. I had to help somehow, but what could I do against the small army below?

Once again, Cephus had outsmarted us. This time, it seemed he'd finish us once and for all.

Chapter 7

Options, Justin, options!
There had to be something I could do to save the others.

There were simply too many enemies for me to fight. A diversion wouldn't work for the same reason. On the other hand, I still had two aces up my sleeves. Since neutralizing the crystoid was out of the question, the Stasis bombs would have to serve another purpose.

The mutants were brainwashed to fight relentlessly until they won or died. The ground troops, however, were Cephus's loyal followers. To make the biggest impact, I had to hit the enemy where it hurt the most.

"By command of Tain Prahven, you have one minute," a seraph said in an imperious voice. Wearing black armor with extra-wide shoulder-pads and a breastplate molded like six-pack abs, he stood with the rest of the loyalists behind a shield of fliers. "Surrender peacefully and you will be spared."

"What a pompous jackass," I muttered. Thankfully, the enemy was breaking the rule that had gotten my allies into this mess. They weren't looking up. Depending on how the mutants were wired, they either took verbal commands or Cephus had some sort of remote control wired into their heads. If I had to guess, it was more likely the commands were verbal, even if transmitted using a communications gem.

Taking out as many loyalists as possible meant the fliers below wouldn't receive any orders until someone else took control. If I had to make another guess, the loudmouth down there was the one authorized to command the fliers.

"Thirty seconds until your destruction!" Tain Prahven, aka Commander Asshat, shouted. "Submit!"

That was my cue to stop thinking and start doing. I dove over the lip of the vortex, the relentless grip of gravity and the speed of the broom quickly taking me to terminal velocity. I detached the Stasis crucibles and let them fall. So focused were the enemy on the building, that not a one of them glanced up as I pulled out of the dive.

One of the ground troops looked up at the last minute, eyes flashing wide, arms going up in the classic *My spaceship is about to crash into an asteroid!* position. He didn't have a chance to shout a warning before the crucibles exploded and a boiling gray cloud of energy flooded across the square outside the building.

The fog swept through the back ranks of the enemy, freezing them into lifelike statues. I'd never seen Stasis directly kill anyone, meaning in a few minutes, those statues would come back to life. Though vicious enemies often forced my hand to kill in cold blood, I still hated it. The faces of many I'd slain still haunted me at night, and now I had to do it again to save my friends.

Considering what Cephus and his people had done to Eden, I was prepared to live with it this time.

Drawing upon the aether pack, I raked a claw of Brilliance across the stricken loyalists. They exploded like ice statues. I sliced the armor off Tain Prahven and destroyed the gem on its collar. Keeping him alive seemed prudent since he might prove valuable for questioning. Though rows of the mutant fliers closest to the building remained unaffected by the Stasis, they didn't move a muscle as I mowed down their ruthless controllers.

Several of the loyalists slumped to the ground as the Stasis wore off. Tain Prahven bare-chested and barrel-bellied without his muscle armor staggered upright and began screaming, "Kill him! Kill him!"

Without the gem to transmit, the fliers didn't move.

I bared my teeth. "You're not the puppeteer they're looking for."

Prahven flung orbs of Murk at me. I batted them aside contemptuously with a shield and then knocked him silly with a fist of Murk.

Screaming in fear, the conscious loyalists ran for their lives. Still not down for the count, Prahven ran away with them. There were too many for me to take on by myself, so I let him go. I found his armor and plucked the red gem from the collar. It looked similar to the one Cephus had worn when I met him. I channeled a spark of Murk into it, but nothing happened.

I took the gem for later study and turned back to the building. Wading through a forest of silent fliers, I reached the front of the building just as Elyssa and the others charged out of it weapons and magic at the ready.

I threw up my hands before they started blasting helpless soldiers. "Wait!"

Elyssa's eyes widened. "We couldn't see what was going on out here."

"We were trying to find the aether supply tunnel," Flava said. "Many of the larger towers have special underground corridors to channel aether energy for the building utilities."

"I used the Stasis bombs on the loyalists," I said. "Right now, the fliers don't have anyone controlling them, so we have to act fast."

"Agreed," Elyssa said. "Retreat!"

"No!" I jabbed a finger at the crystoid. "This might be our last chance to disable that thing. Cephus was probably watching all this through his commander's gem. He probably has more fliers on the way."

"But you dropped the bombs," Elyssa said.

"They wouldn't have been enough." I jammed the rocket stick into its sheath. "Who here besides Lanaeia can channel Brilliance well?"

Flava, Joss, and Otaleon raised their hands.

"Lanaeia, Joss, and Otaleon you're on team Brilliance." I needed equal numbers for what I had in mind. "Now I need three strong Murk channelers."

Out of all the raised hands, I chose Flava, Nailan, and Philas, then looked around at the eerily still mutants. "I want everyone else except for you, you, and you"—I pointed out three of the beefiest looking Darklings—"to remove the aether packs from these fliers and retreat

54

back to the rendezvous point." I motioned to the three I'd singled out. "You'll come with us."

The other Darklings got to work prying off the mutants' armor to get to the aether packs. It would take them a while, but we needed to remove every advantage from Cephus's forces that we could.

I set off at a jog toward our objective. "Time to disable that crystoid."

Elyssa ran beside me. "Why did you ask if they could channel Brilliance?"

"This crystoid is massive, babe." I bit my lower lip. "I need every ounce of power I can get for this one."

When we crested the mountain of rubble and laid eyes on the crystal meteor, everyone let out a collective gasp, including me. Close up, the crystoid looked even larger than from the air. Considering the volume of raw aether flowing into this thing, I was surprised it wasn't the size of the city. Then again, Cephus might have made the ones here different than the ones that hit Eden. He could have limited their growth so he could neutralize them himself once he took total control of the city.

"How do we help?" Flava asked.

"I need those who are the strongest in channeling Brilliance on my right. The rest of you on my left." Once everyone assumed their positions, I continued. "Lanaeia and Flava, put your hands on my back. The rest of you put a hand on the back of the person next to you."

"We are linking," Flava said. "Like your mother showed us."

I nodded. "I need you to channel everything you can through each other and into me. Those on the right channel only Brilliance, and those to my left concentrate on Murk." I pointed to Elyssa and the other three volunteers. "I need you to hold onto me. Once I hit that thing with Stasis, it'll try to suck me in like a magnet."

Elyssa's eyes filled with worry. "A crystoid a quarter the size of this one nearly drained you dry, Justin."

"This is gonna work," I said.

"But your mother said linking too many people together is dangerous." She gripped my hand. "It could burn you out."

"It's the only way to focus enough Stasis," I said.

"What if the aether packs run dry?"

"Pray they don't." I gave her a stern look. "Do your duty, Templar."

Steel shone in her eyes and the worry vanished behind a stern façade. "As you wish." She motioned the other three Darklings into place and ordered them to hold down my legs. Elyssa wrapped her arms around my chest and whispered in my ear, "I've got you, my love."

"Wonder twin powers, activate!" I shouted.

Flava and the others frowned.

I cleared my throat. "That means to start channeling."

"Ah," they murmured.

"Destroyer, I have activated the wonder twin powers," Flava said.

"As have I," Lanaeia added.

One by one, my Seraphim allies began to channel the forces of destruction and creation through the chain and to me, the focus. Power ignited my blood and filled my flesh with the deep cold calm of Murk and the burning powerful rage of Brilliance. My flesh felt ready to evaporate with the raw energy roiling inside.

Raising my hands, I released the energy into my palms, coalescing a sphere of burning white in my right, and ultraviolet in my left. My hair felt as though it was standing on end, and my eyes watered from the sheer effort it took to keep my mind focused. My inner demon growled with delight and rammed against its cage, eager to grasp the power sizzling just out of its reach. My mind faltered, unable to maintain focus on both events. The door opened a fraction and my demon half surged.

It was like holding up the roof of a collapsing house with my hands while fighting off a tiger with my feet. If I concentrated too much on one or the other, I'd be crushed or eaten.

"Justin!" someone shouted.

Elyssa's strong arms gripped me tighter. "Justin, I'm here. You can do it."

You and I have had this conversation before, I sent to the traitorous demon half.

Power, destruction! It sent back.

Why is my demon half an idiot? I had to do something fast. Splitting my attention came hard, especially when dealing with this much power. My head ached. Half my body felt frozen and the other two thirds felt ready to burst into flames. I couldn't channel this much energy for much longer. Focusing everything I had into one swift kick, I booted the tiger in the nose and slammed the cage shut, then quickly returned my focus to the collapsing ceiling.

A croak of pain burst from my raw throat as I threaded the Murk and Brilliance into a massive sphere of Stasis. With a cry of relief, I poured a thick gray beam of energy toward the center of the crystoid. The agony in my body abated as it no longer had to contain the power. The moment the Stasis hit the crystoid, an invisible force jerked my body toward it.

Elyssa and the others grunted. We slid inches closer, but my anchors dug in their heels and our forward momentum stopped.

"It's working!" someone shouted.

The surface of the crystoid cracked, its violet and white hues turning a sullen gray at the outer edges. But the power flooding into me weakened, abating slowly but perceptibly.

"The aether packs," I shouted. "They're running out of power."

The gray spread slowly from the outside in, two yards, ten, fifteen. It was halfway there. My teeth ached and my throat felt as if it were on fire.

"Incoming fliers!" someone shouted. "The mutants who left earlier have returned."

The orbs of primal force unraveled and vanished. Where once there had been a rushing river of power, only a dry, cracked riverbed remained. I slumped in Elyssa's arms. "We're out of juice."

"Was it enough?" she asked.

The core of the crystoid pulsed ultraviolet and white. Ten yards across, it still looked as healthy and malevolent as ever though the outer two thirds were ashen gray. "I don't think so," I croaked from a raw throat. "It's still alive."

I looked up and saw squads of mutants on approach, fists glowing with Murk. Our aether packs drained, we'd be powerless to stop their attacks once they closed within range.

"Justin, can you run?" Elyssa asked.

My legs felt weak, but firm enough to get the flock out of there. "Yeah. We've done all we can."

"Down into the crater," Elyssa said. "Go, go, go!"

We picked our way down the piles of destroyed buildings and took cover in the shell of a smaller structure as the mutants flashed overhead. Shards of Murk rained down, bits of shrapnel pelting us.

"We're trapped," Flava said. "Without aether, how are we to fight back?"

True, we were out of aether, but with the crystoid still functional, there was plenty to be had. I unsheathed the rocket stick and flicked open the seat and fins. "I'm going to fly into the aether beam. That'll give me enough power to at least divert their attention."

Elyssa gripped my arm. "Justin, there must be forty fliers! It's suicide!"

"No, it's a rational transaction. One life for all of yours." I was tired and aching from my previous effort, but I still had my demonic strength to fall back upon.

"We will not let you go," Flava said as Murk crystals smashed against the rubble outside our shelter and pelted us. "There must be another way."

"Then tell me what it is." I gripped the rocket stick. "Once I have aether, I can channel a shield. I'll be fine." I hoped I could live up to that boast since my insides felt like boiled spaghetti.

Shouts rose from outside and two fliers plummeted to the ground. The attacks on our position ceased. I peered outside and saw the rest of our small army equipped with the confiscated aether packs. While some of them shielded against the airborne attackers, others fired volleys of Murk at the fliers.

"Get up the hill to that shield!" I shouted as I boarded the rocket stick.

"Where are you going?" Elyssa said.

I showed her my teeth. "To finish off that blight."

58

Her lips flattened into a line. "We'll cover you."

"Love you." I gave her a kiss and took off.

"Up the hill!" Elyssa shouted, and led the charge to safety while the remnants of the Tarissan Legion fought to protect them.

I had one more shot at this thing. If I failed, we were done for.

Chapter 8

I flew up and into the aether beam still emitting from the core of the crystoid. Like flying from a cold dark cave and into a beam of warm sunlight, energy flooded my body, but was I too weakened to handle it? The fliers were currently too occupied with fighting the ground forces to spare a moment for me, so I spun to face the crystoid. Locking my legs around the rocket stick, I drew upon the primal forces of destruction and creation and threaded them into Stasis. When the sphere of gray grew as large as my torso, I willed it toward the glowing core.

The reaction jerked me down so hard I flipped upside down on the rocket stick, clinging by the backs of my knees for dear life. Despite the precarious situation, I didn't dare stop channeling, pouring everything I had into the infernal meteor below.

Something stuck my back, but the Nightingale armor held. Another attack slammed my leg and I nearly lost my grip on the rocket stick, but I couldn't look away, couldn't lose my concentration. A flier silently fell, and then another. Brilliance sizzled past me as another flier swooped in. A beam of Murk intercepted him before he took another shot.

My legs began to slip and the rocket stick sagged from the strain of holding me aloft. Slowly, it sank toward the pit. The crystoid seemed to suck up everything I had. I heard Elyssa shouting my name, but I couldn't spare even a split second of attention for anything else.

I have to finish this!

I tried to summon more power, but my floodgates were already wide open.

Out of the corner of my eye, I saw dozens of fliers gliding my way. Sweat trickled down my face and rained from the tip of my nose, freezing into tiny crystals when it hit the sphere of Stasis. The rocket stick dropped another few feet, engine whirring at top speed. Another twenty yards and I'd hit the crystoid.

Touching a smaller one had nearly turned me into a mindless malaether zombie. I didn't want to think what one this huge would do to me. In a few seconds the fliers would kill me or the crystoid would.

The stink of burnt electronics stung my nose and the rocket stick died. Without an anchor to hold me up, the magnetic pull on the crystoid jerked me mercilessly earthward.

Shouting as I fell, I refused to stop channeling. The meteor rushed to meet me, crystal spikes ready to spit me like a pig. The Stasis finally suffused the core. The center sagged. With a dull roar, the meteor collapsed and I smacked into a mountain of gray dust and sank. Crystallized ash filled my mouth and nose and another threat immediately replaced the crystal spikes.

Blindly, I thrashed, still upside down, the rocket stick tangled between my legs. I was going to choke to death. I tried to find firm purchase, but it was like climbing a hill of goose down, sagging and slipping away. My lungs burned and panic gripped my heart, burning through my remaining oxygen.

I tried to gasp for air and only filled my mouth with brittle soot. I wanted to scream as terror strummed my insides with sharp claws, whispering, "You're going to die."

A soft voice reached me. *You will be okay, my friend. Stop struggling and find the cold calm that will help you.*

Who is that? I sent, shocked out of my panic.

No answer came, but then I sensed the cold calm lingering gently on my senses. It wasn't the cold of death, but the chill of creation. *The aether is back.* I drew it in focusing on my skin as I'd done before. Channeling Murk from every pore, I created a shield and shoved away the mountain of dust in all directions until I sat in a small dark void.

I hacked up a lungful of gray dust and took a breath of delicious air. When the dizziness faded, I channeled a small orb of Brilliance to light the area. Despite being buried alive, I felt oddly safe, like a child hiding beneath the bedcovers from the monsters in the room.

The luxury of remaining hidden wasn't something I could afford. I had to reach the surface and help Elyssa and the others. I channeled a thick rod of Murk from the bottom of the sphere, thrusting it down until it hit solid earth, then used it to push my bubble upward. When it burst from the ash, I widened it so it would have the surface area to roll across the top.

Using it like a gerbil sphere, I ran and rolled the big bubble until I finally reached the side. Enemy fliers circled overhead attacked, but with aether back, our people were able to respond in kind.

Tears trickled down Flava's cheeks as she struck down one of the fliers and Nailan looked away as another enemy slammed into the ground and rolled to a stop. Cephus was forcing these people to kill their own.

Clutching the rocket stick in one hand, and channeling a shield with the other, I struggled up the rubble and reached my friends.

Elyssa wrapped her arms around me. "I saw you vanish into the ash. I tried to go down there, but we're under constant fire."

"I'm fine," I assured her.

"The aether is back," Flava said. "Can you get your army?"

"I need to reach Kdosh and find out why the Alabaster Arch there isn't working," I said. "It might be another crystoid."

"If there's another crystoid, the skyway won't work," Flava said. "There are three connections between here and the skylet. The last one is in Ooskai Valley, still an hour away from the arch by skyway."

Legionnaires shifted position and channeled another shield as the fliers adjusted their pattern of attack.

"How far on foot?" I asked.

She shook her head. "You can't reach Kdosh on foot."

"I can fly the rocket stick—"

"Through the Great Barrier Vortex?" Flava gave me an incredulous look. "You'd never survive the journey."

"Well, we've got to reach it somehow," I said. "Staying here is no longer an option. We need to evacuate."

"And abandon the city?" Nailan said, aghast. "But our duty—"

"Your duty is to take back the city," I said. "If we can reach Kdosh and activate the arch, I have an army waiting on the other side in Eden."

"We will go," Flava said, wincing as enemy attacks exploded against the shield. "Today marks a victory, but we need an army to defeat Cephus."

Philas put a hand on Nailan's shoulder. "I agree, sir."

"What about the rest of your scouts?" Elyssa said.

"They know to return to base," Nailan said, "but they will not know what happened to us if no one returns to tell them."

"I will go," a seraph said. "Give me your orders and I will relay them."

Nailan nodded grimly. "Tell them to continue gathering intel and care for the prisoners." He selected a group of ten more legionnaires. "Go with him and protect each other. We will return, Creator willing."

They splayed their fingers in salute and then raced off toward the city, channeling shields to protect themselves from any pursuing fliers.

A new form of panic hit me. "Your scouts still have Nookli!"

Nailan's brow furrowed. "Do you speak of the device you gave them?"

I nodded.

"I am certain they will keep it safe."

I really wanted to get my phone back. "How am I supposed to find Indian restaurants?" I whimpered.

Elyssa groaned. "Let's get ready to move out."

Flava ordered her people into a phalanx. "Link with each other and keep us shielded," she said. "Move out!"

We retreated at a steady pace. The fliers followed, relentlessly firing at us with mindless devotion. With aether back in production, the legionnaires were able to thwart their attacks, while the rest of us took down as many attackers as we could without killing them.

Though the mutants had the advantage of flight, we were no longer powerless against their attacks.

Unless Cephus devised something else, the forces of Eden should have no problem defeating his minions. Then again, unless we wanted the wholesale slaughter of citizens on our conscience, we'd have to beat them without lethal force.

About thirty minutes into our trip, fliers began tumbling out of the sky. Legionnaires caught as many as they could on cushions of Murk, but it was impossible to save them all.

"What is happening?" Flava said, face red with tears after she failed to catch one of the fliers.

"They've been attacking us non-stop all this time," Elyssa said. "Their bodies couldn't take the strain anymore."

I looked up and realized the sky was clear. We stood at the fringe of the wasteland, damaged buildings only a few yards away.

"Check the fallen," Flava ordered.

I knelt next to the nearest one and pulled off the helmet to reveal a young sera beneath. Her skin felt ice-cold to the touch, and no breath came from her lips. I felt around the seam on the side where the chest plate joined the back armor and found a latch on the inside near the waist. It clicked open and Elyssa tugged off the chest plate.

Flava pressed a hand to the sera's shaved head and closed her eyes. Lips trembling, she pulled away, face red with rage. "He drove them to death," she hissed. "I will kill this monster with my bare hands. I will see his blood spilled."

"The Void take him." Nailan spat.

The legionnaires checked the other fallen fliers and returned with the same grim news. They were all dead, driven past their physical limits by a monster.

"Death is too good for Cephus," I growled.

"Gladly will I give it to him," Flava replied. "Death may be too good, but life is far too great for him to draw another breath if I have a choice."

"Agreed," Nailan said.

I stared at the bodies littering the wasteland between us and the mountain of rubble in the distance. They deserved proper rites, but it would have to wait. I decided that decision wasn't mine to make, and looked at Flava. "We're on a tight schedule, but if you think we need to bury the dead—"

She shook her head. "We will honor the dead with victory, the sooner the better."

I nodded. "Then let's go."

We traveled down empty streets, the vacant buildings towering tombstones for a city once bustling with Darklings. I thought I glimpsed movement, a fleeting shadow here, a face vanishing behind a corner there, but we came across no other signs of life.

It reminded me of the Gloom, a shadow copy of the real world where floating brains called minders gathered the dreams of the living and spun them into aether, the source of magic. This city was as desolate as the Gloom version of Eden my father and I had been trapped in. There, we'd found Serena and her Gloom fortress where she conducted her mad experiments. After I'd defeated her BFF, Daelissa, she'd probably sworn vengeance on me, the destruction of the Darkling nation part of the price.

I hoped we'd be able to pull the citizens of Tarissa back together again once we finished off Cephus. I didn't know the state of the rest of Pjurna, but we'd need every able body to bring the Brightling Empire to its knees and finally unite Seraphina under a combined government. If we could bring peace here, we'd avoid a replay of the Seraphim Wars and secure peace for Eden.

For now, I'd be ecstatic to return to Eden and see my friends again.

We reached the waist-high stone pedestal with a gray gem on top of it. The tall pearly gates guarding access to the skyway had been torn loose and sat in a heap to the side.

Flava knelt and ran a finger down a gate. "Our people were desperate to escape, but travel to Kdosh was forbidden." She stood and gazed into the sky beyond. "I pray none of them were on the skyway when the crystoid disabled it."

I glanced over the side into the swirling vortex of aether holding up the massive skylet and shuddered at the long fall into oblivion.

"Let's pray the skyway works," Nailan said. Holding out a finger, he sent a jolt of Murk into the gem.

A misty road of clouds unfurled into the air, stretching into the distance. I tentatively tested it with a foot and found it to be firm. "I hope Cephus doesn't have a spare crystoid."

Elyssa grimaced. "Wish I'd brought the parachutes with us just in case."

"I don't think I could live with myself if everyone else fell to their deaths around us," I said.

She sighed. "I suppose you're right."

I took Elyssa's hand and we stepped onto the clouds. I visualized our destination. *Take us to Kdosh.* Like a conveyer belt, we began to move forward.

The others stepped on behind us and we soon gathered speed, flying across the land and hopefully toward salvation.

Elyssa turned and gasped at the rays of dawn touching the horizon. "It's beautiful."

I wrapped an arm around her and enjoyed the receding view of the floating city of Tarissa. The flowing organic structures at the outskirts gave the illusion it had never suffered the destruction we'd witnessed in the center. I wondered how long it would take to rebuild and how long to repair the psyches of its citizens.

Then again, they were accustomed to constant war with the Brightlings. Maybe they'd be more resilient than I thought.

I sat down and a cushion of clouds formed under my backside. Elyssa's eyes flashed with surprise. She followed my example and a misty chair coalesced beneath her.

"Get some rest," Flava told her people. "It has been a long night, and our road to redemption has only begun."

The thought of sleep brought a wide yawn with it, though the scary thought of the skyway vanishing beneath us made it hard to sleep.

Elyssa squeezed my hand three times. *I love you.*

I squeezed back.

"Does the rocket stick still work?" she asked.

66

I removed it from its sheath and looked it over. It still smelled of fried electronics, but when I twisted it on, it whirred faintly and hovered in place. "Wow, I guess they build these things to take a beating."

"I'm sure Shelton gave us the best," Elyssa said as I folded it back into a slender rod and put it back.

"Wish we still had yours," I said. "If a crystoid is blocking the Alabaster Arch, I may have to fly to the skylet."

"I was thinking the same thing." She frowned. "What if it's not a crystoid, but something else?"

"What else could it be?" I said.

"Remember when Serena blocked the Alabaster Arches by keeping a portal open to Seraphina with one close to the Brightling Empire?" she said. "That locked up the whole network."

"Yeah, but my mom was able to sense it." I shrugged. "This time she said the alignment seemed right, but it refused to open."

Elyssa tapped a finger to her chin. "What about the trick with the Mega Chalon?"

The Chalon was a small orb, the key to attuning the arches to different realms. Adam Nosti, one of Shelton's magic hacker buddies had managed to bind three Chalons into one big one and overpower Serena's control.

"Adam already tried that and it didn't work," I said. "Didn't you get the memo?"

She snorted. "I must have missed that briefing."

"I doubt it. We just had so much information thrown at us before this mission, you probably forgot."

Elyssa bit her lower lip. "I don't like the idea of you flying up there alone. You need help disabling a crystoid, especially if it's as huge as the one in Tarissa."

"We'll figure out something," I said. "Put on your thinking cap, Templar."

She punched me lightly on the shoulder. "It's always on."

I hoped we could come up with something, or this would be a long trip for nothing.

Chapter 9

I remembered something from my first trip on a skyway and a mischievous impulse took over. *Show me the ground,* I thought in Cyrinthian. The clouds beneath us vanished.

Elyssa shouted in surprise, startling awake some of the snoozing Darklings as the window beneath us displayed a thousand-foot drop to a great plain of red grass below.

I stood on the seemingly thin air and chuckled. "Cool right?"

She punched me hard in the thigh. "Real funny, mister."

I dropped back into the cloud chair and enjoyed a good laugh. "Sorry, couldn't resist."

Crossing her arms, Elyssa summoned a scowl and focused her glare on me. "You know I'm going to get you back for this, right?"

I pecked a kiss on her nose. "Looking forward to it."

Mountains climbed on either side of us as we entered the Ooskai Valley where Nightliss, Daelissa, and their parents were forced to move during the Great Exile. Demanding equal representation on the Trivectus, the Darklings had risen up against the ruling Brightlings. Things hadn't worked out so well, and most of them had been banished from Zbura, across the oceans to the furthest land from the Brightling nations—Pjurna.

I couldn't help but think of the parallels to our world, how the British had once used Australia as a prison. Then again, Seraphim history far preceded much of Eden's. It certainly hadn't made them any better than humans, though.

"So beautiful," Elyssa said, now enjoying the window beneath us. A sparkling green river wound through a forest of aquamarine trees. A roar echoed through the forest. Golden doves exploded like glitter from cover and burst into the air, pursued by something long, black, and scaly.

A gasp burst from my mouth as a flying black reptile streaked in pursuit, snatched a dozen birds in its maw, then dove into the river and vanished. "W-was that a dragon?" I said.

Elyssa's violet eyes were huge. "What else could it be?"

I wanted to ask Flava, but she and the others were asleep. "I saw a huge flying dragon the first time I was here."

"Where?"

"It was actually on a live-action holographic map of the Great Barrier Vortex Cephus showed me." I stared intently at the river but didn't see any signs of the creature.

"Do people still live down there?" Elyssa asked.

I pointed to the mountains in the distance where buildings clung to the cliff. "Nightliss told me this is like the suburbs for Tarissa."

"How do they get to the city if this skyway is restricted?" Elyssa asked.

"There are other skyways near the mountains." I shielded my eyes and found a long stone arch several miles ahead. "I think that's the last relay for the skyway system out here."

"That must be a two hundred-foot drop for us." Elyssa's gaze wandered back and forth. "How are we supposed to get down if the skyway ends there?"

"It'll probably work like the skyways in Tarissa." I flattened my hands and moved them horizontally. "When you're travelling on a skyway and you need to get off somewhere, you visualize where you need to go and"—I veered one hand from the other and simulated a smooth descent—"a cloudlet forms and takes you to the building or ground."

"Wow, talk about the perfect mass transit system." Elyssa glanced back at Flava. "I'm going to wake her up just in case."

Flava blinked awake at a gentle nudge and stood. "We are at the last relay." She shook Nailan. "Wake the others."

"At once." He walked back along the skyway shaking the others with his foot.

"What happens if it ends here?" I asked Flava.

"Walking is not an option," she replied.

I held up a finger and waggled it. "One does not simply walk into Kdosh."

Elyssa grimaced. "How are we supposed to get there?"

Flava looked west. "To reach Kdosh, we need the aid of the Mzodi—the sky fishers."

"Couldn't I just fly the rocket stick to the skylet?" I asked.

Flava shook her head. "The aether vortex would swallow you whole."

We were a few hundred yards away from and above the massive stone arch bridging the valley. Zooming my vision, I spotted the pedestal with the gray gem in it—presumably the relay. "When will we know—"

A vibration in the skyway answered my question before I could finish it and the cloudy road ahead dissolved into mist.

"The last relay is unstable," Flava said. She clenched her teeth and narrowed her eyes as if concentrating. "I cannot make the skyway stop."

"Can we run back?" I asked.

Her eyes lit. "Everyone run back the other way!"

My simple-minded idea actually worked, but not as well as I'd hoped. The Imperial Skyway was built for speed, and even at a sprint, we were like pugs on a giant treadmill. I drew in aether and was ecstatic to find it in ample supply.

"Who can fly?" I asked.

"We are all practiced with wings," Flava said. "But we cannot soar like Cephus's fliers."

"You don't need to fly," I said. "Just glide to the arch."

"I can't do it!" a young seraph said. "I can only channel one wing!"

I flicked out the rocket stick and turned it on. "Get on the seat. Push the stick down gently to descend, pull up to climb, and lean to the sides to turn." I made sure the stabilizing gyro for novice fliers was on.

The seraph took it and leapt on. "Thank you, Destroyer!"

The steady sprint was starting to take a toll on the others. "Channel your wings and glide!"

Sweat poured down Flava's face. She held up a fist. "Remember your training!" Ultraviolet wings blazed to life at her back and the backs of the others.

A seraph stumbled and flipped off the end, his cries fading as he vanished into the forest far below.

"Jova!" someone shouted.

A sera screamed and lost her footing. I grabbed her wrist at the last second. Her body bounced along the skyway as it tried to tear her from my grasp. I channeled a burst of Murk into her. "Grow your wings!"

She flailed with her other hand, trying to catch her balance. "I cannot!"

"Do it!" I roared. I sent another surge of Murk into her.

Wings burst from her back, slicing holes through the cloth armor eliciting a shriek of pain. The sera's sweaty hand slipped from mine and she tumbled away, screaming.

"Eoriss!" Flava cried.

The sera tumbled through open air, an ultraviolet meteor streaking to earth.

"Spread your wings!" I roared in my full demonic voice.

At the last minute, her wings unfurled and the air caught her. She skidded onto the wide arch and rolled to a stop.

I would have breathed in relief, but I was starting to pant already.

Elyssa didn't look tired, but even she was sweating. "Should I flap my arms to get down?"

I managed a smile. "No, I got you."

One by one the other Darklings spread their wings and spiraled down to the arch below. I sucked in aether and imagined wings on my back. It was like trying to pee at a public urinal while a crowd watched me from behind. I suddenly knew how Eoriss felt.

Sucking in aether like a vacuum cleaner, I imagined wings springing from my back. I felt an itch on my shoulder blades and focused on the itch. I had to activate the magical muscles in my back. "Just like wiggling my ears," I muttered. Unfortunately, I'd never been

71

great at that. Even the great Barnaby Farnsworth, a fourth-grade prodigy who could wiggle his nose and ears at the same time had been unable to teach me those valuable skills.

My left foot slipped off the end of the skyway. I flopped on my belly and the skyway threw me off like a treadmill on the highest setting. Elyssa shrieked and tumbled into the air an instant later.

Wings, now! The itch on my shoulder blades flared into knifing agony as pinions of pure energy erupted from my back. Blazing white furled to my right, and ultraviolet to my left. I pumped a fist in the air. "Booyah!"

"Celebrate later, Justin!" Elyssa shouted.

I reached out a hand for Elyssa. She was inches too far away but the stony arch was far too close for comfort. I only had seconds before we both splatted. I spread my wings and slowed enough for Elyssa to catch me. I wrapped my arms around her waist and flared my wings.

The wind caught them and Elyssa suddenly felt five times her weight as gravity tried to rip her away from me.

The air exploded from Elyssa with a big, "Oof!"

We hadn't smashed into the arch, but we had another problem. I was way off course and too low. I saw Flava waving frantically from the arch, but there was no way we'd reach it. Instead, we were headed for the forest below.

"Find the cliff trail!" Flava shouted. "We will wait for you!"

She vanished from view as my last desperate attempt to reach the stone bridge failed and we flew beneath it.

Elyssa gripped my wrists. "The trees, Justin, the trees!"

I flapped my wings, trying to gain altitude, but smacked into one of the aquamarine trees I'd admired from above. Elyssa grunted and grabbed a branch. I tumbled backward, my wings slicing through the branches like butter. Using my demon-like reflexes, I grabbed a limb and hung on until I could get my bearings.

Red grass and glowing flowers carpeted the forest floor below. I looked up and saw Elyssa gracefully navigating the patch of sliced branches toward me, swinging and leaping like Lady Tarzan herself, so I shimmied down the rest of the trunk to the ground. The forest whirred with insect life. A huge silver owl stared at us from its perch in another tall tree, and something rustled through the bushes to my left.

Elyssa landed next to me and immediately focused on what was most important. "Ooh, is that a glowing flower?" She held out a finger toward something that looked like a combination between a sunflower and a lightbulb.

I grabbed her arm and jerked it back. "Haven't you ever seen alien movies? That's how people die!"

"From glowing flowers?" She quirked her lips in regret, but backed off. "Well, I suppose it could be poisonous." Her eyes lit again. "Wow, look at that owl!"

"Ever notice how the animals here look similar to the ones in Eden?" I said. "I don't think that's a coincidence."

"I'm certain there's some cross-pollination of species," Elyssa said in a lecturing tone. She knelt to inspect a small blue lizard. "That's odd."

"What is?" I asked.

"It has something on its back."

I picked up a twig and poked the reptile. Wings spread from its back and blurred into motion like a hummingbird. Hissing angrily, the lizard glared at us and flicked out its tongue before flying away.

"That wasn't very nice," Elyssa said.

"Yeah, I don't appreciate being hissed at."

She rolled her eyes. "I mean poking it with a twig."

"What if its skin was poisonous?" I said. "I didn't want to touch it with a finger."

Elyssa groaned. "I'll bring biohazard suits next time we explore a strange new world."

"Ha, ha." I jabbed a finger to the left of the tree we'd descended. "The cliff is that way. Let's go."

"Uh, no it's not." Elyssa motioned straight past the tree. "It's that way."

I looked up and spotted the rocky face through the tree canopy. "Guess I got turned around when I fell."

She grinned. "Yea, you get turned around a lot."

I stuck out my tongue. "Whatevs."

"Don't stick out your tongue." Elyssa feigned a concerned look. "You might poke something poisonous."

I swiped a hand at her but she giggled and dodged it.

We juked around a clump of giant mushrooms and followed a trail of red grass between the trees. A bright yellow fox leapt atop a stump and watched us curiously. It mewled like a wounded cat then vanished into the foliage.

"So that's what the fox says."

Elyssa clasped her hands together. "How adorable."

I wasn't so sure the wildlife was trustworthy. "Don't try to pet anything. It might bite you."

"Someone's paranoid today."

"I didn't beat the Queen Bitch from Hell only to die from a poisonous flying lizard or a cute yellow fox that morphs into a monster and eats you." I looked around warily for signs of other strange creatures, but spotted only a purple-speckled owl watching us curiously from a tree.

Elyssa snorted. "We need to get you on medication pronto."

I looked up at daylight poking through the trees and wondered what was going on in Eden right now. "I hope Shelton had fun at his bachelor party."

"Maybe he postponed it until you get back." Elyssa squeezed my hand. "I really don't think he'd let you miss out."

"We're nowhere near Kdosh and don't even know if we can get the arch working if we ever get there." I booted a rock and sent it skittering through the grass. "Now I've missed out on the bachelor party, and there's no way we'll make it to the wedding."

"Because Shelton's wedding is more important than saving Tarissa," Elyssa said in a sarcastic tone.

I stopped walking and looked at her. "If we can't enjoy the little things in life, then what are we fighting for?"

She opened her mouth but the retort died on her lips. "You're right." Elyssa sighed. "I'm sad we missed it too."

A little knot formed in my throat. Shelton had once tried to arrest my father and hand him over to the Overworld authorities for a bounty. Another time, he'd reluctantly helped rescue my father from vampires and then kept him in a safe place after Underborn, the most notorious assassin in the Overworld marked him for death. I didn't know exactly when Shelton and I became best friends, but we'd been through so much together, we were practically family. It really sucked that I was missing out on some of the most important days of his life.

I cleared my throat and took a deep breath. "I'm adding this to Cephus's list of crimes, right below trying to destroy Eden."

Elyssa pushed through a thicket and stopped. "We're at the cliff."

I stepped beside her and looked up at the steep rock face. The stone arch seemed impossibly far away. Didn't Flava tell us to find a trail?"

"Yeah, but I don't see one."

Elyssa gripped a small outcropping of rock and hefted herself up a few feet. "We might be able to boulder to the top."

I shook my head. "It'd be like climbing the Cliffs of Insanity, but without a thick rope and a giant to carry us." Try as I might, I couldn't see any way up.

We were stuck.

Chapter 10

Thankfully, I already had a Plan B. "Remember the hotel in Thailand?" I said.

Elyssa's eyebrows arched. "How could I forget? Can you climb all that way with me on your back?"

I nodded. "I dragged my dad up a cliff at the Three Sisters while Nazdal tried to eat us, so I think I can manage it with you."

"What if I try to eat you?"

"I would lose my concentration, but for other reasons."

Elyssa leaned forward and traced her tongue along my earlobe. "Can I do that while you're climbing?"

I swallowed hard and shifted the crotch of my Nightingale armor. "Where are we again?"

She laughed and walked behind me, lacing her arms around my neck and her legs around my waist. "I'm ready when you are." Her lips nibbled my neck. "Well, what are you waiting for?"

"You're making it hard for me to walk." I gathered my wits and flung a strand of Murk up the cliff wall. Like a web, it stuck to the rock. I willed it to contract. The web jerked us like a rubber band, launching us thirty feet up the rock wall. Using the momentum, I flung another web and yanked us up again.

"Whee!" Elyssa cried. "This is amazing!"

I laughed. "It's only fun when you're not running from a tsunami or hungry Nazdal."

"How far up can you throw a web?" she asked.

"Fifty feet at most." I grunted as the next strand tugged us upward. "Beyond that, it doesn't stick as well." I flung out another rope. Just as it contracted to pull us up, the section of rock it attached to crumbled.

"Fart bastards!" I shouted as we reversed course toward the rocky ground two hundred feet below. My reflexes responded before my brain, and another strand of Murk caught the cliff just above. We jerked to a stop and hung for a moment.

"Did you just say 'fart bastards'?" Elyssa said in an amused voice.

I wiped sweat from my eyes with a free hand. "How can you ask me that after we almost fell to our deaths?"

"I don't know," she admitted. "It all happened so fast."

A deep breath helped to calm my nerves. "Upward and onward."

Elyssa kissed the back of my neck. "My sexy rock climber."

I channeled a rope and began climbing again. "I'm about to take you back into the forest and go Tarzan on you."

"Me Jane," she whispered in my ear.

"You're going to get us killed," I groaned.

"I'm giving you a reason to live," she replied.

"My testosterone levels are off the charts." Another strand jerked us closer to the stone arch. "Junior is rubbing uncomfortably against the cliff."

She giggled. "Want me to shield it with my hand?"

"That's it, we're going back to the forest." The last aether rope jerked us up and over the lip of the stone arch. I landed heavily on my feet and stumbled.

Elyssa climbed off my back. "Aww, I thought we were going back down."

Flava and the others saw us and ran over. I stood slightly behind Elyssa so they wouldn't see the awkward bulge in my skintight armor.

Elyssa looked down and snorted. "Someone needs a cold shower."

"Shush, you evil woman." I looked at the approaching Darklings and plastered on a casual smile. *Down, boy, down!* Junior seemed to sag with sadness and deflated.

The Darkling I'd lent my rocket stick handed it to me. "Destroyer, I think your rocket stick is broken."

"Broken?" The odor of fried electronics stung my nostrils.

"It turned off during my descent, but thankfully, I was only a few feet from the ground." He looked down. "I am sorry."

I tested the switch, but the rocket stick didn't respond. "It's okay." I didn't like being grounded, but there wasn't much I could do about it.

Another seraph pushed past the first. "Did you see Jova below?"

I stood up and shook my head. "I'm sorry, no."

"He landed only a hundred yards from you," he replied, voice rising with agitation.

"He fell near the river," Flava said. "I am sorry, Axo, but he's gone."

"I wish to look for him."

Flava's lips tightened into a line. "Do you think your brother would want you to abandon the mission and look for him?"

"I do not care what he would want!" Axo said. "I will not abandon family!"

"We are your family," Flava said. "Your brothers and sisters who have fought by your side. Do you remember what Jova said before our attack on the crystoid?"

Axo squeezed his eyes and looked down. "Yes," he whimpered.

"If I die, I pray you fight on. Victory brings honor to the living and dead. If Cephus wins, the dead will be poured into mass graves and forgotten." Flava gripped Axo's arm. "Brother, I do not wish to be forgotten."

Nailan raised a fist overhead. "Remember the dead!"

The others roared the mantra.

Axo wiped tears from his eyes. "My only regret is that the Destroyer could not save him as he saved Eoriss."

His words stung, the venom making my heart so heavy I couldn't breathe. There were so many I hadn't been able to save—Vallaena, Nightliss, all those who fought in the wars. I knew it wasn't my fault, but every loss added another weight and this asshole wasn't helping matters.

Eoriss stared at him with open-mouthed horror. "How cruel to say such a thing, Axo! Jova was too far away for the Destroyer to reach."

78

I took a deep breath as anger burned through the regret and let it harden my heart. "We've all lost loved ones and seen more than our fair share of death and destruction." Turning my gaze on Axo, I held back the sharp rebuke I wanted to deliver and settled for something softer. "I'm sorry for the loss of your brother, but we have a mission to save thousands in Tarissa and perhaps the entire realm of Seraphina."

Demon flames ignited in my eyes and I held Axo's hard look until he shrank away. "If you care nothing for honor, leave us."

The seraph looked down and shivered. "I am sorry, Destroyer. I will not forsake my duty."

I nodded and turned to Flava. "Let's move out."

She nodded. "As you command, Destroyer." Flava pointed to the southern side of the arch. "The Mzodi often dock their ships at the town of Ooskai."

"What exactly are these sky fishers?" I asked.

Flava touched the gem on her uniform. "They harvest the gems from the depths of the vortexes where the extreme forces cause the aether to crystallize."

I examined the faceted green stone. "Oh, I thought the Darklings made the gems themselves."

"Life as we know it would be impossible without gems," she said. "Though gems can be safely harvested from the land around a vortex, the Mzodi brave the deeps where the most powerful crystals are formed."

I had visions of pirates flying galleons into tornados, tossing nets, and hauling in a bounty of booty. "What do their ships look like?"

A smile creased her lips. "They really must be seen to be appreciated."

I was stoked. "We're going to see angel pirates on flying ships!"

Elyssa's face scrunched. "I don't know how you went from sky fishers to sky pirates."

"Just a logical progression," I assured her. I hooked my arm in hers and started hustling over the stone bridge. "I hope their captain has a peg-leg and an eye patch. Shelton's gonna be so jealous."

Elyssa tossed a bucket of cold water on my enthusiasm. "I'm picturing a bunch of old men with fishing poles."

"Stop it!" I gave her a hurt look. "You're destroying my fantasy land."

The stone arch melded into a road when we reached the plateau at the top of the cliff. A wide crystal dock jutted from the side of the cliff. Beyond it sat a tall round house nestled in a stand of aquamarine trees. A stairway in the back trailed down to the edge of the plateau where a wide deck faced the valley.

I nudged Elyssa. "Imagine having breakfast with that view."

"Beautiful," she murmured. "It's too bad we can't stick around and explore. I'd love to hike the valley."

The main street of Ooskai offered a peculiar variety of domiciles. Though most were constructed of shiny black Murk, their shapes ranged from a mundane square and perfect sphere to a bizarre house that resembled a boot.

I pointed out the latter to Elyssa. "I wonder if the old woman in the shoe lives there."

She tilted her head in wonder at one shaped like a giant snail shell. "They obviously don't believe in cookie-cutter designs."

Flava stopped in front of the large house near the dock. It might have looked like a normal two-story house except its proportions were warped, as if viewing it through bent glass. The sera charged the gem where a front door might usually exist and waited.

A moment later the wall misted away to reveal a gray-haired sera. "What does one of the city wish in these parts?" she asked in Cyrinthian.

"Tarissa is destroyed," Flava replied. "We seek passage to Kdosh."

The sera didn't seem surprised. "The price for your sins, city dweller."

"It's like rednecks versus city slickers," I whispered to Elyssa.

"The Destroyer has come as promised," Flava said. "He will help us atone for our sins."

The sera narrowed her eyes. Her gaze quickly latched onto me. "He is different."

I waved my hand. "Hey, I'm the Destroyer, but you can call me Justin." I tried to sound ominous, but my voice cracked because her intense stare made me nervous. "Can you help us get to Kdosh?"

The sera frowned. "I will ask Mother." The doorway solidified into a wall.

I tapped Flava on the shoulder. "I take it they don't like city dwellers?"

"They believe we aspire to be like the Creator himself with our buildings reaching to the heavens and our magical advances." She wrinkled her nose at the village. "They consider this meager living virtuous."

"Some things are the same no matter where you go," Elyssa said.

A shadow flitted across the ground drawing our eyes up. Something I could only describe as a golden winged cat settled on the ground. About twice the size of its domestic cousins and unapologetically majestic, it stalked around us, green eyes wary.

"How beautiful," Elyssa said, not wasting a moment to crouch and summon the thing. "Here, kitty, kitty."

It seemed to think she was okay and rubbed its head against her knee, a purr like a saw deep in its throat.

"What is that?" I asked.

"A felix," Flava said. "They are common companions, though this one is particularly beautiful." She knelt and started talking cutesy gibberish—probably what passed for "Here, kitty, kitty," in Cyrinthian.

"My god, a flying cat?" I wondered what passed for dogs around here. "No wonder I haven't seen any squirrels." Elyssa beamed a pleading smile at me, but I cut her off before she could ask. "No, we can't keep him."

She pouted. "Aww."

"Mother will see the Destroyer."

I jumped and turned toward the sera. "What about Flava?"

"Only you," she said.

"Is it safe?" I asked Flava.

She raised an eyebrow. "I should hope so, for the mighty Destroyer."

Embarrassment heated my face. "Well, you never know."

Elyssa gripped my hand. "You're right. Don't let your guard down."

I pecked a kiss on her lips and stepped through the doorway. The sera charged a gem on the inside and a wall filled the space.

"This way." She walked down a flight of stone steps, through a cool tunnel with a musty smell to it. The corridor ended on the wide deck I'd seen from the bridge. A short balustrade provided the only protection from walking straight off the cliff edge and plummeting to a violent end.

The sera motioned to two empty chairs next to a table. "Sit."

"Where is Mother?" I asked.

"She will come." The sera turned and walked back into the tunnel.

Instead of sitting, I walked to the stone railing and looked out at the blue valley, taking in the lovely view now that I had a moment to rest. Wings flapped behind me. I turned and saw the golden cat fly in for a landing.

"I'll bet Elyssa's disappointed," I said with a chuckle. I scratched it behind the ears. "You are beautiful, I'll give you that." I sighed and sat down at the table. Since nobody else was around and I was more than a little nervous about meeting this person who might hold the key to reaching Kdosh, I did what any sane person would do and started talking to myself.

"Where is this mother I'm supposed to meet? I wonder if I should call her mother too?" I shook my head. "Nah—mommy? Mum? Mamacita?" I strained my brain for more synonyms and nearly had a stroke when the felix flowed like liquid gold into the upright shape of a woman.

Piercing green eyes stared at me through a curtain of lustrous blonde hair that I was still scratching as if she were a cat.

I jerked my hand back like it'd been stung and I stumbled backward over the chair, babbling apologies.

The sera pushed the hair behind her ears, revealing fair skin and—I gasped like I'd just been punched in the gut. "Nightliss," I whispered, afraid I was seeing a ghost, and that if I moved it would go away. My eyes stung and the vision of my dead friend blurred.

"I am not Nightliss," the sera said without emotional inflection.

I wiped my eyes and saw it was true. This sera could be either Nightliss or her evil twin sister, Daelissa. Upon closer inspection, she was neither, standing a fraction taller, her nose a bit wider, cheeks a bit higher. That was when the truth hit me.

"Nightliss told me you were dead." I said it in a flat tone, unsure what to feel.

"Perhaps to her I was," she replied in a soft voice. "Neither of my daughters wanted me."

Looking at someone with such a likeness to my dear friend reopened the fresh wound of her death. Emotions jumbled inside me. I wasn't sure how to act or what to do. There was one thing I knew for certain.

I had to tell the mother of Nightliss and Daelissa that her daughters were dead.

Chapter 11

I started with an easy question. "What's your name?"

"I am Kaelissa," she said. "Stories from the city reached my ears months ago. They tell of another great war in the mortal realm and the fall of my daughter who would rule Eden."

I hesitated. This was the part where I should avoid telling her how Daelissa died so she could find out later from someone else and plot her revenge. I decided to skip all that and tell her up front so I could judge her reaction and decide for myself if I should take care of business right here and now.

"I couldn't let Daelissa rule Eden so I killed her."

Her eyes turned liquid jade. A blink sent tears rolling down her cheeks. "And Naelissa?"

"Who?"

"Nightliss changed her name to sever her familial ties." Kaelissa looked down. "She was a troubled child."

"She died saving Eden."

Kaelissa continued speaking as if she hadn't heard me. "Our daughters were the best of friends until Daelissa became old enough to see how the Brightlings treated the Darklings." She sat down and motioned me to do the same.

I played along. "That was when Daelissa decided she was going to become a Brightling."

Kaelissa frowned. "Become a Brightling? She was born one."

I shook my head. "No, she was a Darkling like her sister and parents." I tapped the back of my right hand. "She implanted a prism in her hand so she could channel Brilliance. From that day on, she refused to channel Murk."

I seemed to have wounded some motherly pride because Kaelissa's lips tightened. "This is a lie."

"After her death, I found the prism in her hand." I softened my expression. "I'm sorry, Kaelissa, but your daughter faked it."

She leaned back, shock replacing the doubt. "She migrated to the Brightlands and left us forever. I thought she had died in the First Eden War." Kaelissa took a deep breath. "Thousands of years passed, and recent stories from Zbura reached us in this far away land. Tales told of a new Empress who returned from Eden to raise an army."

It took me a moment to remember that in this realm, they called the First Seraphim War the Eden War. "Yes, that was Daelissa," I said.

"My sweet Daelissa," she said. "My beautiful child."

"And Nightliss?" I asked. "What about her?"

"She was rebellious, always fighting with her sister," Kaelissa replied. "Daelissa despised Pjurna, as did my husband Hjoeruss and I. Naelissa preferred it here. She said it was a chance for Darklings to weave their own destiny."

I didn't like to hear her talk about my friend that way. "Where is your husband now?"

"Oh, he died in an uprising many thousands of years ago." She might have been discussing the weather for all the emotion in her voice.

"Nightliss thought you were dead all this time." I couldn't get over the incredible likeness between this sera and her daughters, but appearances were where the similarities ended. Kaelissa obviously played favorites and I couldn't help but form an intense dislike for her.

"I dearly wish I'd been able to see Daelissa again." Kaelissa sniffed and wiped at damp eyes. "Perhaps even Naelissa would have grown out of her troubled youth by now if she hadn't died."

My back stiffened. "Nightliss died a hero." I repressed the urge to defend my friend's honor and shifted to the most pressing subject. Much as I might dislike Kaelissa, we needed her help. "I was told you might help us arrange for passage with the Mzodi."

Kaelissa raised an eyebrow. "They seldom take passengers." Her brow furrowed. "Whence do you travel that you require a sky ship?"

"Kdosh." I could tell she had more questions so I gave her a rundown on Cephus's activities. "Eden was attacked with crystal meteors, crystoids, that threatened to destroy all magic. He used the same weapons on Tarissa to destroy the city legion and take over the government."

"I take it he was unsuccessful in destroying Eden?" Kaelissa said, a faint note of disappointment in her voice.

"Yes," I said firmly. "Now we're here to destroy him once and for all."

She pursed her lips. "What is your ultimate goal?"

"Kill Cephus, rebuilt Tarissa, unite Seraphina." I shrugged. "I know it doesn't sound like much."

Kaelissa frowned. "You remind me of Naelissa. She wished to unite our people, but the war only drove us further apart."

Once again, I resisted the urge to punch a female in the mouth and steered us back on topic. "Will you help us with the Mzodi?"

Her eyes gazed into the distance. "I will ask on your behalf, but I cannot promise their acquiescence."

"How often do they come here?"

"A ship is due tomorrow morning," Kaelissa said. "If you require food and lodging, I suggest you speak with my servant, Djola."

"The woman who led me in here?" I asked.

She completely ignored my question and put her hand over mine. "Would you tell me about my daughters?"

I felt certain she only wanted to hear about the exploits of Daelissa, but decided to indulge her. "Can I tell the others about our situation first?"

"Of course." She motioned to the tunnel. "Djola will see you out."

Djola sat upstairs near the door, two small gems pinched in her fingers. I watched as she channeled Murk through the gems and weaved silky cloth.

"That's really cool," I said.

She flinched and nearly dropped the gems. "How may I serve?"

"Kaelissa requested that you find accommodations for my friends," I said.

She nodded. "At once."

I nodded at the cloth. "May I touch it?"

Djola held it up. "It will be a gown for a newborn baby."

The cloth felt so soft it actually drew a moan from me. "That's amazing."

She smiled. "Thank you. I have been a weaver for over two centuries, but I love it no less than the day I began."

"Wow, that's quite a while." I looked at her graying hair and the fine wrinkles in her skin. At the end of the First Seraphim War, the Chalon had been forcibly removed from the primary Alabaster Arch, the Grand Nexus, and caused a tremendous backlash called the Desecration. It had husked all the Seraphim in Eden, turning them into soul-sucking monsters. In Seraphina, they called it the Schism. The results here had been less severe in the short term, but deadly in the long run.

The children of Seraphim caught in the blast radius on this side no longer lived for millennia, but were reduced to centuries. Those already alive before that time seemed to live on otherwise unaffected. It explained why Kaelissa looked young as ever despite being even older than her late daughters, and why Djola looked so old.

I knew better than to ask her age and kept my curiosity to myself.

"I will weave until the day our creator, the Primogenitor takes me," Djola said. "Creation is the most holy of works."

"Yes, it is." I motioned toward the wall. "Can you open the door for me, please?"

Instead of answering, she had a question. "Is it true you knew my sisters?"

I blinked, suddenly tongue-tied. "You're Kaelissa's daughter?"

She looked down. "I am not what mother wanted, but yes, I am truly her daughter."

"I knew Nightliss well, but not Daelissa." I swallowed a lump. "I only knew Nightliss for a couple of years, but she was like a sister to me." In retrospect, it seemed I'd barely gotten to know her at all. "Do you have other siblings?"

87

"Yes, but most are dead," Djola said in a quiet voice. Her face fell. "I will see to your friends." She activated the gem and opened the door.

Elyssa looked relieved to see me. "What happened?"

"Let's just say I have an interesting surprise for you." I walked to Flava. "Djola will find everyone accommodations. I'm going back to speak with our host."

"Who is this mother?" Flava asked.

"Her name is Kaelissa," I said.

Her eyes widened. "She is of the blood of Issa?"

I tried to understand what she meant, but my brain spit out an error code. "I don't know what that means."

"The ancient Seraphim named their children by matriarchal lineage," Flava said. "The practice was discontinued millennia ago."

"Who was Issa?"

"One of the first Seraphim, according to legend." Flava gazed up at the sky. "She was the progenitor of the line that produced Daelissa."

I had an *aha* moment. "No wonder Seraphim never tell me their last names. It's all built together."

"In the past, yes," Flava said. "Now Seraphim use whatever name they wish."

"Maybe you'll need to use last names," I said. "I think Flava Jones has a nice ring to it."

Flava's nose wrinkled. "It sounds unnatural." Her head tilted slightly to the side. "Who is this Kaelissa?"

Elyssa looked at me expectantly. "Yeah, Justin, spill the beans."

I sighed. "She's the mother of Nightliss and Daelissa."

"Whoa!" Elyssa's eyes flashed wide.

Flava's mouth hung open. "Impossible."

"How much did you know about their parents?" I asked Flava.

"History tells us almost nothing," she said. "They died after the Great Exile, but we do not even know their names."

"Hjoeruss and Kaelissa," I said.

"The blood of Ussor and Issa," Flava said. "It is no wonder they were so strong."

Now that I knew the Seraphim naming convention it got me to thinking about another Seraphim in Eden. Nicknamed Mr. Gray, he'd once been an adversary but turned into an ally. Using his lifelike golems, the gray men, he'd helped us win the war. His real name sounded remarkably like another. "Were Fjoeruss and Hjoeruss related?"

Flava grew more excited. "Do you mean the Fjoeruss who went to Eden with Daelissa before the Eden War?"

I nodded. "That's the one."

"He could be a brother," she said.

"He never mentioned being related to Daelissa or Nightliss." I really wasn't surprised. Fjoeruss was never one to volunteer information if there was no profit involved.

"Back in those days, there were only hundreds of Seraphim, not thousands," Flava said. "I'm certain most of them were related somehow."

Elyssa shuddered. "That's kind of gross."

"No different than the Daemos," I said.

She shivered again. "Still gross."

"What did Kaelissa have to say about the Mzodi?" Flava asked.

"A sky ship is due here tomorrow morning." I nodded toward the dock. "She'll speak with them for us."

"Excellent," Flava said, though her eyes looked uncertain. "I was not certain the villagers would help us."

"What was our backup plan if they hadn't?" Elyssa asked.

"That is a good question," the sera replied. "Without the skyway, the journey through the vortex is perilous."

"If the rocket stick worked," I said, "what would prevent me from flying high over the vortex?"

"The updrafts and turbulence would likely break the rocket stick and throw you to your doom." Flava looked at me as if waiting for my next stupid question.

"Doesn't sound so bad." I shrugged. "Sounds kinda fun, actually."

"Yeah, right." Elyssa snorted. "Going solo on a rocket stick is a bad idea. You'll need our help if there's another monster crystoid up there."

89

I threw up my hands in surrender. "Well, let's hope the Mzodi like us." I blew out a sigh. "Flava, why don't you get the troops settled in? I'm gonna brownnose our host."

Flava stared at me blankly for a moment. "I hope you make her nose very brown if it will help us." She gave me another confused look and walked away.

Elyssa took a turn to look confused. "How do you plan to suck up to Kaelissa, and is that really a good idea?"

"I told her I killed Daelissa."

Her eyebrows arched. "That's not exactly brownnosing."

"Maybe not, but she didn't try to hurt me." I pressed my lips together and shook my head. "Daelissa was her favorite, surprise, surprise."

"I don't think you know what brownnosing is, babe." Elyssa leaned against my shoulder. "Maybe you should've left out the part about how you killed her favorite daughter."

"I wasn't brownnosing then, silly." I took her hand. "I promised Kaelissa more stories about her daughters. Hopefully that'll make her happy."

"Maybe you should tone down the killing of Daelissa part," Elyssa suggested. "Make it sound like you really regretted it."

"In retrospect, I did." I held up my fingers with a tiny space between. "Just a little bit. If I'd used Clarity on her—"

"You didn't even understand what it was." Elyssa set her hands on her hips. "We're not going through this again, are we?"

"Nah." I slashed a hand through the air. "I plan to use it on Serena, Cephus, and any other evildoers."

"That's not a good idea either." She gripped my shoulders and looked me in the eyes. "Clarity makes a person see the bare naked truth about themselves, but it doesn't make them a good person."

"We don't know that," I said. "What if I'd hit Daelissa with it sooner? Maybe she would've stopped."

"The truth for Daelissa was so awful, it killed her," Elyssa said. "I'm not so sure that'll be the case for Serena and Cephus." She shrugged. "You can try it if you want, but they're not insane like Daelissa. They know exactly what they're doing."

"Plus, I can kill those two the old-fashioned way." I punched a fist into my palm. "I just really want to tear Cephus apart, you know?"

"Yeah." Her eyes darkened. "I know exactly what you mean."

We went back inside Kaelissa's house and found her on the deck gazing out at the blue valley. She turned her serene gaze on us. "Your friends are taken care of?"

I nodded. "This is Elyssa."

Elyssa's mouth fell open when she saw Kaelissa's face.

"Is this your wife?" the sera asked.

I cleared my throat. "You wanted to hear about your daughters?"

"Yes, please." Kaelissa looked toward the door and nodded. Djola stepped out with a tray of fruits and a crystal pitcher of something that looked like wine. "Thank you, daughter."

"Of course, Mother." Djola set the table and held out the chairs while we all sat.

Kaelissa gave her a questioning look. "I believe that will be all."

Djola smoothed gray hair behind her ears and backed away. "Of course, Mother."

"Doesn't she want to hear about her sisters too?" I asked.

"She is but a mere shadow fading into dark, not even worthy of our family name." Kaelissa dismissed the question with a swat of her hand. "Hearing about her superior sisters would only make her feel worse."

Elyssa's hand tightened on my leg.

"Isn't that a little harsh?" I asked.

"The truth is often so." Kaelissa's eyes grew sad. "I have given life to so many, but none have risen to the glory of the first."

Poor Nightliss must have been treated like the red-headed stepchild growing up with her gloriously insane sister. I really wanted to light into this sera about how awful Daelissa truly had been, but I didn't think it would do any good. Kaelissa was just as blind to Daelissa's true nature as Daelissa had been. Judging from the odd gleam in her eyes, I had to guess she wasn't all that mentally stable herself.

That didn't bode well for her helping us with the Mzodi. If I rubbed her the wrong way, it meant we could be stuck in Seraphina with no way out, short of a miracle.

Chapter 12

The sera wanted to hear about her favorite daughter, so I decided to give her what she wanted. "Let me start at the beginning." I didn't quite go back to my own genesis when I discovered my sweet blood was a dangerous commodity to have. Instead, I told of the small black cat I'd rescued, and the first time I'd seen Nightliss in human form. She hadn't spoken much English in those days, but gradually grew much better.

Kaelissa seemed disinterested until I reached my first encounter with Daelissa. Her enthusiasm only grew when I told of the many battles with her awful daughter. It was hard—so damned hard—to stomach, but I made it sound like I actually respected Daelissa.

I used embellishments like, "I'd never seen such raw power," or "She was so beautiful I went weak in the knees."

Elyssa's grip tightened with every lie, and I'm pretty sure she gagged a couple of times.

"Yet, I fought because I had no choice," I continued. "My very existence was at stake."

"She was so powerful with Brilliance," Kaelissa said after I finished the tale. "She was no Darkling at all."

I wanted to contradict her as I had earlier, explaining about the prism I'd found in Daelissa's hand, or how completely insane she was, but I held back, certain if I gave her the brutal truth she'd either ignore it or get angry and not help us with the Mzodi.

Elyssa was the one who had trouble letting it go. "Daelissa murdered humans by taking all their soul essence."

"My sweet Daelissa was only doing what she was taught," Kaelissa said. "She was the most beautiful child, so full of love and life." Her lips peeled back in a snarl. "The Brightlings poisoned her mind."

Daelissa was, without a doubt, the most extreme case of bad parenting in the history of the universe, all things considered.

"Tell me more about Daelissa and this Ezzek Moore," Kaelissa said.

The last thing I wanted to do was go into a love story, especially since I didn't know many details. Then again, I could just make it up as I went along. "The first Arcane, Moses, lived for thousands of years and assumed many identities. Long after the war, he was known as Ezzek Moore, and in my time as Jeremiah Conroy. It was during the Roman Empire that he met Daelissa."

"How interesting," Kaelissa said. "Mortal enemies who survive the first war only to meet again in another life."

"Yeah." My tone was anything but enthusiastic. "They didn't recognize each other and became lovers. It was only when Ezzek discovered he was bedding the killer of his wife, Thesha, that he began to plot his revenge."

"A love story for the ages." Kaelissa's face flushed with pleasure.

I wanted to pound my face on the table, but I plastered on a smile instead. "Yeah, a real heart warmer." I kept that smile on my face when I told her how Daelissa killed Moses, then known as Jeremiah. "She incinerated him to ash."

"There is no fury like a sera scorned," Kaelissa said. "I wish you had more details of their history."

"Well, your daughter murdered Jeremiah before he could tell me anything else." I was so done with this terrible mother.

Kaelissa sobbed into her hands. "My sweet little sera."

Elyssa bared her teeth with disgust. "Nightliss was the sweet one."

Kaelissa was too lost in her grief to hear her.

I ate a couple of quintos and drank the sweet wine, giving the sera time to calm down. Elyssa rolled her eyes with disgust and looked ready to leave.

After a time, Kaelissa wiped her eyes with a silky napkin and regained her composure. "Thank you for giving a mother peace."

"Holy farting fairies," I muttered. *How in the hell could a story like that give anyone peace?* "Now that I've told you about your daughter"—I intentionally made that singular—"I'd like to know a little about Seraphina."

She nodded. "Of course, what would you like to know?"

"This first question is a bit personal, but I hope you'll forgive me." I hated asking this question, even of immortals females. "How old are you?"

"I cannot say precisely," she replied. "I was the third generation to be born on Seraphina."

That drew a wide-eyed look from Elyssa. "You knew the first Seraphim?"

She nodded. "The ancient ones lived in Eden before the Sundering. Many of them died, but—"

"Uh, what's the Sundering?" I asked.

"Ah, yes, of course you are too young to understand." A condescending smile stretched Kaelissa's lips. "All the realms were once one earth. The Seraphim ruled the skies and our eternal adversaries, the Sirens, ruled the seas. It was the dawn of mankind, and the mortals lived in complete harmony with nature."

I tried to get a handle on the timeline. "Ten thousand years ago?"

"Perhaps ten times that," she said. "The ancients are not ones who keep time. To them, its passage is like water in a stream."

"Like urine streaming into a toilet?" I said.

Elyssa elbowed me. "What happened next?"

"The Apocryphan," Kaelissa said in a clipped tone. "No one knows whence they came, but they were more powerful than any of us."

"What did they look like?" I asked. "Humanoid?"

She shook her head. "Sometimes, yes, but only when they willed it. I was told their natural form is like a dark vortex of energy and they could change their form at will."

"Creepy," I said. "What did they do?"

"The story is quite long and involved," Kaelissa said, "but their leader, Kathazal, came to us in Seraphim form and told us the Apocryphan had long watched our war with the Sirens and determined it would lead to the destruction of this world. In their benevolence, they decided to declare themselves our rulers." Her hand tightened around a wine glass. "The Seraphim and Sirens fought back, even gaining the help of the dragons and other ancient beasts. The mortals refused to help, for they agreed that stopping the warring between the Seraphim and Sirens was for the best."

Elyssa's lips tightened. "Benevolent dictators usually aren't benevolent once they take power."

"The war against the Apocryphan ended quickly," Kaelissa continued. "They were more than immortal—indestructible. Nothing my ancestors did to harm them had any lasting effect." She paused for a long drink of wine. "For a time, there was peace. The Apocryphan divided the kingdoms among themselves with Kathazal as their leader. Though gender does not apply to the Apocryphan since they can take many shapes and genders, Kathazal was deemed the father of the others."

"Everyone has to come from somewhere, right?" I said.

She nodded. "Perhaps. Posthaneid was the favorite son, and as such, he was given Aquilis, the Siren kingdom. Couriondral ruled Draxadis, the dragon lands."

I had a boatload of questions about the dragons, but bit my tongue so as not to interrupt.

"Every Apocryphan ruled a kingdom—all but the outcast Xanomiel." Her gaze rested on the valley, but her eyes were focused inward. "Though none of the ancients knew for certain, they believe Xanomiel fomented unrest among the Apocryphan, claiming Kathazal planned to give Posthaneid complete power over all the kingdoms. War once again blighted the Earth, every Apocryphan throwing their kingdom against Seraphina and Aquilis."

"Talk about a world war," I muttered.

Kaelissa's gaze refocused on me. "As an outcast with nothing, Xanomiel likely hoped for the end of the world. Instead, the incredible outpouring of destruction fractured Earth, spinning the kingdoms into realms, still together, but separated by a veil of magic."

I put it into scientific terms. "Same place, different dimensions."

"Some ancients believe Xanomiel intentionally created the realms, while others argued Kathazal did it, hoping it would end the bloodshed." Kaelissa shrugged. "No one knows for sure. Thousands died from the breaking, and thousands more were ripped from their corporeal bodies and thrown into a spiritual realm called Haedaemos."

"Whoa," I said. "The Sundering created demons?"

"Indeed," she said.

"Are the Apocryphan still around?" Elyssa asked.

"They exist, though not in any of our realms," Kaelissa said. "The Sirens were the first to breach the divide between worlds and secretly contacted the Seraphim. The Sirens had discovered the spiritual plane and realized it held the key to defeating the Apocryphan. Using what they'd learned from service to their master Posthaneid, they partitioned Haedaemos, creating a sub-realm from which nothing could escape. With the help of the Seraphim, they tricked the Apocryphan and trapped them in this new realm, the Abyss."

A penetrating cold formed in the middle of my stomach. "The Abyssals are the Apocryphan?"

"That is another name for them, yes." Kaelissa seemed to sense something was wrong. "Why do you ask?"

"Are there others in the Abyss besides the Apocryphan?"

"Yes, there are other demons and spirits trapped there." Kaelissa raised an eyebrow. "Why?"

"Because I summoned one and it escaped." I prayed I hadn't screwed up majorly. "It looked like a black vortex with a glowing red eye and humanoid upper body."

"I cannot say for sure," Kaelissa said. "But it is highly likely you unleashed an Apocryphan upon Eden."

That wasn't exactly what I wanted to hear, but Jeremiah's warning about summoning Abyssals rang loud in my ears. In short, he'd told me not to do it just before Daelissa killed him. Other Daemos had echoed the warning, but during a battle with Daelissa, I ran out of options. Her army was decimating mine, so I summoned something powerful to fight her goliath battle golems. We'd won the day, but the Abyssal had broken my control and gone AWOL. I felt pretty certain it hadn't left looking for a college degree so it could get a nine-to-five job.

I looked at Elyssa. "You remember Kaylee Diggs?"

Her forehead wrinkled. "From high school?"

"Yeah. I'll bet she graduated and went to college."

"I don't understand." Perplexity wrinkled her forehead. "What does she have to do with the world being ruled by ancient gods?"

"Kaylee's biggest problem right now is probably deciding whether she wants to go to a party Friday night, or maybe she's worried the hot guy in her class doesn't like her." I sighed. "Must be nice having real world problems like that."

"Yeah," Elyssa said in a resigned tone. "Let's concentrate on unreal world problems so she can stay ignorant and alive, okay?"

I took a deep breath and rewound the story in my head. "So, the Sundering happens, the good guys trap the Apocryphan, and then what?" I asked Kaelissa.

She pondered a moment before answering. "There is far more to that story, but after a time, the realms lost contact. Thousands of years passed, I was born, and the following generations of Seraphim forgot Earth or the other realms ever existed. The ancients instructed those of us who knew to never reveal the past." Her eyes saddened. "Unfortunately, Daelissa discovered Eden and it led to her destruction."

"Technically, my mother found Eden," I told her.

Kaelissa didn't look surprised. "The news I heard from Zbura spoke of you and your mother, Alysea, Justin." She studied me intently. "The halfling son of a demon and angel."

I was surprised to hear her use that term. Most of her kind preferred the term Seraphim. "My father is a Daemos."

"Ah, yes." Her eyes brightened. "The incarnate form of demons. I heard about them during the First Eden War, but never met one."

"You took no part in the war at all?" Elyssa asked.

"No." Kaelissa's gaze retreated inward. "The ancients believed it a mad quest driven by bored youth. That was before Daelissa returned, her powers magnified enormously by mortal souls, and killed the Trivectus." Her chin rose slightly. "My daughter ruled the Brightlings."

"Murder isn't something to be proud of," Elyssa said. "Even if she killed Brightlings."

"The ancients were a different breed," Kaelissa said. "They were neither Brightling nor Darkling, but perfectly balanced, able to channel both forces equally. It was not until after the Sundering that their offspring manifested affinities to one force or the other. Many believed it a curse from the Apocryphan."

I swished the wine in my glass. "Fjoeruss is the only pure Seraphim I know who can channel both forces equally."

Light blazed in Kaelissa's eyes. "How do you know of him?"

I frowned and exchanged a glance with Elyssa. "He was one of Daelissa's companions."

"How very interesting," Kaelissa said. "An ancient helping one who killed so many of his own."

"Fjoeruss is an ancient?" I nearly jumped from my seat. "That's not possible. My mother said he was about her age."

"It makes sense," the sera said in a quiet voice. "The trickster still lives though we all thought him dead."

"Who else knew he was an ancient?" I asked.

"Unless another of his generation lives, I am perhaps the last who knew most ancients." Kaelissa plucked a quinto from the bowl and rolled it in her fingers. "Fjoeruss is not truly his first name—it was Ussor. His greatest love and adversary was Seaa, the golden ruler of the Seraphim."

"What happened to her?" I asked.

"Fjoeruss tried to defeat the Apocryphan by trickery while Seaa resorted to diplomacy." Kaelissa took a bite of the quinto, chewed and swallowed. "Kathazal discovered the trickery and blamed Seaa. He imprisoned and later executed her, thus sparking the Apocryphan War. Fjoeruss went mad with anger. He hid their children in the farthest reaches of the world and only brought them back after the war ended."

"I have a hard time imagining Fjoeruss as a father," I said. "He's kind of an ass."

"He was a father to two children," Kaelissa said. "His daughter bore him a granddaughter who bore him a great-granddaughter, who birthed a great-great-granddaughter—"

I held up a hand. "Okay, okay, I get it. He begat some kids who begat over and over again for thousands of years. I have a family tree too."

"Yes, but his great-great-granddaughter is very important to you. As with many sera, her mother chose to keep her matriarchal lineage and named her—" Kaelissa paused to take another bite of quinto while I waited.

"There's no drama to milk here," I explained. "I really don't care what her name is."

"Alysea," Kaelissa finished, a glint of pleasure shining in her eyes when she delivered that blow.

Fjoeruss was my great-great-great grand-pappy.

Chapter 13

"Say what?" Elyssa shouted.

I shook my head. "No way. Fjoeruss is not my pop-pop."

"Perhaps you should ask Ussor the next time you see him," Kaelissa said. "Perhaps this is why he helped you"—her voice grew very quiet—"end my daughter."

I heard shouts echoing from the village above. Djola raced onto the deck, face white. "Mother, we are under attack."

My brain booted out confusion and invited fear and adrenalin over for dinner. I raced upstairs to the street and stopped dead in my tracks when I saw what was coming into the valley. A massive flock of mutants riding the skyway burst into flight when they reached the end of it, and circled high into the air.

"Must be fifty of them," Elyssa said in a hard voice.

Another group of soldiers further behind the fliers lifted off from the skyway on a cloudlet.

"They followed us," Elyssa said. "Cephus hasn't given up yet."

"Is there a village on the other side of the valley?" I asked Kaelissa as she emerged outside.

"Not for several miles," she said.

"In other words, they're coming straight here," I muttered.

Flava led her troops onto the street and barked orders to them. She turned to me. "We are still exhausted from fighting and traveling. How can we defeat fresh troops?"

Nailan decided to pile on with another dire warning. "There are only twenty-eight of us and nowhere to run."

"I have faced worse odds." Lanaeia brushed a lock of silver hair from her face. "Elyssa, what should we do?"

Kaelissa's brow furrowed. "You are no Darkling, child."

Lanaeia's nose twitched. "How could you possibly know?"

"Your hair, child." Kaelissa said. "Only those touched with the fire of Brilliance will bear such silvery locks." She sighed. "Even my Daelissa would be envious."

Lanaeia's lips curled with distaste.

Elyssa bit her lower lip, a sign she was furiously thinking through our options.

Though aether was plentiful, I'd stretched myself to the limits to destroy the crystoid. Revving my engine that high came with a cost that only sleep or feeding could help. Sleep was better, but human soul essence would do in a pinch. The only human available was right next to me.

I gripped Elyssa's hand. "Babe, I'm gonna need a boost."

"Do you have time?" she asked.

"Maybe." I looked around. "Have you thought of anything?"

"My dad's the military genius, not me," she hissed.

"We cannot flee to the north or west over barren land because the fliers will see us," Flava said. "Our only hope is taking cover in the trees around the village."

Elyssa frowned and turned to Kaelissa "How strong are these houses?"

"They were made to withstand Brightling attacks," the sera replied.

Elyssa's eyes narrowed. "That gives me an idea." She splayed the fingers on her hands. "Justin, start feeding."

I spread my fingers and felt my Seraphim side straining for the soul essence freely offered. White energy trickled from Elyssa's right hand, and ultraviolet from her left, flowing into my fingers and replenishing my energy reserves. Though Seraphim didn't have to feed from others to survive, Daelissa had discovered long ago that feeding from mortal soul essence amped our powers exponentially.

As I fed, Elyssa quickly outlined a plan that sounded just crazy enough to work. There was a dreamy quality to her voice, a side-effect of our connection. Feeding my Seraphim side was tame compared to the sexual lust my inner demon aroused.

We put the plan in motion, racing from house to house and evacuating the villagers. I went first to the boot-shaped abode and sent a jolt of Murk into the gem outside—ringing the doorbell, so to speak—and a weary looking sera appeared a moment later.

"Hostile soldiers are coming," I explained to her in Cyrinthian. "You need to evacuate to the communal hall on the other end of town."

She looked as if she wanted to argue about it, but her eyes locked onto something behind me and went wide with terror. I assumed it was the sight of other Darklings fleeing down the street, but when I turned, Kaelissa's hard stare met me.

"Children, come at once! We're under attack!" The sera ran inside and returned with a toddler in each arm and a stream of kids in tow.

"Is this a nursery?" I asked, but the sera cast another frightened look at Kaelissa and led her young troops away.

A haggard-faced seraph emerged last, dragging a screaming boy. The seraph looked up at the skies and hesitated, possibly considering which was the worst fate—dying or dealing with so many kids. He apparently decided to live and trotted off after the sera, the boy still screaming incoherently.

She really is the old woman in the shoe.

I turned to ask Kaelissa what that was all about but she'd gone back to her house.

Djola ran up to me, panting. "Everyone is evacuated."

"You should join them," I told her.

She looked over at Kaelissa's house, a pained looked in her eyes. "I cannot. I am already a burden to Mother's honor and will not shame her further by running like a coward."

I couldn't imagine how hard it must be for this poor daughter, living in the shadow of a dead sister she'd never known. Daelissa had been insane, but Kaelissa only saw the beautiful Brightling daughter who'd once ruled Eden and Seraphina. Thanks to the Desecration, all of her other children would age and die—all would be inferior, mere shadows of the only child that mattered.

"Why do you live with her?" I asked. "Why not go out and make a life of your own?"

"She is the oldest among us," Djola said with reverence in her voice. "It is an honor to be by her side." Her chin lifted slightly. "I am a child of Kaelissa."

I repressed a groan. *The crazies must run in this family.* "Maybe you should strive to be more like your sister, Nightliss."

"Why should I?" Djola shuddered. "Naelissa forsook her name and betrayed our family's honor." She shivered once more for emphasis and stalked toward her living idol.

"And I thought my daddy issues were bad," I muttered.

Elyssa appeared by my side. "Is it just me, or do you have a bad feeling about Kaelissa?"

"I'm beginning to think Nightliss was the only normal one in that family." I looked around and noticed most of our people were out of sight. "We should get into position."

We jogged inside Kaelissa's crib and transformed the door opening back into a solid wall. I charged the gem inside and imagined how I wanted the wall to change. Several sections misted into circular windows, leaving a thin barrier on the outside that operated like a two-way mirror, allowing us to see out, but to those outside, the house appeared windowless.

The cloudlet with Cephus's loyalist ground troops drifted over the trees and landed in the middle of town, a protective ring of mutants surrounding them. I recognized a seraph with a dozen or more symbols inscribed on his shiny black chest armor tilted his chin and glanced haughtily at the village.

"Tain Prahven again," I muttered. "Guess I didn't kick his ass hard enough the last time."

Kaelissa stepped outside and approached them. "What brings the protectors of Pjurna to our village?"

The commander looked her up and down. "I am Tain Prahven of the Imperial Legion. We seek a band of rebel fugitives who likely passed through here."

"*Tain?*" She raised an eyebrow. "I thought that title died long ago."

"We are reviving the old ways," he said in a pleased tone. "Not many remember them."

A genuine smile stretched across Kaelissa's face. "They do not remember or honor them as they should."

"I don't like how chummy Kaelissa is getting with this guy," I told Elyssa.

The corners of her eyes wrinkled with worry. "She's off script."

Prahven's expression tightened. "If this is true, sera, please honor me with an answer to my question. Have you seen the fugitives?"

Kaelissa paused way too long before answering that question. Her finger rose and pointed north. "I saw a large band of people leave the skyway and head west along the valley rim."

"None of them passed through here?" he asked.

"It has remained quiet as ever, Tain Prahven."

Prahven pursed his lips. "These fugitives seek passage to Kdosh. I find it unlikely they would not come here since the skyway is malfunctioning." A smirk tugged the corners of his lips. "The Mzodi are the only other means of reaching their goal. Do they not regularly call to port here, sera?"

Kaelissa's eyes flashed. "Do you call me a liar?"

Prahven stroked the back of his hand over her cheek. "And if I did, young sera, what would you do?"

Eyes glittering like diamonds, Kaelissa trembled with rage.

"Oh crap," I muttered. "Get ready to give the signal."

"Search the domiciles," Prahven commanded. "Blow them apart if you must, but find the fugitives!"

"I hope Flava can follow through," Elyssa said. "If she doesn't, we're dead."

"If she doesn't, I'm grabbing you and running for the hills." I gripped her hand. "We'll find another way home."

Everything rode on what happened next. The fliers might be brainwashed citizens, forced to do the will of Cephus, but they'd kill us in a heartbeat. Maybe they could be saved, but not at the cost of our own lives. Elyssa had drawn a line in the sand and told Flava and her soldiers they'd have to cross it if they wanted to survive.

The fliers split into squads, each one accompanied by loyalists. Elyssa waited and watched, giving the enemy a chance to spread out. The first squad reached the house across the street. When no one answered, they balled their fists and blasted the outside with Murk, raining blows like a sledgehammer, cracking the crystalline outside.

With Prahven facing away, Kaelissa morphed into her felix form and flew to safety.

Elyssa nodded. "Now."

I extended my forefinger, angled it up and fired off a little sparkle. The reaction to the signal was almost instantaneous.

Windows appeared in the houses, and inside them, twenty-something cornered legionnaires with nothing to lose. Slender needles of Murk caught the loyalists in their unprotected throats, spearing through them like icepicks. Blood spurted from ruptured arteries and bodies fell. The survivors screamed and ran.

Tain Prahven channeled a protective dome around himself and barked orders. The fliers channeled shields and threw themselves in front of the attacks. I caught sight of Flava across the road, pain etched into her face as she mowed down one of the mutants.

"I think she's all in," I said in relief.

Their assigned loyalists protected, the fliers struck out. A group of five linked together, and the center one hurled a massive orb of Murk at the boot house. The structure imploded like broken china, shattering and falling in on itself. The legionnaires trapped inside tried to run, but Mutants cut them down. I fired a torrent of Brilliance, but it splashed harmlessly off the enemy shields.

The linked fliers blew a hole in the next house. The soldiers inside shielded themselves and retreated into the undamaged section, but another blast from the linked fliers smashed through the other side.

I pummeled the enemy again, finally overwhelming a shield and killing a flier, but it wasn't enough. I might as well ram my head against a stone wall for all the good my attacks were doing.

"Stop thinking in two dimensions," Elyssa said. "You're more than a Seraphim; you're part demon."

As usual, Elyssa's advice helped me take a step back. *Remember to look up.* My direct attacks weren't effective. Somehow I had to disrupt the mutant phalanx. Several different plans circled through my head and then I remembered how my father and I escaped from Serena's Gloom fortress.

"I've got an idea, but we have to go outside." I looked around for Kaelissa, expecting her to come up the stairs from the balcony, but found only Djola cowering in a corner.

"I will help," Djola said in a weak voice. "I must help."

"No, just stay inside," I told her. "There's no shame in not fighting."

Djola steeled herself and stood. "I will shield you."

Elyssa grabbed my arm. "You need the protection."

I nodded. "Fine, but be careful." That was all the time we had for words. I misted open the doorway and skirted behind the trees, out of sight of the attackers. "Get ready," I hissed.

Murk hammered on the attackers' shields sounding like a drummer gone mad. Houses exploded and legionnaires died. Mutants fell, but not nearly fast enough. I opened the window in my soul that connected me to Haedaemos and my demon half. I found a minor demon lurking in the spirit realm and snared it.

How'd you like to wreak some destruction?

It quaked with anticipation which was just what I had in mind. I imagined a portal opening at one end of the enemy lines. A small patch of the crystal street melted into black goo. The attackers were too busy looking at the horizontal plane to notice what was happening right at their feet.

I envisioned what I wanted to happen and punched the ground.

A huge shard of rock in the shape of a shark fin exploded from the ground and rammed straight down the line, splitting the seam between the backs of the mutants. Loyalists screamed, their bodies thrown into the air by the huge fin while the mutants were shoved apart, breaking their phalanx. The fin vanished back into the earth, leaving a giant furrow and mass confusion behind.

I pumped a fist. "Shark bowling for the win!"

Prahven spun toward me, face contorted with rage. "You will not escape here alive, Destroyer!"

Flava's people took advantage of the confusion, spearing fliers with Murk before they rose, precise stiletto attacks finding the seams in the dark armor. Elyssa rammed a loyalist with her shoulder and ran a sai sword through his throat. Legionnaires burst from the houses, swords in hand and began killing as many enemies as possible before they recovered from my surprise attack.

Prahven suddenly seemed to realize his fliers were at a severe disadvantage on the ground. He touched a gem on his uniform and the fliers rose, leaving the loyalists unprotected.

I summoned the demon once more, focusing on the ground beneath Prahven, but his dome protected him from all sides, and the demon portal refused to open. Rather than attempting to blast through his shield, I decided to counter it and threaded a sphere of Stasis from Murk and Brilliance.

Blasts of Murk rained down as the fliers turned their attention on me. Djola channeled a shield overhead, and Elyssa dove beneath it as the aerial assault began. Flava led her troops back into cover, but four fell before reaching safety. Loyalists shielded themselves and retreated toward their leader.

Prahven's eyes narrowed when he saw the Stasis forming. "Kill him!" he shouted to the loyalists. "Kill him now!"

The loyalists drew swords and attacked. With Flava's people pinned down, the odds were five to one. Djola couldn't help us since she was shielding our heads from the hail of Murk, so that technically made the odds seven and a half to one which was all the math my brain could process at the moment.

The other thing it quickly grasped was the need to retreat back inside the house. I stopped channeling Stasis, but before we could run, the loyalists blocked our way.

Elyssa twirled a sai sword in each hand, a savage grin on her face. "It's about time you fought your own battles, cowards!"

Since she said it in English, I translated for them.

Prahven scowled. "You'll see just how cowardly we are when we cut out your hearts, boy."

I looked over my shoulder. "Djola, can you hold on?"

Sweat poured down her face and every blow on the shield drew a wince, but she looked up and nodded.

"Ready, babe?" I asked Elyssa.

A cute growl rumbled in her throat. "More than ready."

The loyalists raised their swords with a roar and charged.

I channeled a shield over my left arm and formed a blade of pure Brilliance in my right hand. Elyssa shifted into a ninja stance and bared her teeth.

Our last stand had begun.

Chapter 14

We had one advantage and I hoped to make it count. The trees in front of Kaelissa's house funneled the loyalists between them, allowing only three to attack us at once. Our advantage wouldn't last long once the bulk of the soldiers circumvented the trees and surrounded us, but I was determined to make it work.

Two loyalists aimed their hands at one of the trees and hammered the trunk with violet energy. The trunk exploded into splinters and toppled. Other loyalists pounded it with attacks, leaving behind a trail of pulp and branches. Just like that, our protection was gone.

The enemies raised black crystal swords and charged.

The hail of Murk from the fliers overhead ceased since Prahven didn't want to kill any loyalists. Djola collapsed to the ground, exhausted. Elyssa met two attackers at once, her sai swords singing as they deflected and redirected simultaneous attacks. I caught a heavy blow on my Murk shield and parried a thrust from another loyalist.

Elyssa caught the swing of a sword from a fifth attacker just inches from my head. She ducked, spun, and swept the legs from another. Her sword darted into the unprotected space of his armpit. The seraph cried out and went silent in the space of a second as the blade ruptured his heart.

Roaring, I rammed an attacker in the chest with my shield. A loyalist sword blurred for my head. I caught it with my energy blade then kicked the attacker between the legs. The impact drove him five feet in the air and he screamed like his daddy-sack just exploded.

"Guess who's not having kids anytime soon?" I shouted. My blazing sword whooshed, slicing through the loyalist's neck at the apex of his flight. His body tumbled one way, head rolled in the other. "You, bitch!"

Elyssa ducked beneath simultaneous attacks from both sides. The loyalists parried each other and flashed confused looks at each other. A sai sword in either hand, Elyssa thrust upward between the seams in their armor. Sharp metal punched through soft flesh where the legs joined the groin. Their battle cries went up a dozen octaves to porcine squeals of agony.

"If you're looking for free vasectomies, you've come to the right place!" I blocked another blow and kicked a loyalist so hard he rammed into a tree and went still. Three more loyalists leapt over the bodies of the fallen and pummeled me from all sides. It was all I could do to shield myself. My demon and Seraphim attributes gave me incredible reflexes, but that didn't give me much of an advantage over other Seraphim—especially not three of them.

That was when a fourth enemy joined the party.

Elyssa seemed to be doing fine dispatching her seven and a half attackers, but the mass of bodies shoved us apart so we could no longer protect each other. Djola was in no shape to help, and god only knew where Kaelissa was.

I considered throwing up a dome shield, but that would only delay the inevitable. I needed more arms and more swords. Since I didn't possess lizard DNA, that wasn't gonna happen. A memory of battle flashed through my head. *I have something better than extra arms.* Pulling it off while fighting would be the trick.

Summoning more aether, I envisioned what I needed to happen. My shoulder blades itched. A powerful blow from a loyalist knocked me off balance and sent me sprawling. I released my energy blade so I wouldn't accidentally cut off my own head and turned my tumble into a somersault. A quick roll avoided another sledgehammer attack. A backward flip dodged a blow meant to crush the family jewels.

"Hey, I'm not the one who needs sterilizing!" I shouted and blurred away from another attack.

I had a few seconds worth of space before the enemy rushed in to fill the void. The itch in my shoulder blades suddenly felt like daggers slicing through flesh as my dark and white wing unfurled from my back.

The loyalists staggered to a halt. I released the channel on my shield and flexed my wings. Just for show, I flicked my left hand and channeled a dark sword. Flicked my right hand and unsheathed a blade of blazing white destruction. A savage grin stretched my mouth. "Come get me, you little bitches."

One by one they smiled back as spheres of white destruction coalesced in their right hands. It didn't take a genius to realize Cephus had equipped his people with prisms so they could channel Brilliance.

My grin faded. I couldn't parry energy attacks with two energy swords. "You just totally ruined the moment for me," I shouted. "I was going to look so cool for my girlfriend, but no, you had to go and ruin it!" As I shouted, I morphed the dark sword into a shield again and ran forward.

Brilliance speared from enemy hands and splashed against my shield. They might have prisms, but these dudes weren't very strong with destruction and they knew it. Their swords came up to meet mine and the spheres of white energy vanished. I transformed my shield back into a sword and loosed a savage cry.

Blades of energy met those of ultraviolet crystal. I flexed my left wing and parried a thrust meant for my back. I spun and whipped my white wing at another attacker. The destructive energy sliced deep into his armor. Duck. Parry. Thrust. I leapt over a low swing, flapped my wings and flipped over the attackers.

My sword of Brilliance speared one seraph through the back. Blood spurted and sizzled. I slammed another loyalist to the ground with a wing, leapt on his chest and buried both swords in his throat. As he gurgled his last, I flipped backward, over the attacks of the other loyalists. Before they could spin to face me, I sheared off their heads with a savage swipe. Headless bodies dropped to their knees and toppled.

I braced for more attackers, but when I looked back, only bodies littered the ground. Elyssa spun and delivered a roundhouse kick to one last seraph. Before he could rise, she leapt and drove her swords through the broken armor on his back. His bloodcurdling scream went silent.

A wide-eyed Djola emerged from behind a tree. "I have never seen such vicious fighting."

"You okay?" I asked her.

"Yes, I believe so."

Elyssa wiped angelic blood from her face. "We need to finish Prahven."

We raced through the trees and came back to the street. A handful of fliers hovered over a building, firing volleys at legionnaires inside, but their attacks splashed off the defenders' shields.

Prahven was nowhere to be seen.

Elyssa grabbed my shoulder and spun me around. "Look!"

I spotted Prahven and a handful of loyalists retreating into the sky aboard a cloudlet.

"The son of a bitch got away again," I growled. "Let's fight off the rest of the fliers."

Before I could focus on the remaining enemies, a volley of dark energy slammed into a flier's helmeted head with a loud crack. The stricken flier tumbled to the ground like a lead balloon. Another flurry streaked through the air like guided missiles, smacking mutants in the head and dropping them like flies. A beam of Brilliance sheared through the armor of two mutants like a hot knife through butter and the last of the fliers slammed to earth.

I turned and saw Kaelissa standing on the roof of her house. She wiped her hands and grimaced as if she'd just touched a dirty toilet seat. With a graceful flip, she dismounted the roof and landed next to us.

"Why didn't you help us before?" I said. "We could have ended the fight without so much carnage."

"Do not ask me to perform such menial acts," Kaelissa replied, face flushing red. "Had you been up to the task, I would not have interceded."

"Up to the task?" Elyssa said. "People died because you vanished and didn't help."

113

John Corwin

Kaelissa ignored the comment, rubbing her hands furiously on the silk material of her dress as she walked among the fallen. She knelt next to a dead loyalist and plucked a diamond-like prism from the palm of his hand. "Is it a sign? Will our ancient greatness soon return?"

"What do you mean by that?" I asked.

"Dual channeling," she said. "No more Darklings. No more division." Kaelissa's eyes glowed white. "Unity at last."

"That's what we're striving for," Elyssa reminded her. "After we beat Cephus, we'll reunite the two empires."

Flava emerged from the rubble of a house, followed by Joss and Otaleon. Nailan sprinted down the road, trailed by Lanaeia and two others. I looked around for other signs of life, but found only the stillness of death.

"Are we all that is left?" Lanaeia said in a despairing voice.

"Everyone, look for survivors," Flava said.

We raced from house to house, removing bodies. I heard a groan from beneath a pile of crystalline Murk and tossed aside large chunks. A bloodied Axo stared up at me. Blood trickled from the corner of his mouth, and the breath rattled in his throat.

"Flava!" I shouted. "I need help, now!"

She ran over and touched the stricken seraph's chest.

Axo bared his teeth in a bloody smile. "The Destroyer's curse sits heavily upon my family," he rasped. "I am the last. Our city in ruins. At least I will see my brother."

Flava looked at me and shook her head. "He is too badly injured."

"Put him in a stasis spell," Elyssa said.

"I don't have the strength." Tears trickled down Flava's face. "I am exhausted from battle."

Blood bubbled from Axo's mouth. "The Destroyer has failed—" his body jerked and foam spilled from his lips. With one final spasm, he went still.

I got up and backed away, my head feeling light, stomach sick. Lanaeia's slight form darted in my path and embraced me.

"You are no destroyer, Justin," she said in a faint voice. She looked up at me. "You are a fighter and a savior. Never forget this."

114

We were down from twenty-eight people to six. Our success relied on the good graces of the Mzodi and Daelissa's insane mother. If ever I needed a hug, it was right then. I wrapped my arms around Lanaeia and closed my eyes, allowing the real magic to soothe my grief and shine a light into the dark future.

"Thank you, Lanaeia." I managed a smile. "How did you know I needed a hug?"

A smile brightened her face. "It is the most powerful magic Nightliss taught me."

"Yeah." Salt stung my eyes. "She was a good hugger."

Lanaeia released me. "I will be sure to practice in case you need another."

We continued the grim task of digging through the rubble and found Philas trapped in a small pocket beneath a destroyed house.

"It's a miracle you survived," Elyssa said.

"I ordered my people to run," the seraph said sadly. "I did not make it out in time, but I survived and they are all dead."

The sheltering villagers began to poke their heads out of the buildings at the far end of town. The sera from the boot house ran down the road, eyes wide with horror. "Where will I keep the children?"

"You will manage," Kaelissa said in a hard voice, "while we rebuild."

The other sera looked down. "Of course, mistress."

That drew a raised eyebrow from Elyssa and several others in our group.

The children began to file out of the building at the end of the road. Without the pressure of battle looming, I took a better look at the brood and began to see a disturbing pattern. Many of them bore a resemblance to someone, but it wasn't the sera I'd mistaken for their mother.

I looked back and forth and noticed others in my group coming to the same realization. "Those are your children, Kaelissa."

She seemed unruffled by my observation. "Our bloodlines were tarnished by the Schism, our immortality lost." Kaelissa regarded a round-eyed girl with no particular tenderness. "I will recreate a pure breed, but I need the proper mate. So far none have produced suitable offspring."

"Woman, you just turned the crazy dial up to eleven." I saw my disgust reflected on the faces of my other companions.

Djola sprang to her mother's defense. "She will make Seraphim great again! Our people will rise from the ashes and once again build cities in the sky."

I threw up my hands. "Whatever. It's not as if breeding like rabbits is a crime." Wrinkled foreheads and raised eyebrows met my analogy. "Just get us onboard with the sky fishers tomorrow and everything will be hunky dory."

"I will gain you passage," Kaelissa said. Her eyes wandered to Lanaeia. "Were you turned into a husk during the Schism—the Desecration?"

"Yes." Lanaeia's face tightened. Daelissa had treated her like a red-headed stepchild, and looking at Kaelissa had to be as unsettling for her as it was for the rest of us. She pointed to Joss and Otaleon. "They were also husked."

"Has it affected your children?"

"I have not tried for children," Lanaeia said.

Kaelissa looked at Joss and Otaleon. "Does your seed remain viable?"

The seraphs' faces paled and they backed away a step.

"What's the deal with the personal questions?" I asked.

Kaelissa stepped closer to Joss and ran a hand through his blond hair. "I would have you plant your seed in me. Perhaps our ancient blood will overcome the curse."

Joss gulped. "I'm not certain—"

"It is my price for the destruction of my village," Kaelissa said, looking at me. "The Mzodi will refuse aid unless I endorse you."

"I will do it," Otaleon said, clearly unnerved by the prospect. He wiped away a trickle of sweat.

Kaelissa's nose wrinkled. "I think not. I would like this child to have golden hair, not a dull brown."

"Talk about rude," Elyssa said.

116

I stepped between Kaelissa and Joss. "Are you really going to stake the fate of Seraphina on your need to breed?"

"If our people do not regain immortality, they no longer deserve to exist," she said in a quiet voice. Kaelissa smiled faintly. "I will be taking my tea on the balcony once you reach a decision."

Djola stiffened. "I will prepare your tea at once, Mother." She hurried away.

Kaelissa gave Joss one last look over and strolled through the devastated village back to her undamaged house.

Joss stared after her for a moment. "She is as lovely and every bit as insane as Daelissa."

"The question is, how dangerous is she?" Elyssa murmured. She bit her lip. "Did you see her power with Brilliance?"

I nodded slowly. "Unlike Daelissa, I don't think she used a prism for it."

"But she's a Darkling," Elyssa said. "How is she so powerful with Brilliance?"

"I have no idea," I admitted.

Elyssa turned to Flava. "Will the Mzodi help us if Kaelissa doesn't put in a good word?"

"They are notoriously reclusive," Flava said, "living deep in the Great Barrier Vortex and only visiting border towns to trade gems." She looked grimly toward Kaelissa's home. "I think we need all the help we can muster."

"Surely if we tell them the stakes, they'll give us a lift," I said.

"Perhaps," Flava said. "I don't think they like the land folk."

In other words, I was going to have to push poor Joss into making snu snu with Kaelissa or our mission was toast.

Chapter 15

Before I could come up with a way to broach the subject, Joss spoke. "I will do it. Kaelissa is a delight for the eyes, and I do not have to talk with her."

Elyssa groaned. "Men. I swear to god you would all jump in a pit of spiders if a beautiful woman was involved."

I wrapped an arm around her. "Like the time I traveled to another realm, destroyed their government, and raised an army so I could bring back a healer to save a beautiful woman?"

She stared at me for a moment. "Well, when you put it like that, I guess this is pretty tame."

"Hey, it's not like Joss is taking one for the team," I said. "Provided Kaelissa doesn't go black widow on him and kill him afterward."

Joss's eyes went wide as manhole covers. "Do you believe it a possibility?"

I got the attention of Kaelissa's brood keeper. "She doesn't kill her mates, does she?"

The sera sagged. "No. All the seraphs of Ooskai have mated with her and all still live. Their deepest regret is she gives them only one chance to prove their worth."

Elyssa grimaced. "That's just gross."

Otaleon patted Joss on the back. "Enjoy yourself."

Joss nodded nervously. "It has been over two thousand years."

Lanaeia's eyes softened sympathetically. "Yes, it has been a very long time."

Flava shared a horrified look with Nailan and the other legionnaires. "How have you survived so long without?"

"Well," Lanaeia said shyly, "I was a husk for most of that time."

Joss smiled and departed for Kaelissa's house. "I think he'll last thirty seconds."

"Two minutes," Elyssa said.

Otaleon snorted. "I'll be surprised if he's able to disrobe in time."

We all shared a good laugh in the middle of the half-destroyed village, where the dead outnumbered the living. God knows we needed a light-hearted moment. Then it was time to start the grim task of cleaning up and burying our comrades.

Joss didn't reappear for several hours, during which we time moved the bodies to the small graveyard on the plateau to the south. Lanaeia dug graves in the hard soil by plowing the earth with Murk. Though she was a Brightling, it appeared her dual channeling skills had progressed well.

A crew of villagers brought out long cylinders resembling telescopes but with gems for lenses. Some were as thick as a finger while the largest stood nearly as tall as me. By channeling Murk through tube with a large red stone, they dissolved the crystalline rubble into mist. Within two hours, they'd cleared away one house and started building a new one by channeling through a blue gem nearly six feet in diameter.

Ultraviolet rays swept back and forth along the ground, laying a cloudy foundation that solidified into the shiny black chrome material I'd grown familiar with in Tarissa.

Joss emerged from Kaelissa's house looking flushed and a bit rumpled. Otaleon and I met him in the street.

"Did you go through every step of Kama Sutra in there?" I asked.

Otaleon chuckled. "We expected you much sooner."

Joss grinned. "Apparently, there are some things I remember about my previous existence before the Desecration."

"How to make love for sixty seconds and then talk for several hours?" Otaleon said.

"Let's just say Kaelissa will be more than happy to endorse our voyage with the sky fishers." Joss ran a hand through his tousled hair.

"Apparently, this is the first time in centuries she has actually enjoyed coitus."

Elyssa appeared at my side. "How was she?"

Joss cleared his throat uneasily. "Let us just say that in between sessions, she rambled about her ambitions." He looked into the distance. "She hopes to raise an immortal Empress."

"What if she has your child?" Elyssa said. "Will you want to see it?"

Joss flinched. "I hadn't thought that far ahead."

Elyssa groaned. "Sex apparently reduces males of every kind to short-sighted stupor."

"Of course I will want to see the child," Joss interjected before Elyssa could badmouth every male in the universe. "If Kaelissa does not want it, then I will gladly take it."

"How does she even know if the child will be immortal or not?" I asked.

"Flava told me a good healer can detect if the child will be short-lived," Otaleon said. "There is a darkness in the genes of those affected by the Desecration that cannot be purged."

That got me to thinking about all the husked Seraphim we'd revived. The Desecration had affected the Seraphim in Eden much differently than those here in Seraphina. "Can Flava test the reborn to make sure they didn't lose their long lifespans?"

"She tested me and found me free of the malady," Otaleon said. "It is possible the method for restoring us from husked form also purged whatever affects the lifespans of the Seraphim here."

"Are you otherwise healthy?" I said. "You're not shooting blanks or anything?"

The term obviously didn't compute because his forehead pinched into a confused V.

"You're not sterile," I clarified.

"I did not ask her to check that," Otaleon said.

"Though he'd like to test it with her," Joss said with chuckle.

"Ooh, Otaleon likes Flava?" I said.

Otaleon sighed. "She is a beautiful sera who has proven herself fierce in combat and a great leader. What more could a seraph ask for?"

I thought back to the earlier conversation about how important the matriarchal lineage was to the angels. "I take it women—seras—are the ones who make the moves here?"

"Perhaps during our time," Otaleon said. "It seems things are more uncertain now."

I expected Elyssa to make some smart remark about how it was better with women in charge, but she passed up the opportunity. Eyes pensive, she sighed. "Too bad Daelissa had to make females in charge look bad."

"You should speak with Flava," Joss told Otaleon. "We are at war and the odds are one of you will die before it ends. Do not let the opportunity pass you by, brother."

"I agree," Elyssa said, voice somber. "You never know what tomorrow brings."

As if on cue, Flava stepped from the southern tree line, face smudged with dirt from burying the dead. She joined our group and said, "It is time for final rites, if you would like to join us."

Otaleon touched her shoulder. "Of course."

She patted his hand. "Thank you."

As the sun dipped in the west, we walked up the incline to the plateau and regarded the rows of headstones. Lanaeia sat on a boulder, shoulders sagging, face pale with exhaustion. Even her silvery hair had lost some of its luster.

Flava called our small group to order and began. "We were once more than a mighty thousand strong, and in one fell swoop, reduced to a hundred. From a legion to a century in the space of a moment. Over the months, our numbers dwindled as Cephus's minions hunted and killed us. Once again we have been reduced, and now we are only a handful."

She let that sink in for a moment. "Though our numbers are small, our will to fight and win is great. Cephus has no loyalty but to himself. His evil will die, if not by our hands, by the hands of Eden's army. Today, we celebrate those who sacrificed all for the love of Pjurna and her people."

Flava knelt and splayed her fingers, palms facing the ground as was common when Seraphim greeted each other. The rest of us mimicked her.

"May the skies receive your souls and your lives find peace on the ethereal plane." Flava squeezed shut her eyes. "Amen."

"Amen," Nailan and Philas said, and the rest of us chimed in right after.

Flava rose and wiped away tears. "Thank you for coming."

I gave Elyssa a confused look as the small gathering dispersed. "Did she say amen?"

"Sure sounded like it," she said. "I didn't follow everything since it was in Cyrinthian, but that last word sounded pretty familiar."

"Weird." I took her hand and led her away from the others to the far end of the plateau where it ended in a cliff overlooking a seemingly endless plain of red grass. A tall boulder shielded us from the cool breeze, but still allowed us to see into the distance.

Elyssa leaned against me as we sat in silence and just enjoyed being with each other. It felt as if we'd been in Seraphina for weeks and not just a few days, and I'd been jonesing for some alone time with her.

I lifted her chin and brought her soft lips to mine. She tasted sweet, and sent fire rushing through my veins. "You missed a little blood on your forehead," I told her.

"Sorry, I washed off in a hurry," she said.

I chuckled. "Doesn't bother me." I wet my thumb and wiped away the blood.

"I hope the Mzodi can help," Elyssa said. "I don't know about you, but just thinking that every day Cephus is brainwashing more and more of his people makes me sick to my stomach. I can't wait to end this."

"Daelissa was bad," I mused. "She killed humans just to feed off them, but it wasn't like she consumed hundreds a day. I mean, what if Cephus's brainwashing is irreversible?"

"All those people lost forever," Elyssa murmured. "Justin, that's awful."

"Cephus is just like Serena." The comparison seemed so clear in my head. "They're both scientists but without a heart or compassion to guide them."

"They have power but no ethics," Elyssa said. "Though they're not really scientists since they practice magic."

"Well, whatever you call magical scientists," I said.

"Those words are complete opposites." Elyssa managed a small smile. "I'm sure you'll come up with a good name soon enough."

"What I mean is they experiment with magic." I shrugged. "They're researchers."

"Well, whatever they are, they're extremely dangerous," Elyssa said.

"True that." I kissed her cheek. "I wish I knew what to expect on Kdosh. If it's another huge crystoid, we're in trouble."

"What's keeping Cephus from launching another wave of crystoids once our army arrives?" Elyssa said. "Removing the first round from Eden took a massive effort. What's keeping him from launching another salvo to keep us from invading?"

"That's a question I've been wondering myself," I admitted. "If he started preparing from the first day he met me, that gave him about four months to mass produce crystoids."

"He hit the Tarissan Legion just a few weeks after they arrived," Elyssa said.

"All he needed was a couple crystoids for that," I reminded her. "He probably used what he had here first. Since the crystoids beam all the energy back to his base, it left him sitting pretty while everyone else suffered and died."

"So it took him about three months to produce the ones he used in Eden," Elyssa said.

"That'd be my guess." I thought back to the final tally Cinder had given us. "At least two hundred crystoids were launched, but only a hundred and thirty or so actually made landfall and grew."

"In other words, his manufacturing process isn't very efficient." Elyssa tapped a finger on her chin. "It probably took him three or four months to make that many."

Cold fingers coiled around my heart. "It's been nearly three months since the invasion."

"Which means if he's been making more crystoids all this time, he might have another volley ready to go."

Any shred of optimism I'd had before evaporated. "All he needs is one crystoid to keep us from returning to Tarissa. I got up and started pacing. "If he launches another at the skyway terminus in the city, then it doesn't matter if we open the arch on Kdosh because we can't transport an army without the skyway."

"If we clear the crystoid on Kdosh, that gives us clear sailing at least to Ooskai," Elyssa said.

"Yeah, but Tarissa is on a massive floating island above a vortex," I reminded her. "We can't march overland because there's no way to fly the army up to the city once we reach it."

Elyssa pursed her lips and remained silent. "Logistically, the other Alabaster Arches are too deep in Brightling territory for us to use."

"Then there's his threat to open a portal to the Void." Just thinking about the Beast made my skin crawl. "Cephus said it would be ready in days."

"Whether it's crystoids or the Void, we have to figure a way inside his fortress fast." Elyssa bit her lower lip. "How are we supposed to punch a hole in his barrier?"

"We're thinking about this too magically," I said as an idea struck me in my thick skull and trickled into my forebrain. "Why use magic when we have Victus Edison and Science Academy to help?" I clapped my hands with excitement.

"Calm down, cowboy." Elyssa grabbed my hand and pulled me back down to earth. "Are you suggesting we use battle bots?"

"If we can't use the skyway, we'll use lots and lots of rocket sticks." I sketched out the plan in my head. "I know we can't transport everyone and everything with rocket sticks, but we could land enough

124

people in Tarissa to destroy another crystoid and guard the end of the skyway."

"Totally," Elyssa agreed enthusiastically. "It's too bad we can't fit airships through the arch."

"Yeah, I talked with Victus about that. He said he could probably break them down and reassemble them on this side. The envelopes are the problem."

Elyssa frowned. "Envelopes?"

I nodded. "The balloon part of the airship."

"I thought that was the nacelle."

"Don't get me started," I groaned. "Do you know how many times Victus corrected my airship terms when I spoke with him about it? He's brilliant, but he's a condescending jackass, too."

She grunted in agreement. "Rocket sticks sound doable. All we need to do is maintain a foothold on Kdosh to thwart any attempts to shut down the arch."

I leaned against her and felt the weight slide off my shoulders. "I feel much better about our chances now, but—"

Elyssa combed through my hair with her fingers. "But what?"

"We still need the sky fishers." I looked up at the dark clouds gathering in the dusk. "I hope Kaelissa can deliver."

Without another means of aerial transportation, we were stuck.

Chapter 16

Elyssa and I spent the night in Kaelissa's house, but the village brood mother remained out of sight. Djola brought us breakfast the next morning, but remained elusive when we asked about the Mzodi.

"What time do they usually get here?" I asked.

"They arrive when they arrive," she said and backed out of the bedroom.

"You know how much I love vague replies," I muttered.

Elyssa bit into a loaf of panari and shrugged. "She probably doesn't know."

After breakfast, we went outside and were stunned to see most of the houses already rebuilt—some of them with new additions or geometry.

I looked at the new three-story version of the boot house. "I wonder how long it takes to build a skyscraper."

"I'd like to know how hard it is to change the color." Elyssa glanced around at the shiny ultraviolet domiciles. "I like dark purple, but it gets a bit old."

A loud pop jerked my attention to the west where sparkling aether lit the sky. Another magical flare soared into the air and popped like fireworks.

"I think the sky fishers are here," Elyssa said.

Kaelissa emerged from her house and walked toward the stone arch, Djola following close behind. Flava ran from a dome-shaped house, eyes wide and alert.

"What was that?" she asked us.

"Our last hope is arriving," I said dryly, though my nerves squirmed like a pouch full of snakes.

The rest of our shrunken entourage joined us on the street in short order and we set off down the street to the valley bridge.

Kaelissa waited at the edge of the cliff where the wide dock nestled between the rock face and the bridge.

I stepped beside her and looked west, but a thick bank of clouds spoiled an otherwise clear morning. "Are they far?"

"No," she replied. "I suggest you remain back while I speak with them. They are not very welcoming to strangers."

The sound of children laughing and playing caught my ears. I looked back and saw the ward of Kaelissa's many offspring herding them down the road toward the dock, probably to see the spectacle.

"We'll step back when they get here," I said.

Kaelissa nodded, her eyes never leaving the west.

I followed her gaze but the only thing in sight was the thick bank of clouds drifting unnaturally fast toward us. The clouds shimmered and slowed. A forked tongue poked through the mist. Behind it emerged long reptilian muzzle and wide organic curves. Four large Seraphim wings flapped majestically, pinions moving in perfect unison to drive the ship forward and keep it aloft. Large gems along the wooden hull shone with an inner light.

Now clear of the cloud, the vessel resembled a whale with the head of a dragon and the wings of angels. Its construction seemed primarily of wood instead of Murk, though a crystalline sheen around the hull hinted at something in between.

The crew raced along the upper deck. Shouted commands echoed across the distance as the Mzodi prepared to dock.

Elyssa tugged on my arm. "Justin, let's back off."

"B-but look at that thing," I stuttered. "It's amazing!"

"Admire it from a distance," she ordered.

With a long, drawn-out sigh, I walked it back a good distance and waited.

The ship glided into port and rotated to face west while slowly drifting down to land on the dock. When it touched down on its wide flat hull, the wings flickered and vanished and a long ramp extended to shore.

A tall sera with wide shoulders and hips appeared at the top of the ramp, eyes surveying the village. She frowned when she noticed us, but proceeded down the ramp to speak with Kaelissa.

"I was kind of hoping for sky pirates," I muttered, "but she doesn't have a peg leg or an eyepatch."

"Or a parrot," Elyssa added.

Kaelissa and the presumed captain spoke for several minutes then the latter raised a hand. A side section of the hull folded away to reveal a cargo hold filled with glittering jewels.

"Oh my," Elyssa said softly. "I want to touch those so much."

"Admire them from a distance," I said with a grin.

Elyssa pressed her lips tight and glared at me. "Don't make me hurt you."

I held up my hands in surrender. "I'm sure we'll get a chance to look at the goods when Kaelissa negotiates our passage."

Two stocky seraphs carried a large tray from within the hold and set it at Kaelissa's feet. I zoomed my vision and saw gems of various shapes and sizes on the tray. Djola knelt and inspected each gem while Kaelissa spoke with the captain.

"I really wish she'd waited to conduct business after getting us onboard," Elyssa said.

I was itching to walk over and talk with the captain myself, but decided my interference could ruin our chances of passage. After painstakingly examining the goods, Djola stood and whispered in Kaelissa's ear. The ancient sera nodded and motioned at the children.

"What's that about?" Elyssa murmured.

We soon realized horrific truth when the captain selected several girls from the crowd. One of the stocky seraphs guided them toward the cargo hold.

"They're trading those kids!" I said. "What kind of monster is Kaelissa?" Before Elyssa could respond, I raced to the dock and skidded to a stop in front of Kaelissa and the others.

"I told you to wait," Kaelissa said coldly.

"You're trading children for gems?" Outrage crackled in my throat. "They're your own flesh and blood!"

The captain stared at me. "This is not your affair, stranger."

"Maybe not, but it's wrong." I bared my teeth. "Don't make me take them back by force."

"The only thing wrong here is your interference," the captain replied. "Look at the children." She jabbed a finger toward the girls. "Look!"

I saw them standing inside the cargo hold, waving and smiling at their siblings as if they were about to embark on a Disney cruise. "I'm looking."

"Do they look frightened or sad?" the sera asked.

"No, but you could've told them there's free ice cream and candy on the ship for all I know." I sensed movement behind me and saw Flava, Lanaeia, and the others forming up. A dozen of the ship's crew gathered at the top of the ramp and I knew there was about to be a smackdown.

"Release the children," Flava said. "I cannot allow such barbarism to go unchallenged."

"Leave us and mind your own affairs," Kaelissa hissed. "You fools have no idea what is going on here."

"I know I'm about to open a can of whoopass," I retorted.

Kaelissa's forehead pinched with confusion at the untranslatable word.

I walked toward the girls and held out a hand. "Come to me."

They backed away and hid behind the crewman.

"We're going to save you," I said. "We won't let the bad angels take you."

"Your interference ends now!" the captain shouted and slashed a hand through the air.

The crew charged down the ramp with a roar. Elyssa and the others drew weapons and formed up around me. I summoned aether and gathered enough energy for a deadly strike.

"Enough!" someone shouted from the top deck.

Everyone paused in mid-attack and looked up. A pale sera with blazing orange hair stalked down the ramp. A tight black coat lined with silver lace outlined a thin frame. Jade green eyes bored into the would-be brawlers, causing the crew to look down and back away, faces blanched.

The sera stormed up to me and spoke in a deadly quiet voice. "We are taking these girls from an uncaring mother and giving them to loving parents who cannot have children of their own. Now, if you are opposed to such charitable acts, I will gladly fight you here and now. Otherwise, I suggest you control yourself and leave my crew alone."

I glanced at the frightened girls cowering behind the crew and down at the glowing orb of destruction coalesced around my fist. "Why in the hell didn't someone just tell me what was going on in the first place?"

The orange-haired sera glared at the person I'd mistakenly assumed was the captain. "What did you tell him, Illaena?"

The other sera looked away. "I told him it was none of his concern."

The captain nodded. "I see." She offered a slight bow to me. "Apologies for the misunderstanding..." She looked at me expectantly.

"Justin," I said and splayed my fingers toward her.

She hesitated when she saw the fingers, then spread hers in a token gesture. "You may call me Cora."

"Captain Cora?" I said.

"We don't use such formalities," she replied.

I turned to Elyssa and explained in English what Cora had told me in case the meaning had been murky.

Elyssa tucked away her swords. "I love her hair. It's so vibrant!"

Cora's lips stretched into a wide smile which quickly vanished. She turned back to Kaelissa. "Is everything in order?"

"Yes, Cora," the ancient sera replied. "There is another matter to discuss."

I decided to jump straight in, figuring I couldn't do more damage at this point. "Can you give us a ride to Kdosh?"

Cora raised an orange eyebrow. "You wish to reach the arch?"

"Desperately," I admitted. "I have to reach the Alabaster Arch."

Her eyes filled with interest. "Are you not from this realm?"

I gave Kaelissa sideways glare. She'd told us these people didn't care about outside affairs, but Cora certainly had a lot of questions. "I'm from Eden," I answered.

Her lips parted and her eyes widened. "I will gladly help."

"I thought you said they would be hard to convince," Flava said to Kaelissa. "You said we couldn't gain passage without your help."

"You made Joss sleep with you," Lanaeia said.

"I would gladly do it again," Joss said, drawing a chuckle from Otaleon.

"Kaelissa is right," Cora said. "We prefer to keep to ourselves, but this is another matter."

"You're aware Cephus usurped power in Tarissa?" I said.

"Of course," Cora replied. "Even in these troubled times, we travel the world, trading our wares and trading in rumors."

Flava gasped. "You trade with the Brightlings?"

"Yes." Cora gave her a sharp look. "Despite what Darklings think, not all Brightlings are evil."

"Flava doesn't believe that either," Lanaeia said. "But the Brightling Empire has been at the borders of Pjurna, waiting for a chance to invade."

Cora nodded. "War is the most constant thing in any world." Sadness flickered across her face.

"Agreed," I said grimly. "We have an army waiting to dethrone Cephus and restore the rightful rulers to Pjurna."

Cora held my gaze for a moment then nodded. "We depart soon. Gather your belongings and meet back here."

"I think we have everything we need," I said.

"Our journey here has been hard," Flava said. "We have lost many loved ones and carry only the armor and weapons on our backs."

"Very well, then." Cora looked at her crew. "Prepare for departure."

The people who'd been ready to fight us moments earlier stormed back up the gangplank while the crew with the girls vanished inside the hold, the wooden hull growing in behind them.

131

"Come," Cora said, and walked up into the ship.

I turned to Kaelissa. "Thank you for your, um, hospitality."

She stared at me for a moment, head tilting slightly to the side, then spoke. "Our paths will cross again."

I wasn't sure if that was a promise or a threat. "Take care." I turned and led my entourage up the gangplank.

The decking, a dark-grained wood, was carved into a semblance of dragon scales.

"This is amazing," Elyssa said, kneeling and running her hand along the wood.

"Who thought up the idea of a whale dragon hybrid?" I asked. "Do they even have whales on Seraphina?"

Cora tilted her head slightly and hesitated. "It is a fanciful design, but it also serves its purpose."

She hadn't exactly answered my question, so I threw out another one. "Is this real wood, or did you weave it from Murk?"

She turned to her first mate. "Illaena, show them to their quarters."

The tall sera nodded. "Of course." She didn't even bother telling us to follow her, but marched down a ramp inside the bowels of the whale dragon. A sullen white light suffused the wide hallway below. The wooden walls were carved into the likeness of vines that looked so real, it seemed I could uproot them from the walls. Spiky black trees, complete with limbs and leaves, supported the ceilings, and the doors seemed to be woven from brambles.

"How cool is this?" Elyssa said.

Lanaeia ran a hand along the wall and gasped. "I have never seen such lovely work."

"There is no other ship like the *Evadora* in the fleet," Illaena said proudly.

"There's a fleet of sky ships?" I asked.

She ignored the question and slid open a nearby door. "The cabins from here to the end are yours."

Flava stared at the sliding door. "Why are there no gems to open the doors?"

"Perhaps you should ask Cora your incessant questions," Illaena replied and stomped away.

I met Elyssa's questioning gaze, but waited until Illaena was out of sight before speaking. "Riddle me this—why and how is there a wooden sky ship when nearly everything in Seraphina is made with gems and crystal?"

Flava put a hand to the wood and closed her eyes. "How strange. I sense life within the very walls."

"The wood is alive?" Elyssa asked.

Flava nodded. "I have heard of the Mzodi and their flying ships, but never have I heard of one crafted from living wood."

"Just what I needed," I said. "Another mystery."

Elyssa nodded "I don't know if you noticed or not, but when I complimented Cora in English—"

"She understood what you said," I replied. "I don't know about you, but not many Seraphim speak English."

"Most of us do," Otaleon said, glancing at the exceptions, Nailan and Philas.

I heard a loud whoosh and my stomach dropped as the ship lurched up into the air. "Holy barf burgers." I grabbed the door frame and hung on until the ride smoothed out.

Joss looked a bit green. "I think I will go to the deck for some fresh air."

I felt a bit unsettled myself. "Everyone settle in and rest up. We don't know what's waiting for us on Kdosh and we need to be ready."

"Agreed," Flava said. She walked down the hall and entered the last door.

I stepped inside the open door and propped the malfunctioning rocket stick in a corner. A standard cloud bed occupied the middle of the floor, though I wasn't sure we'd have time to utilize it.

"Now what?" Elyssa asked.

"Cora," I replied simply.

"Huh?"

"I'd like to ask her a few questions." I leaned against the wall and folded my arms. "I'm about eighty percent sure she's not Seraphim."

Chapter 17

Elyssa blinked. "Cora's not Seraphim?"

I shook my head. "Did you see her response when I spread my fingers for an angel greeting? Have you ever seen anything in Seraphina made from real wood besides the trees?"

"No, but why does that make you think she's not Seraphim?"

"I can't put a finger on it, but I'd really like to figure it out." I stepped into the corridor.

"We don't have time to unravel every mystery in the universe, Justin." Elyssa hooked her arm through mine. "Is it really that important?"

I stopped and turned to her. "If she speaks English, that means she's either from Eden or has spent considerable time there."

Elyssa frowned. "So what?"

"What if she's one of Serena's agents?" I glanced around to be sure the hallway was empty. "What if she's a last ditch effort to keep us away from Kdosh?"

"I see your point." Elyssa rested her chin on the top of a fist. "She could be one of Serena's Arcanes, though it's highly unlikely."

"I may be way off base," I admitted, "but at this point, I'm not taking any chances. Cephus and Serena have outmaneuvered us too many times. For all we know, this ship is headed in the wrong direction."

Elyssa gripped my hand. "Then we shouldn't waste any time."

Something pricked my hand. "Ow!" I jerked it back. A vine on the wall darted out like a snake and struck Elyssa before I could react.

Her violet eyes went wide. "What was—" her eyes drooped and she slumped in my arms.

My legs turned to jelly and we both fell to the floor. Just before I lost consciousness, it seemed the deck itself opened like a mouth and swallowed us whole.

I jerked awake on a bed of rough purple grass in a glade surrounded by crooked black trees. Soft white light shined down from a small moon overhead. Warm flesh pressed against my arm. I rolled over and found Elyssa snoozing next to me.

"Eden has seen tough times recently," said a female voice somewhere in the darkness. Cora stepped into the moonlight. "The Seraphim War was another interesting footnote in a long history of violence."

I leapt up and sprang toward her, but vines wrapped around my wrists and legs and pulled me back. With a roar, I ripped loose an arm, but something stung my neck and all the strength left me.

"Please, Justin, do not struggle." Cora sat on a low boulder, hands in her lap. "I wish you no harm. In fact, I will see you through to Kdosh."

"Who...are you?" My tongue felt like a slug, the words like melted marshmallows in my mouth.

"I am simply a person who remembers when the world was young, when the world was whole, when the world was torn asunder." She smiled. "I was once a queen, but am now banished from my own realm. A mother, torn from her own child."

My mind, foggy from the drug in my blood mustered an idiotic reply. "But you look so young."

Cora ran her fingers down a silver chain around her neck and rubbed a green pebble at the end. "Ever am I so."

"Unnhh," Elyssa groaned. She jerked to a sitting position, eyes glowing violet. "Justin, where are we?"

"Safe," Cora said. "Please, child, let me explain."

The stuff I'd been injected with wore off, and my head cleared. This time, I opted not to attack the strange woman. "What realm are you from?"

"The land of Lyrolai, the forest, the glen, the glade—all the lands of the forest folk." Cora tucked the pebble back into her shirt. "Like the others, our realm was fractured from Earth during the Apocryphan war. Many lives were lost, and our mortal brethren were separated from us."

"You're elves!" I gasped.

Her brow furrowed. "The fairy tale creatures you refer to were perhaps born out of our legend." Cora shrugged. "Lyrolai, the realm of forest, where our folk lived in harmony with nature, was chosen, unbeknownst to us, as the center point for a great undertaking."

"I'm lost," Elyssa said. "You're from a realm called Lyrolai?"

"Once it was thusly named," Cora replied. "The Sirens saw the sundered realms slipping far apart, never to reunite. They unilaterally decided this was unacceptable. Using the ancient magic taught them by Posthanied, they ripped our realm apart to create an anchor stone which now holds all the realms in tight orbit."

Elyssa and I exchanged confused looks.

I rose slowly so as not to draw another stinger. "The Sirens destroyed Lyrolai and killed everyone there?"

"Not everyone," she said. "The broken land now exists in eternal twilight. No longer Lyrolai, it is now called the Glimmer."

The Glimmer? "How did you get into Eden?"

"It was not easy. The rift between the Glimmer and Eden is guarded, but I discovered a way around the sentinels." Her fingers found the green pebble around her neck again. "I went through a crack in the world and emerged in a place you call Queens Gate."

"A pocket dimension?" My jaw went slack when I realized what this meant. "The pocket dimensions are in the Glimmer?"

"Not precisely." She released the jewelry and pressed her palms together. "The Glimmer touches all the realms. What you call a pocket dimension is actually where Eden intersects my realm. In a sense, it is a juxtaposition of our two worlds."

"But it's underground," I reminded her. "How does it have a sky?"

"Think of it as a fractured part of your realm, a remnant of when the world was whole." Cora pressed her fingertips together.

136

"Everywhere the Glimmer touches another realm, you will find these pocket dimensions."

I was a bit disappointed to discover they weren't actually in a separate dimension after all, but it raised a whole host of other questions. "Can you show me how to reach the Glimmer?"

"Perhaps someday," she said with a smile. "I believe you have bigger fish to fry."

Elyssa pursed her lips. "Sounds like you're good with the English lingo."

Cora nodded. "I lived in Eden for many centuries, and I have always been quick with language."

"How long have you been in Seraphina?" I asked.

"Months," she said. "I slipped through an Alabaster Arch once the Grand Nexus was repaired. The sky fishers found me on Kdosh and took me to their home." Her eyes lit with delight. "I knew at once I would rather spend my eternity here than in Eden. The mortals have all but ruined a once beautiful wilderness. Now it is the land of concrete, its natural splendor marred."

"You said you have a child?" I asked.

Cora's smile faded. "A daughter, but she lives in the Glimmer. Once I decided to remain here, I returned to the edge of the realm to gather seeds from my homeland so I could recreate it here." She waved an arm toward the moon, and it grew brighter until its glow illuminated a vast space filled with crooked black trees, thorny vines, and large glowing flowers.

I said the only thing that made sense right then. "We're in a flying whale-dragon ship with a forest in its belly, run by angel pirates with an elf pirate as their captain!"

Elyssa blinked a few times. "What do you mean by pirates?"

"They hijack gems from the sea," I said. "I guess it's legit and all, but basically we're now officially sky pirates."

Cora's forehead pinched into a confused V. "We aren't pirating anything."

"Well, you kidnapped us for one thing," I said. "Pirates kidnap people, though I'm totally fine with being kidnapped by sky pirates."

"Anyway," Elyssa said, steering things back on course, "Why did you kidnap us, Cora?"

"The crew believe I am a Seraphim like them," she said. "They treat me like family but I fear their opinion might change should they discover I am not like them."

"You grew this ship out of wood from the Glimmer and they still think you're one of them?" I asked.

"They believe it is another form of Seraphim magic," she said. "A lost art."

"Your secret is safe with us," I assured her. "Just get us to Kdosh."

"We will arrive within the hour," Cora said. "Unfortunately, you will find another problem waiting when you arrive."

"I knew it." I pounded a fist on my leg. "There's a crystoid blocking the skyway."

She tilted her head slightly. "I don't know what a crystoid is, but, no. The pedestal powering the skyway on Kdosh was destroyed. We can provide you with the gem to repair it, but it will take a week."

"A week?" I threw up my hands. "I saw workers rebuild houses in a few hours. Why would it take so long to repair the pedestal?"

"The pedestal takes no time at all," she said, "but linking the gem to aether and charming it to create the skyway takes a very delicate touch and a team of skilled magic weavers."

I thought back to what one of her crew had told me. "The Mzodi have a fleet of sky ships, right?"

"Yes, though they are nothing like the *Evadora*." She pursed her lips. "You wish the Mzodi to provide transport for your army."

"Can you?" I asked, trying not to sound like a beggar but failing.

"I will speak with the others," she said. "Many of them prefer to leave civilization well enough alone."

"Those girls you took from Kaelissa," Elyssa said in a soft tone. "Do you do that because of your daughter?"

A tear trickled down Cora's cheek. "I can provide happy homes for the children forsaken by Kaelissa, though I failed in my own right as a mother."

"Why don't you go back to the Glimmer and get your daughter?" Elyssa asked.

"My travels to Eden unleashed a great evil in the Glimmer." Her face paled. "If I return, my sweet Evadora will die."

"That's your daughter's name?" Elyssa asked.

"Yes." Cora traced a finger along a vine. "The ship and her name are all I have of my home realm."

I sensed another quest on the future radar and did my best not to care. As usual, I couldn't resist. "What's this evil in the Glimmer? Could our army help you conquer it?"

Cora's eyes widened. "No. You would throw away the lives of all who tried to interfere." She raised a hand and the black vines beneath my feet writhed, weaving together into a nearly perfect semblance of Cora, complete with flowing hair and blinking eyes. "Imagine your fight is not with people, but with the land itself. A forest of death, or"—the arm of the vine statue extended and a drop of venomous-looking fluid dripped from a thorn at the tip of the finger—"eternal sleep in twilight."

"This evil could defeat a massive army?" I said. "What if we burned the forest?"

"Absolutely not!" Cora shouted. She gaped at me in horror. "Such a crime would be even more evil than the one who sits on my throne."

Elyssa leaned forward, eyes pensive. "Who sits on your throne?"

"My reflection," Cora murmured. "In every account she is me, but without mercy, without kindness." She blinked as if coming from a trance. "The Glimmer has a perverse effect on my people, granting them immortality, but taking from them every trace of emotion. It was only in Eden I once again discovered how to feel."

I grimaced. "What a living hell. Eternity without feeling?"

She nodded. "Yes. Our oracle told me the balm to our wounds lay in Eden. If I found love, it would lead to our salvation." Her lips trembled. "I found love, but it only led to my exile and the ruin of my realm."

"Evadora's father?" I asked. "Was he your love?"

"Yes." Cora's voice trembled with misery. "It is too painful to speak of."

Elyssa stood. "I'm so sorry." She walked slowly to the grieving woman and put a hand on her shoulder. "Maybe the oracle spoke of another love."

Cora wiped at her red eyes and nodded. "Perhaps. There are many possibilities, but prophecy often lacks specifics."

"Tell me about it," I muttered. "There was a time I felt like everything I did was already decided." I chuckled wryly. "Things turned out okay before going to complete crap again."

"I kept abreast of Overworld events," Cora said. "I wasn't certain your forces would prevail against Daelissa."

"I hate to change the subject," I said, "but can you ask the Mzodi fleet to help us?"

Cora stood. "I will send the request. I apologize for accosting you."

Elyssa smirked. "Not the first time it's happened."

"Probably not the last," I said. "As far as kidnappings go, this one was pretty tame."

We followed Cora through the spooky forest of hers, walking up two levels to reach the top deck. A cool breeze met my face and a dull roar vibrated in my ears. Seraphim sailors, most of them female, ran back and forth in response to the shouted commands of Illaena who stood atop a tall platform near the prow.

"Sky pirates," I whispered excitedly to Elyssa. "I wish I had an eye patch so much right now."

"How about a black eye?" she suggested sweetly.

"I will speak with the others and let you know about gathering the fleet," Cora said. "Until then, please enjoy our hospitality."

I touched a tender spot where a vine had stung me. "Think I've had too much hospitality already."

Elyssa laughed. "Sky pirates, remember?"

I wandered over to the railing and felt my jaw drop when I looked over the edge. A massive vortex whirled over a boiling ocean. Gusts of aether mixed with salty mist blew my hair back, leaving a thin coat of brine on my skin. The air within the whirling maelstrom glittered as if a million fairies had dropped a load of pixie dust inside.

Hot wind blasted my face and the entire ship shuddered, rising and falling as if riding invisible waves of air. I gripped the railing and felt my gorge rise. Not far from me, Joss puked a load of glurk over the side then slid down to embrace the railing as if it were a lover. Another wave sent us soaring then crashing back down.

Illaena gripped a bejeweled pedestal, fingers working furiously while other sailors manned pedestals near the giant wings on the side of the ship, manually adjusting their angles to fight the brutal turbulence. The ship listed hard right, tilting and groaning as if would fly apart.

Elyssa grabbed the railing, eyes worried.

"This is kinda fun," I said, holding out my hands as if I were riding a surfboard while the deck shifted and rolled beneath me.

"All hands brace yourselves!" Illaena shouted in Cyrinthian. "Aether storm ahead!"

"Yeah, maybe you should hold on too." Elyssa reached a hand for me, but I shook my head.

"I'm fine." I held my footing as the ship coasted up a swell and dove down the next. "I totally could have made it through this on the rocket stick."

The ship literally dropped ten feet then lurched up so quickly, I flopped on the deck like a dying fish and cracked my chin hard enough to draw blood. The ship dropped and rose again, slamming me into the deck.

"Gak!" I shouted, desperately trying to reach Elyssa's hand, but only sliding further away as the ship pitched and rolled as if fighting the storm of the century.

A vine shot out and secured me to the railing just as the entire sky beneath us went pitch black. The ship coasted to a halt and for a brief instant, all was completely silent. Thunder rumbled in the distance and the air grew so cold my breath fogged.

Illaena banged the drum three times. "Pitch port, prepare for storm gust!"

The ship rotated ninety degrees, bringing into view a monstrous black cloud billowing straight for us. My stomach tripped over my kidneys in its haste to get the hell out of Dodge. Just as a scream of terror ripped from my throat, the black cloud slammed into us like a brick wall. The ship creaked and groaned as if it were flying apart and lifted higher, higher, and higher still on the black wave.

"Starboard haul!" Illaena cried.

The crew pulled hard on the pedestals and the ship spun just as the wave crested, and suddenly we were flying down a sheer cliff of dark insanity. Lightning crackled, thunder rattled my bones, and it looked as if we were delivering ourselves into the darkest bowels of hell. We were going so fast, my lips flapped in the breeze.

We plunged through the wall of lightning and death and into bright clear daylight, dust sparkling like glitter all around us. Gems of all sizes and shapes whirled through the air, caught in an updraft of aether so pure, it tasted like honey to my magical senses.

Still shaking with fright, I unclenched my fingers from the railing, leaving imprints and claw marks behind. "W-where are we?"

Illaena marched past, a smirk on her face. "We are in a class five vortex." She nodded over the side. "Look."

I rose on weak legs and peered over the side. The ocean lay far below, visible in the calm eye of the vortex. The air pulsated with aether and what looked like pixie dust. "This is where you harvest gems?" I asked.

Illaena nodded. "The deeper one goes, the larger the gems." She motioned to a group of sailors casting shimmering nets into the wall of black clouds only feet away.

A moment later, they withdrew the net now laden with gems of all types and sizes.

Elyssa's mouth practically watered. "That's amazing. What's the largest gem you've seen?"

"Nearly as large as this ship," Illaena said. "But it was too deep and no nets could ever haul it in."

Cora joined us. "I see you weathered your first aether storm."

I wiped sweat off my forehead. "I didn't realize it was so violent."

"Even the Mzodi still lose vessels to the aether storms." She inspected the area where my fingers had dug gouges into the wood. "I sent the request to the Muhala Kajeen, the leader of the Mzodi. She will return an answer shortly."

I gazed at the violent winds of the black vortex. "Guess Flava was right about a rocket stick not being enough."

The ship lurched. Illaena and Cora exchanged surprised looks.

Gripping the railing again, I said, "I thought this was the eye of the storm."

"That was no ordinary turbulence," Cora said. Her eyes widened. "Prepare for an incursion."

Illaena ran to the central pedestal where she beat the drum four times. A horn wailed near the back of the ship and the crew raced into positions.

"What's going on?" I asked.

Elyssa and I peered over the side with Cora. Far below, a giant blue crocodile with webbed wings burst from the ocean. Thrusting in slow motion, the wings carried the beast higher and higher. Gouts of steam burst from its lean reptilian muzzle. Scales glittering in the glow of aether, a dragon slithered like a flying snake directly for the *Evadora*.

"Draxadis!" Cora shouted. "Draxadis!"

Cora pulled us back from the rail as defenders took our place. "It's another incursion from the Dragon realm, Draxadis. In my first two months here, we saw one dragon. In the last three months, we have fought seven."

"Wait—they're coming here from Draxadis?" The roar of the wind and the strange bellow of the dragon nearly drowned out my voice. "How is that possible without an Alabaster Arch?"

"The vortexes sometimes open rifts to Draxadis." Cora watched as the sailors formed a line, crystal bows cocked and ready. "The Mzodi believe the two realms overlap."

I didn't have time to ask another question before a tremendous boom vibrated the hull and the ship lurched sideways. Elyssa and I tumbled across the deck, skidding uncontrollably toward the railing on the opposite side. A vine snaked around my chest and another snared Elyssa before we flipped over the side and into the vortex.

The ship righted, and I climbed back to my feet. The dragon's muzzle slid into view. Gold parietal eyes rose above the railing, regarding us with cold intent. Though the creature wasn't nearly as big as the earth dragons I'd seen, it was massive enough to do some serious damage. The defenders, anchored to the railing by vines, hurled spears of Murk at the beast. The projectiles shattered against the scaly hide, causing no damage.

The dragon bellowed, a ragged guttural noise as if it had a loose flap of skin in its throat. The spear throwers continued their ineffective attacks, shouting and yelling. They might as well have been toy poodles barking at an angry bull for all the good they were doing.

"How in the hell have they survived this long if that's how they fight?" I shouted above the din.

Elyssa gripped my arm and pointed to another group of defenders. "Look, it's a feint."

The dragon gripped the railing with a clawed foot and clambered onto the deck after the spear throwers. It unlocked its lower jaw like a snake and hissed. Steam sprayed at the defenders who channeled shields to protect themselves. The other group ran up behind the dragon. Using their hands like stirrups, two of them launched a third up onto the dragon's long sinuous neck.

The dragon bellowed and spun, but the defender gripped one of the long horns and hung on for dear life. The spear throwers launched another volley. The dragon lowered its head and hissed another jet of steam. The defender on its head used the moment of stability and swung around the horn, a long sword in hand.

With a loud cry, the defender thrust the sword into the eye of the dragon. The beast unleashed a terrible wail and thrashed wildly. Its tail knocked two sailors across the deck, but Cora's vines snagged them before they fell over the side. The spear throwers backed off from the flailing creature. Dark red blood spurted from the eye, covering the deck in a crimson lake.

Elyssa and I retreated from the carnage. With a ragged sigh, the blue dragon went still, steam whistling from its throat like a tea kettle signaling ready.

The defenders clasped arms and raised their hands in victory.

They never even saw the giant red claw slashing over the railing behind them.

Chapter 18

"Dragon!" I shouted, but my warning was lost to the roar and thunder of the vortex.

Bodies tumbled like rag dolls as the huge claw swept them aside. Another scaly foot slammed onto the railing, and then a red dragon clawed its way onto the deck. If the blue dragon had been the size of a horse, this red one matched an elephant pound-for-pound.

A vine jerked Cora away an instant before massive jaws snapped down on her head. The other vines caught airborne defenders, pulling them away from the new threat, but many of them were bloodied and unconscious from the surprise attack. The dragon snaked across the wide open deck toward Cora.

A wall of vines blocked the creature, but it snapped through them with powerful jaws. Two of the uninjured spear throwers shouted and got the beast's attention, but the kill squad was out of commission, two of them lying motionless near the bow.

I took off my shoes and handed them to Elyssa. "Keep an eye on these."

She dropped them on the deck. "You distract, I'll kill, okay?"

"Hey, don't lose my shoes!" I couldn't wear them for what came next.

"We'll get you new ones if the dragon eats them, okay?" Elyssa drew her sai swords. "What's the plan?"

Drawing upon my demonic nature, I unleashed a little taste of hell and manifested. Black claws pushed out my toenails and fingernails, muscles coiled around my legs and arms, swelling me to twice my height and size. Horns spiked through my forehead

145

momentarily blinding me with pain. I slammed the cage door on the demon to keep myself from fully spawning. The more demon I let out, the stronger I'd become, but I'd lose all control and rampage, doing more harm than good.

Using my claws to dig into the wood and keep my balance, I raced across the deck toward the dragon. The creature lunged at Cora, but her vines kept her just out of reach. The dragon abruptly changed course and fired a stream of red liquid from its throat at the vine. The acrid smell of molten lava stung my nose.

Cora cried out as the hot liquid burned her vine to ash. She thudded to the deck. The dragon raked razor claws at her face.

I streaked across the open deck and threw myself against the monster's foot. The impact knocked the attack off course and twisted the dragon's leg awkwardly. It roared and lost its footing, but the impact also knocked me into a flat spin across the deck. I dug my claws into the deck and screeched to a stop.

"Come get me, you, uh, big stupid dragon!" I shouted, my voice deep and guttural from the demonic shift.

The dragon twisted its sinuous body and rose to all fours, webbed wings spreading wide. Golden eyes glared at me, and a forked tongue snaked between gleaming razor teeth. Curving horns rose behind the dragon's eyes, much like the ones on its dead sibling lying on the deck a few yards away.

Without the crew, the ship drifted to the side. A wing caught in the dark vortex, hurling the ship sideways, spinning out of control. We plunged through the wall of darkness, riding up and down violent wave after wave of air. I dug in my claws, and even the dragon held on for dear life. Another hard gust jettisoned us out of the vortex and into a foggy wonderland.

The dragon growled and looked at me with foul intent. I saw Elyssa using the dead dragon as cover to sneak up behind the new threat. She didn't have a chance without my help.

The dragon bellowed and streaked toward me. I roared and charged.

What in the hell am I doing?

This was like a mouse playing chicken with a steamroller.

146

Sulfur stung my nose as the beast opened its mouth. I dodged left and a stream of lava narrowly missed my face. Using my football skills, I juked right and drove my shoulder into the monster's neck. It was like crashing into a wall made of diamonds. The dragon scales had no give in them whatsoever. I bounced backward and landed hard on my ass. The lava breather arched its long neck and reared back. Quick as lightning, it struck.

I rolled out of the way an instant before razor teeth snapped into me. "You really don't want to eat me!" I shouted, and rolled the opposite way to avoid disemboweling by dragon claws. "I didn't take a bath today!"

The dragon didn't seem to care how I bad I smelled or tasted and chomped down. I twisted away, hot dragon breath scorching my backside. The dragon planted its feet to either side, pinning me between them. I wriggled, but even my demon strength couldn't overcome the power of those legs. Crocodilian jaws lashed toward me.

A beam of brilliance smacked the dragon's snout. The energy refracted from the scales, but it was enough to blind the monster and make it rear back in confusion. Now free, I rolled out of the way and scrambled to my feet. Lanaeia continued channeling a beam of white energy until I dove out of striking distance. Flava and the legionnaires joined her attacks, lancing ultraviolet rays at the dragon.

They quickly realized the dragon scales repelled the damage.

I'd faced monsters like this before—summoned demons or shape-shifting Flarks with natural magic immunity—but that magical protection hadn't protected them from the effects of magic on the environment. I'd used fireballs to spill molten rock on a Flark, but I couldn't set this ship on fire to indirectly attack the dragon.

The only other option was brute force. In my semi-manifested state, I was much stronger than normal, and I'd successfully battled monsters much larger than me. But this dragon was something else, sinuous, flexible, and incredible strong. The dragon scales posed a major problem. Elyssa peered out from her hiding spot behind the blue dragon and pointed at the angry monster bearing down on us.

John Corwin

She needed a distraction and I had to give her one without getting eaten.

"Keep attacking," I told the others. "We have to let Elyssa get into position."

"But it's impervious to magic!" Lanaeia said.

"Trust me, just keep it busy!" I unleashed a bolt of destruction and hit the dragon in the snout, which really seemed to piss it off.

"Rawr!" it roared, and slithered toward us, lava spraying.

I channeled a shield right in front of the molten rock, redirecting it back at the dragon. Scorching liquid splashed in the reptile's face, splashing off the scales like rainwater against a waxed car.

"It's like hitting diamond fiber!" I complained. I tried a different tact. Elyssa used to kick my ass regularly when we sparred, but once she taught me some basic mechanics, I'd improved by leaps and bounds. One of the first things she'd shown me was that it doesn't matter how big something is if you can knock it off its feet.

The dragon ran low to the ground like a lizard, but if I could trip it up, that might give Elyssa the split second she needed. Direct magical attacks hadn't worked, and I sure as hell couldn't ram the thing, but what if I tried something that wasn't a direct attack?

I didn't have time to reason through the alternatives. This was going to be a quick and nasty field test. If it failed, I'd be within nom-nom range of those deadly chompers. Elyssa leapt from cover and raced behind the dragon, preparing to leap onto its back. I had no time to lose.

Watching laser-wielding pirates fighting an army of ninjas had always been a dream of mine. My experience as a newly minted sky pirate versus a dragon was terrifying, but I wasn't about to give the scourge of the seven seas a bad name by losing, especially in front of my girlfriend.

Summoning my demonic rage to bolster my courage, I charged the oncoming dragon and prayed my little trick worked. "Beware the dread pirate Roberts!" I shouted at the top of my lungs.

The dragon licked its lips in anticipation of a demon burger—hold the mayo—and opened its mouth to gobble me whole. At the last minute, I veered right and slid through the pool of dragon blood. As I

148

passed the dragon's left leg, I looped a web of Murk around it and jerked hard. The aether rope jerked taut. The dragon kept moving forward, but its leg didn't. Thrown off balance, it smacked face-first into the deck.

Elyssa leapt for the neck. I scrambled to my feet and shot aether tethers to the dragon's horns and yanked hard. Still stunned, the creature didn't resist. Its neck looped backward, head upside down. Elyssa flipped in mid-air and buried both swords in the dragon's eye on the landing.

The dragon bellowed and shook free of my tethers. The swords clattered to the ground as Elyssa vaulted free.

"The swords aren't long enough!" Cora shouted.

The dragon wasn't dead, but it was done. It raced across the bloody deck and leapt over the side, angry roars fading into the distance. Someone else shouted over the din of the vortex as Illaena and the deck crew reassembled. A rock face appeared through the gloom directly ahead. Sailors jerked on levers and the ship tilted hard left.

Vines coiled around everyone, keeping them from sliding over the side, but the ship wasn't turning fast enough.

"Brace for impact!" Illaena shouted.

Another sailor blew the horn.

Wood crunched. The ship shuddered violently as the starboard side grazed the cliff. I grabbed Elyssa with one hand and held onto the vine with the other. The aetherial wings on the right flickered off. The ship hung suspended in the air for a brief pause and then the bottom fell out.

My stomach journeyed to the top of my throat but it didn't stop a scream from escaping first. Wind roared past my ears. The ship groaned and tilted right. I saw Cora, teeth clenched in concentration, directing a vine to carry Illaena and other sailors to the right side of the ship.

The sky vanished in a cloud of whirling aether as we dropped into another vortex. The ship spun and twisted, rolling upside down to face the boiling ocean far below. Elyssa's grip on my arm tightened painfully. She struggled closer and kissed me.

"I will always love you!" she shouted.

"I love you!" I yelled back. "But we're not going to die. We're going to jump!"

"You can't fly in the vortex!"

I channeled my wings and spread them. "Maybe not, but I'm going to try."

The ship rolled again. The vines holding down the dead blue dragon snapped and the corpse slid across the blood and smacked into us. My head rammed the deck and stars flashed in my eyes. When I blinked them open, I saw the dragon corpse crash through railing and vanish over the side.

Elyssa held a vine with one hand, and wrapped her other arm around my waist. The vines holding me down had snapped and Cora was too preoccupied holding Illaena over the starboard side to help me. The blow to my head had disrupted my wings too. I tried to stand, but the ship lurched and shuddered. We only had seconds before we hit water. I grabbed Elyssa, determined to leap off the craft and channel my wings in midair.

A gust of wind blew sparkling dust across the deck. Small gems pelted my face and grit filled my teeth and eyes. We drifted toward the wall of wind at the edge of the vortex. The gems inside would grind us to dust. I couldn't jump off that side of the ship. Somehow, we had to make it to the other side.

The ship rattled and jerked so hard, my chin slammed into the deck and Elyssa lost her footing. The deck leveled out and my stomach dropped like a lead weight. The vortex roared around us, but we had stopped falling. Cora's vines pulled Illaena and several others back onto the deck and I saw the aetherial wings flapping on the starboard side once again.

The sailors cheered, immediately setting to work on the levers. The ship began to rise, wood creaking and groaning as it fought the wind shear. The prow grazed the edge of the vortex and Cora cried out, as if it was her own flesh in the aether storm. When the vessel backed away, the dragon nose was little more than a nub, ground away by the gem dust.

Another group of sailors deployed glowing nets into the roaring winds even as the ship fought the downward pull of the gargantuan tornado engulfing us. The nets hauled piles of gems, sparkling reds, glowing blues, sullen greens, and some that measured six feet across. With one loud groan, the ship seemed to jerk free of gravity and raced upward.

Moments later we hovered over the ocean of whirlwinds and boiling water. Just off the starboard bow hovered the rocky skylet that had nearly killed us. The floating island was small and barren of inhabitants, but with one predominant feature in its center: an Alabaster Arch.

Cora slumped against the railing, eyes dark with fatigue. "Welcome to Kdosh."

Chapter 19

We were finally here.

Illaena landed the ship on the northern side of the skylet and dropped the ramp. Sailors immediately began repairs. The two large gems on the starboard side of the ship used to channel the giant wings had been hastily replaced during our freefall. The collision with the skylet had damaged the originals and contributed to our near-death experience.

The skylet only took a couple of minutes to traverse and I soon reached the Alabaster Arch. "If there's no crystoid, jamming the aether, why isn't the Alabaster Arch working?"

Elyssa shrugged.

The tall stone arch, obsidian laced with alabaster with a wide silver circle around it, sat silent. I held a hand over the Chalon in the control socket. It popped out and hovered just beneath my hand, but willing a portal to open yielded no results. I knelt and willed the silver circle embedded in the ground to close. Aether flooded inside, running static fingers through my hair.

I tried to open a portal, but though the air flickered and the presence of an opening tickled me senses, nothing happened. "Magic definitely isn't the problem. It's something else."

Elyssa's eyes flashed. "I think I know what's blocking it."

I reached a similar conclusion. "A portal-blocking statue."

"That's what it has to be," she said.

"Wonderful." I smacked the back of my hand into the other palm. "Serena must have kept some from Thunder Rock."

"Problem is, I don't see one lying around." Elyssa got down on her hands and knees and looked under a bush. "It's going to take forever to search this entire skylet."

Cora arrived with a crew of sailors to start repairs on the pedestal and gave us a curious look. "Why are you crawling on the ground?"

"The arch isn't working." I stood and brushed dirt off my hands. "There are these small statues that block portals from working and we think one is hidden here somewhere."

"Perhaps I can help." Cora knelt and placed a hand on the ground. The red grass writhed toward her. Even the shrubs and trees seemed to lean her way.

"Creepy," I murmured.

Elyssa was entranced. "Amazing."

"Ah," Cora said a moment later. She stood and walked thirty yards from the arch and flipped a flat stone out of the way. Worms and bugs scattered in the sudden light. Plant roots pulled the soil aside, opening a hole a few feet deep. At the bottom lay a small stone statue shaped like an angel, wings folded, head bowed. A slender root snared the statue and dropped it in Cora's outstretched hand.

"You'd be a real hit on a gardening show," I said.

Cora grimaced. "Television bores me, as do most modern amenities in the mortal world." The roots filled in the hole as she stood and turned to us. "I much prefer the outdoors."

I took the statue and looked at the bottom. Symbols inscribed on the underside were actually musical notes needed to disable the statue. "You don't, by chance, still have those deactivation tones on your phone do you, babe?"

Elyssa scrolled through her phone and shook her head. "I must have deleted them after the war."

My phone still had the tones on it, but of course I'd left it back in Tarissa. "The statues have a three-hundred yard working radius if I recall correctly, right?"

"Sounds right," Elyssa said.

"Cool." I cocked my arm and flung the statue over the edge of the skylet.

"Simple but effective," Elyssa commented dryly. "You're a true genius."

I turned to the Alabaster Arch, too nervous to come up with a witty reply. "Please work." I knelt and sealed the silver circle again then anxiously stepped up to the Chalon.

"It'll work," Elyssa said. "It has to."

I held a hand over the small orb. After a brief hesitation, it popped from the socket and hovered, the intricate pattern of lines along the surface glowing happily. This time I sensed the connection the arch held to its sister in the other realm and sent a simple command.

Open.

The space between the arch columns crackled, alternating between hues of white, ultraviolet, and gray. The scent of ozone tickled my nose. With a loud boom, the air split vertically and flashed open horizontally to reveal a cave lined with small black arches.

Two Templars in black Nightingale armor stood on the other side. The tall one with arms as thick as my legs looked at the other. "Go tell the commander they're back."

The other Templar saluted and raced away. Michael Borathen, Elyssa's older brother, allowed a smile for his sister and stepped through to give her a hug. "You had us worried, Ninjette."

"Believe me, we were all worried," Elyssa said with a laugh as Michael set her back on the ground. "We need an immediate debrief."

"Already in the works." He stepped back and nodded at the other Seraphim, though his gaze lingered on Cora for a moment. "Looks like you've gathered quite a crowd, Justin."

"It's my Axe Body Spray," I said. "Works like a charm every time."

"I will await word from the fleet," Cora said. She clasped my hand. "We will also begin work on the skyway pedestal in case the Mzodi refuse my request."

I squeezed her hands. "Thanks, Cora."

Michael looked around at the red grass, the blue trees, and the tufts of aether drifting up over the edges of the skylet. Usually stoic and reserved, even he seemed amazed by this little taste of Seraphina.

His eyes caught on the *Evadora*. "I don't usually care for debriefings, but I think this one will be interesting."

Flava stepped into the circle around the arch. "Hello, Michael."

He nodded at her. "Welcome back, legionnaire." He stepped back as a platoon of Templars marched through the arch to guard Kdosh.

The rest of her group joined us and Michael motioned them through. I took Elyssa's hand and two steps later, we were back in Eden. I was so happy, I could have burst. I settled for gaily skipping down a long aisle of small black arches, the baby brothers of the monstrous one in the main cavern outside this control room.

We reached the wide center aisle and walked to a niche filled with black arches about ten feet tall and wide. Unlike the other arches, these omniarches could take someone just about anywhere they could clearly envision. An open portal glowed inside one of them. I recognized the underground hangar at Big Creek Ranch, also known as the Templar headquarters for most of North America.

We hurried through and found Elyssa's parents, Thomas and Leia Borathen, waiting on the other side. She ran over and hugged them.

"We were so worried," Leia said.

Elyssa took a deep breath and backed away, her smile fading to seriousness. "Cephus has more capabilities than we realized."

Commander Thomas Borathen gripped my hand and shook it. "Good to have you back."

"Great to be back," I said, and bent over to give Leia a hug.

She kissed my cheek. "We were going to send through reinforcements, but the crystoid holding open the portal went dead and we had no way to send help."

"It's good you didn't," Elyssa said. "Any reinforcements would have faced the same problems we did."

"Speaking of," I said, "let's get this debrief out of the way. I'm dying for a slice of pizza."

Flava and her gang had waited quietly behind us until now.

"Commander, I have grave news about Seraphina," she said. "The Tarissan Legion is lost."

Thomas's eyes flashed. "It sounds like we may have to adjust our plans."

Painted yellow squares demarking portal arrival zones began to flash with activity as portals from all around the world opened.

"I contacted our allies," Thomas said. "Everyone should be here shortly."

Shelton burst through the first portal, Bella right behind him. Wearing his standard leather duster with a wide-brimmed hat and cowboy boots, he looked the same as ever—not at all like a man who was about to tie the knot. He saw me and jogged over. "Holy farting fairies, man, I thought you'd finally gotten yourself killed!" He wrapped me in a one-armed hug and dragged Elyssa in as well.

"This is the second time you've left us behind while you go on a mission to Seraphina," Bella said. The petite Colombian pushed glossy black hair from her face and regarded us severely. "Perhaps I should lodge a formal complaint with the commander."

I chuckled and gave her a hug and kiss on the cheek. "Next time we'll let you and Shelton go by yourselves."

"Yeah, if you want the world to end," Shelton said. "I think I'll just stick to armchair quarterbacking."

I sighed. "I'm sorry we missed your rehearsal dinner and your bachelor party."

Shelton pshawed. "You didn't miss squat. Do you really think I'd do any of that stuff without my best man around?"

"He's been insufferable," Bella said. "Pacing all over the mansion and talking about how inconsiderate it would be if you died before attending our wedding."

Elyssa snorted. "We're not that rude."

Shelton grinned. "Thank goodness. Otherwise Cinder was going to be the best man."

"Let's grab some pizza after this," I said. "I'm sick of eating glurk."

"What the hell is glurk?" Shelton grimaced. "I thought they ate ambrosia in Seraphina."

"I wish." I spotted my parents and little sister emerging from a portal and waved to them.

"Justin!" Ivy cheered and raced over in a blur. The impact of her hug nearly knocked me off my feet. "You're alive!"

I ruffled her platinum blond hair and leaned down to kiss her cheek, though I didn't have to lean down as much as I used to. She was definitely getting taller. "Of course I am. The mission took a little longer than expected."

"That's one way of putting it," my father, David Slade, said with a grin. He squeezed my shoulder. "Your mom was getting worried."

My mother, Alysea, wiped tears from her eyes. "Worried is an understatement." She embraced me and seemed to melt with relief. "We've been through so much conflict, you'd think I'd be used to it by now."

"It's something you never grow accustomed to," Bella said.

I spotted Colin McCloud, the Lycan Nation Alpha stepping out of a portal, and Kassallandra Assad, the beautiful Maedras of the Daemos Nation appear in another one, her blazing red hair braided into something resembling a crown. Thomas walked over to greet the newcomers and everyone began to migrate toward the levitator shaft which would take us down to the conference rooms.

A new portal opened. Through it stepped a tall man with thick black hair and an angular set to his jaw. Neatly groomed eyebrows overshadowed his dark eyes. A black Arcane robe with white ruffles gave him the appearance of someone in charge—which he was. Chancellor Victus Edison of Science Academy, and Arcanus Primus of the Arcane Council saw me and offered a well-practiced smile.

"Justin, I'm relieved to see you back safe and sound." He stepped aside to make room for a tall woman, her black curtain of hair a sharp contrast to skin so pale it looked unhealthy.

Victus's wife, Delectra, still looked every bit as haughty as the last time I'd seen her, but her greeting this time was warmer. "Mr. Slade." She managed a smile and walked with her husband over to me.

Victus pumped my hand and kissed Elyssa's. "We were getting worried when you missed the second deadline."

The scent of brimstone teased my nose—a sign Victus was still playing with demons. I decided not to comment. "Things got pretty hairy," I said. "We'll cover it in the debrief."

"Fair enough," he replied. "It's good to have Eden's hero back with us again."

Delectra absentmindedly pushed her hair behind an ear to reveal a nasty bruise visible even through the makeup on her cheek. "We are pleased you made it back safely."

"What happened to your cheek?" Elyssa asked.

The other woman's dark eyes flared and she quickly rearranged her hair to shield the bruise.

"One of my experiments did not go well," Victus said with an apologetic smile.

I couldn't hold my tongue any longer. "Was it a demon?"

Delectra swallowed hard and answered in a quiet tone. "Yes."

"Ever since the demon uprising, I've been testing new ways to contain those spirits who still manage to slip through," Victus said. "I've met with mixed success."

Elyssa narrowed her eyes at the man, but said nothing.

I saw Shelton and Bella waiting impatiently near the levitator. The rest of the crowd had already gone below. "We should go to the briefing."

"Of course," Victus said. "I'm eager to hear what happened."

Two more portals opened before I had a chance to leave and more familiar faces emerged. Christian Salazar, commander of the South American Templars stepped from one, and Commander Taylor of Australia emerged from another.

Christian offered me and Elyssa a standard Templar salute, hand across the chest. "Welcome home, Commander Slade, Lieutenant Borathen."

I wasn't big on formalities, but Christian wouldn't appreciate a big hug and wet kiss on the cheek, so I obliged him. "Thank you, Commander." I turned to Taylor. "Sorry I didn't get to say hello when I was down at the Three Sisters."

She smiled and waved it off. "I know you needed to get back to HQ quickly." Taylor gave me and Elyssa a warm handshake. "I'm happy you made it back safely."

I half-expected another portal to open and delay us, but it appeared everyone had arrived. We crowded onto the levitator with

Shelton, Bella, and the others and rode it down several levels to the conference rooms.

Shelton chuckled. "Every time we have a war, it's like a family reunion around here."

Nightliss's smiling face journeyed through my mind. I nodded somberly. "Yeah."

Elyssa squeezed my hand, but didn't say anything.

We stepped into a corridor hewn from rock and stepped inside the sprawling war room.

It was time to plan another war.

Chapter 20

"Hey, sis!" Phoebe Borathen, Elyssa's sister, met her inside the door with a hug. Though the two looked almost like twins, they'd been born centuries apart. Both Templars and dhampyrs, they were two of the most skilled fighters I'd ever encountered, not including the tall enigmatic man standing in the corner across the room—Kanaan, the Magitsu master.

He met my gaze and offered a brief nod. Kanaan stood almost as tall as me and looked like his heritage had a few percentage points in Asian, and maybe a little more in Caucasian, but I knew from watching him he was a hundred percent badass. Where I dealt in raw power, this guy served death with finesse. He could do more with his lower-powered Arcane magic than I could pull off with ten times the wattage. Learning Magitsu, the magical martial arts, was something I had on my to-do list, but the forces of darkness had to give me a vacation first.

Captain Takei of the Blue Cloaks gave me a broad smile. "We were rather worried about you and Lieutenant Borathen, Commander Slade."

"Cephus isn't going to be as easy as we hoped," I told him.

He didn't look surprised. "Underestimating an opponent is a sure way to make anyone formidable."

"Sounds like something Kanaan would say," I said with a grin.

He chuckled. "I probably got it from him."

"Justin Slade, my lad!" Colin McCloud barged into the conversation, slapping me and Takei heartily on our backs. He took

Elyssa's hands and kissed them. "Lieutenant Borathen, you're still as fair a lass as ever."

She blushed and smiled. "Thank you, Colin."

The lycan alpha's smile faded after he released her hands. "I'm ready to pay back that son of a bitch, Cephus." He ran a hand down a mutton chop. "I didn't fight a war against Seraphim to let another one blast our realm to pieces."

I put a hand on his thick shoulder. "You'll have a chance soon, Colin."

"Aye, I hope so," he said. "The packs are howling for vengeance."

"Justice is best served with a clear mind," Takei said calmly.

McCloud barked a laugh. "Our minds are quite clear, thank you."

I cleared my throat before the pair got off on a tangent. "It's time to get started."

Before taking my place at the head of the room, I walked to Kassallandra and offered her a slight nod. She curtseyed deeply, eyes on the floor without losing a hint of her royal bearing.

"Anae Kassallandra Assad, your presence honors me," I said, doing my best not to laugh at the absurd social niceties required by Daemos.

Her eyes rose to meet mine, an eyebrow quirked. "The honor is mine," she replied. "This is truly a new day when Justin Slade greets me formally."

"I try to mix it up," I said. "Thank you for coming."

"The war is not as completed as we hoped," she replied. "Cephus poses a serious threat to our realm should he muster another attack."

"Agreed." I headed toward the head of the room where Elyssa had already gone to speak with her father. "We ready?"

"Ready as ever," she said, fiddling with her phone. "Just give me a minute to prepare the maps."

I decided to get the ball rolling and clapped my hands to cut through the din of conversation. "Our mission to destroy the crystoid didn't go as planned."

"You're darn tootin'," Shelton said around a mouthful of donut. "We were about to call in the cavalry."

161

"It's a good thing you didn't," I said. "Cephus has been a very busy beaver." I displayed an image of the dome taken as Elyssa and I had flown past it during mission insertion, and pointed to the shadows of the arch inside. "We suspect this purple arch is how Cephus was able to launch the crystoids."

"It looks purple," Shelton said.

"Probably red," McCloud said. "The Murk just makes it look purple from the outside."

"Whatever color it is, it poses a significant threat," Elyssa said. "During our escape from Tarissa, we were cornered by Cephus and his forces. He asked us to join him because within a few days, he plans to open a portal to the Void."

Shelton's mouth fell open. "Holy Moly. He can't be serious."

"What madman would release the Beast from its prison?" Captain Takei said.

I held up my hands to silence the shocked murmurs. "Does anyone know what the Beast is?"

The looks around the room told me no.

Victus was the only one who didn't look overly concerned, his gaze distant as if scientific curiosity were more interesting than the grave danger of the Void.

"There are few legends about the Beast," Mom said. "Jeremiah said he'd once seen the creature, and it frightened him so much he refused to travel by portal for months."

Shelton held his hat over his chest, eyes wide. "What did it look like?"

Mom shook her head. "He didn't say."

A chorus of groans went around the room.

"That was a letdown," Shelton grumbled.

"Cephus's arch isn't the only concern," Elyssa said. "He's had enough time to construct more crystoids or another secret weapon."

I clapped my hands once to silence the room. "Bottom line—we don't have time to play around."

"We need to be on the attack in less than four days," Elyssa said. "Sooner if possible."

"We came ready to go to war," McCloud said. "Just lead the way."

I continued the story of our escape from Tarissa and our journey to Ooskai. "In this small village we met someone I thought was long dead." I paused to let some tension build. "Kaelissa, the mother of Nightliss and Daelissa."

"She still lives?" Victus asked in a shocked voice.

Murmurs filled the room.

"Alive and kicking and messed up in the head," I confirmed. "She's pumping out kids to fix the Seraphim immortality problem." I caught an embarrassed look from Joss who probably prayed I didn't mention his contribution to the cause.

"An interesting wrinkle," Takei said. "She won't be a problem, will she?"

"I don't think so." I displayed images of the village and people Elyssa had taken during our visit and stopped it on Kaelissa. The murmurs rose to gasps.

"Bloody hell, she looks just like her daughters," Colin said, the hair on his neck rising like hackles. "Let's hope she doesn't have the same aspirations as the crazy one."

Shelton whistled. "Spitting image. I think she looks more like Daelissa."

"She is troubled, but harmless," Flava said. "I do not expect her to help or hinder."

"Agreed," Elyssa said. "My assessment is that she prefers to stay out of harm's way."

I still felt a wild mix of emotions looking at the sera who so reminded me of Nightliss. I almost hoped I never saw her again. I flicked the image away and projected the holographic map of Kdosh. "Thanks to the Mzodi, the sky fishers, we were able to secure passage to Kdosh on a flying whale-dragon ship with a forest inside it."

The murmurs died away to confused silence.

"What's a whale dragon?" Shelton asked.

I flicked to a picture of the *Evadora* and described the ship and crew. "I asked Captain Cora, to request help from the sky fisher fleet. Otherwise, it'll take several days to finish repairing the skyway."

"Holy prancing pirates," Shelton said. "That's the coolest thing since ninjas with laser swords." His eyes lit up. "Do they have sky ship battles?"

Thomas asked a more practical question. "What's the capacity of these ships?"

"The whale ship could probably hold two hundred people." I rotated the image so everyone could see how humans scaled to the large vessel. "I don't know how large the other ships are."

"Who's the lass with orange hair?" McCloud pointed to Cora in the three-dimensional image.

I wasn't sure how to answer. She'd requested I keep her true identity secret from the crew, but what she'd told me seemed too important to keep from the others. That, and my nerdy side was super-excited about what I'd discovered. I felt like a giddy school girl with fresh gossip to dish. I repressed a nerd-tastic giggle and kept my face serious, then baited the hook. "What I'm about to tell you must remain classified."

Shelton rubbed his hands together. "I knew you were holding back."

Thomas raised an eyebrow. "What's the reason?"

"Cora doesn't want her crew to know certain things about her," I explained. "Not that it's anything bad."

Thomas looked around the room. "Whatever is spoken in this room is already privileged information for security purposes, but I recommend we adopt a classified rating for whatever you're about to tell us."

"Recommendation seconded," Victus said.

"Vote by a show of hands," Thomas said, raising his.

Everyone but Shelton raised their hands. He hesitantly did so after Bella nudged him with her elbow.

"The motion passes," Thomas said. "Information regarding Captain Cora is classified. Anyone caught disseminating such intelligence will be banned from future meetings unless and until we hold a vote to declassify."

Shelton frowned, but a warning look from Bella kept his mouth shut.

"Proceed, Mr. Slade," Thomas said.

I dropped the little bomb first. "Cora is not Seraphim." *Bam.*

The statement drew a few raised eyebrows but fell well short of the response to Kaelissa's picture.

I let the suspense marinate a few seconds before dropping the next bomb. "She's also not from Eden." *Boom.*

Shelton didn't let this dramatic pause linger. "You going for an acting award or something? Spit it out already."

"Cora is probably older than all of our combined ages." *Kerblam!* I didn't know if that was true, especially since Kassallandra and my father existed a long time before they adopted corporeal bodies, and my mother had been around a few thousand years as well. Still, it was definitely worth the uproar that followed.

"How is that possible?" McCloud said.

Shelton had turned to my father and was probably interrogating him about his age so he could calculate a number. Even Kanaan looked a bit unsettled.

My mother gave me a troubled look that didn't have to do with age. It made me think she had some idea where I was going with this. It also reminded me of Kaelissa's claim—that Fjoeruss might be my bunch-of-greats grandfather.

I dropped the final thermonuclear factoid on the crowd. "Cora is from a realm called the Glimmer, a place that anchors all the realms together. In fact, the pocket dimensions are actually the points where our realms touch." *KABOOM!*

The room erupted into excited conversation.

Victus raised a hand. "I motion that we declassify any information regarding the Glimmer where it does not pertain to compromising Cora's identity."

"I don't have a problem with it so long as we don't blow the whistle on her," I said. "Motion seconded."

Thomas called for a vote and the motion passed. Everyone in the room suddenly had access to the juiciest gossip known to man and Shelton had the look of a man who planned to milk it as much as I had.

"Let's simmer down, folks." I raised my hand and lowered it. Once it was quiet again, I continued, explaining how Cora controlled nature and what she'd told me about the Lyrolai, the Apocryphan, the Sirens, and so forth. I didn't mention her daughter, Evadora, or her personal issues since I didn't think they contributed to the conversation. I finished up with some fun facts about the Glimmer. "After the Sirens destroyed the realm, they granted the survivors immortality, but at the cost of all emotion. Apparently, the Glimmer folk can regain emotion if they come to Eden, but they also risk losing their immortality."

"Cora lived here for centuries," Victus said. "Does she retain immortality by visiting the Glimmer?"

"I don't know," I said. "I suspect there's something about the realm that makes mortal beings immortal."

"How interesting," he said.

With the big revelations out of the way, I flicked back to the map of Seraphina. "And now back to our regularly scheduled program." I flourished my hands toward Elyssa. "What's the battle plan?"

Without missing a beat, she stepped into the spotlight and switched to a map of Tarissa. Elyssa drew arrows from the skyway terminus. "If the sky fishers don't give us passage, we'll come via the skyway." She dotted the area with icons of blue flying carpets. "The Blue Cloak air forces will sweep forward with our broom attack squadrons to ward off aerial assaults from the fliers."

"You said these fliers are brainwashed citizens?" Takei asked. "Are we using lethal force?"

"I think we have to," Thomas said. "Their conditions might be reversible, but we can't risk losing our own people." He turned to Flava. "What do you think?"

Flava's eyes clouded with sadness. "We would be killing mothers, fathers, and children—citizens my legionnaires are sworn to protect even at the cost of their lives." She looked around the room. "If you saw your own brethren in such a condition, would you kill them, or grant them mercy?"

Thomas turned to Phoebe. "I need casualty projections if we attempt nonlethal force on the mutants."

"I don't have enough data," Phoebe said. "Justin told us that Cephus is creating more of them every day. If we attempt nonlethal takedowns on a thousand, then we're going to be massacred."

"I need more options," Thomas said, looking around the room. "We have lancers, but their range is too short to be effective against flying targets."

"What about magical interdictors?" Victus said. "Without magic, they can't fly."

"They have the aether packs, remember?" Shelton said. "Cutting off magic won't do squat."

"Interdictors don't deplete magic like crystoids." Victus said in a contemptuous voice. "They corrupt it into malaether. This means that even the aether packs would be corrupted."

"Our people would require a token to filter the malaether," Thomas said. "We don't have nearly enough of those to go around."

Shelton glared at Victus a moment then raised his hand. "I have some ideas, but I'll need Adam Nosti's help."

"If you can implement them quickly, let us know," Thomas said. He turned to Flava. "If we can't come up with suitable nonlethal methods, we'll have to use full force."

"I appreciate your efforts, Commander," Flava said coldly, "but I cannot condone the wholesale slaughter of Tarissan citizens, no matter their state of mind."

"I'm not asking you to condone it," Thomas said, "but you also need to understand that Cephus poses an immediate threat. If he opens a portal to the Void or launches another salvo of crystoids, he'll kill thousands more. I will not sit idly by and allow that just because he's using civilians as shields."

Shelton grunted. "Talk about your moral dilemmas."

"The loss of civilian life would be regrettable," Takei said. "But we must act swiftly and decisively before Cephus launches another offensive."

"Approaching from the skyway means we'll be facing the brunt of Cephus's defenses," Elyssa said. "If the Mzodi help, we can flank Cephus's defenses and assault his fortress before his forces react." She zoomed in on the giant purple pimple in the city center. "The shield is powered by aether wells—the equivalent of Arcane aether generators—and can probably withstand a barrage of crucibles."

"That's where we come in," I said. "I once broke out of the fortress using Stasis, but it took everything I had to make a hole big enough for me to fit through. I'll need all the Seraphim we can muster to link and pound the fortress with one huge blast of Stasis. That should create a gap for our ground troops to exploit."

"Once the ground troops are in, their priority targets will be the aether wells around the perimeter." Elyssa circled the locations. "At least half of them need to be down for the shield to fall."

"There is a flaw in that plan," Flava said.

Elyssa turned to her. "Which is?"

"There are backup aether wells belowground." She walked to the front of the room and rotated the angle of the holographic image to ground level. Barely visible through the Murk barrier, the aether wells resembled flat circular pods bulging a foot out of the ground. Flava drew circles staggered between the aboveground wells. "In order to lower the barrier, the wells above and below must be destroyed."

"How do we reach the underground targets?" Thomas asked.

Flava pointed to the building door. "The only access to the underground is through the Ministry of Research."

"Are there any sewer tunnels in the city?" Thomas asked.

Flava's forehead wrinkled. "Sewers?"

"They don't use plumbing," I explained.

"Huh?" Shelton said incredulously. "Where do you put all your sh—"

Bella elbowed him. "Harry!"

"There are aether conduits," Flava said, "but they are barely large enough for a person to crawl through."

"It's an option," Thomas said. "Are they dangerous to use?"

She shook her head. "No, they merely contain concentrated aether for the buildings to utilize."

"What if we cast an interdiction field over the fortress?" Shelton said. "If we corrupt the aether, the wells will fail."

"The interdiction field can't breach the Murk barrier," Flava said. "The device would corrupt the aether outside the dome, but not inside. Even so, aether wells can convert malaether back into aether."

"How in the world do they do that?" Shelton said.

"They use purifying gems," Flava explained.

"That's one tough zit to pop," Shelton grumbled. "Once the Stasis breaks a hole in the shield, how long do we have before it closes back up?"

"A few seconds at most," Flava said. "Any of our troops inside would be trapped."

Elyssa shook her head and stared at frozen image. It was a look I knew all too well. She was stumped.

"Welp." Shelton clapped his hands once. "We're screwed."

I couldn't have said it better myself.

Chapter 21

The room fell silent, mental gears churning as everyone looked for a weakness in Cephus's defense.

"An elemental could tunnel beneath the fortress," Kassallandra said. "We could destroy the generators below while other forces attack those above."

"The barrier extends underground," Flava said. She drew an egg-shaped oval around the holographic image.

"Damn, I was gonna suggest trolls," Shelton said. "They can dig through anything."

"Perhaps we could cut off their food supply," Thomas said. "I don't like the idea of a siege, but it might be our best alternative."

"The Ministry has greenhouses where they grow food." Flava flipped to an overhead view of the complex and circled a pyramid-shaped building. "We also believe they stockpiled for years in preparation for Cephus's plan to overthrow the government."

"I'm getting real tired of hearing what we can't do," Shelton said. "What *can* we do that'll be super-effective?"

"There's an old trick we used back in the first war," my father said, a sly grin tugging at his lips. "When the Brightlings used dome shields to protect their troops, we'd let loose a few rats inside."

His comment raised eyebrows around the room, except for Mom's. The amused look on her face told me she knew what he was talking about.

"Are you suggesting we blow a hole in the shield and infest the Ministry with rats?" McCloud said.

"Something bigger," Dad said. "Demons."

"It was a clever ploy," Kassallandra said. "Unfortunately, once the enemy caught on, they were able to counter it."

"The Ministry is also a lot bigger than the shields we dealt with," Mom said. "But with enough Daemos, it could work."

"Please clarify," Thomas said.

"Demonic infestation," Dad said. "We can summon crawlers, scorps, and all sorts of nasty buggers inside the barrier as long as we have line of sight vision to the target area."

"Just like the way Justin snagged the Chalon through a shield." Shelton whooped. "I can't wait to see how Cephus's buddies react when a crawler is chasing them down."

"Can you direct the demons to attack the aether wells?" Elyssa asked.

"That wouldn't be the most efficient use," Dad said. "We'll want to summon as many hard hitters as we can and cut them loose to wreak havoc, not micro-manage them. Just a few crawlers are hard to control."

The image of Cephus's people being ripped apart, souls sucked from their bodies by crawlers sent shivers up my spine. Unfortunately, it seemed the best way to attack the problem. "Can we possibly unleash enough Hell in Heaven to drive Cephus out of the dome?"

"Only a few of us can pull through the really nasty demons," Dad said. "Everyone else can concentrate on hellhounds. I figure we could really shake them up. If we're lucky, someone in control of the shield might panic and open it to escape the mayhem."

Elyssa stopped drawing lines on the hologram and shook her head. "We shouldn't count on that. Instead, we treat this as a diversion while our Seraphim cut a hole through the barrier."

"Yeah, but once our people are inside, the crawlers and scorps are gonna eat them alive," Shelton said.

"We would need to scent our units with brimstone," Kassallandra said. "The scorps and crawlers would be less likely to attack."

Shelton snorted. "Less likely ain't much of a guarantee."

"The Daemos could lead the charge," Dad said. "Once inside, we can control the creatures we summoned and banish them if necessary."

Elyssa bit her lower lip and stared at the floating map. "It sounds risky, but I don't know of an alternative."

I cleared my throat. "We still have the problem of holding open the barrier long enough to allow the ground troops inside."

"You don't have enough Seraphim?" Elyssa asked.

"We need to combine the power of twenty Seraphim into one big battering ram of Stasis." I thrust my hands forward. "To do that, one person has to be the focus, and has to handle all that energy."

Elyssa tilted her head. "Are you saying you can't handle that much power?"

I waggled my hand in a so-so gesture. "When everyone was linked into me to destroy the crystoid, I had to fight to regulate the two opposing forces into perfect balance. I barely managed it with six Seraphim. I'm just not efficient enough with Stasis to handle more."

"Why not break into smaller teams and carve smaller holes in the barrier?" Thomas said.

"Because the smaller holes would only stay open for seconds at a time," I said. "What we need is someone who is powerful and really good with Stasis."

"Oh god," Shelton groaned. "Are you really thinking what I think you're thinking?"

"Yeah." I caught a pained look from Mom who knew exactly who I had in mind. "We need Mr. Gray."

Victus, for one, looked delighted. "Fjoeruss, the creator of the gray men?"

"All attempts to contact him after the war have failed," Thomas reminded me. "Even our best agents were unable to locate him during the crystoid crisis."

"He was never all that enthusiastic about choosing sides during the war, either," Shelton said. "You sure we really need him?"

"He's the most powerful Stasis user I know of." It just so happened I knew one promising way to find him, but I didn't want Victus to get wind of it. His favorite hobby was designing mutant monsters like the tragon in Queens Gate. I didn't want him collaborating with Fjoeruss and learning the secrets of creating lifelike golems.

"Looks like we have a lot of angles to cover," McCloud said. "We need contingency plans in case this fortress assault fails."

"Agreed," Thomas said. "The Custodians are already working on such a plan in the event of another crystoid attack."

"What we need are more ideas about containing Cephus." Elyssa zoomed out the holographic map. "There must be some way of cutting him off completely."

"Sounds impossible," Shelton grumbled. "The entire city is floating on aether."

"It appears we need time to strategize," Thomas said. "I suggest we adjourn. If you have any ideas, consult with Lieutenant Borathen."

The meeting broke fractured into individual conversations and some attendees drifted out of the door.

I sidled up to Elyssa. "Well, Lieutenant, is seems you have your job cut out for you."

"I don't know how we're going to do it." Elyssa stared at the frozen image of the barrier. "At best, we can prevent Cephus from kidnapping more citizens and turning them into mutants. After that this turns into a siege."

I didn't like the sound of that. "There's nothing we can do to stop him from his evil plans?"

"We might be able to stop a crystoid launch, but if he opens a portal to the Void, all we can do is sit back and watch." Elyssa's forehead creased with worry. "We have to crack that egg."

I wracked my brain for some unorthodox manner to reach the objective, but aside from building a gigantic excavator, didn't reach an epiphany.

Shelton squeezed through the dwindling crowd and sat on the edge of the table next to me. "I know this ain't the best time to bring this up, but we'd like to have the rehearsal dinner tonight if you have time."

Elyssa smiled. "Are you kidding me? We haven't had a break since we left for the mission. I need a diversion."

"Wonderful," Bella said as she joined us. "It is good to have you back home."

My stomach rumbled at the thought of normal food. "Please tell me you're having pizza or burgers."

Bella shook her head. "We're having Colombian food—empanadas, arepas, and plenty of plantains."

"I wanted pizza too," Shelton murmured. He quickly grinned when Bella gave him a sharp look.

I checked the time and was shocked to discover it was only two in the afternoon. "What time do we start the festivities?"

"Six," Shelton said.

"Anything I can do to help?" Elyssa asked.

"Oh, there's plenty," Bella said. "But you have far more important things to plan."

Elyssa turned off the holographic map and picked up her phone. "No, I need some downtime to help me think. Cooking or putting up decorations sounds like just what I need."

"I'm going to get a late lunch." I patted my pockets for my phone and remembered once again it was still vacationing in Seraphina. "Who's up for pizza?"

Shelton's hand shot up. "I'm in all the way."

"I'm not hungry," Elyssa said. "Why don't you two enjoy some boy talk while Bella and I prepare for tonight?"

"Okay." The words were barely out of my mouth when Shelton grabbed my arm and pulled me out of there.

I dragged my feet. "Hey, I didn't get to kiss Elyssa goodbye."

"Plenty of time for that later." Shelton grinned. "I can't wait to get my hands on beer and pizza."

"Harry, don't destroy your diet!" Bella called after us.

He pulled me around the corner. "I'm pretending I didn't hear that."

"Since when are you on a diet?" I asked.

"Since a week ago." Shelton groaned. "Bella doesn't understand that I have a high metabolism." He patted his stomach. "The pounds just melt off even if I'm just sitting around."

I looked at his slightly round belly. "No more donuts?"

174

"No more pancakes. No more donuts." His eyes filled with agony. "I have to eat turkey sausage instead of bacon for breakfast!"

"Maybe you could ask someone to turn you into a vampire," I suggested. "Eat all you want then."

Shelton's nose wrinkled. "And have to drink blood? No thanks." He shuddered. "Already grosses me out when Bella drinks her occasional goblet of blood. I'm just happy dhampyrs don't have to drink it as often as vampires."

"Doesn't bother me," I said. "I usually let Elyssa sip right off my neck."

"You're lucky you don't scar easily." He flashed white marks on his neck. "Turns out my delicate skin doesn't like fangs." We boarded the levitator and rode it to the hangar level.

Several delegates from various factions still remained. My parents were speaking with Kassallandra, probably about the plans to summon demons inside Cephus's fortress. Victus nodded his head at a tall thin man standing next to a small boy I recognized as Conrad, Victus's son. The boy looked too pale to be healthy, his frame thin and frail.

A portal opened in one of the yellow squares and a Templar hurried through. His eyes locked onto me almost instantly as he jogged over. "Commander Slade, a woman from Seraphina is requesting to travel here."

"Cora?" I asked.

He nodded. "Yes, sir. She claims to have news."

"Please let her through." My stomach knotted. Had the Mzodi decided to join us?

He jogged back through and a moment later, Cora appeared.

Victus stopped talking at once and stared at her. I could almost hear the gears grinding in his head.

"Man, I hope this doesn't take long," Shelton said. "I'm starving."

Cora drew in a deep breath and grimaced. "I can barely smell the trees from here."

"We're in an underground hangar bay," I explained. "Would you prefer to go outside?"

"No." She waved a hand past her nose.

"Hey, I'm Shelton," Shelton said and extended a hand.

Cora gripped his hand, but didn't shake it. "A pleasure."

Shelton looked at her orange locks. "Do you dye your hair?"

As if in response, her hair shaded dark green and bounced back to orange. "Not precisely."

"Cool," he murmured, eyes wide.

"Anyway," I elbowed Shelton to the side. "Do you have good news?"

Cora smiled. "The Muhala Kajeen has agreed to help. She believes the rapid increase of Draxadis incursions are caused by Cephus's new arch. When they heard of the latest attack on the *Evadora*, it took them little time to reach a decision."

I sighed with relief. "That's great. How long will it take the fleet to reach Kdosh?"

"They dock in the morning." Cora looked left and stiffened. "What is wrong with that boy?"

Shelton glanced at Conrad. "Bad parenting and a pompous ass for a father."

Victus saw Cora looking his way and took it as an invitation to approach along with Delectra and the tall thin man. "Greetings, and welcome to Eden. You must be Cora." He flourished a bow and made no move to shake hands. "I am Victus Edison, and this is my wife, Delectra."

Cora never broke her gaze from Conrad. "This is your boy?"

Delectra raised an eyebrow. "Yes. Our apologies, but he has always been a sickly lad."

The Lyrolai woman knelt next to him, her eyes soft. "No, he is not sick. This is something else."

The thin man I didn't recognize stepped forward and pulled the child away. "It's time for your medicine, Conrad." He smiled, but his bushy black eyebrows and rumpled attire gave him a somewhat sinister look.

Cora rose, eyes flashing. "And you are?"

"Dr. Rufus Cumberbatch at your service." Cumberbatch bowed briefly. "Now, come boy. We really must away."

"I would love to hear more about the Glimmer," Victus said.

Cora's eyes hardened and she turned to me. "You told them that which I asked you to keep secret?"

Embarrassment flushed me with heat. "Uh, technically you said not to tell your crew." I held up my hands. "Besides, I told them it's classified information."

She glared coldly at me and spoke in a hard tone. "I will return to Seraphina."

"I'm sorry," Victus said. "I shouldn't have mentioned it."

"I do not blame you," Cora said.

I took her by the arm and guided her away from the others. "Please, I thought it was okay to tell my own people."

She pulled her arm free and faced me, eyes glittering. "Why would you betray my trust?"

I struggled for an excuse. "I had to tell them who you were. They had to know they could trust you."

Cora's stony gaze held mine. "Do you trust me?"

"Yes."

"Do they trust you?" she asked.

I'm an idiot. My throat went dry. "Yes."

"Apparently, I can no longer trust you." Cora shook her head slowly like a disappointed mother. "I do not think the Mzodi should help someone untrustworthy."

"No, please reconsider, Cora." My voice trembled with desperation. "Your crew won't find out from my people, I promise. I really didn't think—"

"That much is obvious," she said, icicles dangling from every word. "We will complete work on the skyway and part ways."

"Is there anything I can do to change your mind?" I asked. "Please, let me earn back your trust."

"Good luck in your endeavors, Justin." She turned and stalked toward the portal zones.

My heart thudded like a timpani drum and my chest felt hollow. I looked at Victus and felt rage building inside. It was almost as if he'd done it on purpose, but why would he sabotage the war effort?

Victus looked at me with some alarm in his eyes. As Cora passed him, he stepped in her way and bowed his head ever so slightly. "My son would dearly love to see your ship. May we come visit it?"

Cora's gaze snapped toward Cumberbatch and the boy as they waited on a portal to open. She stared so long, Victus seemed to wonder if she'd gone catatonic. At last she answered. "Only you and your son may visit. I will be available tomorrow evening."

Delectra raised an eyebrow. "What about me?"

Cora tilted her head slightly as if realizing the other woman was still there. "What about you?"

"Thank you," Victus said quickly, bowing again. "I'm sure Conrad will love it."

"Yes," Cora said faintly. "Perhaps." She snapped her gaze away from Conrad and headed to the open portal leading to the Three Sisters way station, Delectra staring after her with open contempt.

Shelton got in Victus's face. "You're a real calculating jackass, you know that?"

"Step away from my husband," Delectra growled. "Or I will throw you away."

Victus feigned innocence. "I didn't realize you weren't authorized to tell anyone her secret, Justin."

"You knew better," I said, "but you're always looking for an angle, Victus." I had a feeling visiting Cora with his son was another angle.

"We agreed to declassify anything regarding the Glimmer, so long as it didn't involve Cora," he said. "I thought it was fine to ask her for more information."

"Or maybe you asked to declassify it so you could piss her off," I hissed. "What do you have to gain from this?"

"Apologies, Justin." Victus held out his hands in supplication. "I spoke before thinking."

"Yeah, right," Shelton said. "That was premeditated as hell." He grabbed my arm. "Let's go eat before this jackass makes me lose my appetite."

Victus managed a troubled look, though Delectra ruined it by casting murderous glares at Shelton.

178

"What am I going to do?" I said in a pitiful voice. "They were going to help us, damn it! Now we have to use the skyway. By the time it's fixed, Cephus will have opened a portal to the Void."

"We'll figure out something," Shelton said. "If they're staying to repair the skyway, we have time to change her mind."

"How?" I threw up my hands. "I have nothing she wants."

"Flowers and chocolate always work," Shelton said. He grinned. "C'mon, man, chin up. We've faced tougher odds before. How hard can it be to change a woman's mind?" He frowned. "Never mind. I think we're screwed on this one."

I groaned. "What will I tell the others?"

"Just tell them she decided not to help."

"No." I shook my head. "I'll tell them. Maybe Elyssa or Thomas can figure out something."

"Maybe so." Shelton crossed his arms. "Now, for more important issues—what are we gonna eat?"

I pushed away the troubled thoughts and headed toward the row of dark sedans parked along the back wall.

"I've got half a mind to run against Victus in the next election," Shelton said. "You'd endorse me, right?"

"Yeah, if you can change Cora's mind." I mustered a wan smile.

He snorted. "I'd have more luck pulling a rabbit out of my ass."

The car on the end was one Elyssa and I used on a regular basis. The door opened when I touched it, and a fake engine noise thrummed to life. Though the automobile was designed to blend in, it could camouflage itself and even fly if necessary. Though I wasn't looking forward to Atlanta traffic, I decided to enjoy a nice normal drive through the outside world.

"Where's Cinder?" I asked as I steered us toward downtown. The thought of pizza helped me swallow the lump of regret in my throat. Shelton was right—we'd faced tougher obstacles before. *I can fix this.*

"The minute he found out you were back, he said he had some finishing touches to put on my bachelor party." An apologetic grin crossed his face. "I know it's probably gonna be the worst one in history, but at least we can hang out one more time before the big day."

I barked a laugh. "I'm actually curious to see what he's got in mind."

"Dude, this is Cinder we're talking about." Shelton shook his head. "This is the same golem who thought he could build himself a golem girlfriend."

"Well, at least he cares enough to try."

Shelton hissed air between his teeth. "Yeah. I think he sort of understands how to care."

I circled back to my original reason for asking about Cinder. "I need you to call him for me."

"Right now?" Shelton looked out the window as Antico's Pizza appeared.

"Yeah, no time to waste." I gave him a conspiratorial look. "I think he's our best hope for pulling out the big guns. We need to find Fjoeruss."

Chapter 22

I pulled into the parking lot and saw two open slots. Before I could get there, a shiny black BMW whipped in and double-parked right over the white line. A man in a black suit with a red power tie got out.

Shelton leaned out the car window. "Hey, buddy, how about parking in between the lines?"

"And risk getting my new car scratched?" the man said. "No way."

"Don't make me do it myself," Shelton said.

"You touch my car and we'll have a problem," the man replied. "I'm a lawyer and I'll sue your ass back to the Dark Ages."

"You mother fu—"

"Hey!" I grabbed Shelton and jerked him back inside the car.

"But—"

"Just hush, okay?" I told him.

The lawyer smirked. "That's what I thought."

I clenched my teeth and got out of the car. "How about I make this easy for you." I walked over to his car and gave it a nice firm shove. Rubber squealed and smoked as the car slid to the left, positioning it right between the lines as god intended it.

"What—how?" the lawyer gibbered. "That's impossible!"

Shelton slid into the driver seat and piloted our car into the now-open parking spot.

I wiped my hands together and grinned at the lawyer. "Next time you park like that, I'll wad your car up into a ball and shove it up your ass, okay?"

Shelton roared with laughter. "That's a good one, man."

The lawyer pulled out a phone. "I'm calling the cops!"

Shelton discreetly slid out his wand and flicked it. The phone sparked and smoke poured through cracks in the screen. "Aww, man, this just isn't your day, is it?"

"My new phone!" the lawyer wailed.

We left him crying in the parking lot and ordered pizza at the counter.

Shelton called Cinder while we waited on the pizza and asked him to meet us. The brick ovens in the community seating area made the room several degrees warmer, but not enough to be uncomfortable. We found a couple of chairs at the table closest to the door and waited on the food.

"I feel a little guilty for shoving that guy's car," I told Shelton when he ended the call. "I should know better than to exhibit my abilities in front of noms."

"Meh." Shelton waved it off. "That guy was a grade-A douchebag. Even if he tells anyone, who's gonna believe him?"

A man with slicked back blonde hair and a friendly grin stepped into the seating area. I did a double-take because he looked exactly like—"Cinder, is that you?"

He stepped up to the table and extended a hand. "Hello, Justin, it's been a while. I took an omniarch portal directly here since Shelton said you needed to speak with me."

I shook his hand and marveled at how warm it felt. "It's been less than a week since I saw you."

"Whoa, I like the new look, buddy." Shelton slapped Cinder on the back. "You still hitting up the night clubs?"

Cinder stood stiffly at the end of the table. "Indeed. The patrons are intriguing, and I've learned a great deal about human mating rituals."

"Uh, sounds a bit creepy," I said. "How did you make your skin warmer?"

"I have been experimenting with methods Fjoeruss told me about." Cinder turned to Shelton. "I assume the wedding will proceed as planned?"

"Yep." Shelton took a sip of his beer. "Rehearsal dinner tonight, wedding tomorrow."

"Man, we're really cramming it in, aren't we?" I said.

"There will be a great deal of cramming in," Cinder said. "Tonight we will be cramming at the bachelor party."

Shelton snorted. "What are you going to be cramming, Cinder? Strippers?"

"After watching numerous movies based on bachelor parties, I determined including strippers would be a poor decision." The corners of his mouth tugged down into a gruesome frown. "It seems they usually end up in car trunks or buried in the desert."

Shelton buried his face in his hands in a vain attempt to muffle his laughter.

"No strippers is probably a good idea," I agreed, barely able to keep the grin off my face. Before he could reply, I quickly changed subjects. "Speaking of Fjoeruss, do you know how I can contact him?"

"I apologize if it sounded like I spoke with him recently, Justin." Cinder managed a stiff shrug. "I have not directly heard from him for months."

"What about indirectly?" Shelton asked.

"In exchange for letting him study how I achieved consciousness, he agreed to share his secrets for creating gray men." Cinder stepped back as a server delivered the pizza, though his eyes never left Shelton. "After I fulfilled my part, he assigned one of his gray men to contact me on occasion with information."

"He didn't just hand over the entire recipe?" I asked.

Cinder shook his head. "Fjoeruss is rarely straightforward. His methods are puzzling, but interesting."

"Delegating one of his golems to contact you doesn't sound that puzzling," Shelton said.

"You would be correct," Cinder replied, "but to learn the secret of changing skin color, I had to find the golem hidden in a field of tulips in Holland. For answers to making realistic skin, I had to wrestle women in a mud pit at a bar in Nevada."

My jaw dropped. "Are you kidding me? How does any of that help?"

"I believe he wished to show me by example," Cinder said.

"Next time you have to mud wrestle women, let me know," Shelton said. "I've got to get a video of that."

I pressed my lips together to repress a smile. "The important question is, did you win?"

"I was told to lose," Cinder said. "Afterward, the golem with my answers emerged from the crowd and gave me instructions."

I hated to derail the amusing conversation, but we could talk about the adventures of Cinder at the bachelor party. "Getting back to Fjoeruss, can you think of any way to contact him?"

"The last gray man I spoke with is still in my lab," Cinder said. "Once I have gathered all useful information from him, he will presumably return to Fjoeruss. Perhaps I could ask the golem to pass along a message."

"I hope that works," Shelton said.

"May I deliver the message to the golem?" I asked.

Cinder nodded. "Of course."

"Why don't we just follow the golem?" Shelton said.

"I doubt the golem will return to Fjoeruss's current location," I said. "Besides, you know how picky he is about people just dropping by."

Shelton wolfed down a slice of pizza. "Yeah, wouldn't want to get dropped by his elite golems."

After lunch we took the car back to the ranch and from there traveled through an omniarch portal to the underground mansion in Queens Gate. A new one was being built aboveground where the old one had once stood before Daelissa's forces destroyed it and murdered Jeremiah Conroy. The underground one was almost an exact replica and had more or less been my home ever since the war started.

The omniarch sat in a small round cavern. The stairs leading up to the old cellar had been cleared of rubble and were even now being worked on by crews. We went the opposite way, out a door, through a wide corridor and into a large gauntlet room used for practicing magic. Cinder had set aside a portion of the room for his lab.

The gray man sat in a chair, face expressionless, eyes staring straight ahead. Aside from slicked back silver hair and the gray cast to its skin, the golem looked the spitting image of Cinder. Then again, so did all the gray men. Forged in the likeness of their creator, Fjoeruss, they were some of the creepiest creations I'd ever seen—aside from Cinder.

"Never understood why Fjoeruss likes having an army of clones," Shelton grumbled.

"Oh, he has plenty of other ones," I said. "When Mom and I tracked him down at his headquarters last time, I found out the janitorial staff were all golems."

"Four-oh-five, I have need of your service," Cinder said to the motionless golem.

The thing stood and turned its unnerving stone gaze to him.

"I need you to deliver a message to Fjoeruss," Cinder said, seemingly oblivious to how creepy the other golem was. "Justin Slade will give you the message." Cinder stepped back.

"Tell Fjoeruss that unless we have his help, another crystal meteor event could occur," I said. "Even worse, Cephus may open a portal to the void with a new arch he's constructed. We need help breaching a Murk barrier protecting Cephus, the one who attacked Eden."

The golem replied in a dull monotone. "You will receive help by tomorrow."

I felt my forehead pinch. "Fjoeruss is coming?"

The golem didn't answer.

"Well, at least it's something," Shelton said.

"I suppose." I turned back to the golem. "Did Fjoeruss anticipate us asking for help?"

The golem stared blankly ahead.

"I require information about emotion," Cinder said.

"What do you wish to know?" the golem replied at once.

Cinder looked at me. "Apparently, it was only authorized to answer something specific."

"Classic Fjoeruss," Shelton grumbled.

"It's more than I'd expected." I walked around a curtain and found lifelike limbs and torsos spread out on the floor. "Yeesh!" I jumped back. "It's like a shop of horrors in here."

Shelton stepped around and jumped back. "Christ Almighty, Cinder. Can you put this stuff away when you're finished working on it?"

"Apologies," Cinder said, scooping up arms and legs and dumping them into a chest. "I forgot how unsettling this might look."

"Did you make these?" I asked.

He nodded. "I am practicing making parts now."

Shelton took off his hat and scratched his head. "Next thing you know, he'll make his own girlfriend."

"That is one of my goals," Cinder replied calmly. "The last step—creating the spark—will be the most difficult for me since I am incapable of magic."

"I'm sure you'll figure out something." Shelton slapped his hat on his head.

I went back to the mansion and was instantly accosted by a vicious hellhound. Cutsauce was the first hound I'd ever summoned. He was also the size of a small Chihuahua and not very bright. I picked him up and let him happily lick my face, his brimstone-scented breath making me feel right at home.

"Did you miss your daddy?" I said. "Who's my happy pup?"

He yipped and wiggled in my arms. I put him down and he followed me upstairs where I flopped into bed and took a much-needed nap. Elyssa woke me with a good hard shaking since her tender kisses apparently hadn't done the trick.

"Ungh—is it time already?" I groaned.

"It's time." She brushed her lips across mine. "Up and at-em, sunshine."

I felt groggy and almost put off telling Elyssa about the bad news, but procrastinating wouldn't make it easier. "Before we get started on the festivities, I need to tell you something."

Elyssa's eyes narrowed. "Tell me what?"

"Victus let slip to Cora that I told the council about her background." My throat went dry. "She'd just told me the sky fishers would help. Now they won't because I was an idiot."

She pursed her lips and nodded. "Cora is pretty upset, I guess."

"Yeah." I ran a hand down my face. "She agreed to finish repairs on the skyway, but we just lost a huge advantage."

"Tell me exactly what happened."

I told her everything in detail and waited with bated breath in the hopes she knew of some way to help.

Her forehead wrinkled. "What's this about Victus's boy, Conrad?"

I shrugged. "Cora seemed kind of taken with him for some reason."

"That's odd. I wonder if he reminds Cora of her daughter." Elyssa bit her lower lip. "I think we should go visit her tomorrow after the wedding. Maybe we can convince her to help."

"Should I bring flowers and chocolate?" I asked, standing up and stretching.

Elyssa shrugged. "Wouldn't hurt." She slapped me on the butt. "Now, go get ready."

I showered and tossed on jeans and a button-up shirt then went downstairs.

"My lovely little lamb!" A curvy blonde gripped me in a tight hug and kissed me on the cheeks. "It's been too bloody long."

"Stacey!" I kissed her on the cheek. "It's been months."

She loaded a sigh with regret and released me. "Children are taxing, love. It seems I never have a chance to leave the house."

"Where's Ryland?" Elyssa asked.

A smirk tugged Stacey's lips. "He's tending the twins so I could escape and do my bridesmaid duty."

I chuckled. "I'll bet he loves that."

"Oh, he quite enjoys it," Stacey said.

"You certainly don't look like you've had children," Elyssa said.

"My stomach was so stretched, I thought it would never pop back into shape," she said. "I couldn't even shapeshift during the third trimester." As a felycan, Stacey could morph into most feline shapes.

Her mate, Ryland, was a lycan which made them a somewhat unlikely pair that had worked out quite well.

I grimaced. "Seems like it would be kind of rough on the fetuses if you shifted into panther form."

"Perhaps." Stacey traced a fingernail down my arm. "When are you lovebirds having children?"

"Uh—" Panic flashed through Elyssa's eyes. "Not now. Not for a while. I mean, we're not even married yet."

I tried not to laugh and failed. "Someone's a little flustered."

"Someone's about to get punched," Elyssa shot back, violet eyes sparkling.

Another blonde stepped through the front door. "Stacey!" Katie Johnson ran across the foyer and gave the felycan a hug. Once she pulled away from her, she repeated the performance with me. "Justin!" Hug. "Elyssa!" Another enthusiastic hug.

After the hugs were over, Shelton came into the foyer. "We're ready to get started."

"Lead the way," I said.

We went into a rarely used part of the house and into the grand dining hall. The front half of the long room had been rearranged with rows of chairs replacing the long tables, and a raised platform where the ceremony would take place.

Thomas Borathen stood at the front of the room, face set in stone while Bella spoke with him. She turned and saw us and motioned us forward. "Come, everyone get into positions. The commander doesn't have time to spare."

"Your dad is marrying them?" I asked Elyssa.

"As head of the Templars, he's ordained," she said. "Though there are plenty of others who could do it just as well."

"At least they didn't request to use the Church of the Divinity," I said, talking about the church Daelissa's Exorcists had used for their nefarious activities.

Elyssa put a finger to her lips. "Don't give Shelton any ideas."

I spotted Adam Nosti and his girlfriend Meghan Andretti up near the front. I shook his hand and pulled him in for a bro-hug while Meghan exchanged greetings with Elyssa.

"Sounds like we have a real challenge with this Cephus guy," Adam said.

"Remember when you hacked the shield protecting the Chalon?" I asked.

He chuckled. "How could I forget? If you're asking if I can hack through a Seraphim shield, the quick answer is, I don't think so."

"Damn." I bit the inside of my lip. "I know the magic is different than what Arcanes use, but I hoped it might have some similarities."

"Seraphim magic is primal, the energy woven into different uses," Adam said. "Arcane magic is flexible and requires spells to make full use of it. If something is made from a spell, it can be hacked."

"Makes sense," I said. "Is there a way to counter Seraphim magic with Arcane spells?"

"That's an interesting question," Adam said. "It's something I've been working on."

"Hey, enough with the war talk," Shelton said. "This is my special day."

Adam snorted. "It's the rehearsal dinner, not the wedding."

"Every day is Shelton's special day," I said.

"Finally, the fairy princess wedding you've always wanted," Adam said with a grand wave of his arms.

Shelton's face turned bright red and the women burst into laughter.

"I apologize, Harry," Cinder said. "I did not realize you wished a fairy princess wedding or I would have planned a more suitable bachelor party."

That only brought more laughter which, of course, went completely over Cinder's head.

Bella brought everyone back under control and divided the bridesmaids and groomsmen then instructed us how to proceed. I'd never been to a nom wedding, so I didn't know what to expect. It turned out to be pretty simple—lining up in the hall outside and escorting in the bridesmaids. Thomas quickly ran through a rehearsal of the ceremony, and we were done.

Butler golems brought in the food afterward, heaping platters of empanadas, flat arepas, and enough beans and rice to feed an army. I was just digging into the chicharrón—thick pork bacon—when my ears popped, as if the air pressure had suddenly changed.

I caught a confused look from Elyssa and saw Stacey looking around.

"You felt that too?" I asked Elyssa.

"It's like an omniarch portal opened nearby," she said.

"But we have portal blockers around the mansion," I said. "The only way in is to use the omniarch itself."

A bad feeling inserted itself between my stomach and my heart. I pushed away from the table. "Something isn't right."

"It must have been close," Elyssa said.

Much to the alarm of the others at the table, I leapt up and ran into the hallway. I didn't find a portal, but I found what had come through the portal. A malaether crucible sat on a pedestal, the malevolent energy swirling and crackling inside. On the pedestal was a note that simply read: *From Serena with love.*

Chapter 23

The glass globe looked exactly like the malaether crucible Serena had made away with at the end of the war right when I started the final boss fight with Daelissa. Though it wasn't large, it could nuke the entire mansion if the glass broke. Thankfully, it looked intact, leaving me to wonder what sort of message Serena meant to send. What really sent a cold chill into my chest was how easily she'd pulled this off.

I channeled aether into my body, ready to throw up a shield at a moment's notice.

"Oh, god," Elyssa breathed. "Why didn't she set it off when she had the chance?"

"No idea." I examined the pedestal from a distance.

The rest of the group joined us a moment later.

"Son of a buck-toothed vampire," Shelton shouted. "Can't they give us a moment's peace around here?"

"Where are the portal-blocking statues?" I asked him.

"Last I remember, there's one in the middle of the west wing, same with the east, and another tucked into the chandeliers inside this hallway." He peered at the string of chandeliers lining the tall ceiling and pointed to one about thirty yards behind the pedestal with the bomb. "I think it's in there if I recall correctly."

"Who placed them?" I asked.

"Templars," Elyssa said. "They did it during the war for obvious reasons."

"I need to check the statue." I started walking around the pedestal when Adam shouted and grabbed my arm.

"Wait!" He pulled me back. "Something's wrong with the floor."

I looked down but didn't see anything different.

Adam took out his wand and flicked it through a pattern. Soft white light shone from the tip. Dark patterns appeared on the floor where the light touched it. "A triggering ward," he said, shining the wand all across the hall. Shadowy symbols floated like dark ghosts in the air and on the walls. His nostrils flared and he spun around. "Oh, crap."

"What?" I said.

"Nobody move." Adam shined the light behind us to reveal more symbols in the air behind us and all along the walls and ceiling. Only the floor where we stood was clear of them. "We triggered the wards when we walked in here. If we try to walk through any of them, it'll probably set off the bomb."

"If I read those runes correctly, this thing is designed like a roach motel," Shelton said. "You can check in, but you can't check out."

"Yeah, it's a one-way rune," Adam said. He swept the light back and forth, revealing runes between us and the crucible, giving us no way to defuse it.

Shelton growled. "Son of a—I'm gonna kill Serena with my bare hands."

"I will gladly help," Bella said, mustering a cute scowl that wouldn't scare anyone, even though she could easily back it up with magic and enhanced dhampyr strength.

Thomas Borathen stood calmly near the back of the group, an occasional blink the only sign he hadn't gone catatonic. "Serena knew we'd all be here tonight." He stepped forward and looked at the pedestal. "Somehow she disabled the portal-blocker and received an image of this hallway so she could open a portal here."

"When was the last time anyone checked those portal-blockers?" Shelton said.

"Probably not since the war ended," Elyssa said. "There was no need, or so we thought."

"Cuckoo!" A high-pitched warble echoed through the hall.

"Where the hell did that come from?" Shelton said.

"Cuckoo!" Something fluttered down from the chandelier where the portal-blocking statue should have been and landed on the crucible. A clockwork bird, brass gears and insides visible, tilted its head and gazed at us with creepy glowing eyes.

"I think I know how she pulled it off," Shelton said in a worried voice.

The bird's metal feet tinkled on the crucible. "Cuckoo!" It tapped on the glass with its sharp beak.

Everyone, except maybe Thomas, shouted and jumped back in alarm.

"You've got to be kidding me!" Shelton said. "Death by cuckoo?"

Adam took out his arcphone and flicked through spells. "Shut up and start scanning, Harry."

"I'm on it," Shelton grumbled, taking out his own phone and scrolling through a list. "Try the rune decoder we wrote for the Darkwater job."

"Already using it," Adam said. "Try to find a backdoor in the code."

"Nothing so far," Shelton said.

"Cuckoo!" the bird struck again.

"It's striking every minute," Bella said.

"It's not hitting the glass hard enough to break it," Stacey said.

"Yeah, but after a dozen pecks in the same place, that crucible is going to crack," I said. I drew in more aether. "If it comes down to it, I might be able to shield us."

"At this range?" Elyssa said. "You barely held together a shield at the fringe of a malaether explosion, and that was with your mom helping."

"What else can I do?" I said. "I have to try something."

Bella frowned and looked at the floor. "Adam, were there any runes on the floor?"

"Maybe we can dig," I said, converting some of the built up power into destruction.

"Don't do it," Shelton said. "We're boxed in on all sides. If you breach the floor, you'll set off the ward."

"Cuckoo!" the beak pinged against the crucible. A thin crack formed in the glass.

"What if I crush the bird with Murk?" I said.

"You can't channel or cast magic through the rune," Shelton said.

Another idea hit me. "I'll summon a hellhound."

Shelton's eyes lit up. "Try it."

I reached through my demon half and found a minor demon spirit. Focusing on a section of floor behind the crucible, I imagined the hellhound emerging there. It was like ramming my head into a brick wall. Tears of pain blurred my eyes and I lost the connection.

"Dammit, she even demon warded it," Shelton said.

"Found something!" Adam said. "Looks like Serena missed something crucial in all the coding she jammed in here."

Shelton dropped to his knees next to his friend. "I see it."

"What is it?" I asked.

"Twenty-one, twenty-two," Stacey counted the seconds to the next strike.

"One of the runes is in the wrong order," Adam said. "We can exploit it to insert our own runes and break the wall."

"Try this snippet," Shelton said.

Adam took the arcphone and projected a series of runes into the shadow runes in the air. The ghostly images slid aside and made room for the new code.

"Fifty-eight, fifty-nine," Stacey continued.

"Cuckoo!" Another peck against the glass. A spider web of cracks raced along the surface.

"One more hit and we're done for," Elyssa said. She gripped me in a tight embrace and kissed me. "I love you."

"I love you too," I said, "but I'm not letting us die."

"What can I do to help?" Bella said. "Can I strengthen your shield?"

"I'm going to form a sphere," I explained. "We'll roll with the blast."

"Do you know how fast we'll travel?" Shelton said as he watched Adam push more code into the rune. "We'll fly out of here quick enough to achieve orbit."

"Escape velocity, sure," Adam said. "But we'll go the wrong direction and splat against a wall."

Thomas spoke quietly with someone on his phone. "The closest Templars are coming, but they won't make it in time."

"Why don't they open a portal here?" I asked.

"The portal blocker is back on," he replied grimly. "Serena must have reactivated it after dropping off the bomb."

"Vindictive bitch," Stacey said. "Though I suppose hell hath no fury like a woman scorned."

"I think we're way past scorned with her," I said.

Stacey looked at her arcphone and held up the timer for all to see. "Twenty seconds."

"I put Commander Salazar in command in case of my death," Thomas said.

Elyssa hugged him. "I love you, Dad."

His crystal blue eyes didn't betray a hint of fear, but they didn't mask the sadness lurking there. "I love you too, daughter."

Not long ago, he never would have uttered such words. Thomas had lightened up on his oh-so-serious ways, but the forces of darkness hadn't really given him a break to play the loving father.

"Oh crap," Adam said.

I threw up a shield as time ran out, channeling Murk into a dense dome around us.

"Cuckoo!" The bird smacked the crucible and everyone gasped.

Jagged cracks joined the ones already present, but the vessel held.

"Hurry!" Bella said.

I dropped the shield and Meghan began a new countdown on her phone.

"Almost there," Adam said. "Almost there."

"Insert the code break right there!" Shelton said.

"Where?" Adam frantically searched the smoky runes.

Shelton jabbed a finger toward a section. "Right freaking there, man!"

Adam quickly projected a new line of code from his phone. "That's it, we did it!"

The ghostly runes began to fade.

"Serena really made a rookie mistake with that one," Shelton said.

Adam whooped. "Time for her to go back to school."

"Uh, Harry?" Bella stared at the runes as they contorted into a new shape, a holographic image of Serena, blond hair pulled back into a tight bun, a smirk on her face.

"Goodness, you really are gullible, aren't you, Harry Shelton?" Serena sighed. "Don't fret, you wouldn't have broken free anyway."

"Daelissa lost!" I shouted. "Get over it already, Serena."

The image was apparently a recording, not a live transmission, because Serena's floating head didn't acknowledge the outburst.

Adam furiously tapped on his arcphone but he looked up, face drawn with defeat. "We're done."

The countdown on Meghan's phone hit twenty seconds. I thought about what Shelton had said if I created a sphere around us, how we'd be shot like a bullet. Enclosing us in a shield probably wouldn't work, but what about enclosing the bomb? *No, that would increase the explosion.* Just like gunpowder encased in paper made the explosion that much bigger, wrapping the malaether bomb in Murk would only stop our destruction for an instant before the pressure burst the bubble.

But what if I did what a gun barrel did—direct the deadly force anywhere but at us? It was our only hope.

"If I channel through the barrier, it'll trigger the bomb, right?" I said.

Adam wiped sweat off his forehead. "Yes, why?"

"Wish me luck." I drew in a torrent of aether and threaded Murk and Brilliance into Stasis. Whirling my hands, I twisted the Stasis into a long funnel.

"How is Stasis supposed to stop it?" Shelton said.

"That's just the inside." I didn't have time to explain further. The next part would have to be fast. I thrust my hands forward and stretched them apart. The funnel twisted through the rune barrier and engulfed the crucible while at the same time stretching all the way up to the high ceiling. I instantly channeled a thick tube of Murk around the swirling foggy mass.

196

Serena's face burst into laughter and faded away. "Goodbye, little Slade."

"Cuckoo!" I couldn't see the bird since it was inside the Stasis, but the sound of shattering crucible glass echoed. A loud bang made everyone except Thomas jump with fright.

I braced for the explosion, but aside from fizzling lights, nothing happened.

"Did the Stasis neutralize it?" Shelton said.

I maintained the channeling just in case and shook my head. "I couldn't channel nearly enough Stasis to counteract a malaether bomb. It was just enough to soften the blow so the blast would travel up the barrel and through the ceiling."

Adam picked himself up off the floor and stared with confusion. "I don't get it. What happened to the boom?"

I just knew it had to be a trick. "Everyone get out of here, now."

"Wait," Thomas said. "I think I know what this is."

"Seems pretty obvious to me," Shelton said. "That crazy bitch wants us dead."

"Remove the funnel, Justin." Thomas stepped toward the area where the runes had once been.

I decided to trust his instincts and released the threads. The Murk and Stasis faded away to reveal the broken crucible and the cuckoo bird lying on the floor next to the pedestal. A rod with a stiff flag jutted from the shards. Like a fake gun with a Boom! sign sticking from it, the malaether bomb had its own message for us.

Farewell heroes of Eden.

"What the hell does that mean?" Shelton said. "She had us dead to rights."

"She didn't want to kill us," Thomas said. "She wanted to send a message."

"I don't understand the message," Bella said. "She could have killed some of our most important leaders tonight."

"True," Thomas said. "But then she would still have David Slade, Alysea, and plenty of others to worry about who would have turned their sole focus on finding her."

"Let's not forget she's just crazy," Shelton said.

197

"Crazy like a fox." Adam shook his head. "Why tonight instead of the wedding tomorrow?"

"She must have assumed it would be easier to crash the rehearsal dinner," Elyssa said.

"It's not like the crowd will be much bigger tomorrow," Shelton said. "Just a few extra people."

"Our security has grown lax," Thomas said. "It was a foolish oversight on our part."

"Won't happen again," Elyssa said. "I'm ordering a review of protocols."

"I still have a really bad feeling about this," I said. "Serena didn't do this for nothing."

"Agreed," Thomas said. "I'll have the mansion swept."

"Does this mean the bachelor party is cancelled?" Cinder said.

Shelton blinked and stared at the golem before bursting into laughter. "Are you kidding me? After this, I need a drink."

"I'm certain you will enjoy the mimosas tonight," Cinder replied.

Even Elyssa looked a bit disgusted by that. "Mimosas at a bachelor party?"

Bella snickered. "La vida loca."

Templars rushed into the grand hallway, swords out and raced all the way up to us. "Sir, what's the sitrep?" the first asked.

"Contained," Thomas replied. "I need this scene forensically examined, and the mansion swept from one end to the other."

"I'll debrief them," Elyssa said. She gripped my hands. "I think it's time you boys went to the bachelor party."

"We'll start our own party after Elyssa is done," Stacey said.

"I dunno," Shelton said. "I mean, we coulda been killed. Maybe—"

I still felt giddy with adrenalin and fright and wondered if maybe we shouldn't call it off.

"Nonsense!" Bella said. "Go have fun."

"What are you going to do?" he asked.

Stacey smirked. "Darling, do you really want to know?"

Shelton got a wild look in his eyes. "I know you two used to do some crazy stuff back in the day, but try to tone it down, okay?"

Stacey tilted her head back and laughed.

"We don't know how to tone it down," Elyssa said. "We're about to get cray-cray."

Adam and I snorted at the frightened expression on Shelton's face. We each grabbed an elbow and escorted him away, Cinder right behind us.

"I studied bachelorette parties in an attempt to refine the selections for your celebration," Cinder said, "but brides tend to get much wilder than the grooms."

Shelton gulped. "Wilder than strip clubs and hookers?"

"Much wilder," Cinder said. "Do not fear, Harry. I believe this will be a cray-cray time for you." He said it in such a deadpan tone it caused me and Adam to burst into fresh laughter, though we both sounded a bit hysterical from the brush with death.

"A very wild time," Adam said in a trembling voice.

My hands shook, and I felt cold. I could hardly wait to get out of there.

Chapter 24

Cinder took us back to his lab where he made us change into tight black outfits with capes that reminded me of Templar armor, except this material didn't feel like it could protect me from a toothpick. Then he brought out a pitcher of sangria and board games.

"I thought we were having mimosas," Adam said in a voice tinged with regret.

"Hopefully, sangrias will be just as enjoyable," Cinder said.

Shelton gulped down a cup. "Man, I need a stiff drink after Serena's nasty prank."

I took a sip and savored the sweet fruit-laced wine. "Wow, this is really good."

"Thank you," Cinder said, and laid out the board games on the table. "Would you prefer Chutes and Ladders, or Candyland?"

"Oh god." Shelton face-palmed. "We're really doing this aren't we?"

"Well, hey, at least it's safe." Adam twirled to flare his cape. "Nothing like playing board games after thinking you're gonna die."

"Chutes and Ladders." Shelton sounded on the verge of tears.

"Excellent," Cinder said. "For each chute you fall down, you must drink a shot."

"Of sangria?" Adam asked.

"Precisely," Cinder replied. "Who will go first?"

Shelton looked so miserable that I volunteered. "I'll go."

Cinder placed the spinner in the middle of the table. "Proceed."

"You know, there's a half-decent strip club I know of," Adam said. "Maybe after a round of this we could ditch the capes and check it out."

Shelton brightened a bit. "Yeah, that sounds like a real bachelor party."

Cinder's expression didn't change. "That will be fine after we play this game."

I flicked the spinner. It stopped at three and I moved my pawn. Adam and Cinder went, then Shelton glumly thumped the spinner to take his turn. "I'll bet the women are gonna live it up tonight."

The lights flickered and the sound of boots stomping down the corridor outside reached our ears.

"I must request that no matter what happens tonight, you abstain from using magic." Cinder handed each of us thick black rods about six inches long with runes inscribed on the end.

"What the heck are these?" Shelton asked.

Cinder gripped his rod. "Remember, no magic."

The rest of us exchanged confused expressions. A dozen men in robes raced around the corner and stopped. Holding rods like ours, they flicked them and blazing energy swords extended from the ends with a buzzing thrum.

"Holy farting fairies," Shelton whispered with excitement. "Am I dreaming?"

"By the order of the Emperor, we are here to destroy you," the leader of the group said, and charged.

Shelton flicked on his own blazing sword and shouted, "Long live the rebellion!"

Adam, Cinder, and I followed suit, and with a roar, charged the enemy. The battle was quick and furious, the enemy relentless. Though one of the attackers hit me with his light sword, it did no damage. When we struck them, they dropped like rag dolls.

After defeating the emperor's minions, we discovered a princess was in trouble and followed Cinder up a winding corridor that exited into the grass field behind Arcane University.

A ship with a large forward saucer and long nacelles waited. There was just room enough for four in the cockpit—a captain's chair, two gunner positions, and a science station. Shelton hopped in the captain's chair and we flew up toward a large black orb hovering above the Dark Forest.

A swarm of starships rose from the trees and attacked.

"Shields up, weapons online!" Shelton commanded.

"Shields at one hundred percent," Cinder said from the science station.

"Weapons ready," Adam and I said.

The first wave attacked. The ship shuddered violently with every hit.

"Lock lasers on target!" Shelton shouted. "Fire!"

Though it felt like our ship was being pounded to pieces, it held together as we fought a pitched battle against impossible odds and finally passed through the enemy armada.

As we drew closer to the black orb hovering in the night sky, Adam rotated his chair to face Shelton. "Sir, it's a moon."

Shelton leaned forward, eyes narrowed with intensity. "That's no moon, ensign. It's a battle station."

Lasers erupted from the battle station.

"Shields at thirty percent," Cinder reported.

"Divert power from auxiliary systems." Shelton walked between the gunner seats and held on as the ship shuddered. "It's time to save the princess."

By the time we finished with the scripted adventure Cinder had prepared for us, it was nearly two in the morning and we piled back into the lab, laughing and unable to stop talking about how much fun it had been for us to live out a collage of every geek's fantasies.

"Was that Princess Ardala we saved?" Adam asked. "That costume she wore was definitely from the seventies."

"It was awesome, dude." Shelton gripped Cinder in a one-armed hug. "Man, that was the best bachelor party of all time."

Cinder managed a genuine looking smile. "I thought you might like it, Harry, especially considering your collection of science fiction shows and movies."

"How did you pull it off?" Adam said.

"I used my limited golem creation abilities to make the characters," Cinder said. "Students at Science Academy helped me craft the space ships."

"It was perfect," Shelton said. "Thanks."

Cinder's eyes actually softened, as if he were experiencing true emotion. "You are welcome, Harry."

"Better than a strip club," Adam added.

"No doubt about that." I stifled a yawn. "I'm gonna hit the sack, guys."

"Night," Adam said.

"Yeah, me too." Shelton slapped Cinder once more on the back and we went back to the mansion.

Elyssa had just gotten out of the shower when I came inside. "Let me guess, strip clubs and debauchery," she said.

"Couldn't be further from the truth." I grinned. "How about you?"

"Pole dancing lessons." She rolled her eyes. "Took us about ten minutes to get better than the instructor. Stacey did a routine that had the teacher begging her for lessons."

I snorted. "I'll bet. How did Meghan do?"

"She just watched," Elyssa said. "Meghan isn't exactly the partying type."

"Yeah, she can be a bit of a killjoy." Meghan was a Templar, but not the agile fighting kind as far as I knew. She probably didn't want to look foolish with two dhampyrs and a felycan showing her up.

"After pole dancing we took twerking lessons," Elyssa continued. "It's a lot harder than it looks."

My tired body perked up. "Wanna show me?"

She leaned against the door frame and bounced on her legs, but her bottom refused to join in the dance. "I can't get it to jiggle!"

"Too much muscle," I said, enjoying the show.

"You think?" Elyssa slipped into boy shorts and lay down on the bed.

My mouth was already watering from the twerking demo. "Let's practice together."

She licked her lips. "I'm game."

The next morning, we joined Shelton, Bella, Adam, and Meghan for breakfast in the kitchen. Bella let Shelton make his usual pancake breakfast for the occasion, much to his relief. The big topic of the morning was the bachelor party.

"Wow, I can't believe Cinder pulled it off," Elyssa said. "I wish I'd been there."

"You prefer fighting starship battles to twerking?" Bella asked.

Elyssa laughed. "Any day of the week."

Cutsauce yipped and looked up at her expectantly. She dropped a piece of bacon on the floor and he gobbled it down in an instant.

"By the way, the security sweeps for the mansion came back clean," Elyssa said. "The portal blockers will be checked every hour."

"That's a relief," I said. "Just the thought that Serena could pop in at any minute scares the hell out of me."

Shelton ate a lot less than usual and kept tugging on the collar of his T-shirt as if it was too tight.

"Looking a little pale, buddy." Adam commented. "Didn't get enough sleep?"

Shelton gulped some orange juice. "Nah, I'm fine."

Elyssa and Bella exchanged a knowing look.

Stacey arrived moments later, Ryland and the twins in tow. The boy looked like a miniature version of Ryland with bushy brown hair sprouting in all directions. The girl, an adorable little blonde with big innocent eyes toddled behind her mother, bouncing up and down on her toes and exclaiming loudly in baby-speak when she saw us.

"Come here, you precious little thing!" Elyssa said, and scooped up the girl. "Alana is growing so big already."

Little Tyler hid behind his father's leg and peeked around at the commotion.

"Hey, Ryland." I exchanged grips with the lean, muscular lycan. "Looks like fatherhood is treating you well."

Ryland chuckled. "Best thing that ever happened to me."

"Who's the cutest wittle munchkin?" Bella peppered kisses on Alana's face and the girl giggled. "You are!"

Adam knelt next to Tyler. "How's it going, big man?"

The boy squeezed between Ryland's legs and looked out with wide brown eyes.

Ryland swept him up and held him in one arm. "He's a bit shy until he gets to know you."

Shelton still sat at the table, eyes a bit wild as he watched the women gush over Alana.

"I think reality is hitting him right now," Adam said in a conspiratorial whisper.

I snorted. "I don't think he's ready for kids anytime soon."

"I can't wait to have our own little Harry running around," Bella said.

Shelton's face went from white to green. He gripped his coffee mug with shaking hands and guzzled the steaming liquid.

Adam and I snickered.

"What's so funny?" Shelton said.

"Your expression," Adam said. "It's priceless."

"Hey, I like kids," Shelton said, pushing to his feet. "Kids are great."

Adam elbowed me. "Look, I think he's having a panic attack."

Everyone burst into laughter.

The other guests began to arrive around noon—my family and Elyssa's, Cinder, and Katie Johnson along with two of our high school friends, Ash and Nyte.

"Justin!" Ash gripped me in a full-blown hug, while Nyte settled for a manlier one-armed chest-bump.

Nyte ran a hand through his short carrot-colored hair. "When we heard you were overdue from your mission in Seraphina, we got worried."

"Yeah, things got intense," I said. "Thankfully, we got some help and took care of business."

"We've got the feeder corps ready to march," Ash said. "They're pretty excited to be needed by Seraphim again."

"Yeah, well, the Tarissan Legion isn't very large anymore," I told them.

Katie's face fell. "I'd heard rumors, but Commander Salazar hasn't told us much."

"There's only a handful left," Elyssa said. "Don't repeat that outside of here, please."

"Oh no," Katie whispered. "That's awful."

"What happened?" Nyte asked.

"Cephus wiped most of them out with a crystoid," I said and let that sink in a moment before continuing. "Don't worry, though, we're going to need the feeders to rebuild the legion and to reinforce the entire army."

Ash grimaced. "Sounds like we're starting over."

"There's a lot of work to be done," Elyssa said. "For now, let's focus on today. I don't want to spoil the mood for Bella's wedding."

Katie nodded and managed a wan smile. "Yeah, let's perk up and move out."

Ash chuckled. "Spoken like a true Templar."

"That's exactly what Commander Borathen says right before a battle," Nyte said with a huge grin.

I went upstairs and got dressed then met the rest of the wedding party in the hallway outside of the grand dining hall. Shelton already stood at the front of the room looking pale and nervous. It was strange seeing him in formal Arcane robes, snug and black with white ruffles on the chest and sleeves. His hair was combed neatly to the side and, for once, he was clean shaven.

"Hardly looks like Shelton," Adam said.

"He cleans up nice," Meghan commented. "A shame he dresses like a cowboy most of the time."

"I like the cowboy look," Elyssa said. "It suits him."

I turned to Adam. "You've known him longer than all of us. Why does he always wear a wide-brimmed hat and leather duster?"

He shrugged. "There's a lot he doesn't talk about, even with me."

I thought back to the revelations about Shelton's childhood during my brief tenure as a student at Arcane University. "Seems like he had it rough."

"He's changed a lot since you became friends, Justin." Adam put a hand on my shoulder. "Shelton is a nicer jackass than he used to be."

Elyssa laughed. "I can agree with that."

"Shelton is a bit of a rogue." Stacey tapped a finger on her chin and looked at the groom. "But he's also brutally honest, and I've always admired that about the man."

"Yeah, he doesn't mince words," Adam agreed.

Flava and Lanaeia walked around the corner and approached us.

"I am curious to see a mortal wedding ritual," Flava said. "Would it be acceptable for us to observe?"

"Sure," Elyssa said. "Go have a seat."

"I wonder if it will be as wonderful as the weddings in romance novels," Lanaeia said as they left us to join the murmuring crowd inside.

The small orchestra began playing an unfamiliar but soothing melody that cued our entrance. I hooked arms with Stacey, since she was the maid of honor, and led the procession down the aisle. We split at the front and took our positions at the podium.

I put a hand on Shelton's shoulder. "You hanging in there, man?"

He nodded and took a deep breath. "I hate dressing up."

"It'll all be over soon," I assured him.

Shelton wiped away a bead of sweat from his forehead and his voice cracked when he spoke. "Yeah, I know."

Once the wedding party was in place, the orchestra changed to a spirited rendition of Mozart's *Wedding March*. Bella stepped through the doors and Shelton's heavy breathing caught in his throat. His bride looked beautiful in a white dress that hugged her curves and contrasted with her olive skin. Despite her age, Bella looked like a college girl getting married for the first time.

"She's beautiful," Shelton murmured. "I'm the luckiest man alive."

Stacey sniffled and wiped tears from her eyes. "This is so bloody romantic."

Bella smiled, her violet eyes twinkling with delight at the stunned look on Shelton's face as she slowly paced down the aisle. Elyssa looked at me, a look of love and adoration on her face. I wanted to kiss her so badly, it hurt.

"This is very touching," Cinder whispered behind me. "I offered to sing a romantic love song before the ceremony, but Bella requested we keep it short."

Adam snorted. "I'd pay to see you sing, Cinder."

Thomas Borathen cast a warning look our way that rocked us back on our heels and shut us up.

Bella reached the podium and took Shelton's hands, and the ceremony began.

"We are gathered here today to join Bella Pizarro and Harry Shelton in holy matrimony," Thomas said. "If anyone objects to this marriage, let them speak now or forever hold their peace."

I braced myself as visions of another sneak attack from Serena flashed through my mind. Elyssa looked tense as well, perhaps thinking the same thing.

"Nobody better object, or I'll blast them!" Ivy shouted, bringing a wave of laughter from the audience.

Thomas waited until the noise died away and continued. He led the bride and groom through the usual questions and, moments later, made it final. "I now pronounce you husband and wife. You may kiss the bride."

Shelton no longer looked nervous or pale. He looked happy, like a man who'd opened a door to his future and found out it would be wonderful. I tried not to think about the new war, about how many people would die, or Cephus's terrible plans, but the thunderclouds on the horizon were almost upon us. There would be no honeymoon for the newlyweds.

I just hoped they both survived what was to come.

Chapter 25

After the reception ended later in the afternoon, Shelton took his bride through an omniarch portal to eke out a meager honeymoon in the Caribbean while the rest of us got back to business.

"The question remains, how are we going to break through the shield?" Elyssa said to me and Thomas as we studied battle plans in the war room back at the Ranch.

Thomas rotated the holographic map projected above the table. Icons representing the various factions of the army surrounded the wasteland at the city center, but the plan for moving the troops closer had stalled until we could figure out a reliable way to break through the shield and hold it open for troops to funnel through.

Squadrons of Blue Cloaks on flying carpets would blockade the air to prevent any airborne attacks from escaping the fortress while the rest of us built a beachhead within the city. Thomas had decided a wider perimeter would be safer in case another crystoid attack slipped past our aerial defenses.

"You should speak with Cora about the Mzodi fleet," Thomas said. "Despite her personal issues with you, Cephus poses a threat to all of Seraphina, especially if he can truly open a portal to the Void."

"Any tips about how to approach her?" I asked.

Thomas nodded. "With great humility."

"Cap in hand? On my knees?"

"If she's reasonable, she'll understand the threat Cephus poses," Thomas said. "From what you told me, she cherishes Seraphina and the Mzodi. I believe she'll help for their sake if nothing else."

"I think she's being a bit butt hurt about it, myself," Elyssa said. "On the other hand, her secrets weren't ours to tell."

"I thought it was important at the time." I shrugged. "Guess I got a little exuberant."

"You, exuberant?" Elyssa's jaw dropped open in mock surprise. "Say it isn't so."

We left Thomas to contemplate the logistics of the attack and headed up the levitator to the hangar bay and the portal zones. I heard footsteps and spun around in anticipation of the help Fjoeruss had promised, but it was just a Templar racing through on his way to deliver an important message, or perhaps dashing for a toilet after an unfortunate dinner of spicy Indian food.

"You're a little jumpy," Elyssa noted. She acknowledged the salute from the Templar on duty at the portal station. "Portal to the Three Sisters, please."

"At once," the soldier replied.

"Fjoeruss's golem said we'd receive help today," I said. "I hope it's not one of his tricks."

"Do you think he'll show up?" Elyssa asked.

I shrugged. "No telling with him. Our army is useless if we can't breach the fortress shield."

The air above the yellow square split open, revealing the control room at the Three Sisters. We stepped through the gateway and travelled thousands of miles from Atlanta to Australia in the blink of an eye. We stepped out of the niche lined with omniarches and walked down the large center aisle to reach the Alabaster Arch rising high above the smaller black arches all around it.

The portal to Seraphina was still open so we stepped through onto the skylet of Kdosh. A stiff breeze bent the tall red grass to the side. Clouds of aether in shades of red and gold billowed up from the vortex below, casting sunlight in brilliant hues.

The *Evadora* crouched like lurking monster on the north side of the island, clawed feet holding the flat-bottomed hull several feet off the ground. I saw Victus and Conrad leaning over the railing at the top deck. The boy looked amazed, and for once, seemed awakened from the stupor he'd demonstrated on the last occasions I'd seen him.

210

Delectra stood at the bottom of the ramp leading to the ship, a sullen frown on her pale face.

"Looks like someone didn't get the tour," Elyssa murmured.

I hoped that wasn't a bad sign for us. "I forgot Cora was giving a tour. We should wait until it's over."

Motion at the base of a nearby tree drew my attention to Cora's first mate, Illaena. The sera wore her black hair in a tight ponytail. Her tight red uniform stood out nicely against her dark olive skin and outlined wide muscular shoulders and thick legs. She looked as though she could leg press a bus.

Illaena rose and splayed her fingers in greeting. "Well met, Destroyer and Elyssa."

"Howdy, Illaena." I spread my fingers toward her. "Call me Justin, please."

"I would know what you did to draw the wrath of my Captain," the sera said, wasting no time getting to the point.

I didn't see any use beating around the bush. "I betrayed a secret."

"She has many secrets," Illaena said. "We have often wondered if she was royalty in her home realm."

Elyssa's eyes flashed. "What do you mean by that?"

"Cora would have us believe she is Seraphim, but clearly she is not." Illaena folded her arms across her chest. "She is a good captain, wise and patient, but when it comes to her homeland she is somewhat irrational."

"Why don't you tell her you know?" I asked.

"If she wishes to tell us, she will," the sera replied.

"We figured out she wasn't Seraphim during the trip here," Elyssa said. "She told us about herself, and asked that we not tell the crew."

Illaena raised an eyebrow. "Did you tell anyone on the crew?"

I shook my head. "No, but we told some people on our war council. Cora found out and rescinded her offer for the Mzodi to help us."

The first mate nodded. "I understand why she is vexed with you."

"Me too," I said. "But we really need the help of the sky fishers, and I think you need us if you don't want to be overrun by dragons or worry about Cephus unleashing the Beast in Seraphina."

"We are in agreement," Illaena said, "but I am not the one who needs convincing."

"Can you help us?" Elyssa said. "At least tell Cora that the crew knows she's not Seraphim."

"Would that I could," the sera replied, "but admitting that would not mend Justin's honor. Only he can do that."

"In other words, you'd rather lose your homeland than speak a few simple words to gain us the help we need?" I stepped closer, maybe in an attempt to intimidate, but Illaena stood nearly as tall as me, and she didn't look the least bit cowed by my nearness.

"Death is better than dishonor," she said in a tone that brooked no argument.

"I'm sure you'll feel that way when a dozen dragons tear your ship apart and disembowel your friends right in front of you," Elyssa said. "When your captain has her head bitten off as the *Evadora* plummets in flames to the ground."

I added my own two bits. "How honorable is it to become dragon poop?"

Elyssa gave me a disbelieving look. "Really, Justin?"

Illaena looked a bit unsettled for once. "It is not a pleasant prospect, but I cannot interfere."

We'd obviously hit a brick wall that Illaena wasn't willing to break through or climb over. That didn't mean others on the crew wouldn't be willing to help. I saw Victus walking down the ramp. Conrad lingered at the top with Cora who gave him a hug and then sent him on his way.

Victus spotted us near the portal and headed over without waiting for his son to catch up. Delectra waited on Conrad, an uncharacteristic smile on her face as he ran for her open arms.

"I wish you luck," Illaena said, and walked away.

"Good news," Victus said as he drew near. "Cora is amenable to helping us again. She seems to enjoy children."

Certainly more than you like kids. I tried not to get my hopes up. "Did she actually say the fleet would join us?"

Baleful Betrayal

"Not in so many words, but she said she'd reconsider." Victus put his hand on my arm. "Perhaps it's not a good idea for you to talk with her. She's still a bit miffed."

I pulled my arm away. "Are you forgetting who told her in the first place?"

Noticeable anger, though quickly quenched, flashed in Victus's eyes. He flashed a plastic smile. "If you truly blame me, then let me be the one to mend fences."

I wondered if he'd told Cora anything else to piss her off more. "I think I'll take my chances."

Hand-in-hand with Conrad, Delectra approached, her step noticeably lighter, face flushed with happiness and a rare smile. "He had a wonderful time, Victus. Can he do it again soon?"

Victus maintained his smile and shook his head. "I don't know, dear. Why don't you give him his toy and we'll be going?"

Delectra's face fell. "But, I thought—"

"Really, dear, we must be going." Victus's voice sounded strained, as if he were barely holding back anger.

A tear trickled down his wife's cheek as she removed a small blue object spiked on all sides like a sand burr, though it looked soft rather than sharp. She gave it to Conrad who rolled it in his hands.

"My favorite toy," he said, and suddenly seemed to lose all interest in the world around him.

Victus gripped Delectra by the upper arm. "Good luck, Justin." He stepped through without waiting on a reply, pulling his family along with him.

Elyssa hooked her arm through mine and led me toward the ship. "Something is horribly wrong with that family."

I couldn't stop thinking about the odd change in Conrad the moment he started playing with his toy. "That's the most emotional I've ever seen Delectra."

"Yeah, it's like something switches off and on inside that woman." Elyssa shuddered. "Must be mental issues."

I suspected it was something else. The odor of brimstone hung around that family like they used it for body wash. Being half demon myself, it was an odor I'd grown used to. Though others found it

213

unpleasant, most of my kind actually liked it. But not all demon pheromones were made equal. What I smelled on Kassallandra was far different than what I sensed on my father.

In short, some demons smelled worse than others. Whatever nether creatures Victus dealt with smelled sour and slightly rotten. I'd confronted him about demons before, and he'd freely admitted he consorted with them. As an adult, he was free to do so, but if his association with infernal spirits was negatively affecting his son, I had to put a stop to it. Now was not the time, but soon. We might need Victus and his battle bots for the war, but I wouldn't let that stop me from ensuring his son was safe.

Elyssa nudged me and nodded up. Cora stared coolly down at me from the top of the ramp.

"Permission to come aboard," I said.

Cora didn't answer, instead walking slowly down the ramp to meet us. "I thought I made myself clear, that I didn't wish to speak with you."

Her comment rubbed me the wrong way, but I struggled to remember Thomas's advice. *Be humble.* "I'm sorry I dishonored myself, Cora. I spoke without thinking and betrayed your confidence to others." *Should I drop to one knee? Nah, too melodramatic.* I met her gaze and held it. "Forgive me, please, and don't punish the entire realm of Seraphina for my mistake."

Cora pursed her lips and seemed to look inside me, probing for sincerity. "Well spoken, Justin, but it does not absolve you."

Damn, she's stubborn! "Can you punish me alone and ask the Mzodi to help our army?"

"I have already considered it," she said. "My decision to rescind the offer of help was perhaps too hasty."

I tried not to let the relief show on my face. "Thank you, Cora."

"Do not thank me yet," she said. "You must accept your punishment."

I felt like a student sentenced to a paddling in the school hallway. "Whatever it is, I accept."

"Bravely met, but I will give you a chance to back out," she said.

"If I did, would that mean the Mzodi would no longer help?"

"This realm must be saved despite my disappointment with you." Cora crossed her arms. "Should you decline, however, your dishonor would be complete."

Elyssa squeezed my hand three times. *I love you.* She knew I'd do the right thing.

But what if she wants to paddle me? I had an unholy fear of paddles, especially the ones with holes in them that sucked your butt cheeks through and doubled down on the pain. That fear stemmed from the childhood trauma of a severe whacking I'd endured at the hands of Mr. Buck McGillicuddy in sixth grade. With my supernatural powers, a paddling wouldn't hurt much at all, especially compared to what else I'd been through.

I swallowed hard. "Name your price."

She held out a small green pebble similar to the one she wore on her necklace. "You will travel alone to the Glimmer and deliver a package to my daughter, Evadora."

"Alone?" Elyssa's tone took great issue with that condition.

Cora's face softened. "Your love for him is admirable, Elyssa. Should you choose to accompany him, you may. Please know the risk may be great."

"I'm used to that," she said. "When do you want this done?"

"Now," Cora replied. "War brings great uncertainty, and I would hate it if Justin died before fulfilling his oath."

"What are the risks, and how do I reach the Glimmer?" I asked.

Cora held out the flat of her hand. "Press your hand to mine if you agree to fulfill this."

I pressed the flat of my hand against hers and flinched when vines beneath her robes spread along her arm and bound our hands together. A thorn extended from the top and pricked each of our fingers, drawing blood to mingle between them. The vines vanished and Cora withdrew her hand.

"The oath is sealed by nature, bound by blood." Cora licked the blood from her finger.

I looked at the blood on my finger. "Uh, do I have to lick it?"

She nodded. "Lick it, Justin."

Uneasily, I licked the blood off my finger. "Hey, that didn't taste so bad. In fact, it tasted kind of good."

Cora looked satisfied. "Having tasted my blood, if you break your oath, you will have no honor."

I had a feeling she meant that in a literal way, but had no intention of backing down. "Tell me what to do and how to survive this quest."

Cora motioned us to follow her onto the ship, and then led us down into her inner sanctum for cups of sweet nectar. "The best way into the Glimmer starts in Queens Gate. From there you travel through the reflected world and into the crack in the world."

By the time she finished explaining the dangerous route from our world to hers, how to safely navigate the Glimmer, and how to find her daughter, I felt a deep sense of dread pooling in my lower gut. This wasn't going to be a cake walk. The package she gave us was bound in leaves and vines.

"May I ask what this is?" Elyssa said.

"A tear catcher," Cora said. "A gem master crafted it for me, and I have spent years filling it for Evadora."

Elyssa's forehead wrinkled. "With tears?"

"Be sure she opens it," Cora said. "When she does, all will become clear."

I pocketed the small green stone and stood up. "We'll start right away."

"May the moon shine favorably upon you," Cora said. She held my hands and kissed the tops of them, then did the same for Elyssa. "The blessing of the Glimmer Queen keep you safe."

"I hope that's more than a saying," I said.

"It is a very real blessing," Cora said. "But it will only last twenty-two hours."

My forehead pinched. "Why not twenty-four?"

"I always tell people less so they don't cut it too close," she replied.

"Wait, others have tried this before?" I asked.

She nodded. "Three others have braved the Glimmer, though not to visit my daughter. They sought fragments of the anchor stone."

216

"What happened to them?" I asked.

"Naeve, most likely," she said. A tremble passed through her shoulders. "Is it strange I call her by my name?" The question seemed directed at herself, not us, so we didn't answer.

"We'd better get started." Elyssa gripped my hand. "Cora, please make sure the Mzodi fleet gets here."

"They are already on the way and should be here tomorrow," Cora said. "No matter what happens to you, they will help your army."

Elyssa set the timer on her phone and the seconds began to count down.

Chapter 26

When we arrived back in the underground hangar at the Ranch, I noticed a small squad of gray men standing at attention near the cars.

"Sir, they marched through a portal that wasn't one of ours," the Templar stationed at the portal zone informed us. "One of them told me it had a message for you."

"Thank you," I told her. "We'll take it from here."

I jogged over to the golems and spoke with the closest one. "Are you the help Fjoeruss promised?"

One in the center of the front row stepped forward and spoke in a monotone voice. "We embody the power you seek, but we must touch the barrier for two minutes to bring it down. Once down, you will have ten minutes before it is restored."

"How do I command you?" I asked.

"Verbally," the golem replied. "For further help, please say 'instructions'."

"Instructions," I said.

"These golems are programmed to accept a wide range of verbal commands," it said in a lecturing tone. "The command 'move' plus a direction will tell the golems to move in a certain direction. The command 'attack' will instruct the golems to attack the shield. Manufacturer's warning: These golems are not enhanced for other forms of combat and will break if used in such a way." It stopped speaking and stepped back into formation.

"Twenty golems," Elyssa said. "I hope that's enough."

"Can you believe he put a warning label on these things? I said. "You'd think he was afraid I'd sue if they didn't work as advertised."

218

"I'm sure it amused Fjoeruss," Elyssa said. "We need to inform my father about our mission before we go." She checked the time. Only fifteen minutes had passed, but that might be the difference between life and death if things went wrong in the Glimmer.

We took the levitator down to the war room and found Thomas still poring over data with Cinder.

"It appears Fjoeruss sent us help," Cinder said.

I waved away further explanation. "Yeah, I saw the golems. Cora agreed to help with the Mzodi fleet."

Thomas raised an eyebrow. "I sense a 'but' in there somewhere."

"We promised Cora we'd to go to the Glimmer and deliver a package to Evadora," Elyssa said. "She requested we do it before embarking on war."

"It appears with Fjoeruss's golems we have the final pieces of the puzzle in place," Thomas said. "If they take down the barrier, we can do the rest."

"Cinder knows how to use the golems," I said. "Just in case you need to move them before then."

"We should be back by the time the Mzodi fleet arrives," Elyssa said. "If we're not, you need to go without us."

The commander nodded. "I know." He strode across the room and shook my hand. "Good luck." He turned to Elyssa, embraced her, and planted a kiss on her forehead. "I'll see you soon."

She smiled, eyes growing misty. "I'll see you soon, Dad."

"If you see my parents, please let them know," I said.

"I believe they went with Kassallandra to meet with other Daemos leaders," Thomas said. "There appears to be some fracturing among the houses."

"As usual," I muttered. "Is it Yuuki this time, or Godric?"

"Both," Thomas said. "Your father and Kassallandra can handle the problem."

"I hope so." Dealing with Daemos politics was about as much fun as smashing my balls with a ballpeen hammer. I took Elyssa's hand. "Let's git 'er done."

She chuckled. "With such a commanding redneck tone in your voice, how could I refuse?"

219

We went back up to the hangar bay and requested a portal leading to the Fairy Gardens behind Arcane University. That earned us a puzzled look from the portal coordinator, but she obliged without question. The portal opened in front of Colossus Stadium since that was the closest image she had on her arcphone, but it was good enough.

The portal winked away after we stepped through it, leaving us before the massive gates leading inside the stadium. The gates hung open, displaying the sorry state of the field inside. Cracked mud and blasted boulders, the remains of stone goliath golems, littered the arena. I resisted the urge to walk inside and revisit a place I hadn't seen since the latter days of the war. It was one more nagging item on a long checklist that needed repairs, but it was low on our priorities.

Elyssa and I headed left down the wide walkway, its surface cracked where the massive tragon had tromped on its way to help us destroy the aforementioned golems. Even the outside of the arena was pocked with black marks that looked like burnt blood.

The walkway ended at a black iron fence which, in turn, led to a gate. We went inside the gate and headed down a path that led through a thick forest and eventually to a burnt-out mansion Shelton had destroyed during a flight with a shape-shifter named Mr. Bigglesworth. We stopped short of the forest and detoured toward the pond just outside the forest. I expected the Lady of the Pond to leap up from the water and ask us our business, but either she was on vacation, or she didn't care I was about to violate her watery home.

"I hope I remember all of Cora's instructions." I took the pebble from my pocket and gripped Elyssa's hand. "Ready?"

She looked uncertainly at the water. "I'm going to be really mad if this doesn't work."

"I doubt Cora would punk us." I spoke the magic words and rubbed the stone. "As above, so below." We jumped into the water.

The surface rushed to meet us and swallowed us whole without a splash, without a sound. For an instant there was a void. My guts seemed to turn themselves inside out and I felt the urge to puke, but it passed so quickly, it barely had time to register. Open air hit me, followed shortly thereafter by the ground.

Baleful Betrayal

Elyssa landed lightly on her feet. I stumbled forward and caught myself with one hand.

I stood and examined myself. Everything seemed to be in place, but I felt disconnected from reality, as if I'd fallen down the rabbit hole.

Elyssa turned in a circle. "Looks the same."

The world rippled like water and I staggered, my senses thrown off balance. "Yeah, not the same." After a moment, my equilibrium returned and everything seemed hunky-dory. We walked to the edge of the forest. Looking into the darkness, I felt a terrible foreboding.

"Scary," Elyssa said. "This reflected world is creepy as hell."

I gulped. "Good thing I have the cure for a sense of impending doom."

She sidled closer to me. "What's that?"

"Just follow my lead." I took Elyssa's hand and started skipping through the forest. "A-questing we will go, a-questing we will go, hi-ho the merry-o a-questing we will go."

Elyssa joined me for the second round of singing and we burst into laughter when we reached the other side.

"It worked," Elyssa said. "I'm not nearly as scared as I was before."

"Skipping and singing usually works," I said. "It also confuses the monsters lurking in the dark."

The blackened ruins of the grand mansion spread out before us and some of my levity faded. Shelton had demolished half the structure with a huge flaming meteor in his futile attempts to kill the Flark, Mr. Bigglesworth. I still remembered it like it was yesterday.

"We should hurry," Elyssa said. "Remember what Cora told us about the reflections."

Cora had warned us about the soulless denizens of this world—reflections of ourselves who, at this very moment, were racing to catch us and steal our souls. I shivered and jogged around the back of the mansion. Behind a stand of trees, we found the crack in the world. I'd had my fill of crawling through dark tunnels during the terrifying journey into the bowels of El Dorado, but it seemed dark tunnels hadn't had their fill of me.

221

Elyssa and I dropped to hands and knees and crawled inside, our way lit by a small orb of light I channeled. Once we reached the end of the tunnel, my stomach completely abandoned me, dropping like a rock at the sight of the rift. Cora's description hadn't done it justice.

"Oh god," Elyssa said, and pressed her back against the tunnel wall.

I got down on my hands and knees and peered down into the bottomless expanse of stars. In addition to being bottomless, it was also topless and sideless. The only hint that I wasn't about to commit my body to the wastes of outer space was the crack in the stars about a hundred yards across from us.

"Cora, if you ever wanted to prank us, now is not the time," I muttered, and ran my hand out into the void and found something solid but invisible. "There's a bridge." I couldn't hide the relief in my voice.

Pale-faced and ashen, Elyssa reached out a hand and felt it too. "I think I'm going to be sick."

I gripped her hand. "I've never seen you so scared."

Her violet eyes grew large. "Falling through an endless void, wasting away and helpless to save yourself—doesn't the thought terrify you?"

My gorge rose at the thought. "Why did you have to tell me that? No I'm going to have nightmares."

Elyssa jerked. "We have to go. Our reflections will catch us if we don't hurry."

Faced with such terrors as this void, I'd almost forgotten about the other horrors somewhere out in this reflected world rushing to catch us and steal parts of our souls.

I took Elyssa's hand and we stood. "One, two, three, go!"

We ran. The invisible bridge kept us from a fate worse than death, and brought us safely to the other side. We entered the crack there and crawled through the tunnel. Emerging on the other side, we found a world of crooked black trees and purple grass that writhed like snakes as we walked through it.

The looking pool, a black foreboding pond, waited in the middle of this surreal scene. Wasting no time, I rubbed the pebble and reversed the previous incantation. "So below, as above."

We jumped.

Another flip-flop of my innards, my entire body seemed to turn inside out. We sailed from the pond and landed heavily on the other side. I rolled to my feet and staggered in a semi-circle as my ear canals struggled to find balance. Elyssa grimaced and grabbed a nearby tree for support.

I stumbled on something hidden in the tall purple grass and fell on my ass. The thick scaly blades felt waxy to the touch. As I pushed to my feet, another sight stopped the breath in my throat. A huge green moon hung suspended above a mountain shaped like a crooked witch's hat. Sparkling like jewels on a necklace, the other realms encircled the green hunk of rock Cora called the anchor stone.

White clouds swirled in blue skies on one world, while another glowed sullen red with streaks of black. Zooming my vision on the spectacle, I saw a desert realm, one that looked like a giant snowball, and one that was black as night. Hovering above the moon like a specter was a swirling darkness that could only be one thing.

"The Abyss," I murmured.

Elyssa followed my gaze. "Have you ever felt insignificant as a speck of sand?"

"Right now." My throat felt dry, senses numb. "Is this real?"

"Yeah." Elyssa blinked and shook her head. "We need to head to the Soul Tree." She took out her arcphone and studied the directions Cora had given us.

I climbed up a nearby tree, careful of the thorns and spikes on its bark and looked over a forest of similar trees. Though I wasn't high enough to get a true view of the land, our target was clearly visible on the horizon, a massive umbrella of white branches spreading like the protective arms of a mother over her children.

The tree looked miles away from the crooked mountain. "If the queen lives in the mountain, why would Evadora be way over at that tree? How could a little girl survive the wild?"

"Nature is her domain," Elyssa said. She motioned me down. "Let's get moving."

I dropped to the ground and we headed past a large glowing mushroom and onto a narrow trail between the trees, their twisted branches forming a dark tunnel lit only in spots by glowing fungi. The glow only made the shadowy forest look even creepier, so I channeled another sphere of light and sent it hovering over our heads. "I still think a flying broom would have been primo for this mission."

"Cora said it would expose us to the queen's eyes," Elyssa said. "The last thing I want to worry about is the plants rising up against us."

"Yeah, but if the queen controls nature, wouldn't every animal around here be spying on us?" The deeper we went into the forest, the darker it seemed, so I sent my light ball floating higher to illuminate more of the path ahead.

The branches above us burst into a cacophony of squeaks and a flurry of wings. I screamed at the top of my lungs and threw up a shield around us. My screamed trickled off to a croak when I realized a flock of birds was the source of my terror. One of them landed on the shield and looked down at us with curious feline eyes. Webbed black wings like those of bats flapped as it gained balance, but its body resembled a bird, and its head, that of a house cat.

"I don't know what frightened me more—you or the bird things," Elyssa said.

I peered closer at the little monster. "Freaky." I lowered the shield and the bird-cat—did that make it a bat or a card?—flew away to join the rest of the flock circling overhead. "I hope those aren't the minions Cora warned us about."

"They're kind of like flying cats," Elyssa said. "I think they're cute."

"Cute as a felix?" I asked.

"There's cute, and then there's beautiful." Elyssa shook her head. "Knowing that felix was Kaelissa somehow cheapens the experience."

I noticed something white reflecting from beneath the trees and sent the light ball questing deeper off the path. It revealed a mound of bones several feet tall. Some of the skulls might have come from small horses. I sucked a breath between my teeth. "Holy farting cats. I think those things are carnivorous."

"Duh, they're cats," Elyssa said, though she seemed a bit more wary all of a sudden. "If they eat such large prey, maybe they wouldn't be good pets."

I imagined them swarming over an animal like piranha, stripping flesh away like a sandblaster. "Let's hope they don't eat people."

"I say we pick up the pace," Elyssa said, looking up at the swarm. "Just in case."

Our walk turned to a jog over the rutted uneven ground, spiky limbs trying to snag our Nightingale armor as we passed by. The armor responded as it would to a knife, hardening to deflect the thorns.

When we reached the edge of the forest, the bent bough of a giant tree arched off the edge of a cliff, bridging the gap between our side and the other. But when I stepped closer to the edge, my knees went weak as jelly. Cora had told us about this shattered world. She'd warned us about the treacherous land. Nothing could prepare us as we gazed over the cliff and into the infinite vastness of space.

Chapter 27

The giant tree provided a nice wide bridge, but I felt weak with fear knowing a void waited to swallow us up if we fell. As Elyssa had noted at the rift, falling forever between the stars seemed worse than death. When we reached the middle where the top of our tree entwined with one from the other island, we stopped to gape at the mind-blowing view. Chunks of land hovered in a sea of stars as far as the eye could see, the big green moon crowning the mountain in the center.

The Soul Tree looked close as the crow flies, but remained miles away by foot.

"How can such a place exist?" Elyssa said. "I can't believe the Lyrolai survived when the Sirens tore their world apart."

"There shouldn't be an atmosphere," I said. "These plants should all be dead without sunlight, and anyone who did survive is probably stark-raving mad."

"Then again, there shouldn't be a huge moon with realms orbiting it either," Elyssa said. "This place is like stepping behind the props at a play and seeing they're made from cardboard."

"All the world's a stage, and we are merely players," I murmured. The moon looked close enough to touch. "Never thought a Shakespeare quote could be taken so literally."

"Much as I'd like to gawk, we should hurry." Elyssa checked her phone. "Only a little over twenty-two hours left."

I looked along the path of islands and bridges leading to the destination. "That should be plenty of time."

Elyssa threw up her hands. "Great. You just jinxed us."

I face-palmed. "Sorry, wasn't thinking. Maybe we should run for it."

"Uh, maybe once we get off the bridge." Elyssa backed away from the edge. "I wouldn't want to trip."

We had to walk along a wide branch where the tree from the other island met ours, leaving only a three-foot ledge between us and oblivion. I hugged the bough and made my way to the other side. Once there, we carefully walked to the bottom and then set off at a run on solid ground through another tunnel of trees.

A scrubby yellow plain unfolded before us on the other side. Miniature ponies grazed peacefully in the distance. I was just about to comment how cute they were when a hissing to my right sent me scampering sideways.

What could only be described as a giraffe with six legs and a serpent's head munched on the spiky trees. Its playmate stared down at us, fangs bared and hissing. It skittered toward us, but when it came to within a few yards, it stopped and stared. Its companion stopped chewing, the webbed wing of a flying cat hanging from its mouth.

"I didn't think snakes chewed their food," Elyssa whispered.

I backed away from the new monsters. "Is that really at the top of your mind right now?"

"Why didn't it attack us?" she said.

"Cora's blessing." Though she hadn't specifically told us what the blessing did, I assumed it prevented the monsters here from chowing down on us. I decided it was worth testing. Besides, I could probably shield myself before the giraffe spider ate me. I walked toward the creature. It hissed, but backed away, nearly tripping over its friend.

"What's the matter?" I shouted. "Scared of little old me?" I ran forward and it stumbled over its own feet in the haste to get away. I shook my fist as it ran. "That's what I thought!" It suddenly occurred to me that when a person seemingly scared away a big monster in the movies, they always turned around to find something even larger standing behind them.

When I spun around, the only scary thing I saw was Elyssa's glare.

"If the blessing really keeps us safe, we need to hurry," Elyssa said. "I don't want to be here when it wears off."

We sprinted across the plain through a herd of miniature ponies. They whinnied and galloped out of our way. Several of them snapped razor teeth in our general direction, but made no move to pursue. After carefully crossing the next tree bridge, we found the path on the other side blocked by brambles.

I poked and prodded, but the patch blocked off the rest of the island. "Should I burn it?"

Elyssa shook her head. "That would be a bad idea. Remember how upset Cora got when you even mentioned fire?"

"How else will we get through this?" I asked.

"Use something other than fire," she said. "Pry an opening."

Simple but effective. "I'm glad you have enough brains for both of us."

"Just barely." Elyssa knelt and examined the patch. "I don't see any weak spots."

"I'll make a weak spot." I channeled a wedge of Murk slightly taller and wider than me and pushed it forward. The briar patch crackled and resisted, bending unwillingly out of the way as I formed a tunnel of Murk. I maintained the barrier until we cleared the patch. When I released it, I expected the brambles to collapse and cover the exit, but they remained where I'd left them.

"Not that I'm complaining, but this doesn't make any sense." I touched a bramble. Brown and stiff, it felt like it should have broken instead of bending.

"Nothing in this place makes sense." Elyssa tugged my arm. "Let's go."

We continued our run and started up the next tree bridge.

Elyssa paused to look at the broken land when we neared the top. "I wonder where all the people are. I don't see houses or anything."

"Maybe they live in the trees or underground." I hadn't given it much thought. "From what Cora said, not many survived the breaking of the realm."

"It's like being on a wild safari without a guide." Elyssa navigated the narrow branch at the top. "I'm not sure if I like it or not."

Several miles and two bridges later we reached the Soul Tree. It looked big from far away. Up close, it seemed large enough to house a city in its branches. The trunk measured at least a hundred yards in circumference, and the bough rose hundreds of feet before massive branches sprouted off in all directions.

Wispy white leaves resembling sheer strips of cloth dangled from the limbs. Cora hadn't explained why this was called the Soul Tree, but it definitely emanated an aura that both soothed and frightened me.

Something big and hairy moved in the branches. It looked down at us and growled. Elyssa's hand tightened on mine. Cora had told us to expect this, but that didn't make the next part easy.

The creature scampered down the tree trunk and leapt to the ground. *If the Yeti was real, it would look something like this.* Standing eight feet tall with shaggy white hair and fangs as long as my hand, the monster's wide nostrils flared, drawing in our scent. It stepped closer, smelling the back of my neck.

"Just don't sniff my ass and we'll be okay," I muttered.

After pacing around me, it dropped to all fours and loped toward the tree, vanishing between the large roots. Moments later, it returned with a small girl tucked under one arm and set her down.

"Oh my god, she's adorable," Elyssa gushed.

Evadora looked up at us with eyes too large to be human. Long green hair hung to her shoulders, and her skin held a silvery sheen.

Elyssa knelt. "Evadora?"

The girl replied in a language I'd never heard, her voice as cute as any little girl's. Unlike other children I'd seen, she didn't smile or frown at the strangers, nor did she betray any other kind of emotion I'd expect.

I took out the package and handed it to her. "Cora sent this."

Evadora looked at the package, face still as stone. She touched the vines holding the packaging. They unbraided themselves and dropped to the ground. The leaves unfolded, like a flower blossoming, to reveal a small crystal bottle glowing with an inner light. Evadora looked up at the Yeti thing and said something in a questioning tone.

The beast replied in a rough voice and tapped a long brown claw on the cork in the top. The stopper popped loose when Evadora tugged on it. The beast spoke in the strange language once again, and the little girl nodded. Carefully, she tipped the bottle into the palm of one hand. Tears piled like frozen drops of water. Each glowed a different color—yellow, red, green, and some of those in-between colors paint manufacturers invent so women think they're better than men.

Evadora plucked one tear from the pile, a sunny glow emanating from it, and funneled the rest back into the bottle. She placed it on her tongue. Her eyes widened and a smile spread across her lips. She corked the bottle and jumped up and down, giggling and clapping her hands.

Elyssa laughed. "The tears gave her emotions!"

Evadora hugged her leg, looking up and talking rapidly. Elyssa knelt and gave the little girl a big hug. "You are just too cute! Can we keep her, Justin? Please?"

I snorted. "I think Yeti here would have something to say about that."

As if responding to me, the shaggy beast nodded sagely and said something even though it had to know we couldn't understand it. Its gaze turned to us and it pointed back the way we came.

I understood that. "I think it's time for us to go."

Elyssa checked the time on her phone. "Looks like we'll make it out of here with plenty of time to spare."

"Now you're the one jinxing the mission," I said with a grin.

We waved goodbye to Evadora, but the girl was too busy playing and leaping around to pay us any attention. We headed back at a jog, though taking the time to cross the tree bridges carefully.

"I'm so ready to be out of this place," I said as we headed through the bramble forest. "Something about the void all around us makes me feel agoraphobic."

"Fear of the environment?" Elyssa looked around uneasily. "I completely agree."

"I wonder if the Void Cephus wants to reach is something like this." I imagined a realm of nothing but insubstantial darkness and it terrified me even more than the Glimmer.

We were about halfway through the briar patch when I felt a sting on my neck.

I blinked and Cora appeared before us, face so expressionless as to be carved in marble. I tried to talk but my words were too slurred to understand. "Wh-wheee?"

"Uhh?" Elyssa grunted.

I sluggishly turned my head to face her. She looked paler than normal and a black vine hovered near her neck, a sharp thorn glistening with green fluid.

"You are from Eden," Cora said in a monotone voice. "My sister sent you, did she not?"

Fear surged in my chest, but wallowed in the mud of my grogginess. "Naeve." I pushed the word out slowly like a drunkard at the end of a binge.

"Why did she send you?" Naeve asked.

It took Elyssa a few tries, but she finally got out, "Gift for Evadora."

The Glimmer Queen stared unblinking at her. "What sort of gift?"

"Tears." My tongue slowly unglued itself from the roof of my mouth. "Emotions."

"A dangerous gift indeed," Naeve said. She leaned toward me and sniffed. "Almost gone."

"What is?" I asked.

"Cora's blessing." Naeve walked around us, inspecting our bodies like slabs of meat. "It must be quite a curse to deal with emotions. They were Cora's undoing, and perhaps they'll be yours."

Elyssa struggled with a question. "What do you mean?"

The vine venom seemed to be wearing off because my mouth no longer felt like I was talking underwater. "Are you going to kill us?"

Naeve shook her head. "Cora has already done that by sending you here." She stood in front of me. "Do you think it was coincidence these vines blocked the way to the Soul Tree?"

231

As my limbs thawed from the effects of the venom, I looked around and realized that by pushing apart the brambles, I'd tripped an alarm somehow. I almost threatened her with magical violence, but bit my tongue. If she knew what I could do, all she'd have to do was prick me with another thorn and that would be that. The venom in those things must be incredibly potent to knock out someone with my recuperative abilities.

"You intend to let the Glimmer creatures kill us," I said, keeping my voice as emotionless as hers.

"The Eden folk despoil nature." Naeve ran her fingers through Elyssa's glossy black hair. "They care only for themselves, not the creatures of the woodland. One day I will venture to Eden and reverse what man has done. For now, I will allow my creatures to sample what is to come."

"How do you know what man has done if you've never been to Eden?" Elyssa said.

Naeve brushed her fingers across Elyssa's full pink lips. "I know much of what Cora knows. After all, I possess half her soul."

I could tell from the wild look in Elyssa's eyes, she wanted to push away Naeve's hand, but her limbs wouldn't cooperate.

The brambles crackled and retreated away from us on all sides. A massive condor swooped down and landed behind the queen. Its beak parted and unleashed an ear-splitting screech. Naeve walked up its wing like a ramp and perched in a saddle of vines on its back.

"How interesting it would be to possess emotion right now," she said. "Humans love to hunt for sport. Perhaps I would enjoy watching my children rend you apart."

"Maybe Evadora will let you have a sip from her bottle," I suggested, rubbing my wrists to get the pins and needles sensation to go away. "I wouldn't want our horrific deaths to deprive you of enjoyment."

Elyssa staggered forward as she began to regain control. "Why are you doing this?"

Naeve blinked. "Did I not make myself clear, child?" She patted the red crest on the condor's head. With a great beating of wings, it took off into the air and began circling far above.

Elyssa checked her phone as the final seconds ran out. "I jinxed us."

"We'll get out of this." I squeezed her hand. "Are you okay to run?"

She took a deep breath. "Other than dying of thirst, I'm fine."

"We're halfway home." I shook the numbness from my limbs. "All we have to do is get past carnivorous horses, spider giraffes, cat bats, and nature itself."

"Piece of cake." Elyssa patted her shoulders where the hilts to the sai swords usually rested, but Cora had asked us not to bring weapons.

"I know Cora asked us not to harm anything here, but I don't see a choice." I cracked my knuckles and rolled my neck. "I'll do whatever it takes to get us back alive."

Elyssa stretched. "I'm ready when you are."

We set off at a jog, scanning the environment for hazards. A screech from the queen's condor echoed in the lonely twilight, sending shivers down my spine. At the next tree bridge, we continued our ascent at a quick pace, hoping to make it back to solid ground as fast as possible.

The branches where the trees met crawled with dark wings and a cacophony of high-pitched mewling. The most dangerous part of the crossing was blocked by cat bats.

Chapter 28

"Retreat," I said.

"What good will going back do?" Elyssa asked.

"We're about to find out." I withdrew to the window of my soul and almost immediately sensed Haedaemos. It made sense this border realm was much closer to the spirit world than even Eden. "What's the one thing cats don't like?"

"Water," she said. "Did you bring a firehose?"

I reached for a willing spirit and located a minor entity that fit the profile I wanted. "What's something else cats don't like?"

"Having their fur petted the wrong way." Elyssa narrowed her eyes. "You realize how hard it will be to do that when they're swooping at us and gnawing on our faces?"

I rolled my eyes. "You're being intentionally dense, aren't you?"

She gave me an innocent look. "Who, me?"

Directing my concentration to a spot of earth, I ordered my new minion to spawn. As it clawed its way from the netherworld and into this one, I found another demon spirit and directed it to manifest. Within minutes, two hellhounds the size of Great Danes burst from the ground and howled. The first one snapped at me. I stood my ground and bared my teeth at it. It snarled and lunged. I grabbed it by the neck and slammed it on the ground.

You are mine! I sent to it.

It bucked and snapped but couldn't break my iron grip. Finally, it whined and looked away from me. The other hound trotted over and sniffed my butt, then rolled over on its back for a good belly rub.

"That one sure is a softie," Elyssa said.

"Meet our secret weapons, Snapper and Bugsy." I rubbed Bugsy's tummy then stood and looked up the bridge. Hellhounds could shapeshift into different forms, but making them grow wings wouldn't enable them to fly. During my early days of summoning hellhounds, I'd experimented quite a bit to learn their limitations. Morphing required an intimate knowledge of physiology. Just because I knew what something looked like didn't mean I could command the hounds transform into it.

More often than not they could mimic the appearance, but if I didn't imagine the joints and everything else properly, they wouldn't be able to move. In other words, I couldn't launch my own fleet of flying dog bats, but I also didn't need to. Hopefully the big brutes would keep the cat bats away from us.

Scare away the cats at the top of the tree. I told them.

Bugsy woofed excitedly. *Cats!* He loped up the tree bridge, Snapper right on his heels.

I waved Elyssa to follow. "Let's go."

The cat bats exploded from the tree as the massive hounds closed in. Swooping and hissing, they stayed just out of reach. One of them dove at me. Snapper leapt and snatched it from the air like a hairy Frisbee and crunched down. Bugsy batted another from the air with a big paw, his face alight with puppy delight.

I kept threads of aether on standby in case I needed to channel a shield. If the swarm really wanted us, it would be hard to stop them. We reached the other side of the bridge and ran across the plain of yellow grass.

The stomp of hooves and whinnies rose with a cloud of dust a few hundred yards away to our right. The two spider giraffes skittered toward us from the left. Directly ahead, a herd of small beige elephants charged out of the trees. Behind us swarmed the cat bats.

The condor screeched.

"Remind me to shoot that stupid bird," I growled.

Elyssa's head swiveled as if she were watching a tennis match. "We're going to need more hellhounds."

"Hellhounds won't do much against those small elephants or the ponies." I'd have to use destruction to carve a path. I fired a blast of

Brilliance straight ahead. The energy splashed harmlessly off the thick hide of the elephants. "Crap."

"Understatement of the year," Elyssa said. "We'll have to juke them."

"Hang on." I had Plan B in the works, but if it didn't work, it'd be a doozy. I didn't have much time, so I latched onto the fiercest minor demon I came to first. It writhed and struggled in my psychic grasp, trying to crawl free. I amped up my willpower and held it in place long enough to project my attention on the ground ahead.

The presence of the infernal creature pressed like lead bricks on my mind. I'd only summoned a crawler once as practice, and it had nearly taken off my head. Now I remembered why I hadn't tried again. Though it was nothing compared to the Abyssal, holding onto it and controlling the hellhounds was no minor feat. The black ooze writhed as my summoned creature began to form.

A flash of pink was the only warning I had as one of the ponies rammed into my leg and sent me rolling. My connection with the crawler sundered and I landed in a heap. Elyssa picked up the little pink pony by its left legs and flung it toward its herd. It bowled through a dozen of them, slowing their advance. I pushed unsteadily to my feet and saw something that was definitely not a crawler rip its way from primordial black ooze.

Dozens of faces trapped beneath rubbery black skin screamed and writhed as if trying to escape their prison of flesh. A body like a scorpion with a stinger of crocodile jaws followed the gruesome head of faces. A newly summoned monster scorp rose up before the elephant herd and screeched in challenge. I didn't have time to see what happened next because the rest of our magical little pony friends were nearly on top of us.

I counted at least thirty—too much mass to stop with a simple shield. The hellhounds howled and leapt to the fore, jaws snapping. The ponies whinnied and bit back with razor sharp teeth. Though the hounds outweighed them individually, they stood no chance against the collective.

Raising a finger, I fired a thin beam of Brilliance. It smoked against the hide of a purple pony, but didn't penetrate. The pony squealed and bucked crazily. "Magic isn't going to cut it against these things."

"I can tell," Elyssa said. "Your hounds are getting pulverized."

Elephantine trumpets of pain tore my attention back to the monster scorp. Its tail chomped down on one mini-elephant while its claws snapped the head off another. At three-times the size of its attackers, and behind the protection of shiny black chitin, the scorp didn't seem to have any problems.

I couldn't say the same for us. Snapper shook off five ponies and tore the guts from another, but Bugsy went down beneath a pile, his terrible yelps going silent. His doggy spirit would return to Haedaemos, but his physical body was done for.

The cat bats saw their chance and dove at us. Elyssa round-housed one pony and snapped the neck of another as they broke past the hellhounds. I fired off a torrent of Brilliance. Smoking cat bats spiraled out of the air with yowls of pain.

I pumped a fist. "Magic finally puts one on the scoreboard."

Elyssa leapt and spiked her feet down atop a charging pony. The little monster's snout plowed into the dirt. She looked up, face wet with tears, eyes haunted. "Why is that evil bitch making me kill ponies?"

"I didn't realize it was so traumatic for you." Two more ponies galloped at me. I flipped over them and booted one in the backside, slamming it into the other one.

"I love ponies!" Elyssa dodged a charge and stared down a red pony. "Please don't make me do this."

The monster flashed fangs and whinnied. Gobs of hellhound flesh hung from its jaws.

"These aren't the ponies you fell in love with," I said. "Don't expect them to crap rainbow-flavored ice cream or nuzzle you for affection."

"I know." Sadness weighed her voice. "Vicious little perversions."

Loud hisses told me the fourth threat was almost upon us. I rolled to the left as a cobra head struck where I'd been. The other spider giraffe lunged at Elyssa. She picked up the red pony and slung it at the other monster's face. The cobra head chomped down on the unexpected meal and chewed on it.

I risked a glance toward the scorp. Blood and gore coated the path we had to take and only a few elephants remained. A torn-off scorp leg twitched, but the rest of the demon scorp looked undamaged aside from chunks of missing chitin. I'd completely lost my link to the creature which meant it would try to kill us the moment it had a chance. It was too tall to leap over and too low to the ground to slide beneath. Spiky black trees blocked us to the sides, so that left us little choice but to run straight at it.

The ponies finished off Snapper, rending the poor hellhound to a grease spot and turned to us. The spider giraffes finished munching on the carcasses of the ponies and skittered toward us with evil intent. The cat bats clustered and swooped around for another attack.

"Plan C," I announced and grabbed Elyssa's hand. We ran pell-mell toward the scorp.

"Plan C?" she shouted over the roar and din of hisses, whinnies, and mews behind us. "I didn't even know there was a Plan A or B!"

"We're going to run over the scorp." The demon rotated on its remaining five legs and snapped its gore-stained claws. "Try to avoid the claws!"

"Maybe we should skip to Plan D." Elyssa's gaze focused on the demon, no doubt visualizing the safest path to victory.

I couldn't stop looking at its horrific face of many faces and wondering if mine would be trapped inside if it ate me.

Images of claws rending me to Justin stew flashed through my mind and I realized the scorp was talking to me. Unlike hellhounds, these things didn't use words. I sent back an image of it lustily tearing into spider giraffes accompanied by a nice red wine, hoping it might think they were a more tantalizing target. It stubbornly sent another image of it ripping into my guts.

Are you mad at me for summoning you, or just grouchy? The monster sent no response, probably because it didn't understand, but more likely because it didn't care.

I closed in on the scorp, juking left and drawing its attention solely to me. The scorp turned just enough to offer its side to Elyssa.

She jumped atop a leg and ran across its back. I glanced over my shoulder and saw the herd of death closing in. Drawing upon Murk, I channeled a sheet of slick ice on the ground and then leapt to the side.

The spider giraffes and my little ponies of death hit the ice. Legs motoring furiously on the slick surface, they skidded right into the monster scorp with a resounding symphony of whinny-hiss-screeches loud enough to wake the dead. I swept the air with a blast of Brilliance, driving away the cat bats, and then clambered atop the heap of snapping jaws, hissing cobra heads, and the screaming demon faces. The scorp's tail stabbed down at me as I ran across its back. I dove forward and rolled off the armored back, landing heavily on the ground.

Elyssa jerked me out of the path of another stab that sliced a nearby tree in half. Before the scorp could skitter after us, the rest of the monsters on its flank took out their frustrations on the demon.

The queen's condor screeched in displeasure. I raised a fist at it but Elyssa jerked my hand back. "Don't piss her off unless you want the vines and trees to attack us!"

I grudgingly nodded and looked around at the crooked forest as we raced through it. "Yeah, we're not out of the woods yet."

Elyssa rolled her eyes. "Save the smartass remarks for later."

We stopped at the edge of the forest and looked uneasily up at the next tree bridge. A flock of the giant condors circled overhead.

I pounded a fist into my palm. "This just isn't fair."

"Got any flying demons up your sleeve?" Elyssa asked.

"No." I stared up at the next obstacle. "If those birds are magic resistant, there's no way we'll get past them."

"We'd have to hijack one," Elyssa said grimly.

"How are we supposed to do that with the queen controlling them?" I asked.

She sighed. "Scratch that idea."

"All they have to do is knock us off the bridge." I imagined those huge wings and claws beating and tearing at us as we tried to navigate the narrow branch connector at the top.

Elyssa's eyes lit with an idea. "What if they can't see us?"

I frowned. "Is this camouflage armor?"

239

She shook her head. "No, but you can make fog, right?"

It had been a while since I'd messed with the forces of nature. I'd created a monstrous tornado that nearly killed my own people. Fjoeruss had taught me the basics of elemental magic, but he hadn't taught me how to make fog. Then again, I didn't have to blanket the area to keep the birds from seeing us.

I took a quick headcount of our adversaries. The sound of hoofs pounding behind us told me we didn't have much time to make a move before the rest of the Glimmer gang caught up to us. Four condors—eight eyes to cover.

"I hope this works," I muttered.

"You never answered my question," Elyssa said. "Are you using fog?"

"No, I'm going with something a bit more localized." I glanced back down the path and saw the spider giraffes, ponies, and the surviving mini-elephants racing our way. "Be ready with a Plan E if this doesn't pan out." I dashed toward the tree bridge.

Elyssa pulled even with me as we raced up the incline. "Is this Plan D?"

The Condors saw us coming and unleashed a chorus of warbling screeches that made the hair on my neck stand on end. They attacked when we were nearly to the top. I thrust out my hand and channeled a sticky strand of Murk similar to what I'd used to climb buildings, but focusing this one into a thick glob.

It smacked into the lead condor's head right above the beak and coated its eyes. With a surprised cry, it veered left and thudded into the tree bridge. The bough shook violently, throwing me and Elyssa off balance. She screamed and vanished over the edge.

"Elyssa!" I dove after her and caught her hand.

I tried to grasped a branch, but my fingers missed and our momentum carried us both over the edge and into the sea of stars.

Chapter 29

A condor's beak snapped, narrowly missing me. I almost wished it hadn't, as Elyssa and I plummeted into infinity. The gust of wind from its wings twisted me around. I saw the bough of the tree bridge only yards away and fired a strand of Murk at it. The webbing caught. We hung suspended for a moment and then swung beneath the tree.

Elyssa gripped my arm with her other hand. "Justin, watch out!"

I already saw the next condor swooping in at us, flies caught on a spider web. "Hold onto my leg!" Elyssa shifted her grip, freeing my arm. I flung out my hand and fired another glob of Murk. It smacked the bird across the eyes, saving us from the sharp beak, but not from the impact.

The condor's big ugly head crashed into us jarring me all the way down to my bones. I screamed. Elyssa screamed. The bird screamed. Stars blurred as we spun crazily and swung on the strand of aether fast enough to loop up around the tree. The magical rope ran out of length and we slammed onto the top of the tree bridge.

I groaned woozily. Elyssa rolled on her side, grabbing her ribs. All but the queen's personal condor had vanished from view. I staggered to my feet, blood drooling from my mouth.

"Babe, can you walk?" I touched Elyssa's side and she cried out in pain.

"My ribs," she croaked. "Help me up."

I scooped her into my arms. A painful twinge in my knee protested as I ran. Elyssa groaned and squeezed her eyes shut. Angry squawks sounded behind me, but I didn't dare look back. All I had to do was keep moving forward as quickly as possible. My gimpy knee caused me to stumble when we reached the ground, eliciting another shriek of pain from Elyssa.

"Almost there," I told her. "Almost there!" We passed through the final tunnel of trees. "Grab the pebble from my pouch and rub it."

Elyssa gritted her teeth and nodded. She found the pebble and rubbed it as we neared the water. "As above, so below," she groaned.

The queen's condor swept into view and landed near the edge of the pool. I expected her to stop us, or deliver a killing blow. Instead, she simply said, "Well met, mortals."

Her emotionless gaze was the last thing I saw as I leapt into the looking pool. Darkness took us in its cold embrace and my guts wrenched with nausea. When the ground rushed up to meet us, I landed hard on my injured knee but managed to remain upright.

"Son of a Salisbury steak!" I shouted, limping in circles to ease the pain.

"Let me down," Elyssa groaned.

I set her gently on her feet. Her deathly pale face and the tears streaming down her cheeks told the story. "Can you walk?" I asked.

She took a few steps, nodded. "Let's go."

I remembered we didn't have time to dawdle, thanks to the soulless versions of ourselves now coming this way. Elyssa began to jog, whimpering every step of the way. Broken ribs were no fun—I knew that from experience.

"You sure you don't want me to carry you?" I asked.

She shook her head and spoke through clenched teeth. "Hurts just as much."

We made our way back to the crack leading from the reflected version of the Glimmer and into the rift. Despite the vertiginous void of space beneath our feet, we soldiered onward to the crack on the opposite side of the starry bridge and crawled through.

Elyssa was gasping by the time we emerged in the reflected version of Queens Gate. She put an arm over my shoulder. "Carry me."

I cradled her again and ran around the ruined mansion and through the dryad forest. As we emerged from the trees, two figures blocked our path, black eye sockets smoldering with darkness.

Our reflections.

Elyssa's reflection held her ribs, face contorted in a grimace. Mine limped forward, hands grasping with longing.

My good knee went weak. "The pebble, babe!"

"So below, as above," Elyssa hissed.

I ran straight for the reflections. Their lips stretched into horrific smiles as they saw their prize coming straight into their grasps. With Elyssa in my arms, I couldn't use magic, I couldn't dodge around them. Hoping my reflection couldn't instantly mirror everything I did, I waited until the last instant and then leapt as high as possible.

I sailed over my creepy doppelganger. He leapt straight up, fingers grasping, but barely missed my foot. I almost overshot my target, hitting the water only inches from the other shore. We flew back into the real world, all the momentum from my jump translating into even more air. I bent my knees on landing, trying to reduce the jolt to Elyssa.

She shrieked and slumped in my arms, mercifully passing out from the pain. I set her easily on the ground and used her phone to call for a portal. "This is a medical emergency," I told the portal coordinator. "Hurry, please!" I texted an image of the area and seconds later, a portal opened.

I sighed with relief. We'd survived the Glimmer and fulfilled our promise, but the true battle lay ahead.

While healers tended to Elyssa's wounds, I met with Thomas and debriefed him on the Glimmer.

"This Glimmer Queen sounds extremely dangerous," he said. "If she decided to launch an attack on Eden, it could be catastrophic."

"Especially if she brings those cat bats with her," I said. "It would be cat-batastrophic."

Thomas stared unblinking at me for a moment to let me know he wasn't amused. "One problem at a time."

"It seems like we have a line of bad guys waiting in the wings." I was going to list them all, but Thomas's raised eyebrow let me know he was focused on the current priority. "Is Victus bringing robots?"

"His robot crews are disassembling airships and taking them through the arch for reassembly." Thomas projected the holographic image of a weaponized airship under construction. "I anticipate we'll have at least three of them ready to go for the mission start."

"Which is?"

"The moment our troops and supplies are boarded," he replied. "The Mzodi fleet arrived a couple of hours before you returned and we've been loading them ever since."

"Kdosh must be awfully crowded right now." I imagined the island couldn't hold more than a few hundred people at a time.

"Even with the flying ships, we'll be lucky to fit everyone onboard." Thomas switched to an overhead map of the island. Curving arrows showed two courses leading to the north and south of the city. "We'll flank Cephus's fortress from both sides. Once we've secured a beachhead, Daemos forces will begin summoning demons on the other side of the barrier to throw the enemy into disarray. That should give Fjoeruss's golems enough time to do whatever it is they're supposed to do."

"I believe they're filled with Stasis."

"But you have no way of knowing for sure."

I shook my head. "If Fjoeruss says they can do the trick, I believe him."

"There's no room for mistakes," Thomas reminded me. "Our people will be most vulnerable when they're up against the shield wall. Without the golems, there is no breaking through that barrier."

I sat on the edge of the table and stared at the image of the enemy fortress. "Then we'll just have to make sure nothing goes wrong."

We left unspoken just how impossible that would be.

Elyssa greeted me with a smile when I entered the healing ward. I peeked beneath the white robes and winced at the deep purple bruises running up her left side. "Ouch."

"I don't feel the pain right now," she said in a dreamy voice. "They gave me something to drink."

"You may have to stay behind tomorrow," I said. "You need time to heal."

"No." The declaration cut through the fuzz in her voice. "I sent for Flava to accelerate my recovery."

"Alrighty, then." I stroked her fair cheek and kissed her forehead. "When will she be here?"

"Soon." Elyssa yawned. "How many plans did it take for us to get out of the Glimmer?"

"I think Plan E was the last one." I counted on my fingers. "Five plans."

"What about the plan to leap over our reflections?"

I grinned. "Fine, six plans."

Elyssa clasped my hand and held it to her cheek. "How are the battle plans for tomorrow?"

"Finalized." I gave her the short version.

"Sounds like my father used the attack pattern I recommended."

"He used almost everything you recommended." I kissed her forehead. "How does it feel to be the favorite child?"

"Hah." Elyssa's eyelids drooped. "That would be Michael."

"Not anymore." I watched her until she drifted to sleep then leaned back in the chair and waited for Flava to come.

I blinked awake and saw Flava covering Elyssa with the robe. She looked over at me. "You looked so peaceful, I didn't want to disturb you."

I wiped the gunk from my eyes. "How is she?"

"Healed enough to throw herself into harm's way again." Flava turned in her chair to face me. "You went to Cora's realm?"

"The Glimmer." My mouth felt dry as cotton so I found a pitcher of water and poured myself a glass. "I had to deliver a gift to her daughter."

Flava pursed her lips. "To atone for breaking a promise to her."

"Technically, I didn't break my promise, but yeah, I should've kept my big mouth shut." I took a swig of water and felt relief melt into my parched throat. "I guess it gives you one more thing to bust my balls about."

Flava looked puzzled. "Why should I wish to destroy your genitalia?"

"You're mad about me not coming with the army to Tarissa in the first place. You blame me for the destruction of the legion." I resisted the urge to slam the glass down on the night stand. "I did this for Cora so she'd bring the sky fisher fleet to help us."

"My accusations were wrong. Commander Borathen told me many things I did not know." Flava's lip trembled. "Before our army left, the commander warned Ketiss that Cephus had long planned the sequence of events leading to the murders of the other Trivectus leaders." Her eyes focused on the past. "He told Ketiss that assaulting the stronghold before we'd had time to recover from the war and assess the situation would be a mistake."

"Ketiss didn't tell you any of this?" I asked.

She shook her head. "Ketiss simply told me he believed a quick offensive was necessary and that we would free Tarissa before the forces of Eden arrived." Flava reached a tentative hand and touched my arm. "If we had but waited, the legion might still be alive."

I shook my head and looked away. "I wasn't there for the Darklings. I ran away from war, from responsibility."

"But you came back when you were needed."

I blew out a derisive laugh. "I came back after a crystoid nearly leveled the island I was vacationing on."

"You returned and you destroyed the crystal menace." Flava's hand tightened on my arm. "You returned to Seraphina and you will once again lead us to victory." She smiled. "Don't you see, Justin? You are always there for people when they need you most. You are here for us now."

Her logic held a certain amount of appeal. True, I'd put my head under the covers and hoped someone else could clean up the mess before I had to pull back on my combat boots and go fight the Seraphim. The question remaining in my head was, would I have returned to Seraphina to unify the Seraphim if the crystoid incident hadn't happened, or would I have been content to procrastinate for a few centuries?

It was a question I couldn't answer. Things being the way they were, I guessed it didn't really mater.

"Cephus wanted to cripple us, to keep us out of Seraphina," I said. "His attacks have directly contributed to our return." I put a hand over Flava's. "I just want peace, but the bad guys won't give me a break."

She smiled. "Then we will have to break the bad guys, Justin."

I couldn't have put it better myself.

I carried Elyssa home and tucked her into bed, then curled up next to her, glad to finally get some rest. For the first time in weeks I didn't dream about Nightliss's final words to me, I didn't replay the horrors of war over and over in an endless nightmare. What Flava told me must have connected with the part of me that felt such awful guilt.

Because I slept like a baby.

Breakfast the next morning was a big affair. Shelton and Bella returned early in the morning from their short honeymoon and whipped up pancakes, bacon, freshly squeezed OJ, scrambled eggs, and mimosas.

Meghan, Adam, Stacey and Ryland joined the four of us and we enjoyed each other's company despite the battle looming ahead.

"Ever notice how Shelton conveniently leaves out the part where Justin threw him in a dumpster?" Adam said as we relived some early adventures. "He always skips to the part where the vampires attack."

Shelton polished off another piece of bacon and shrugged. "It's not something I enjoy remembering."

"I don't think you actually remember it." Bella giggled. "Probably because Justin knocked you out."

"Justin was so sweet and innocent back then," Elyssa said with a sigh. "Now he's all growed up."

I groaned. "Can we talk about something that doesn't involve me throwing Shelton in a dumpster?"

"But it's my favorite story," Adam said.

Cutsauce yipped at Shelton as he grabbed another piece of bacon. Shelton held the treat out and laughed as the tiny dog tried unsuccessfully to jump high enough to reach it. Adam flicked his wand and knocked the bacon out of Shelton's hand with a spell.

"No torturing the pup," Adam said.

I got up and rubbed my hands together. "It's time we reported to our duty stations."

"Aww," everyone chorused, but they finished off their food and began cleaning up.

I hugged Stacey goodbye and shook Ryland's hand.

"I do so wish we could go," Stacey said. "I could get a babysitter for the little ones."

"While you go off to fight a war?" Meghan set her arms akimbo. "That's awful! What if you died?"

Ryland wrapped an arm around Stacey. "Maybe I ought to tie her up just in case."

Stacey smiled suggestively. "That sounds deliciously fun, my dear."

Meghan's face turned bright red. She grabbed a couple of plates and vanished into the kitchen.

Before long, we were ready to go and went to the mansion's omniarch. I opened a portal directly to the Three Sisters where the rest of the army filtered through the Alabaster Arch. My stomach tightened with apprehension.

The countdown to invasion had begun.

Chapter 30

Elyssa and I spotted my parents and walked over to them while Shelton and the others joined the Arcane forces rallying near the front of the control room.

"Where's Ivy?" I asked.

"Yuuki asked us to help House Wakahisa hunt down a gang of rogue vampires who have been kidnapping Daemos in an attempt to duplicate the blood serum made by Maximus." Dad cast an uneasy glance at Mom. "Ivy developed a crush—"

"On a young incubus," Mom finished. "Your father decided it was okay for Ivy to remain behind and come when House Wakahisa rendezvous with the last ship out of port a few hours from now."

Dad pumped a fist threateningly. "Don't worry, I told that boy what would happen if he broke my daughter's heart."

I snorted. "Ivy would burn him to pile of ashes."

"That's more or less what I told him too." Dad grinned. "At least I never have to worry about pulling out the shotgun with my daughter."

Mom sighed. "I don't like leaving our impressionable young daughter with a pubescent incubus."

"Ivy may be thirteen," I said, "but she can take care of herself."

Elyssa grinned. "I'd be more concerned about the boy."

The group of us walked over to the Alabaster Arch. Auxiliary forces raced back and forth between the control room and Seraphina, carting supplies and siege units between realms. We stepped through the portal and onto Kdosh. A breath caught in my throat at the sight awaiting me.

"Wow." My jaw went slack.

A glossy black sky ship floated just off the skylet, ramp extended to take on passengers and equipment. Wide and flat on the bottom with bulging curves and sharp fins along the sides, it looked more like a spaceship than anything terrestrial. Pulsating gems studded the bottom and sides of the hull. Unlike Cora's ship, it had no wings to keep it aloft. Though I was no sky ship expert, it seemed likely the gems had something to do with its feat of magical levitation.

All it needs is a skull and crossbones on the side and it'd be perfect.

Three other similar ships were docked to other sides of the island, while a fleet of a dozen more of their brethren hovered several hundred yards offshore. Each one bore its name in sparkling Cyrinthian symbols engraved in the crystalline hulls. They ranged in size from that of a galleon, to the absolutely massive mother ship drifting in the center of the formation.

I shivered. "That thing's the size of an aircraft carrier."

Elyssa wiped the side of my mouth. "Stop drooling, babe."

"This is gonna be the coolest invasion ever."

"Holy Hairy, mother of Bigfoot." Shelton came up beside me and took off his wide-brimmed hat in a moment of sacred reverence.

Adam grabbed his friend by the arm as a column of other Arcanes marched past. "Dude, you're not supposed to break formation."

"I'm a freelancer, not an enlisted man." Shelton tugged his arm away. "Can't a man get a moment to appreciate a freaking fleet of flying ships?"

"They are pretty cool." Adam gazed upon them adoringly.

Bella broke formation and stood beside her new husband. "I'll bet the view is even better from the ship."

Shelton slapped his hat back on his head. "Hell yeah." He squeezed my shoulder. "See you guys at the war."

I clapped him on the back. "See you soon."

Elyssa and I watched as our friends boarded the ship straight ahead of us—the *Pstra*, if I read the Cyrinthian correctly. I felt a moment of panic, contemplating how awful it would be to lose another friend in this battle.

It's all a part of war.

I'd do whatever it took to make this battle short and victorious.

Victus stepped up to my side. "Quite a fleet."

"Pretty amazing," I replied. I glanced over where robots worked efficiently reconstructing the nacelles of three airships. "How long will they take to finish?"

"Maybe thirty minutes," Victus said. He motioned toward three containers the size of train boxcars. "Each of those is filled with battle bots. Once the airships are ready to fly, they'll carry the cargo into the city."

The containers sparkled in the sunlight. "Are those made of diamond fiber?"

He nodded. "Impossible to destroy. When the airships set them down, both ends will open so bots can deploy from both sides, using the container as a shield from magical attacks."

"Nice." I didn't much care for Victus, but at least he had both feet in the war.

"Good luck, Justin. Delectra and I will be on an airship." In place of his typical plastic smiles was something far more genuine. "I think celebrations will be in order at the end of today."

"You're really that confident?" Elyssa asked.

Victus looked at her and joy radiated from his face. "Oh, yes. By the end of today, I think it'll be clear sailing from here on out." He shook my hand warmly, his grip lingering as if savoring the moment.

"Wish I could be so confident," I said, a bit puzzled by his behavior. "Good luck, and stay safe."

"I certainly will." Victus turned and walked toward the airships, a skip in his step.

"That was really weird," Elyssa said. "He must be on drugs."

I snorted. "Or maybe he's looking forward to finishing this as much as I am." I took Elyssa's hand and we headed toward the *Evadora*. Cora met us with an expectant look when we reached the top deck.

"Evadora has the bottle," I told her.

A tear sparkled in the corner of her eye. "Did she use it?"

"She tried a yellow one," I said. "Happiness, if I had to guess. When we left, she was skipping around."

Cora wiped her eyes. "Thank you, Justin."

Elyssa cut straight to the chase. "The queen tried to kill us. She had the path warded to alert her if anyone went to the Soul Tree."

"My blessing should have protected you," Cora said.

I shook my head. "Not from the venom in those vines."

"She must have thought I would try to sneak back in," Cora said. "That trap was meant for me."

I wasn't sure if I should be angry or not. I didn't think Cora had intentionally sent us off to die, but she should have warned us if she suspected any traps. "If she has part of your soul, doesn't that mean she thinks like you?"

Cora paused. "In some ways, yes. In other ways, she is much different. Then again, I have been exposed to emotion and she has not."

A horn sounded from one of the other ships. "Sounds like we're ready to get underway," Elyssa said.

"Cast off!" Cora shouted in Cyrinthian.

Illaena relayed the order to the crew, and the *Evadora* sprouted wings. The wood creaked and groaned as the massive ship lifted off of the skylet. The other ships moored to the island raised their gangplanks and drifted higher to join the rest of the fleet.

I decided to impart a nugget of knowledge with Cora before leaving her to tend her duties. "Your crew already knows you're not Seraphim."

Cora's eyes flashed. "Did you tell them?"

"Didn't have to." I nodded toward Illaena. "She admitted it to me when I asked her for help."

Her shoulders slumped. "I wonder why they never told me."

"Because they respect you no matter what sort of being you are or where you come from." I waved a hand around at the ship. "Your crew loves you. Maybe you should respect them enough to admit the truth."

"Perhaps," Cora said. "Others in the fleet might not be so understanding." She tapped a finger on her chin and looked back at

Kdosh as it receded in the distance. "Besides, I may return to Eden for a time."

Elyssa arched her brow. "I thought you didn't like Eden?"

"There is something about Conrad that tugs on my soul," Cora said softly. "I sense a great darkness in him that is not his own."

"He seemed pretty happy during the visit to the ship," I said.

Cora nodded. "Yes. It was almost as if something heavy lifted from him and let him be a child, if only for a moment."

I felt certain it had to do with Victor's political ambitions overwhelming his duties as a father. He loved himself too much to truly love anyone else. Delectra showed some signs of humanity, but having a cold fish like her for a mother couldn't be very nurturing.

"Conrad could use a real family," I told her. "Unfortunately, he's stuck with the one he has."

The Lyrolai woman looked down. "I failed my own daughter. Why should I be any better for him?"

I couldn't answer that question. I wondered where the father was, if he was dead or alive and living in the Glimmer. Instead of asking, I ended the conversation. "We'll let you get back to your duties."

Cora wiped at her red eyes, nodded, and walked away.

The fleet reached the Ooskai Valley later in the day and drifted past Kaelissa's village. A lone figure walked out onto the stone bridge as the *Evadora* sailed through. Blond tresses and a royal demeanor gave away Kaelissa before I even saw her face. She watched us go without raising a hand in greeting or shouting a word of encouragement.

It wasn't like I expected her to cup her hands to her mouth and shout, "Kick Cephus's ass for me!" though a wave might have shown she cared. She seemed as detached as the last time I'd seen her, the last link to her world severed by Daelissa's death.

As we neared the eastern end of the valley, the fleet prepared to split in half, delivering troops to the north and south of the city. Elyssa and I went to the prow and waved at the *Pstra* sailing fifty yards ahead of us. Shelton and Bella stood at the stern talking to a group of people. They saw us and waved back.

"Don't tell me they're letting you steer that thing!" I shouted.

"Of course they are," Shelton boomed back. "Hey, wanna race?"

"Hello, *boy*."

I spun around to see one of Fjoeruss's gray men standing behind me. I was shocked by the venom in its tone. "Boy? What's wrong with you?"

The gray man gripped its slicked-back hair and tore off its own scalp, ripping the skin completely off its face to reveal the leering grin of a madwoman beneath.

"Serena!" Elyssa gasped.

But the gray countenance staring at me didn't belong to the real Serena. "No, it's a golem that looks just like her."

The golem held out its hand, palm up and a holographic image of Serena appeared. "I hope this message finds you well, boy." The short blond woman smiled sweetly. "I am sorry to tell you that the shipment of golems Fjoeruss sent you were waylaid and slightly modified."

Elyssa gripped my arm as the hologram continued to speak

"I also want you to know that I've forgiven you for disrupting my valuable experiments and destroying work that took decades to complete." Serena's right eye twitched and the smile flickered. "Just because I've forgiven you doesn't mean you won't be punished."

Slimy dread burrowed into my guts. "Punished how?"

The recording hadn't been charmed to reply, continuing as if I'd never spoken, but it answered the question in the next sentence. "Should you survive this war, you will never return to Eden. Moments after you departed, my allies and I took control of the Alabaster Arch at the Three Sisters and the Grand Nexus. We rendered the entire network inoperable." Serena smiled. "You and the Eden army are stranded, dear child."

A lump of cold formed in my chest. "No, that can't be true."

Serena smirked. "Farewell, heroes of Eden."

The golem reached for its ear. My hyper reflexes kicked in and time seemed to slow. For the first time, I noticed a bulge of skin beneath the golem's ear. What was it hiding? A button? I didn't have time to find out. I grabbed the golem and flung it overboard. Seconds later, it detonated in midair and the shockwave rocked the *Evadora*.

Illaena and Cora raced to my side.

"What was that?" Cora asked.

My heart thudded. "The golems—where are the rest of them?"

"I believe the quartermaster divided them among the ships," Illaena said. "Why?"

"Warn the other crews!" I shouted. "The golems are rigged to explode!"

Illaena touched a gem on her uniform and issued orders, but it was too late.

An explosion rocked the ship to our starboard side, blowing out the hull where one of the large levitation gems kept it afloat. The gem shattered and the ship listed hard port. I saw the crew frantically working to wrest control but there was nothing they could do. The ship slammed into the valley wall. The hull cracked and caved. People fell from the breached hull, bodies crashing down the cliff, screams fading into the distance.

A shockwave from ahead sent a shudder through the *Evadora*. The *Pstra* veered so hard it began to roll sideways. Bella stumbled backward over the railing. Shelton grabbed her. An instant later, another ship, the *Kjala*, smashed into the starboard side. Both ships crumpled, spiraling down toward the forest a thousand feet below.

"No!" Elyssa screamed.

Everything went silent except for a high-pitched whine in my ear as I watched my friends falling toward the valley floor far below. "No," I whimpered. "No!" I didn't even think, just dove over the side of the ship. My wings burst into fiery form. I furled them around me and dove after the *Pstra*.

Shattering crystal and a chorus of screams caught my ear. I looked up as a smoking sky ship streaked toward me. I spread my wings and veered to the side as the stricken ship glided past. I course corrected and dove for the *Pstra*, diving through the breached hull and into the cargo hold. The ship rolled side-to-side as the remaining levitation gems tried to keep it aloft, slowing its descent. A net broke and empty crucibles bounced loose, some shattering on the floor, others bouncing into me. I fought through them and reached a shelf laden with carpets.

Grabbing as many as I could, I tucked them under one arm and raced back to the breach. Rather than relying on my poor flying skills, I leapt up and caught the broken floor of the next deck with one hand, pulled myself up, and leapt up again. The forest loomed closer and closer as the ship spiraled in slow motion to its doom.

On the top deck, the Seraphim crew leapt off the sides, spreading their wings and gliding away. I saw Shelton and Bella helping a wounded Seraphim from beneath a section of broken decking. Grim-faced Templars held onto the railing, knowing their journey would soon end.

I raced over and tossed the carpets on the deck. "Get out of here!"

Shelton's eyes flashed with gratitude. "You came for us, man."

"Yes I did, now shut up and fly!" I dragged an unconscious Templar onto a carpet as his comrades boarded the other ones and began to take flight. "How many more onboard?"

"Twenty soldiers trapped on the third deck," one of the Templars answered.

I jabbed a finger toward the remains of the *Kjala*, its prow wedged in the hull of the Pstra. "Rescue survivors over there."

The Templars each took a carpet and flew toward the other ship, grabbing the wounded from the deck. I snuffed my wings and raced below deck. A section of deck two had collapsed into the level below, blocking the way for escape. I channeled a wave of Stasis, turning the tough crystal into brittle glass and punched my way through it.

Part of the hull broke free, revealing the forest floor looming even closer. This entire ship would be a heap of shattered crystal within the next minute.

Chapter 31

The ship fell in slow motion, but not slowly enough. I didn't have long to rescue the trapped Templars. Fear renewed my efforts. I rammed through more debris and found the stranded soldiers.

"Follow me!" I turned and ran back up the ramp toward the top deck. The Templars followed in orderly fashion, carrying their wounded and keeping calm, as if this was something they did on an everyday basis. I showed them the pile of carpets.

One soldier raced to the pile and handed them out quickly. Someone paired with wounded and the carpets took off one-by-one. The last soldier hopped on a carpet and looked at me expectantly. "Sir, are you coming?"

I shook my head, suddenly realizing I hadn't even thought to get on one myself. "Yes." I hopped onboard and the carpet lifted off. We flew free of the wreckage and watched as the *Pstra* and *Kjala*, hulls locked in a deadly embrace, crashed into the trees with a tremendous boom.

Dozens of other carpets floated nearby, some of them bearing five people, far more than their rated load and unable to rise any higher. We drifted close to one and took one of their passengers. Other carpets followed our example until most of the weight was evenly distributed. Small crystalline boats with the markings of their mother ships hovered nearby like life rafts. A lump formed in my throat when I found Shelton and Bella waving at me from a nearby carpet.

Hot tears stung my eyes and I waved back. So long as I drew breath, I would do everything in my power to save my loved ones.

If only I could have saved Nightliss.

"Thank you, sir," one of the Templars said, a broad-shouldered man with a scar across his cheek. "You saved a lot of good people."

I saw the grateful looks on the faces of people trained to face death and suddenly couldn't speak. *Great, now I'm going to cry in front of Templars.* A few deep breaths melted the knot and I hoped they took my silence for grim resolve or heroic stoicism.

We flew up to the *Evadora* and Elyssa ran over to hug me. "How many ships?" I asked, not wanting to hear the answer.

"We lost nearly half," Elyssa said, voice breaking.

I looked out over the railing. Four ships looked undamaged and had docked with other damaged ships to keep them afloat. Our once mighty fleet was reduced to a pale shadow in one fell blow.

I'm going to kill you, Serena.

Where Daelissa had once ruled with brute force, her former lapdog attacked with ruthless deceit. At least with Daelissa you could see the attacks coming from a mile away. My face burned with anger, but my heart sagged like lead in my chest. *Why didn't I see this coming?*

Was Serena really so much smarter than all of us? After the attack at the mansion, we should have been prepared for anything. How had she remained a step ahead?

Elyssa seemed to know what I was thinking. "Justin, nobody could have foreseen something like this."

"How could she hijack Fjoeruss's gray men?" My fists clenched painfully tight. I wanted to smash and break things, but Serena had already done that for me.

Behind us, I saw the three airships we'd left behind on Kdosh slowly catching up with the fleet, the battle bot containers swaying gently beneath them. The first airship came to a stop over the *Evadora* and paced us. A container thudded onto the deck and both ends slammed open. Battle bots poured from both ends, gears and motors whining in syncopation.

I waved my arms at the airship. "Hey, we don't need help now!"

"What is Victus doing?" Elyssa said. She touched the comm pendant on her uniform. "Airship Delta One, we do not need battle bot assistance. I repeat, we require no assistance."

The whining electric motors of the bots stopped as the last one stepped into formation, shiny chrome bodies absolutely still. The green lines in their wide visor-like eyes zigzagged up and down like a heart monitor leaving a jagged graph in its wake. The lines flashed yellow.

"Oh crap," Shelton said from beside me. "You've gotta be kidding me!"

The tone in his voice amped the dread factor and it dawned on me that these bots weren't here to help. The lines in their electronic eyes flashed red. "Everyone take cover!"

"New targets acquired," the bots said in cybertronic monotone. "Battle bots attack."

I channeled a blazing sword of Brilliance and sliced off the arm of the closest robot before it could activate the laser cannon mounted on the wrist.

Shelton slammed his staff on the deck and raised a shield an instant before a flurry of lasers slashed the air, leaving trails of smoke and an acrid scent in the air. Two Templars went down with smoking holes in their chests. The rest pressed the attack.

Bella whirled her staff behind the protection of Shelton's shield. "Caliente!" she shouted and leveled the focus toward the closest battle-bot. A lance of green light met the bot's arm cannon just as the robot fired. The arm exploded, throwing the bot back into its comrades and knocking them out of formation.

I leapt over sizzling beams of energy and channeled a massive sledgehammer of Murk in my left hand, wielding it like Thor and crushing a bot with one blow. The blazing sword still in my right hand, I slashed the head from another robot, lashed out with a foot and sent another bot flying back into a group of metal soldiers. Before they could recover, I went berserk, cutting them to scrap metal with my energy sword.

A whining hum caught my attention. Looking up, I saw the blimp's bottom laser cannon swiveling toward the deck. The whine reached a fever pitch and went silent an instant before a ball of red energy exploded from the muzzle and slammed into a group of Templars. Bodies scattered and wood splintered. The airship was too high for me to reach so I raced for the flying carpets.

Black vines slithered up through the air and wrapped around the laser cannon. With a loud screech of metal, the weapon tore free. I saw Cora staring up at the airship, eyes blazing with unbridled fury. The vines wrapped around the engines and pulled the blimp lower and lower.

So intent was she on the airship, she didn't see the battle bots converging on her position. I raced across the deck, ducking and weaving through enemy fire. The enemy bots detected me, torsos swiveling in my direction, arm cannons flicking up. I channeled a sheet of ice and slid on my butt beneath a torrent of laser fire. Whirling my energy blade, I sliced the legs off the bots and then decapitated them to finish them.

Cora looked shaken. "Thank you, Justin."

"No problem. Can you get me up to the ship with a vine?" I asked.

"Not necessary." Choked with vines, one of the airship's engines sparked and exploded. The blimp listed but the tether of vines kept it from drifting away from the *Evadora*. Vines snaked through the holes in the cockpit. The airship drifted low off the port bow. The enemy crew screamed as thorny vines slithered down their throats and tore out their insides.

"Don't kill them all." I gripped Cora's shoulder. "I need someone for questioning."

She nodded. A vine gripped the last crew member and pulled him from the cockpit while the rest of the vegetation released the vessel and let it plummet toward the ground.

The battle bots lay in ruins, bodies now heaps of newly formed scrap metal. One of the sky ships to our starboard keeled hard to port, spilling shiny battle bots into the valley below and slamming into the attacking airship. The diamond fiber container crashed through the railing and pierced the nacelle of the enemy blimp. The vessel spiraled in a drunken loop and plummeted out of sight.

The Seraphim crew held fast to rails and decking with strands of Murk until the sky ship righted itself.

"Smart," Shelton said, breathing heavily.

Elyssa looked at the last remaining airship as it battled with the *Krjast*. "Get us over there!" The crew of the last blimp seemed to realize it was sorely outnumbered and turned away from the sky ship. Engaging its twin turbine engines, it jetted back down the valley too quickly for us to pursue.

The *Evadora* pulled up near the *Krjast*. Battle bots lined up midship, firing volleys of lasers at the Seraphim crew.

"We need to get over there," I shouted.

Cora flung out her hand. Vines shot across the gap between the ships, forming gangplanks.

Shelton's eyes went wide. "Dude, we're pirates for real!"

I held up a fist. "Avast, mateys! Keelhaul the landlubbers!"

Elyssa's forehead wrinkled. "What?"

I clarified with one word. "Charge!"

Templars, Seraphim, and Arcanes ran across the gangplanks swords and staffs raised, a mighty battle cry roaring above the fray. Within minutes, we'd destroyed the enemy robots and secured the *Krjast*.

"Man, that couldn't have been any more epic," Shelton crowed.

Adam compacted his staff into a rod and wiped crusted blood off his forehead. "I think swinging across from the other ship would've been pretty cool."

Shelton tapped a finger on his chin. "True, but these ships don't have masts to swing from."

"I can't believe you enjoyed yourself," Bella said angrily. "People died and the fleet is crippled!"

A sober look came over Shelton's face. "Yeah, I know. Just trying to find a silver lining in this mess."

I choked up a little because my silver linings were standing all around me. My friends had survived, and the woman I loved was by my side.

I'm so selfish.

It was a shortcoming I'd just have to accept. I'd move heaven and earth to save the ones I loved. Much as I wanted to savor the moment, I didn't have the luxury. I took Elyssa's hand. "We've got some loose ends to tie up." We returned to the *Evadora* and found the traitorous crewmember from the airship. Cora had left him bound to the railing.

I already knew the answer to my question, but I had to hear it for myself. I looked down at the bruised man, saw the fear in his eyes. "Why did Victus betray us?"

"You betrayed us," he said in a trembling voice. "Victus discovered your alliance with Cephus. He showed us your plans to take over Eden with a Seraphim army."

Elyssa's mouth dropped open. "That's a lie! Why would we fight off one Seraphim invasion only to turn around and do it ourselves? It makes absolutely no sense."

Something about the man suddenly changed, a flicker of oily black in his eyes, and the distinct odor of brimstone rising above the stench of burnt flesh and wood. He roared and broke free of the vines. Fingers extended like claws, he dove for Elyssa. "My master sends you this parting gift!"

Elyssa deftly sidestepped the charge, flipping the man on his back and then pinning him down with her knees. He snapped his teeth like a rabid dog, unable to arch his neck enough to bite her.

I gripped the man's head and pressed it down. "A demon."

"Just like the crewman from Frankenberg's secret Antarctica base," Elyssa said.

"Victus and his demons." I glared at the possessed man. "He's been playing against us all this time."

"No wonder Serena was able to penetrate the mansion defenses," Elyssa growled. "Victus probably took the portal blocker offline so she could plant the fake bomb."

"She didn't kill us because that would have delayed our departure to Seraphina." I tapped a finger on Elyssa's wrist-mounted lancer. "Knock him out."

A silver dart sprouted in the man's neck and he slumped.

"Serena's note in that crucible makes sense now," Adam said. "She wanted to piss us off, make sure we went to fight Cephus as soon as possible so they could ambush and kill us."

The fleet's flagship, the *Uorion* docked to the *Evadora* during our brief exchange with the possessed man. Thomas and my parents strode across the gangplank.

"What in the blazes is going on?" Dad asked.

"A gray man tried to destroy our ship," Mom said, a look of disbelief on her face. "I can't believe Fjoeruss would betray us."

Thomas gazed at the destroyed battle bots. "What happened?"

"Serena hijacked the gray men Fjoeruss sent." I pounded a fist on the deck. "We were betrayed from the start."

Mom's forehead furrowed with confusion. "How did Serena get the gray men?"

"Because the real mastermind behind this plot helped her." I kicked a robot head and sent it clanking across the deck. "Victus has been in on this from the start and now I think I know why."

Thomas didn't seem surprised. "When we saw the airships attack, I suspected betrayal."

"I knew Victus was ambitious, but did he really expect to kill all of us with the exploding golems and battle bots?" Dad said.

"Therein lies the rub." They weren't going to like what came next. "The gray man on this ship had a message from Serena. After our forces went through the Alabaster Arch, Victus and his people captured and disabled it. According to her, we can't return to Eden."

"In other words, Victus masterminded the crystoid incident to prod us into action against Cephus, knowing we'd throw everything we had against him." Dad rubbed his jaw. "With the entire army trapped in Seraphina, the Overworld is undefended and ripe for the taking."

"We lost most of our equipment when the gray men destroyed the ships," Thomas said. "I can't even begin to count the dead because we simply don't know who escaped and who might still be alive in the wrecks in the valley."

"The Blue Cloaks already launched a sortie of flying carpets and brooms to search for survivors," Mom said. "All we can do now is lick our wounds and push on."

"Not today," Thomas said. "Today we salvage everything we can from the wreckage. I'll evaluate our condition tomorrow and decide when and if we proceed."

"I don't think that's a good idea," Elyssa said. "The longer we wait, the longer Cephus has to multiply his army and fortify his position."

"If we can take his fortress intact, we might be able to use that new arch Cephus built," Dad said. "We won't need the Alabaster Arch to get us home."

"How are we supposed to take the fortress without the gray men?" Mom asked.

I folded my arms and moved the chess pieces in my mind. No matter how I arranged our positions, we'd lost a vital component of our attack on the fortress. "The gray men were our last hope of breaching the shield. Without them, the rest of us won't be able to channel enough Stasis to hold open the barrier."

Thomas looked at the unconscious man at my feet, his icy eyes simmering. "Unless and until we figure out how to do that, Cephus is free to do what he wants."

"All this time, I thought Cephus had cornered himself in that fortress," Elyssa murmured. "He knew what was coming, all he had to do was hope his firewall held long enough."

"What if he's not there anymore?" Dad said. "For all we know, he packed up and left while we were gone."

"What if his entire speech about the Void was a ruse?" I said. "What if he let us escape?"

Elyssa shook her head. "It doesn't matter. We have to take the fortress. If Cephus isn't there, we'll deal with finding him later."

Shelton, who'd been hovering nearby as we discussed the situation dropped in his two cents. "Dollars to donuts he's in Eden laughing his head off with Victus and Serena right about now."

"Our mission has altered," Thomas said in a calm voice. "Elyssa, order search and rescue squads to continue their efforts. I'll send a ship back to Kdosh to verify the Alabaster Arch is inoperable."

"What about Tarissa?" I asked.

"I don't plan to put our army in harm's way," he said. "Cephus nearly wiped out the Tarissan Legion in one blow. We can't go into the city without a plan to get through the barrier."

"Can we send in someone covertly to assassinate Cephus?" I said, desperate for an idea. "Maybe Kanaan—"

"Kanaan was scheduled to come through with the final group of Blue Cloaks," Thomas said. "They never made it through. It's possible they were killed or taken by Victus's people."

Heart pounding, my stomach churned with disappointment and anger. The entire might of the Overworld had been outsmarted and beaten by three people. Victus, Serena, and Cephus had outplayed us and left us to rot in another realm.

The only hope of a way home might be inside the very place we couldn't breach.

Chapter 32

The *Quula-Quay*, a nimble Mzodi skiff, sprinted back toward Kdosh to verify our worst fears, while anyone with a flying carpet or broom swept the valley floor for survivors and equipment to salvage. Even the ships still afloat had lost equipment vital to the war effort. Most of the crucibles onboard the *Evadora* were destroyed, and even if we had plenty to spare, the catapults had all been aboard the *Kjala*.

My parents asked around and confirmed another fear.

"Ivy wasn't on the last ship out of Kdosh," Dad said.

My heart constricted at the news. "She's all alone in Eden?"

"It gets worse," he said. "Houses Wakahisa and Volkov never showed either. I spoke to Kassallandra and we believe Yuuki Wakahisa and Ivan Volkov knew in advance something like this would happen."

Mom wiped tears from her eyes. "They might be in league with Serena."

My knees went weak. "They have Ivy?"

Dad's eyes reddened and he seemed to swallow a lump in his throat. "Yeah, I think there's a good chance of it."

"Oh god." I didn't know what to do with myself, so I hugged Mom and tried not to imagine what Ivy might be going through right now. We couldn't just turn the army around, but if the *Quula-Quay* brought back good news about the arch, I planned to go back immediately.

Since there was little else to do, I spent the next few hours scooping up robot parts and dumping them inside the diamond fiber containers. Cora had wanted to dump the remains, but I convinced her we could still use the weapons and power supplies on the battle bots for something.

Images of Victus's gleeful departing smile stabbed my mind and stoked the furnace of rage in my belly. I'd be sure to shake his hand the next time I saw him, and grip it until I heard bones break.

Shelton held a shiny robot head in his hands and watched the red line blipping back and forth in its visor. "I'd give anything to wrap my hands around Victus's neck right about now."

I crushed the arm of a dismembered robot and then hurled it hard against the diamond fiber container. It didn't even leave a mark on the nearly indestructible substance. "Son of a bitch!" Blinded by rage, I hurled spheres of Murk and Brilliance at the container. The magical energy splashed harmlessly off the surface.

Shelton ran up to the container and kicked it. "Yeah, let that inanimate object have it!" He looked at me and smirked. "Feeling any better?"

"Not really." I forced my fists to unclench and took out some of my frustration by stomping on a robot head. "There, now I feel better."

"Good." Shelton scooped up a tangle of wires and walked them inside the container.

I blew out a breath and followed him inside with an armful of parts. The middle of the container held a pile of parts, but it had been built to hold three or four columns of battle-bots, so we weren't even close to filling it.

I sat down and leaned against the wall. "I hope you and Adam can come up with something brilliant to save the day, because I'm all out of ideas."

"Can't get through the barrier without destroying the aether wells powering the shield," Shelton said. "It's the chicken and the egg, man." He slumped beside me, resting his posterior on a robot head. "Adam sat down with Flava to figure out how the aether wells work. Maybe he'll think of something."

I banged the back of my head against the container, sending a hollow boom through it.

Shelton chuckled. "Maybe if you bang your head hard enough you'll think of something."

I bumped my noggin a few more times against the wall, looked at him, and shook my head. "Nothing yet except a headache."

"Man, I could really go for some donuts right now." Shelton's face creased with worry. "Do you think I'll ever get to eat one again?"

I opened my mouth to answer when the pounding ache in my head dislodged an idea from the dark recesses of my mind. The idea tumbled among all the useless thoughts and dead synapses, coming to rest right next to the light switch of bright ideas. The lightbulb came on. I sucked in a breath and pounded a fist on the wall. "I've got it." I leapt to my feet and burst into maniacal laughter. "I know how we can beat Cephus!"

Shelton didn't have time to answer because I raced out of the container and took the gangplank across to the *Uorion* where Elyssa and her father were debating options in a war room that smelled of sweat, despair, a little like wet dogs.

"Bloody damnation," Colin McCloud bellowed. "We can't just sit here forever. The wolf packs are ready for the hunt."

Kassallandra stared at him with fiery red eyes. "If you're quite finished with the tirade, I suggest you think about other practical issues, namely food and water."

"There's a river and plenty of animals in the forest below," McCloud answered. "Maybe the Daemos are too high and bloody mighty to hunt their own food, but we lycans can provide for ourselves."

"And to think I spoke with Victus before departure." Captain Takei said. "He was returning to Eden, ostensibly to say goodbye to his child."

"I knew he was a bloody liar," McCloud said. "I just didn't think he was a traitor to boot."

"Food is not the only problem." Komad Rashad, leader of the vampires, flashed his fangs. "We did not bring enough blood for a protracted siege because we thought there would be a supply line from Eden to the front lines."

"Plenty of blood to go around," McCloud said. "I'm certain the Daemos would be willing to let you snack on them."

"Absolutely not," Kassallandra said coldly.

The hulking felycan leader, Saber, gave me a steady look the moment I entered. His eyes narrowed, but he said nothing. He rarely spoke, though I suspected it was because he had the patience of a lion stalking its prey.

Thomas watched the exchange as the faction leaders offered ideas and traded barbs. He apparently seemed willing to let them air their frustrations for now, though I also suspected he didn't have any ideas of his own to overcome the primary obstacle.

I pushed in between McCloud and Captain Takei and banged a fist on the table. "Who here wants to kick Cephus's ass so hard he craps out of his eye sockets?"

McCloud shook his head sadly. "We all do, lad, but we're just pups howling in a thunderstorm until the barrier around his fortress comes down."

I bared my teeth in a fierce grin. "Victus gave us exactly what we need."

Elyssa leaned her hands on the table. "The battle bots?"

"But they're destroyed," McCloud said. "Even if they weren't, how would they get us through the shield wall?"

I turned to Thomas. "I'm so confident this will work, that I think we should get underway right now so we can strike the fortress at dawn."

Thomas pursed his lips, touched the comm pendant on his uniform. "Please ask the captain to move out the fleet."

"Yes, sir," someone said on the other end.

I felt almost giddy with optimism as I rubbed my hands together and told the others how we were going to breach Cephus's last defense.

Our fleet arrived in Tarissa, shadows flitting across the brilliant moon. With our forces considerably less than when we'd first departed, Thomas decided to keep everyone together. The Blue Cloaks departed in sorties of flying carpets the moment we arrived, scouting ahead and deploying all-seeing eyes across the city to monitor enemy movements.

I worked with other crews to ready our trump cards for the big showdown.

Thomas emerged from the flagship with a group of Seraphim dressed in the loose, flowing garb of the Mzodi. Among the sky fishers, I only recognized Illaena and Cora.

The group walked over to me and stopped. Cora waved a hand toward me. "Muhala Kajeen, this is Justin."

A sera with a long black cape stepped forward and eyed me. "I regret not formally introducing myself before." She offered a faint nod. "I am Xalara, descended from Ara herself and the Muhala Kajeen of the Mzodi."

I wasn't sure if I should bow or not, so I simply returned the same nod she'd given me and splayed my fingers in greeting. "A pleasure, Xalara."

"The Mzodi council has voted to continue rendering aid," Thomas said. "They will establish a supply line to help keep our troops fed and provide transportation."

I gave Xalara a deeper nod. "Thank you."

"Cephus must be stopped for the sake of all Seraphina," Xalara said. "It is our hope that we may provide a decisive edge in the battle."

"I am sorry about the loss of your ships and crew," I said.

"We are heartbroken by the loss of so many lives caused by the treachery of a few." Xalara's eye's hardened. "We are not a vengeful people, but those responsible for betrayal must be punished." She turned to Illaena. "You have something for Justin."

Illaena stepped forward. "We did as you asked and found a gem that amplifies Stasis channeling." She held out her hand to reveal a flat gray jewel the size of her palm. "It was the best we could find on short notice."

"Thank you." I hoped it was enough.

"Everything ready?" Thomas asked.

I nodded. "The skiffs have their cargo onboard. We just need to get everything in position."

"Captain Takei said the skies and ground are clear all the way to the fortress." Thomas looked at the silhouette of the city against the moon and frowned. "I suspect Cephus withdrew his troops to lure us closer so he can finish us off."

"He doesn't think we can get through the barrier," I said. "We have to breach before he attacks."

Shelton and Adam emerged from the tent we'd been using as a workshop. "We've got twenty bots operating," Adam said. "The rest were too scrapped to work with."

"Rejiggering the friend or foe system was tricky, but I think we got it." Shelton touched the screen on his arcphone and a line of battle bots marched out of the tent. "Battle bots halt!"

"By your command," the robots said in cybertronic harmony.

I turned to Thomas. "Looks like we're ready to go."

Commander Borathen touched the comm pendant on his uniform. "Faction leaders, forward until dawn."

Howls and mighty roars rose in the distance as the lycans and felycans received their moving orders. Squadrons of flying carpets bearing Blue Cloaks rose into the air. Silent columns of Templars began marching toward the goal.

I clapped Shelton and Adam on the backs. "Good luck."

Shelton snorted. "We're gonna need every last scrap we can get."

Elyssa and I boarded flying brooms while Thomas and his command staff boarded the command platform, an octagonal-shaped dais with a pedestal in the center and modules from which the command staff could quickly relay any orders Thomas gave.

Shelton ordered the battle bots to board the skiffs—large flying carpets designed to carry cargo—and our group took off toward the city. A low deep thrum vibrated in my ears, barely audible at first, but growing louder the closer we came to the objective.

The sun peeked over the horizon by the time our forces closed in on the wasteland at the middle of the city. The barrier around Cephus's fortress rose like a purple wart, glowing in the dawn. Daemos sent hellhounds and other familiars questing for traps in the open space between us and the objective while Blue Cloaks and Arcanes checked for wards.

There was no hiding our approach. Even if Cephus didn't have a form of surveillance outside his fortress, all it took was someone with eyes peering through the shield dome. Whether it was the darkness or a change in its composition, the barrier appeared almost transparent rather than translucent, offering a clearer view inside than when we'd first arrived days ago.

What I saw gave me chills—and not the good kind. Towering in the center of the wide plaza outside the Ministry of Research stood the arch, larger even than an Obsidian Arch—large enough for even the larger Mzodi ships to fly through. With the dome transparent, it no longer appeared purple, but blood red. Cephus had created something both awesome and terrifying, and it seemed to be powering up.

I jogged over to Mom where she waited with the other Seraphim, Lanaeia, Joss, Otaleon, Flava, and remnants of the legion. "Mom, have you seen an arch like that?"

My mother shook her head slowly. "It's unlike any arch I've ever seen."

"The dome was opaque for a long time," Nailan said. "It wasn't until you arrived that the dome became translucent enough to see what was inside."

"Why would Cephus make the dome transparent now?" Lanaeia asked.

Otaleon kicked a loose chunk of rubble. "To intimidate us."

Lanaeia brushed back a lock of windblown hair from her face. "He threatens this entire realm with the Void."

Joss clenched a fist. "He is taunting us with destruction."

The dome shimmered and the deep thrum grew louder and I knew why the shield was transparent. "Cephus is powering the arch with his aether wells."

Elyssa snapped her fingers. "The more power it draws, the weaker the shield."

"We need to attack now," I said. "If we let Cephus activate that arch it'll be too late."

"Agreed," Elyssa said. "We're nearly out of time."

I touched the comm pendant on my Nightingale armor. "Commander Borathen, we need to press the attack now."

"I agree," he replied. "Prepare to move out."

A horn echoed through the canyons of the dead city and another horn answered. Flying carpets laden with Blue Cloaks lifted into the air. Squadrons of flying brooms bearing Arcanes rose behind them. Lycans howled and hellhounds responded with a dreadful chorus. A drum beat a steady tempo and Templar soldiers marched out from the cover of the buildings and into the wasteland from the west, their tempo matched by the elite vampire units or Red Cell from the south.

A dark cloud of enemy fliers funneled from the roof of the Ministry of Research, twisting and rising from the top of the dome and forming a phalanx over the fortress. Enemy ground troops gathered but remained safely inside the dome.

Flava hissed. "The cowardly bastards."

Staring up at the flying forces, I had to wonder if Cephus had captured every surviving citizen of Tarissa and arrayed them against us. "There must be five hundred of them."

"More," Lanaeia said. "I hope the Arcanes are up to the task."

"There's no helping it." Much as I wished to reform the Skywraiths and help our aerial units, we had something more important to do.

Beams of deadly energy streaked across the sky as the Blue Cloaks and Arcanes engaged the mutant fliers. Smoking bodies fell to earth as the deadly dance of war began.

Chapter 33

The main body of our troops reached the midpoint and another horn rang out.

"That's our signal." I turned to Shelton and Adam. "Move out the bots and ready the battering ram."

"On it," Shelton said. He turned to Adam and shouted, "Move out the bots and ready the battering ram!"

"Christ Almighty." Adam put his hands over his ears. "I heard Justin the first time."

I gathered the Seraphim around me. "Be ready for anything."

"The day will be ours," Lanaeia said.

Flava took my hand in hers. "We are yours, body and soul, Destroyer."

Melodramatic much? I repressed a sigh and smiled. "Then let's go kick some ass."

We raced on foot behind the Templar troops, covering ground quickly and reaching the outside of the dome. Loyalists standing inside the dome leered at us as we approached. I spotted a single concerned face among them.

Tain Prahven.

Shouts arose and loyalists cleared the way for a tall figure with a flowing black cape embroidered with the symbol of the Void. Hair dark as pitch crowned his head in the Roman fashion, combed straight down. He regarded me with a pleasant smile—a politician's smile that reminded me of Victus.

"We meet again, Justin." Cephus clasped his hands and regarded me through the barrier as if we were old friends once again united, even as the screams and cries of dying men echoed in the air above us where the Blue Cloaks fought his fliers.

I halted my people twenty yards from the barrier and stared suspiciously at the usurper. "Want to make this easy and give yourself up, Cephus?"

"I only want to restore the might of the Darkling nation," he said. "The religious zealots made us weak, Justin. If I had another way to do it, I would, believe me." Cephus held out his hands imploringly. "Believe it or not, you and I have the same goals, friend. We both want to unite the Seraphim under one government and bring peace to this war-torn realm."

God, he sounds so damned reasonable. I steeled myself against his act and shook my head. "Maybe, just maybe, we could have come to terms before, but the crystoid attack put you number one on my crap list."

"I was against such an attack," he said. "Serena and Victus approached me with a plan to defeat the Brightling Empire. The magic-draining crystals sounded reasonable, but when they launched the attack, they did it against Eden." Cephus held up his hands helplessly. "I tried to stop them, Justin, but the damage was done."

I felt a hand grip my arm and turned to see Flava staring at me, eyes warning. "I didn't forget," I told her softly. "Be ready to join." I turned back to Cephus. "Do you suggest I stand here and talk to you while your arch powers up?" My voice rose with anger as I spoke. "Do you think I'm going to just let you kill us like you did Ketiss and the Tarissan Legion while you pretended to negotiate peace?"

Baring my teeth in a feral grin, I stepped closer to the barrier. "Prepare your sphincter, Cephus, because we're about to rip you a new one." I thrust my fist into the air. "Wonder Twin powers, activate!"

This time, everyone knew what to do and joined. As the crimson arch thrummed louder and louder, I imagined our time growing shorter and shorter. We had to do this quick.

"Do you really think you can break through the barrier?" Cephus said. "You'll never hold it open long enough to get an army through." He looked at the approaching Templars. "Speaking of which, your forces are looking rather puny, Justin. I do hope nothing happened along the way here."

Spheres of Brilliance and Murk blossomed in my hands like miniature stars, swelling larger and larger. I funneled the energy into a huge ball of Stasis and flung it at the shield. The gray cloud soaked into the Murk barrier. Cracks raced up and down the ultraviolet wall. Loyalists drew swords and prepared themselves.

But they weren't ready for what we had coming.

As a thirty-foot section of the barrier turned gray as lead and crackled, I shouted the command. "Battering ram is a go!"

Shelton echoed the command and the battle bots raced past, the battering ram at the ready. Cephus's eyes grew wide as dinner plates when he saw them coming.

"Thanks for giving us the key to the fortress," I shouted as the battle-bots rammed the diamond fiber container they'd arrived in through the weakened section of the shield. The Murk shattered and the container slammed through, bowling over loyalists and creating the perfect tunnel for our troops to race through as both ends of it thudded open.

The barrier reformed around the diamond fiber, unable to penetrate its magic immunity. The container was wide enough to hold several rows of battle bots and wide enough to allow two roaring columns of Templars to stream through it.

I grinned at Cephus. "Happy Independence Day, asshole!"

His lips curled into a snarl. "Hold them at the bottleneck!"

The loyalists tried to hold the wave of Templars back, but dozens had already crowded inside the dome. While they were busy there, I channeled another sphere of Stasis a few yards west of the first breach. The shield cracked and the battle-bots rammed through another container. Another stream of Templars poured through the new breach.

The crimson arch pulsated, jagged bolts of energy arcing across the columns as it raced toward startup. "Move out!" I cried and raced south to create one more breach for the vampire forces.

Cephus paced us on the other side of the barrier. "None of this matters," he shouted over the din of battle. "I discovered a new use for the portal magic the crystoids utilized." He waved a hand at the crimson arch. "I made an arch that can open portals to any realm or anyplace within a realm, Justin!"

That stopped me in my tracks. "Who taught you how to do that?" I wished I could reach through the barrier and yank him closer by his stupid cape.

"Soon the true master of the realms will come through my portal, Justin." Cephus's face lit with delight. "The power of the Void will rule supreme."

"You'll kill us all!" At that moment, I realized Cephus's true madness.

Flava jerked on my arm. "Justin, don't listen to him!"

"Oh, I'm completely serious," Cephus replied. "The beast will be released from his eternal prison and the Void will rule the realms."

I stumbled over a pile of rubble and caught myself. A quick look back told me the Templars were pressing hard against the loyalists, but they weren't making nearly enough headway to reach the crimson arch. I held up a fist and the others formed a chain. Power swelled in me and I blasted the barrier with more Stasis. The battle-bots rushed up from behind and crashed the last container through the shield.

The Red Cell, rushed forward, but I decided not to wait on them. "We have to reach the arch," I said. "We've got to shut it down."

"We are with you," Lanaeia said.

"Joss, Otaleon, keep us shielded." I turned to Flava and Lanaeia. "Blast everyone who gets in our way. Nailan and Philas, while we divert the loyalists, I need you to sneak through and find out how to deactivate the arch."

Elyssa whirled her swords. "What are we doing?"

"We're going to make a hole if we can and get to the arch." I summoned globes of Brilliance and Murk. "Move out!"

We charged through the container, Joss and Otaleon leading the way with shimmering shields of Murk. Loyalists flooded the other end of the container, attempting to clog it. Flava and Lanaeia poured forth a torrent of destruction. Flesh charred and seraphs screamed in agony. I formed a blazing sword and Elyssa and I cut a furrow of death through the enemy.

The loyalists lost cohesion and retreated from the container where the advantage of numbers would be theirs. Blood slicked the bottom of the container and fallen bodies made footing treacherous. We pushed outside and found a wall of soldiers waiting.

"Everyone form shields and push!" I shouted. "Make room for the vampires."

Elyssa pressed herself behind me while the others channeled wide shields. We formed a Spartan phalanx and pressed up against the enemy.

"Heave!" I shouted. We shoved forward, bodies locked into one offense unit. The enemy lines skidded back. "Heave!" I shouted again. With a roar, we pushed again and the loyalists lost another foot. We had three feet of space from the container but we needed more.

Towering above the fray, light flickered inside the crimson arch. *We're almost out of time.* "Give it everything you've got!" I roared. "We've got to break the line!" I tensed every muscle in my body and drew upon my demon side. Muscles snaked around my arms, my legs, swelling my body larger. Stabs of pain impaled my forehead as horns sprouted.

Drawing a deep breath, I bellowed the command in a guttural demonic voice. "Heave!"

With a unified roar, we pushed forward and the enemy stumbled back ten feet. I heard the almost silent patter of feet and a rush of wind as the vampires poured into the freshly made space. The loyalists were decently trained and had Seraphim magic on their side, but they weren't prepared for the Red Cell vampires.

Precision strikes with swords found the neck seams in the enemy armor. Blood spurted and the loyalists fell like wheat. I looked back and realized Nailan and Philas had already left. Using my sword of Brilliance, I cut a path through the enemy soldiers toward the flashing columns of the crimson arch. We sliced through the lines and finally emerged in the open square.

I spotted a black cape flapping in the wind as Cephus raced toward the Ministry of Research. Once inside, he could easily lose himself in the maze of corridors and tunnels. He probably had an escape plan already mapped out. As the only person who could shut down the crimson arch, I wasn't about to let him escape.

"Help Nailan and Philas with the arch," I told the others. "I'm going after Cephus." I didn't wait another second and blurred across the square in hot pursuit. A host of enemy fliers lifted off from the roof of the building and swooped toward me. I didn't have time to stop and engage.

Shards of Murk crashed into the ground all around me as I dodged back and forth between attacks. Cephus, a hundred yards in front of me, was nearly to the entrance. There was no way I'd reach him in time.

Two flying brooms streaked overhead. Shelton and Adam flung out their staffs and fired webs of energy at Cephus. His feet tangled and he went down in a heap, sliding across the ground.

"Woot!" Shelton shouted. He and Adam flew past each other, exchanging high-fives then engaged the fliers.

"Great job!" I caught up to the snared usurper and dropped to a knee. I wanted to gloat so bad it literally hurt. But I had no time. "How do I turn off the arch, Cephus?"

He smiled calmly at me. "I'll never tell you."

I jerked him off the ground by his super cape and let him choke for a few seconds in front of the infernal flames burning in my demon eyes. "Tell me, or I'll eat your soul."

"Never," he croaked. "Your new master comes."

I slung his bound form over a shoulder and raced toward the crimson arch. "We'll let you be the first to meet your new master."

"No!" He bucked and writhed.

"What, are you too good to meet the Beast?" I roared.

I found the others fending off loyalists near the arch while Elyssa and Flava worked on a dais with several gems embedded in it.

"We can't figure it out," Elyssa said.

Flava pounded the top. "There must be a pattern to the gems."

I set Cephus down in front of the arch. "Tell me how to stop it or you'll be the first thing the Beast sees when he comes through."

The seraph stared at me, calm smoothing his features. "I will gladly welcome him."

That wasn't the answer I'd hoped for.

"We have to destroy the arch," Flava said.

I waved my hands imploringly. "No, we can't do that. This arch can open a portal to any realm. It might be our only way back to Eden."

The thrumming in the arch reached a fever pitch. "Oh, Christ," Shelton said. "Do something and hurry!"

Elyssa gripped my arm. "We have no choice, Justin."

A loud boom rocked the air and a portal split the air between the columns. There was no world to be seen on the other side, just pitch black emptiness. A wail of intense sadness and longing echoed from the other side. There was no telling how close or far the source of that sound was. Distance might not even be a thing in the Void.

Cephus struggled to turn. "I'm here, master! Your servant beckons you to take this broken world!"

A long note of despair sang out from the void, this time noticeably closer. It was like listening to a depressed whale in a karaoke bar, except whatever was making those sounds was definitely not a friendly denizen of the deep.

I looked at the arch and over at the control pedestal. *Without the Alabaster Arch, this is our only way home.*

If we didn't shut this thing off, none of us would have a chance of getting home.

The wailing changed to a roaring bellow. A gust of foul-smelling air blew from within the portal and we were out of time. "Destroy the arch!"

Lanaeia, Flava, Joss, Otaleon, Nailan, Philas and I took aim at the base of the arch and opened up with everything we had. Shelton and Adam aimed their staffs and fired gouts of destructive energy. The stony material began to glow, but it was so thick, our attacks weren't doing enough.

"Farting fairies on a pogo stick," Shelton yelled. "We're not doing squat."

"We need more firepower." Adam took out his phone and tapped on the screen. Battle bots raced to the scene and unloaded their lasers on the thick arch column. The shield dome flickered and vanished as the Daemos completed their task of disabling the aether wells powering it.

Thomas's voice sounded through my comm pendant. "What's coming through the arch?"

"Master, come for me!" Cephus shouted. "Come for me!"

"The Beast," I told Thomas. "We've got to destroy the arch, but it's made from the same stuff as the Obsidian Arches, and we can't put a dent in it."

The battle had all but stopped. The bodies of mutant fliers and loyalists mingled with those of vampires and Templars. An unnatural silence fell as a heavy breathing and the sound of flesh dragging across a rough surface emanated from the portal within the arch. The base of the arch glowed cherry red where we'd attacked it, but we'd barely scratched it.

Cephus's face lit with joy. "Your loyal servant is here." He unsteadily rose to his feet. "Save me from the religious zealots, master."

A swarm of pure black swept out of the portal and engulfed Cephus. His scream cut off almost instantly and where he'd once stood was nothing except a wailing black presence.

Shelton's face blanched and he backed away as did the rest of us. More of the dark swarm crept through, a shrieking sound slicing through the still air and causing my heart to skip several beats. I tried to make out the individual forms making up the swarm but it was like staring into oblivion. My eyes couldn't focus on the shimmering darkness.

Stretching like a tentacle, the swarm came for me. I threw up a shield and the darkness splashed against it, rebounding against itself and reforming.

"Justin!" Elyssa grabbed my shoulder.

The void swarm pummeled my shield relentlessly though it could have easily just flowed around it. Every attack drained energy from me, leaving brittle cold down to my very core. I dropped to a knee as my power waned and then the swarm swept in to consume its prey.

Chapter 34

More shields sprang up to protect me. Flava, Lanaeia and the other Seraphim overlapped their shields. The moment the swarm hit their barriers, however, they gasped in unison.

"It drains energy," I gasped. "Can't stop them long."

One by one the others staggered back as the energy-leeching things stole their power. Joss lost his shield first, followed by Philas and Nailan.

"Retreat!" I said. "Get out of here!"

Shelton gripped me under the arms and dragged me back. "You think I'm gonna just leave you here?" He grunted. "Man, your demon form needs to lose some weight."

My mother leapt to the fore and fired a withering blast of Brilliance at the swarm. Ashes drifted through the air, but there were always more of the swarm to take the other's place. The Beast, or whatever it was, consumed everything she fired at it.

Blue Cloaks swooped in on their carpets and unloaded on the monster, but nothing seemed to stop it. I realized then with horror what the Beast was—or at least it was the only thing that made sense. The Beast and the Void were one and the same. Wherever it existed, only it remained. If we let it loose here on Seraphina, it too would be nothing more than the Void Swarm.

"Nothing is hurting it!" Shelton shouted. "We've got to destroy that arch!"

But it was too late. More tentacles reached through, wailing, buzzing and roaring in my ears. We couldn't reach the arch through the sheer mass shoving its way free. And then I saw the massive bulk of the *Evadora* streaking our way, Seraphim crew members leaping off the sides and gliding to the ground on blazing wings.

"Holy farting fairies," Shelton gasped. "Run away!"

"Run for your lives!" Adam shouted.

By now, I'd recovered enough energy to follow his panicked instructions. Elyssa grabbed my arm and everyone scattered. With a tremendous boom, the *Evadora* slammed into the crimson arch. Wood groaned and stone rumbled as the titanic vessel demolished itself against the massive structure.

I stopped and looked back as the dust cleared and saw the arch still standing. "Oh god, we're doomed."

The portal crackled and flickered. With a brilliant flash and ear-bursting explosion, the gateway into the Void vanished. The swarm fell to the ground like flies. The hull of the *Evadora* lay in pieces against the crimson arch, its forest spilled out on the plaza. Vines writhed like dying snakes and tree branches flailed wildly.

Illaena ran to the remains screaming, "Cora!" over and over.

"Did she really fly that ship straight into the arch?" Shelton said.

Adam shook his head with wonder. "Dude, that was epic."

"Let's help them find Cora," Elyssa said. She snapped her fingers in front of my face and I jerked from my stupor. "Seraphina to Justin. Come in, Justin."

I nodded. "I don't see how she could've survived that impact."

We rushed over along with dozens of others and began combing through the wreckage. Arcs of energy crackled across the columns of the crimson arch causing people to jump in surprise. Bubbles with images of strange landscapes appeared and popped at random intervals making everyone nervous as the search operation moved closer to the damaged structure.

"It's creating interdimensional warp bubbles," Adam said. "Very unstable."

"Unstable as in it might blow up at any minute?" Shelton asked.

Adam shrugged. "I've never seen anything like this before."

"I have." I tossed aside a chunk of wood and looked beneath it. "Remember when I ended up in El Dorado by accident?"

"Yeah, you tried to use a broken arch to travel," Shelton said.

John Corwin

"I don't know if keeping this arch around is a good idea," Adam said.

Shelton gave him a disgusted look. "How else are we supposed get home, genius?"

"Look me in the eye and tell me that a malfunctioning arch that could open a portal back to the Void again is a good thing." Adam set his arms akimbo and stared at his friend. "Would you rather be alive, or devoured like Cephus?"

"Uh—" Before Shelton could answer, I spotted movement near the arch.

"Hang on." I ran toward a cluster of vines unbraiding and separating to reveal something inside.

Cora broke free of the vines. Face bruised and bloody, she looked like she'd gone nine rounds with a heavyweight boxer.

"Cora!" I turned and shouted at the others. "I found her!"

Cora staggered to her feet. "How is this arch still standing?"

"They're a lot tougher than they look," I said. Before I could close the remaining distance, an interdimensional bubble swelled in front of me. Hot arid air swept across my face from a desert plain. Another bubble blossomed right behind Cora. "Watch out!"

But it was too late. Still woozy from the crash, Cora staggered backward over her own vines. The bubble swallowed her and she fell into a field of brilliant flowers.

"Justin!" she shouted, her voice muted as if she were underwater.

Before I could shout back, the bubbles popped and a lightning storm of magical energy played back and forth along the arch columns. A loud groan and crumbling of rock were the only warnings we heard as the crimson arch began to topple slowly toward the remains of the *Evadora*.

"Run!" I shouted. "Everyone run!"

The search party scattered, people fleeing the massive crumbling arch. I grabbed Shelton and Adam as they struggled through the mountain of wreckage and dragged them after me. The arch slammed into the earth. The massive columns broke and rolled. The ground rippled beneath me and I fell, sending Adam and Shelton tumbling.

284

Dust and rubble scattered past, stinging my skin. When the air cleared, I turned and saw nothing but broken stone and the demolished remains of the *Evadora*.

"We ain't never getting home," Shelton said.

Adam got up and dusted off his clothes. "Never say never."

"Never," Shelton said again.

I hoped he was wrong.

Thomas gathered the war council in the lobby of the Ministry of Research so we could go over our next steps. "We confirmed that the Alabaster Arch on Kdosh is no longer working," was the first thing he shared.

Colin McCloud groaned loud enough for it to echo across the room. "Don't we have the great Alysea Slade, the woman who repaired the Grand Nexus, to fix it?"

"It's not that simple," my mother replied. "For all we know, Serena deployed portal-blocking statues in Eden, making it impossible to open a portal from here to there."

"Can we open portals to other realms?" McCloud asked.

"Right now the arch isn't working at all," Mom said. "Then again, I haven't been back out there to look at it."

"Our Arcane engineers are looking it over," Thomas said. "In the meantime, there's plenty to do here."

"A city to rebuild," Lanaeia murmured next to me.

"The Brightling army may attack if they discover how weakened the Darkling nation has become," Thomas continued. "To that end, we need to put the citizens of Tarissa back to work repairing the damage, and reconstructing the legion." He displayed a holographic map of Pjurna and indicated the blips where the other Darkling legions held the Brightling army at bay. "We need to contact the rest of the armed forces and rethink a long-term strategy. If we're to unite the Seraphim people, we have a lot of groundwork to do."

After the meeting, I took a levitation shaft up to the roof and followed the curve of the domed building to the peak. The building had been much lower than the towers all around it the first time I'd come here, but now it stood alone in the wasteland of the city center.

The shattered remains of the *Evadora* looked like so much scrap amongst the red rubble of the crimson arch.

It made me think of Cora. I wondered where that interdimensional bubble had taken her and hoped she was safe wherever she was. Adam told me that the likely reason for so many dragon incursions from Draxadis were because of the crimson arch creating unstable dimensional bubbles. Just because the bubbles vanished from this area didn't mean they were gone, it simply meant they'd relocated.

It was a lot to soak in. How had Cephus and his allies managed to build an arch unlike any I'd seen? Had they found the blueprints or kidnapped a Siren? Thinking back to Kaelissa's stories about the Apocryphan, it made me wonder if the Abyssal demon I'd unleashed had anything to do with it.

I felt certain we'd only scratched the surface of Serena's deceit. We had to find out how they'd managed to create the crystoids and the sky portals if we stood a chance of ever going home.

The one person I couldn't stop thinking about was Ivy. For so many years, I hadn't even known she existed. Only after my eighteenth birthday had my father told me I had a sister. I'd spent so much time earning her love and trust, and now she was stranded all alone in Eden surrounded by backstabbers.

Unless I figured out a way back home, I couldn't do anything to help her.

"Need some alone time?"

Elyssa's voice made me start with surprise. "Why do you have to be so ninja silent when I'm deep in thought?"

"I like sneaking up on you." She sat down next to me and snuggled against my shoulder. "I guess we have a new zip code now."

"Yeah." I managed a wry chuckle. "Wonder where we register to vote."

"My father thinks we'll be here until we can gain access to another Alabaster Arch." Elyssa sighed. "That means fighting the Brightlings."

"Whatever it takes, we have to do it fast, though." I felt my knuckles crack as my fists clenched with frustration. "Ivy is all alone in Eden."

"Maybe not," Elyssa said. "She's powerful enough to escape danger, and she still has Stacey and Ryland to go to."

My hopes lifted slightly. "She is a handful."

"She'll blast anyone who tries to hurt her." Elyssa patted my arm. "I know she's young, but she can more than take care of herself."

"Ivy's naiveté is what worries me," I said. "What if she's gullible enough to be led around?"

"No way," Elyssa said certainly. "That girl doesn't trust many people in this world, and for good reason. After all, she had Daelissa as a mentor."

"In other words, we should be more concerned about the people of Eden than Ivy."

Elyssa smiled. "I really think so, babe."

"Well, I feel a little better." I rested my face in my hands and groaned. "Can you help me find a good pizza joint now?"

She laughed and trailed off into a sigh. "I think Nightliss would be happy."

My eyes stung. "Sad too, considering the state of her nation."

"We have a long row to hoe, but I'm looking forward to it."

I took in the vista of the unbroken towers in the distance and saw lights glowing in some of the windows as the sunlight faded to dusk. With the crystoid plaguing the city gone, this place could once more come to life. While I could never bring my sweet friend, Nightliss, back from the grave, I could work hard to bring back her nation from the brink of destruction. It looked like we'd have to work hard and fast so we could rescue Eden from my little sister.

Ivy, I hope you're okay.

Squeezing Elyssa's hand, I kissed her cheek and pressed my forehead against hers.

Victus and Serena might feel safe and smug, but a reckoning was coming. It might be a month or a year from now, but one day, I'd find a way home, and they would regret it.

Today we had a nation to rebuild, and a world to unite.

John Corwin

###

I hope you enjoyed reading this book. Reviews are very important in helping other readers decide what to read next. Would you please take a few seconds to rate this book?

For the latest on new releases, free ebooks, and more, join John Corwin's Newsletter at www.johncorwin.net!

Meet the Author

John Corwin is the bestselling author of the Overworld Chronicles. He enjoys long walks on the beach and is a firm believer in puppies and kittens.

After years of getting into trouble thanks to his overactive imagination, John abandoned his male modeling career to write books.

He resides in Atlanta.

Connect with John Corwin online:
Facebook: http://www.facebook.com/johnhcorwinauthor
Website: http://www.johncorwin.net
Twitter: http://twitter.com/#!/John_Corwin